THEIR ROMANCE BEGAN
WITH A FANFARE . . .

Copper's love affair with the stunning Joss Parker was the talk of the town . . . and the scandal of Scotland Yard. But Copper didn't care. Joss had turned his head. Her voluptuous figure, fearless candor and shrewd business sense had won his heart. Until her new nightclub started attracting the right people and the wrong money.

Suddenly the lovebirds weren't singing the same tune. Joss lay quietly dead in a pool of blood. And it looked like Inspector Copper was guilty of murder.

AND ENDED WITH A FUNERAL DIRGE.

MURDER INK.® MYSTERIES

SCENE OF THE CRIME™ MYSTERIES

A *Murder Ink.*®*Mystery*

COPPER GOLD

Pauline Glen Winslow

A DELL BOOK

Published by
Dell Publishing Co., Inc.
1 Dag Hammarskjold Plaza
New York, New York 10017

Dell ® TM 681510, Dell Publishing Co., Inc.

ISBN: 0-440-11130-7

Reprinted by arrangement with St. Martin's Press, Inc.

Printed in the United States of America

First Dell printing—March 1981

In memory of Stanley Glen
and Ray E. Winslow,
for whom Diogenes
lifted his lamp.

At one time the British monetary unit was a troy pound of silver, which became known as the pound sterling. The term 'sterling' is believed to derive from 'Easterlings,' the name given to North German merchants who established a hansa, or trade guild, in England in the thirteenth century. Their coins were noted for their reliability as to uniform weight and fineness.

During most of the eighteenth century, England was legally on a bimetallic standard. Later, the one-pound coin became the gold sovereign. The pound is no longer tied to either silver or gold. At the time of this writing, the pound sterling is worth less than half an ounce of silver.

Without even knowing it ourselves, we were ransomed by the small change in copper that was left from the golden coins our great-grandfathers had expended, at a time when morality was not considered relative and when the distinction between good and evil was very simply perceived by the heart.

ALEXANDER SOLZHENITSYN

COPPER
GOLD

A LITTLE NIGHT MUSIC

The telephone rang at three A.M. CID Chief Superintendent Capricorn lifted the receiver and blinked into the dark.

'Guv?' The voice was familiar. 'Got a tip for yer. Take it easy with Brixton Jim. Otherwise, they're going to make it awkward for Flash Copper, see?'

There was a click at the other end. The voice was gone.

Capricorn had been fast asleep, pursuing a master criminal in a landscape that changed faster than he could run—from England to Europe, from Europe to Asia—and when at last he had his villain well within his grasp, it changed again, back to England, but to an England so transformed he didn't know it. For all that, the tired detective found himself at once wide awake. He groaned and lit the bedside lamp. The sight of the familiar room, his treasured paintings and old furniture, failed to lift his spirits from the melancholy of the dream. The telephone call had been ominous. Reaching for a cigarette, he remembered there were none. He had stopped smoking. Again.

The caller had been no threatening stranger but one of his regular informants, Gyppo Moggs, a 'snout' who would ring up with a bit of information, always at night, in hopes of a future favour or a small reward. Flash Copper. Capricorn rubbed his eyes. Not the way he liked to hear his friend and colleague re-

ferred to. He had worked with young Copper for
many years now and liked and trusted him. But the
villains had given him that name since his flamboyant
love affair with a former barmaid, and now it was
used by the Force.

Just two days before, Capricorn had walked
through Soho on his way to his car which he'd parked
in Golden Square. The stalls in the market had been
packing up, but the vegetables tumbled in the gutter
were rotting quickly in the summer heat. A brilliant
Red Admiral fluttered from some nearby garden to
feed on the putrescent fruit. The streets were littered
and drab, the shop fronts seedy. Parked at a dashing
angle on the narrow pavement, a gleaming purple
sports car, so new that it looked untouched by a
smudge of soot or a drop of rain, contrasted sharply
with its background and drew the glance of passers-
by.

A uniformed constable on patrol stopped to regard
it, hands clasped behind his back, in rather wistful
admiration until another policeman approached,
busily writing out summonses. He, too, regarded the
car, but with a more businesslike air until the first
man spoke.

'Flash Copper's,' he said succinctly. 'In there.'

He gestured with his thumb to a newly painted
door down the street, topped by a gold-coloured canopy.

The summonser whistled a tune familiar to Capricorn, the son of two music hall families. 'She was only
a bird in a gilded cage.'

'Some bird, that Mrs. Copper,' the other constable
said reflectively.

The two men smiled, shrugged and the summonser
went on about his business, while the first constable
resumed his patrol, soon getting into an altercation
with a stallholder plying her trade without a license.

The Superintendent had looked more closely at the

car as he walked by. A woman's purple-striped silk scarf lay across the leather seat. A cardboard box in the back bore the name of an expensive women's haberdasher. Farther down the street he paused in front of 'Mrs. Copper's' new club. She had made, or caused to be made, many changes on the premises. The door had been scraped and repainted with gold metallic paint. The sill had been covered with brightly polished brass. Neat lettering glittered on the canopy: The Golden Calf.

Capricorn had sworn softly then, and now he swore again, not so softly, in the privacy of his room. It was Joss Parker's club. The license was made out in her name. The lady believed in women's liberation and refused legal marriage. Nevertheless, people thought of her as Copper's wife and the place was known as Copper's club.

Just this day at lunch the Commander, a friend of twenty years' standing, interrupted a discussion of whether he should retire to enjoy his country home and do some work for the county or stay on and become Deputy Assistant Commissioner, to suggest that Capricorn have a word with Copper.

Capricorn had found he couldn't ask, 'About what?'

'There's nothing in General Orders to say that a policeman can't have a girlfriend who owns a club,' he pointed out. 'She's been in that business for years. And they're not married.'

The Commander, moved for a moment to forget his conflicting ambitions, put his cigar down and scowled. 'But he's living with her openly,' he said. 'A CID Inspector. It's hardly edifying.'

The two men had looked at each other uneasily.

As he so often did, Capricorn silently congratulated himself for being unencumbered by a wife, legal or otherwise. Still, he reflected, of all the difficulties caused by women, this was something new. Certainly policemen, like other men, were sometimes attracted to women who would be considered 'unsuitable' by their superiors. But these affairs were ephemeral and carefully hidden from official notice. Copper, on the other hand, deliberately made his union public and treated Joss as a wife. Custom was strong in the Metropolitan Police, and particularly in the CID. Policemen's wives tended to run to form. Usually they were housewives, finding their friends in other police families, but if they worked, their work was not of a sort to embarrass their husbands.

'And Copper's been going it a bit, hasn't he? Don't know how he does it,' the Commander added gloomily, for though he himself had come from a family considered well off in police ranks, and his wife had been a rich woman, like most people in England he seemed to be getting rapidly poorer. Joss and Copper, on the other hand, were indulging in a lot of conspicuous consumption. Flash Copper.

Capricorn shrugged, turned the light off and tried to go back to sleep. It was no use. Tossing restlessly, he decided the room was too warm. He got out of bed and without lighting the lamp went to the window. The heavy curtains were not drawn and the inner curtains were blowing a little in the faintest of breezes. The stale, sour air that burdened London was freshened a little with the scents from his quiet garden. He leaned out. The stars were hardly visible; the moon shone wanly through the haze that still lay over the city; a tomcat howled, importunate.

He stood there for a moment but although his body cooled, his mind remained unquiet. Giving up the idea of going back to sleep, he went to his study and, in the small square book-lined room, sat at his desk and went over the papers he had brought back from the Yard. Brixton Jim.

This was a matter never assigned to him, but something he worked on whenever he had the time. Capricorn had met Brixton Jim, by chance, years before at a dinner in the City, when he was investigating the suspicious death of a stockbroker. Brixton Jim, known to the City as Marcus James, a respectable owner of a warehouse business, was a man inconspicuous at such a gathering, soberly dressed, very slightly balding, a touch of South London in his voice, Capricorn believed, though he had only heard him acknowledge an introduction. Of middle height with a complexion suggesting an indoor life—there was nothing to have kept his image in Capricorn's mind, except a cold shrewd glance, perhaps too shrewd, Capricorn analyzed, for such a modest appearance, and such a conventional, old-fashioned life.

Over the years there had been rumours, hints and suggestions coming from snouts, that Brixton Jim was a financier, entrepreneur and sometime-planner of much of the major crime in Great Britain. But no real confirmation of this had ever been found; his name was never connected to any particular job; no unlucky felon had been able to offer information to help himself; so the upper ranks of command at the Yard had been inclined to dismiss the tales as–fantasy. Capricorn, who believed the underworld knew its own, had started collecting a file on Brixton Jim while he worked on more urgent matters. The charge of fantasy didn't trouble him. He was accustomed to looking for the mechanics behind the most perfect illusion.

The breeze sighed against the study window but the hoped-for rain didn't come. A dry summer and now a dry autumn—the rivers were low. The James family had come from river people: James's father had been a wharfinger and had owned the warehouse in Commercial Road, his grandfather had begun as a lighterman, one of those expert boatmen who know every ripple in the tidal Thames. Before that perhaps the family had come from the river pirates who had preyed on shipping before the great docks were built, and who were occasionally caught and hanged with ceremony at Execution Dock, their bodies exposed for three tides to wash over before they were hanged again as awful warnings downstream at Bugsby's Reach.

Not such a perfect illusion. But Capricorn had to check his imagination. Many fortunes had been made and lost in dockland by many respectable men. James's father had lost his wharves to fire bombs in World War II, and the whole area had been rebuilt and come under the control of the Port of London Authority. Young James had inherited only the house in Brixton, the warehouse in Commercial Road and a few small properties down river. But misfortune turned to his advantage, for he bought warehouse properties elsewhere, on the Mersey, in Harwich and even as far as Bremerhaven, all under the control of local managers. When the Port of London began its decline, James flourished. He now owned part of the container docks at Tilbury, and he was considered by his fellows to be a sharp and successful man. Capricorn had failed to find any shred of evidence against him. At one time he had gone so far as to persuade the now-defunct Ghost Squad to put a man in the London warehouse as an employee. The only result had been a good set of James's fingerprints, which, not surprisingly, failed to match any set on file.

Until, just a week ago, he had found a connection. In the quiet of his study, half aware of the night sounds: the faint breeze rustling the dry leaves, a dog's bark, the distant hum of a car on the road, Capricorn still shuddered. He had certainly not hoped for anything like Barlow Road.

It was a horrible business. The robbery of the East-land bank had been ordinary enough, though smooth, professional and well organized. The thieves had got away with half-a-million pounds worth of gold bullion, and doubtless it would have been out of the country by now or, less likely, hidden for some future criminal purpose, except for the fact that the entrepreneurs of crime, like their honest brothers, were having trouble with the younger generation. Young people were not as reliable as their fathers had been, nor inclined to work to rule. Yet for some jobs youth was essential. The getaway car had been driven by a man with the speed and skill of a racing driver, which, as it turned out later, he was. He would never have been caught except for one error in judgement and one bit of bad luck that had ended in tragedy.

Capricorn took a cigar from the supply he kept for guests and lit it, drawing slowly. All the bright young lads, he thought, who went so casually into crime—'After all, it only hurts the insurance companies, right?'—they should see something like Barlow Road. The driver, according to instructions no doubt, after a smart getaway, had avoided the main roads, where police cars could be expected, and had driven through small suburban streets. What he had done on his own account was to drug himself with amphetamines. The resulting euphoria induced him to travel fast, very fast. His control of the car was good, but not good enough to avoid a cluster of schoolchildren crossing to an ice-cream van. Two of the children were killed instantly, a third, if it lived, would be crippled for life. The driver had gone on without stopping. He had tried to ram through a police barrier and had injured a constable before he was taken at last in the car smeared with blood and full of gold.

In a bid for leniency, while he was still shaken from his own minor injuries, he had quickly named his accomplices and hinted that he had information of even greater value. Capricorn had seen him at Dulwich station, a pleasant-looking young fellow with an open expression and a shock of light-brown hair that made him look even younger than he was. He had been a good racing driver; he didn't seem stupid, and Capricorn wondered at the careless greed that had brought him into this dirty business.

On investigation, it turned out he was not as innocent as he looked. He had no previous convictions but there was a file on him at the Yard. This was certainly not his first job, or the second or third. Quite calmly, he offered Capricorn information against Brixton Jim—in return for a charge reduced to causing death by dangerous driving. There were a half-dozen witnesses who stated that the driver had made no attempt to stop even after he must have seen the children. Capricorn had known many evildoers in his years at the Yard, but this one's calm effrontery and complete lack of remorse had provoked him to an uncharacteristic flood of anger. When he had met Copper later in the endless corridors of New Scotland Yard and had told him about it tersely enough, Copper had recalled, almost with affection, old Judge Satterthwaite who was wont to prescribe the cat.

Copper. Copper had not been working with him on this case, he had been busy with a squad tracking down coiners for Interpol, as well as the Metropolitan Police. As usual, he was doing a good job. No one had ever complained about his work. In his bachelor days, indeed even during his first marriage, his light-hearted, casual attitude toward sex, coupled with his attractiveness to women, had caused raised eyebrows at the Yard, and a wish, often expressed, that he would settle down. The younger men had referred to him, sometimes enviously, as 'The Swingin' Skipper.' Yet now that he had seemed to settle down with the voluptuous Joss Parker, there was more talk, not less.

No one had ever questioned Copper's integrity, but now the snouts were reporting that his name caused sniggers in the underworld, much elbow-poking and mutters about 'bent law'. Of course, the underworld habitually believed officials to be corrupt on the slightest evidence or none at all.

But what the devil was all this about? Capricorn was not going to take it easy on Brixton Jim: if he could get evidence against him, he would act. How could Brixton Jim 'make it awkward' for Copper? It must merely be the harassment that a detective always has to live with. An angry villain would accuse him of falsifying verbal evidence or of planting evidence to get convictions or, on the other hand, of taking bribes and failing to make arrests or arresting on a lesser charge. There could be no proof that any of this was so, but suspicion would be aroused, and the detective's only safeguards were his reputation and the number of arrests he had made balanced against his known ability.

Brixton Jim would never have tried it on Copper, Capricorn thought suddenly, if it wasn't for his flashing so much money about. That Golden Calf. Capricorn would stake his own professional reputation on Copper's honesty. But that club was bound to cause trouble. Damn the Golden Calf. He tried not to think, 'Damn Joss Parker.' And failed.

An hour and a half later, Copper was being roused. He wrinkled his snub nose and stretched his feet out tentatively. Accustomed as he was to waking up in a variety of beds, he first noticed the buttoned leather cushions under a light cover—he was not in a bed. A sofa. He remembered and opened his green eyes to smile up at the woman he thought of as his wife. He was on Joss's sofa, in the private office of the club. It had been too late to go home, and so the sofa. He had asked Joss to wake him when she closed.

She was chattering in some excitement. It had been a busy night. The club was a great success. He looked at her handsome form with content, for Copper had found his ideal woman. Joss was as tall as he and had a fine voluptuous figure, which showed to advantage in her evening dress as she now dealt competently with the electric kettle, making him a cup of tea. She took milk from the small refrigerator that looked like part of the files. Joss had done up this room when she did the rest of the place. If she did a job, he thought proudly, she did it right.

His mind, refreshed after a few hours' sleep, picked up the threads of the working day. His job was almost complete. He had a warrant ready and was about to pick up the Italian coiners who had left a trail of fake Krugerrands across Europe. All was going well, better than he could ever have expected, and for a moment the usually ebullient Copper wondered why he felt less than high-spirited, with the curiosity that another man might feel at waking up to a new ache or pain.

He soon forgot this as he enjoyed his tea—Joss was the only woman he knew who always made it perfectly. Her efficiency was also evident in the tiny but well-equipped bathroom she had put in; the hot water was really hot and the cleaners had really cleaned. When he returned to the office, Joss was locking up her ledger in a desk drawer.

'If it keeps up like this,' she said, with an air of relief, 'I'm not going to have any trouble with the payments.'

Copper felt a slight pang of irritation at that 'I'. But he was being unreasonable, he told himself. Joss was used to thinking as a single woman, and the club was really her venture, although he helped as much as his job allowed. And he had given her most of the money he received from the sale of his London house.

Joss poured herself a large brandy-and-soda to keep him company as he drank a second cup of tea.

'Coming home later?' she asked.

'I'll try,' he promised. 'Bloody paperwork on this job is the worst part.'

'Don't wake me up if you do,' she warned. 'I've got to get my sleep. Can't afford to get my face lifted yet. Got to wait till I'm thirty.'

Copper smiled, remembering she had said much the same at their first meeting, when he had woken her from a sound sleep, and she had rained curses down upon his head. Her face now, as then, was unlined and romantically beautiful in a moist misleading way, for Joss was matter-of-fact and businesslike—so much so that she made him feel abashed when she caught him in some sentimental moment. For Copper, although generally known as cynical and tough-minded, had secret fondnesses for pets and children, Christmas, birthdays and family affection. Strange, he reflected, that Joss's sexual appetite was as lusty as his own, yet she had no taste for the smaller change of love; a casual kiss or hug or the holding of her hand would evoke a look between amusement and resignation.

'Daft,' she would sometimes say, taking him back to his childhood. 'Daft,' he used to say to his mother in disgust, when she took him to the pictures and it was a romance, instead of a war story or cowboys and Indians. 'Lot of daft stuff.'

Joss was still adding up figures on a piece of scrap paper, frowning in concentration. Suddenly, she gave a huge yawn.

'God, I'm tired. But it's going to be worth it, you see.'

'I hope so,' he answered, with a grimace. 'Well, I've got to be going.'

He gave her a friendly slap on her rump and she grinned.

'Try and come home.'

She took his jacket from the back of a chair and handed it to him. Something crackled in the right-hand pocket and he glanced down with foreboding. It was a letter he had been walking around with for a couple of days.

'Oh, for Gawd's sake,' he said, frowning. 'I meant to take care of that. I hate to get behind. I was going to make out a cheque yesterday.' He bit his lower lip. 'Then I had to give fifty quid to Monty at the garage. The headlamp, the new carburetor, and he checked the alignment.'

Joss looked at the name of the sender. 'Give it to me. I'll take care of it.'

'I don't want to bother you,' Copper said.

'No bother,' Joss said briskly. 'And it's all our money, isn't it? One for all and all for one.'

Joss was very good about that, he told himself, as he walked out into the Soho street. Very good. You couldn't find another like her. He hadn't wanted to bring that up. She had her bank loan to worry about. But it wasn't just the garage. There was the mortgage payment on the new house. The loan he'd taken to refurnish. And Joss liked to go out; you couldn't expect her to cook every day. And God, that local place the other night. Joss, her friend Mary and her boy friend. Sixty quid.

The street was well lit. He could see the Aid he was working with already waiting on the corner. Young blood, he thought. Eager. He was usually eager himself, but that cheque business took the zest from the day. One thing and another. His shoulder ached. He had the pills but if he took them he'd be no good for hours. An injection would be better, but he'd run out of the stuff. Mary would get him some more. All this because of a roughhouse with a bruiser who had been unloading the stuff for the Italians. For the first time, Copper had nearly got the worst of it. Getting on. Worried all the time about money. He thought of the customers at the club, chucking it about as if it were water. All the years he'd been on the Force, keeping the country safe for them to live in, and on his pay alone he could hardly afford a few drinks there. Certainly not after the car and the house, the child support—and Greywillow.

Greywillow. He'd had to do it. There wasn't any choice. Joss had been pleasant, as always, but firm.

'I know she's your mother, and you're fond of her,' she'd said. They'd been in the old house then, in the living room Joss found too small. It *was* too small, he had to be fair, he'd always been knocking into the furniture. Joss had done it up, but in the end they'd had to move. An hour further out into the country, and that much further from his mother.

'You know as well as I do that once they start to go senile they have to be taken care of all the time. You don't expect me to spend the rest of my life as a nurse. And even if she wasn't barmy, I wouldn't want her here with us.'

'I know,' Copper had said.

He did know. He was very fond of his mother, which Joss could hardly be, not having known her until her mind had begun to wander, but he had to realize that at the best of times the two women would not have agreed. His mother, who liked proverbs, talked of 'Waste not, want not,' and suggested 'cutting your coat according to your cloth.' Copper's father had been a collector for the gas company, trudging the streets; emptying the meters of their shillings. Copper could still remember the smell, slightly acrid, of the metal on his hands. A kind father, he never came home without some small treat for his wife and son, a bar or two of chocolate, a bag of toffees. His earnings had been small, but the family had never owed a penny. His father gave his pay packet to his mother, and they would open the carefully locked cabinet, with its all-glass front, in the dining room, and take out the wooden box his father had made, with the little compartments, and solemnly put away the different amounts for the rent, the light, the burial insurance. They had needed that insurance sooner than they thought. His mother had been brave and made the most of things; it was only in the last year or two that the trouble had started. She hadn't been so bad at first. If he and Joss hadn't moved so far away . . . But, as Joss had said, she didn't have the temperament to cope with old ladies. Nor, she had pointed out firmly, did she see it as her duty.

Joss didn't believe in duty. She was modern, straightforward, free. Copper reminded himself that that was why he had fallen in love. She was as direct as a man. His neighbours in the suburb where he had lived with Myrtle, his first wife, had certainly raised their eyebrows when Joss moved in shortly after Myrtle had gone. Joss had not cared at all; she hardly noticed their existence. She didn't believe in marriage, either. The only time she had been interested in the idea was on their first real holiday together in the south of France. They had been very happy; his divorce had just come through. And added to that, the bank had been hesitating about his mortgage on the house in Wenmore; bachelors were not considered as good a risk as married men, and Joss certainly wanted that house. By the time they returned to England his promotion to Inspector had gone through. The mortgage was granted, and Joss had decided she wanted a club, which Mrs Copper certainly couldn't own. So she had remained Joss Parker, even to the scandalized villagers.

The Soho street smelled of decayed vegetables and other uncollected rubbish. The dustmen, not officially on strike, were staging a slowdown. They wanted more money, like everyone else. And by the time they got it, it would be no use. Prices would be up again. Irritably, he kicked a dog's bone that was lying in his path. He remembered, for no particular reason, kick-

ing a ball about in the school playground. The best
halfback his school had ever had, the games master
had called him, and he had thought of playing for
the local team when he grew up. When he'd kicked
the goal that meant a win over the boys from Dagen-
ham, his mother had been so proud she'd talked
about it to the neighbours until he'd had to ask her
to stop. Even though he'd torn a great hole in the jersey she'd knitted. Always knitting, she was. Hardly
ever saw her without needles and a ball of wool.
She'd made a cake for him as well, to celebrate. Terrible those cakes were, with the shortages still after
the war. No butter, no eggs, not much sugar and that
dark flour, but he'd enjoyed it, then.

He hadn't been able to get anyone to stay with his
mother in the London flat. And then he'd been sent
up North with Capricorn on a case, and when he
came back the Welfare officer had taken her to St.
Luke's. He shuddered now, thinking about it.

'They take care of them,' the Welfare officer had
said defensively. 'It's the best I could do. It's harder
for the visitors,' she explained, 'than for the inmates.
They don't know.'

St. Luke's had been built in the nineteenth century,
and nothing had been done to it since. His mother
was in a long shabby ward with a group of other old
women in various stages of senility or madness. Va-
cant-eyed, they shuffled about, bent, some strangely
contorted. Slack mouths drooled, and one old woman
emptied her bladder as she walked to the table where
a meal of sandwiches was being served. At the other
end of the ward, a woman screamed frantically, and a
nurse approached with a syringe.

Copper's mother, dressed in a strange assortment of
clothes, none of them her own, over a hospital nightgown, saw him enter. She smiled, her clear blue eyes
bright.

'Hello, son,' she said.

The sandwiches smelled strongly of fish paste. An odour of urine from the toilets without doors at the end of the ward mingled with the ever-present sickly sweet smell of disinfectant. Copper, long inured to scenes of violent death, had just time to get outside the door before he retched up his last meal. Dizzy with nausea, he apologized to a male attendant, who observed him without surprise.

'Visitors always get upset at first,' he said. 'But they soon stop coming.'

Death was one thing. Living death was another. Because of what his mother had been, he couldn't leave her in St. Luke's. It had meant his first real disagreement with Joss. Not a quarrel, he told himself, a disagreement.

Joss had supported the Welfare officer.

'You're being sentimental,' she'd said. That was the worst thing she could think of—she would have called it a sin if she believed in sin. 'Just piling trouble on yourself. They don't know the difference. They're looked after. Wallpaper and curtains and carpets are for visitors, not the patients.'

But when she saw he was adamant, she gave in and helped. Joss had found Greywillow. Efficient Joss. Greywillow was the best there was. A converted private house, well kept. Well kept and costing a third of his pay before taxes.

Between that and the house in Wenmore, they'd had to open a club, whether the Yard liked it or not. When they'd both been working, the money was never enough. Joss had had to leave the Hi-Ho club where she'd done well—there was too much talk. It was known at the Yard that the Hi-Ho was owned by Charlie Bo. Bo seemed straight enough but the Yard would never believe it. A CID Inspector associate with a woman who worked for a relation of a Mafia family? But when she'd worked in an office on salary, they'd run into debt. With taxes the way they were it was no use trying.

Joss had had the idea for the Golden Calf. She'd found the place, and she'd raised half the money. And she was a success. His mother quite liked Grey-willow: she'd been lonely, the nurses said. He went to see her when he had time, which wasn't often. Joss didn't visit. Old people depressed her; she believed in euthanasia for the elderly and feeble.

Oh, what the hell, Copper thought. A spaniel bitch lay dead in the gutter. Run over, obviously. Someone had kicked it aside. He felt suddenly sick and turned away. Down the street a party of late merrymakers were trying to remember where they had parked their cars. Shrieks and laughter jangled in his ears.

He grunted at his Aid and went to wake his foreign villains. They were surprised by the visit, stumbling out into the street still hastily buttoning their shirts, their heavy-lidded eyes blinking sleepily in the lamp-light. The shirts, to Copper's knowing eye, looked expensive: the Italians, quite young, were smartly dressed. One of them noticed that the sleeve of his coat was rumpled, and smoothed it, anxiously, before Copper hustled him into the official car the Aid had parked around the corner.

More worried about his clobber than the pinch, Copper thought, with a pang of fellow feeling—he was a fancy dresser himself. He felt a sudden, sharp reluctance to take his coiners. They had only made themselves some money, the easiest way of all. While they were young enough to enjoy it; before the grief started. At that moment they seemed almost reason-able.

WHO were you with last night?
Out in the pale moonlight?
The raucous voice boomed through Capricorn's sleep, as he woke a second time that night. Not night,

he corrected himself: a grey light was already coming through the window. His mind, still tired, tried to soothe itself. The sound was a radio from a passing car, so noisy it could be heard even in the back of the house. Or a neighbour had maniacally decided to play an old gramophone record just before the dawn. A female drunkard, lost, was pounding on his door.

'Merle! Merle!'

It was useless. A female drinker, or more than one, it certainly was, but she, or they, was, or were, not lost. Nor were they really the Harpies or Gorgons he felt them to be at that moment. No, they were among the few who could claim the privilege of banging on his door, even though they should be decently asleep at their own house in Paddington, or, if not asleep, carousing with their cronies, old denizens of the music halls together with bright young lads of the BBC. The intruders were flesh, they would say dramatically, on his flesh. Or partly. In fact, they were his aunts.

Resigned as always, he got up to let her, or them, in, wondering what new trouble was coming. His aunts disapproved of his way of life and his profession, and a call from them usually meant a plea for some friend in difficulty with the law—drink, drugs or blackmail. He sighed. Capricorn was a conventional man who had spent his early years at the Yard living down the fact that he had been a magician, the son of The Great Capricornus himself. When at last, to his great relief, that had been forgotten, he had suddenly found himself, in the 1970's, known as the nephew of The Magic Merlinos. The Merlinos, who had seemed to him the last dwindling spark of the Edwardian era in the theatre, had emerged, dazzling, the darlings of young and old, the very latest stars in the world of television. The generations had been strangely reversed. Capricorn was now an old fogy, while they were 'trendy' and 'with it'.

It wasn't your sister, it wasn't your ma,
Ah, ah, ah, ah, ha, ha, ha, ha!

The unmistakable holler came from Dolly Merlino, and there she was on his front step looking, as always, like a side of ham crowned by a long red wig, dressed in a long tent of dark-blue satin trimmed with sequin stars and a long cape of purple velvet with ermine tails. She was flanked by his two other aunts, Nelly, more dark and gnome-like than ever in Edwardian black, and Tilly, tall and strange with her long neck and her short, fluffy, incredibly blond hair that came to a point on her small head and her long thin hands with blood-red nails that sawed the air as she accompanied Dolly with shrill, bird-like cries.

'Ah, ha!' Dolly boomed.

'Oo, oo,' Tilly squeaked.

Mercifully, Nelly was silent.

Capricorn let them in without question. They would have come anyway.

'We finished the night up at Freddy Blunk's!' Dolly shouted, as she tanked towards the kitchen. 'Went there after the Golden Calf closed. But he fell asleep in the middle of a song. Moonlight and roses,' she trilled in a ghastly falsetto. 'Caved in over the pianner. Getting on, Freddy,' she said with disapproval.

Capricorn found himself trying to calculate how old Dolly herself must be, even if she were the younger sister, but gave up. His aunts had lied about their age so much, he doubted whether they knew the truth themselves any more. They could only agree that his mother, who had died in childbirth, had been the eldest, and *much* older than any of them.

'Don't you ever sleep?' he asked, as Dolly looked round, disappointed.

'Course,' she said, 'as you well know. Days. Where's Mac? I thought she'd give us breakfast. She can do breakfast, I'll say that for the old cow. The only thing the Scotch know is breakfast.'

'Ah'm here,' came a voice from the doorway. Capricorn shuddered. His housekeeper, Mrs Dermott, had arrived silently as usual, using her own key, and could now have stood for a model of matutinal respectability next to the late-night revellers. Like Nelly, she wore black, in her case to commemorate her widowhood, but her garments resembled those in fashion circa 1940. Her face was grim under her sensible hat with brim and bow: she had detested the Merlinos for over two decades, and she strongly objected to being called Mac.

'If yu'll leave ma kitchen,' she said coldly, 'breakfast will be on the table in twenty minutes.'

But Dolly had found her way to the drinks cupboard and was pouring brandy for herself and her sisters.

'Oo,' Tilly chirped, her talons beating a sharp tattoo on the glass.

'You know she's not supposed to have it,' Nelly said, cross. 'I've been telling you all night, Doll. The doctor said it doesn't go with the stuff he's giving her.'

Dolly had flung herself on Capricorn's Regency sofa, with a happy kick of her stubby ankles. In the lovely, twin-arched room, filled with graceful, beautiful objects, she looked like a gargoyle with legs.

'Oh, it's all right if you fancy it,' she sang, exuberant.

Nelly looked at the thin, wild-eyed Tilly with doubt. 'They only let her out when you promised not to get her too excited,' she said.

Capricorn was hastily making coffee, while Mrs Dermott looked dour. Even he was not supposed to be in the kitchen when she was there. On the other hand, it was better to suffer her wrath than to let Dolly drink herself into more liveliness than she had already. Not to mention Tilly. He saw Mrs Dermott give Tilly a very doubtful look.

For many years, Tilly had been in a home for the slightly mad. The Magic Merlinos had gone on with the three sisters, Dolly, Nelly and Milly. Milly, the pretty one, had left to go to the States, in a period when there seemed to be little future for a magic act, and died there. But Dolly had been determined to make a future in television, and, with the help of her almost-husband Tod, she had. Dolly Merlino was a favourite on the panel shows, a star turn on the variety bills and had her own magic show with Nelly. But they had badly needed the third sister, and Dolly decided to get Tilly released. To Capricorn's surprise, the doctors had been agreeable, possibly because they considered the new drugs effective, or possibly, as he suspected, because the world had become so crazy during Tilly's incarceration that she was now no different from the rest. It was hard to tell what her condition was as she had never been very verbal, and certainly her skill at magic was unimpaired.

'Oh, you'll never guess who was with who,' Dolly said slyly.

Capricorn fetched the tray of coffee while Mrs Dermott rattled round noisily in the kitchen.

'When is a copper's wife not a copper's wife?' Dolly went on and chuckled hugely, showing off a mouthful of impossibly white teeth.

Capricorn wasn't interested in gossip and wondered gloomily how long his aunts would stay. He wanted to get into the shower, and then he wanted to look at the papers about Brixton Jim once more, determined to get the information out of the 'stoppo' driver. Besides, he was sick of hearing hints about Joss Parker.

Mrs Dermott came in and laid the table at the other end of the room, by the window over the garden.

'Porridge?' she asked the aunts distantly.

'Not for us,' Dolly laughed loudly. 'We're magicians, not weight lifters.'

She had cast off her velvet cape and it lay in a tumbled mess on the rug. Mrs Dermott looked pointedly at Dolly's almost bare, flat chest and muscular arms. 'I couldna tell,' she said.

'Oo, oo,' Tilly squeaked and grabbed a bowl of porridge and ate happily, standing by the fireplace.

'Too good-looking by half, is Joss, to be a copper's wife,' Dolly said, deciding to ignore Mrs Dermott, whom she had never been able to best. 'What a figure! Oh, she'd be marvellous in the act.'

Tilly scowled. She clanked her spoon in the porridge bowl ominously. Thin to the point of boniness, she felt threatened by any reference to the charms of more voluptuous women. Dolly, who loved to tease, was well aware of it.

Capricorn hastily assembled his breakfast party into some sort of order at the table while Dolly regaled him with stories of the BBC and ITV—who had left what for where and who was sorry they had, and how all the young girls looked alike, and had no staying power. A young star who had been big two years ago and had gone all the way to the bottom—Sir Hugh Brody had said she would never appear in any of his productions again—had been at the Golden Calf the night before trying to catch the eye of Charlie Bo, who was reputed to have some mysterious influence in cafés and clubs.

'Tried real hard to chat him up, she did,' Dolly said happily, digging toast into her egg yolk, 'but he wasn't interested in *her*. Oh, no. You can see who he's still gone on. Always was, for all a certain policeman likes to think otherwise.'

Capricorn pushed his plate away, and frowned. The Golden Calf was something he hadn't wanted to think about yet, but apparently he had to. Dolly's remarks about Joss were not just an attempt to annoy her sister. If Charlie Bo, a known Mafia character, was a habitué of the Golden Calf, it was something he had to know. He'd better let Dolly tell her tale. It might even be the reason for her unusual visit. She had no love for the police, but was fond enough of her nephew to drop him a hint that would save him from trouble.

'Tell me, Dolly,' he said. 'What's it all about?'

She pushed her lower lip forward and her eyelids sank over her pebble-like eyes. Already she was withdrawing, not caring to be direct. 'Well, you know who,' she said. 'Two years, living in almost-married bliss. Just the time to get restless. Charlie Bo always liked her. And where he likes, he spends. And a certain party likes that. Not enough in the world for her, there isn't,' she added cattily, her weathervane loyalties shifting about.

She helped herself to Mrs Dermott's homemade blackberry jam. Unlike most women who drink deep, Dolly enjoyed her food. Food, drink, men—all her appetites were hearty. 'Never thought I'd like a law,' she said. 'No offense, Merle. But I've always had a fancy for young Copper. Lovely feller.'

Copper flirted outrageously with the Merlino aunts, and his brazen pseudo-pursuit of Dolly, whom he called Scarlett, had won her tough old heart. 'Saucy boy. Makes you want to eat him up. But just the same, he's a law. But Joss now—lovely bit of stuff she is—she's something else.'

Dolly shook her head, refusing coffee. Breakfast was finished. That was all she would say. Informing directly to Scotland Yard was outside her code of ethics. She poured herself a little after-breakfast drink. Serious talk, she indicated, was over.

'Dare say there's nothing in it,' she beamed.

'You've had enough,' Nelly said to Tilly who was covering her face and hair with jam.

'Oh, leave her alone, don't nag,' Dolly said. 'She fancies it, that's all.'

Tilly licked the spoon and tried to slip it in her handbag. Mrs Dermott quietly took it away. Tilly had always been a jackdaw, and Mrs Dermott considered everything that belonged to Capricorn to be in her charge.

Capricorn tried again. 'You don't think Joss is having an affair with Charlie Bo, do you?'

'Oh, affair,' Dolly shrugged her shoulders and laughed. 'Gawd, you are old-fashioned, Merle, the way you talk.' She glanced at the portrait of a woman that hung over the fireplace, a woman with a very English beauty. 'Still chasing after her Ladyship?'

Dolly had always been derisive about his affection for his old friend Rose, the daughter of a North Country clergyman, now Lady Theale, as well as other romantic admirations he had had in the past for various cool, unobtainable beauties.

'Straitlaced, that's what you are, Merle,' she said. 'Even when you was a little boy. Stuffy lot, all your generation. Not like the kids,' she went on happily. 'They're like us. Not a lot of po-faced prudes. Nothing goes over on the telly any more without a bit of bare tit and bum. Not,' she added, 'that they know what to *do* with a bum. You should've seen Marie Lloyd at the old Brit in Hoxton. That was when the Halls was the Halls. Got run in, she did, for her turn 'A little of what you fancy.' Oh, how she played up to the beak. Asked her to sing it, and she sang like a bloody choir boy, and he let her off. But you wouldn't have believed what it was like on stage.'

She sprang to her feet, hitched her skirt up with a sash that she pulled from the protesting Tilly, and exposed her strong square knees and chunky thighs.

Oh, it's all right, if you fancy it,

If you fancy it, it's understood.

She danced about, pumping her hips in a carica-

ture of eroticism and with an abandon that caused
Capricorn to close his eyes. 'Now that Joss, *she* knows
what men fancy.' Dolly threw the remark over her
shoulder rather breathlessly as she pranced on the
rug. 'You should've seen her last night, Merle, with
her dress cut down to here,' she indicated her navel,
'and that pair of hers hanging out, just held up with
a bit of Sellotape, and her shoving it all under Charlie Bo's nose until his eyes were popping out of his
head. She's not doing all that for nothing.

'Oh, it's all right, if you fancy it.' Dolly turned
round, half squatting with her hands on her knees,
swaying her hindquarters vigorously, showing a pair
of large pink flannel bloomers.

Mrs Dermott, who had come in to clear, looked
grimly on.

'Oh, a little of what you fancy does you good.'

FANFARE AND DIRGE

What about a little, or a lot, of what you didn't fancy? Capricorn wondered late that light. He supposed that it did you harm. Nevertheless, that was his lot at the moment. He very much disliked night clubs, he had no taste for exhorting his juniors about their private lives, but here he was, entering the Golden Calf, to observe what was going on and to warn, unofficially, his old friend Inspector Copper. He started when the brazen blond in the cloakroom yelled after him, with roguish cheeriness, 'Hello, sucker!'

It had been a tiring, unproductive and annoying day. A morning spent interrogating the murderous driver, Jack Hake, had brought no new information. The frank-faced, smiling young man, in the absence of a promise regarding a lesser charge, had blithely pretended not to remember his hints about Brixton Jim. He made a show of cooperation by telling what he knew about the other gang members, which wasn't a lot. They were already known to the Yard, and under arrest.

His complete absence of real remorse and his very apparent assurance of his ability to make a trade grated on Capricorn so that he had had to impose a strict control on himself to keep his questioning calm and purposeful. What bothered him with this young criminal, Capricorn thought afterwards, was his assumption that crime, policework and justice were run on purely commercial principles. He had no idea of right or wrong, no notion of responsibility, no idea that justice had anything to do with the consequences of his actions. A good trade was all the young man had in mind, and to him the police were merely fellow traders, the killing of children set on the scales alongside a big arrest, Capricorn becoming a confederate after the act to attain a promotion-bringing capture.

Luncheon brought only a change of woe. Capricorn's old friend Manning of Special Branch had come late for their appointment. A brilliant detective, of nondescript appearance with grey hair and eyes, Manning now had the additional grey of extreme fatigue. Capricorn had been assigned to work with him recently, during an emergency, and they had been successful in rounding up one gang of terrorists, but as Manning told Capricorn, there seemed to be no end to the supply.

Manning was also concerned about a report from Drug Squad. A new wave of drug imports had hit Great Britain, and Drugs was puzzled. The government-run clinics that supplied free drugs to addicts had made that business far less profitable here than abroad. There seemed no reasonable commercial motive for this effort, and the idea of a possible political implication couldn't be ignored.

Full of foreboding, intensified, Capricorn thought, by overwork, Manning muttered over his food. 'They say power comes out of the barrel of a gun. You could add that weakness comes from the end of a hypodermic needle.' He had to rush away and Capricorn was joined for coffee by his Commander, who further depressed him with talk of hints going round about Copper's equivocal position. After luncheon Capricorn had attended an important conference with several squads represented. Copper's name came up again, though at first only for commendation. In-

terpol was involved but Counterfeit Currency sat in,
as the subject was the coiners that Copper had
tracked down. The men would be returned to Italy;
Interpol was satisfied; the Yard was not. Preliminary
investigation had made it appear likely that the men
Interpol had inquired about were only the small fry
of the operation. That left two questions open: were
any of the big fish in Great Britain? And if so, should
the Yard expend its short supply of manpower in
their pursuit?

On the first question, the opinion of Counterfeit
Currency was inclined to be 'No'. They had no
knowledge of any major villains employed in this
business. As they said, it was something new. Of
course, no one could be certain. On the second question, Capricorn weighed in on the affirmative side.
The selling of the fake Krugerrands had been a very
dirty business. The people who had bought them
were not sophisticated investors who knew enough to
trade with established dealers. The coins could not
have deceived anyone with a modicum of knowledge.
They were not, strictly speaking, fakes, but genuine
rands that had been drilled, the gold removed from
the inside, and lead pumped in in its place. A layer
of gold over the drilled portion preserved the look of
the coin, at least to the naked eye, but the weight was
lighter than the full ounce of the original coin.

The coiners' salesmen, minor confidence men, had
found an easy market. They preyed on the elderly,
some gullible small businessmen, a few housewives
with a little money put by. It was simple to play on
the fears of people who saw the pound sterling sinking and heard tales of its coming worthlessness. The
fraudsmen had said that the government would soon
forbid the import of such coins, which had proved
true; and they had gone on to whisper that the well-
known dealers informed the government about purchases, and that any gold bought from them might be

confiscated at a later date. Frugal old men and
women had rushed to put their small savings into the
hands of the thieves, and more than one suicide had
followed when the victims realized they had been
hoaxed.

Not everyone agreed with Capricorn.

'Caveat emptor,' someone remarked cynically.

Sedgwick, the solid, sensible Northcountryman who
was the Superintendent in charge of Counterfeit, took
a more hopeful view. 'Now that gold is down the
public will get over the fever. They know now it's illegal to bring the coins in, and they'll be more on the
lookout.'

Capricorn couldn't agree with either of the speak-
ers. Gold fever was bound to return as the inflation of
the currency continued. Caveat emptor should not
apply. It was not the fault, surely, of elderly and
thrifty Britons, who had worked and saved through a
long life for their old age, that the government had
swollen the currency and made them look for some
other store for their means of survival. And if they
believed the coins to be smuggled, it would only
make them afraid to complain when they found
themselves cheated. But his considerations would be
called political, and outside the province of the Yard.
He was unsuccessful; the investigation was closed,
and he was not happy about it.

Then, after the meeting, Sedgwick buttonholed
him to ask if he would have a talk with Copper.
Capricorn looked at the heavyset, freckle-faced Super
with irritation. After all his years in London,
Sedgwick's voice still held a trace of his North Country origin. Usually it was pleasant to Capricorn's ears
but today it was not. At the moment, Sedgwick was
officially Copper's senior officer. It was his job to
speak to him, if it were anybody's. Sedgwick's mild
grey eyes, gazing at Capricorn hopefully, made him
feel more annoyed than ever.

'Lad's done a first-class job,' Sedgwick said, 'I was pleased as Punch at him getting the step up. It would be a shame now if anything were to 'appen to spoil it. And if you could tip him the wink,' he added, 'well, the sooner the better.'

His gaze slid from Capricorn to study the floor of the corridor, as if it held some special interest. Nobody wanted to think ill of Copper; he had been a respected detective at Central too long for that. Years before a man was made a detective sergeant first-class, let alone an inspector, he was proved to be worthy of trust. Nor did anybody at the Yard *really* think ill of him. It was just that since he had lived with Joss Parker—Capricorn understood. There was something there as intangible and yet as offensive as a bad smell.

He had decided to refuse, even if his Commander had hinted about the same thing. It wasn't his responsibility. Then his sense of fairness made itself felt. He and Copper had been friends as well as colleagues, and that was well known at the Yard. They had worked together successfully on many cases and their personalities, though so different, harmonized well. Certainly it was natural that he should be asked to handle a delicate matter before it came to official cognizance. And, by saying 'the sooner the better,' Sedgwick had made it clear that official cognizance was very close. There was no time to lose.

So he sighed and went on into the club to see what Joss Parker had wrought. She had done well, was his first judgement, and the second was that it must have cost a great deal of money. The dominant motif, of course, was gold. The walls were finished to look like stacked bars of bullion. The ceiling was dark blue like a night sky, with golden coins twinkling as stars. The room was a good size and looked larger, for the bar and tables were of a clear, glass-like material in which more fake coins were embedded. Joss must have planned and opened this place before Copper got his last assignment, Capricorn reflected, otherwise it would have seemed an odd joke. At the far end of the club, a trio of piano, bass and drums was perched on a raised platform playing a melodious jazz. The curtains on either side of the platform were the same colour as the ceiling, and the spotlight was set in a canopy decorated with a huge figure that dominated the room, a glittering, prancing golden calf.

The place was almost full, and although many of the patrons were smoking, the air was quite clear, fresher, in fact, than the air outside. Joss's ventilation system was excellent, and the music subdued. Even though he was rather depressed at the thought of his distasteful errand, Capricorn had to admit to himself that his senses, at least, weren't being assaulted in the way he expected. And the people who had come to worship the golden calf—or was it Bacchus?—were socially a cut above anything he had foreseen.

There were a lot of moneyed young people from good families, a sprinkling of well-known business-men, a few theatrical stars and a cinema actor. Very different, Capricorn reflected, from the seedy Hi-Ho where he had first met Joss Parker. He saw, though, at least one doubtful type—in the middle of a noisy party of young socialites in a corner, was Len Slope, a fairly recent arrival in the West End, who forgathered with the rich though he had no known means of support. He was being very pleasant to the girl next to him, who looked vaguely familiar though Capricorn couldn't place her. He regretted the fashion among young people to find crooks 'amusing'. Then the blond, buxom woman from the cloakroom went to their table, all sparkle and smiles, and leaned over them laughing, momentarily obscuring the un-pleasant Slope from view.

The guests were eating dinner, in accordance with the club's license which permitted drink to be served only with meals. The food was well presented and looked delicious. That meant a well-equipped kitchen. Reluctantly, Capricorn's mind totalled what this must have cost, weighed it against Copper's salary and shuddered. A bank loan? But Joss had never had a business before. She would have needed nothing less than a fairy godmother at the bank to provide all this.

Copper was not visible. Capricorn allowed himself to be shown to the only remaining table, a small one by the wall near the bar and away from the tiny dance floor. Joss was not serving here; that was being done by an efficient-looking, middle-aged man, but she stood at one end, talking and laughing to a customer. She was beautiful, with the kind of beauty that shocks a passer-by into admiration. Her dark hair was drawn back into a knot, a style that only the most assured women could wear. A dress of metallic gold clung to her superb figure. Her magnificent shoulders were bare; she wore no jewellery, her strong neck holding her fine head proudly as if her face were ornament enough, which indeed it was.

Capricorn had always thought her handsome, and considered that she and the red-headed, virile and lively Copper made an attractive pair, well suited to each other. It made him uneasy to observe that she seemed even more of a natural companion for the man who was now standing beside her, laughing at her talk and obviously enjoying the vista of fair flesh before him. Dolly's words rang in Capricorn's recollection.

'That Joss . . . she knows what men fancy . . . she's not doing all that for nothing . . .'

Carlo Bonomi, known in London as Charlie Bo, was older than Joss by ten years, and his body had thickened around the middle. He was still good looking in a dark, fleshy way; his eyes were shrewd and there was an air about him of confident success. Charlie Bo had always had a lot of what he fancied,

Capricorn concluded, whether it did him good or no, and he obviously intended to have a lot more.

Just then Capricorn found himself hailed by Slope, returning to his table from a phone booth. 'Even the Yard is eating here, I see,' he said, in a voice that managed to be obsequious and impudent at the same time. Capricorn remembered that Slope had once given information to the Yard on a small matter, and resigned himself to a not unfriendly greeting.

'Well, it's classy and very reasonable,' Slope went on. 'Wonder how Money Mum does it.'

He looked at Joss, still laughing with Charlie Bo, speculatively.

'I take it you mean Miss Parker,' Capricorn said.

' 'Sright. Known as Money Mum by one and all. Heart of gold, they say. And all the rest of her to match.'

He hung over Capricorn with a confidential air.

'You wouldn't credit it, but I'd run up a little bill, and I was a bit short a while back—not for long, but when I didn't pay up on the dot, our Mum sent a couple of bruisers round to put the arm on me.'

'I would suggest you pay your bills,' Capricorn replied, wondering whether to believe this tale.

'Gawd's truth—or she might send the p'lice, eh?' Slope gave a nasty snigger. 'Well, got to get back to Brenda,' he nodded to his companion at the table, 'You know Brenda,' and he made his way back and sat between the cloakroom woman and the girl whom Capricorn recognized at least as Brenda Grey.

Brenda Grey. He would much rather not have recognized her. Only a few weeks before he had had a letter from her father, General Grey, who had been abroad, asking if there was anything Capricorn could do. The General had been dismayed. His daughter was in London with a 'bad set' as he put it. Capricorn found them to be engaged in amusing themselves by experimenting with cannabis and various sexual arrangements. He was powerless to interfere. Brenda was of age, she had managed to stay clear of the Dangerous Drugs Squad, and whatever life she chose was her own affair.

He would have liked to help. As a young woman, her mother, dead now for many years, had moved the then Sergeant Capricorn to a respectful, if distant, admiration. Isobel Grey had been a charmer, with her long, fair hair and violet-coloured eyes, her elegance and her bubbling sense of humour. Brenda had been a pretty child; she was now a mess. She looked oddly older than her twenty-one years. Her hair was frizzed and dull. Her dress, long and shapeless, looked as though it came from a secondhand shop and gave the impression, even in the soft light, of being not quite fresh. A large jet brooch sparkled sombrely on her shoulder, and beads hung in long rows from her neck. Her glance, once candid and friendly, now rested on Capricorn for a moment and slid away, without a sign of recognition or greeting. She was chatting noisily and seemed over-excited.

He had almost forgotten he was waiting for Copper when he saw him pass Brenda's table, give her a smile and a pinch on her bare arm, then swing around to see Joss and Charlie Bo still engaged in talk at the bar. Copper walked across the dance floor towards them, his pleasant smile fading, and stood beneath the golden calf, his red hair and green eyes glittering in the spotlight. First Joss, then Charlie, became silent. The silence among the three of them seemed to grow and spread uncomfortably, until the leader of the trio, which had been taking a few minutes rest, looked round, nodded, and the music resumed.

Copper saw Capricorn and smiled again, patted Joss on the shoulder and came and sat down. ' 'Ullo, guv,' he said, 'Don't tell me you've been reduced to raiding licensed premises. I knew you'd never make a go of it, with me off on the Italian job.'

His manner was light and jocular as usual, but his humour seemed mechanical to Capricorn, as though his mind was on something else, and to the eye of his old friend he looked tired and dispirited. 'It hasn't been the same without you,' Capricorn rejoined, 'still, I hear from Sedgwick you cleared that job up nicely.'

'For what it was,' Copper shrugged. 'That collar was worth nothing. Whoever organized that job could have another dozen boys working for 'im in a week. Or whenever it suits him.' Copper was far too good a policeman not to have realized that. 'But I under-stand it's a closed case. Well, ours not to reason why.

'You're not drinking,' he observed. He turned and called a waiter. 'Joss won't make any money like this. Or eating. You've got to eat, you know. Unless you've been sent to fit Joss up.'

The waiter presented a long menu. Capricorn, who had eaten dinner, or what passed for it, settled for a brandy and mushrooms on toast.

'Joss is making money?' Capricorn asked. He might as well start now. It would never be any easier.

'She's doing well,' Copper said, obviously proud, though not quite answering the question. He smiled at Joss who had left Charlie Bo at the bar and was having a word with a customer who sat alone and looked, not forlorn, but not happy either. He was a small man, probably in his late fifties, conventionally dressed except for a blue bow tie with white spots. Something about him gave Capricorn the impression that he wasn't English, a European of some sort, a small businessman, alone in England, determined to have a little fun in 'swingin' London' and not quite sure how to do it. He had come to the wrong place. Joss employed no hostesses. The little man had an air both prim and mouse-like and as Joss leaned over him, laughing and displaying a fair expanse of almost naked bosom, Capricorn could have sworn he saw his whiskers twitch.

It was plain why Joss would do well.

'D'you think she'd be interested in selling out?' Capricorn asked, wondering how he could phrase his warning tactfully.

'No. Why should she be?'

'It's causing a bit of soul-searching at the Yard.'

The mushrooms came and they were surprisingly good. Nor did Joss palm off inferior brandy on her guests. Yet her prices, as Slope had remarked, were moderate. If it wasn't for all that gold, Capricorn thought, and those wretched imitation coins that reminded him of the day's grief, he would think this club quite a civilized place.

'It's nothing to do with the Yard,' Copper said shortly.

Capricorn put his fork down with a sigh.

'Now, you know if you were married to Joss they could give you an either-or. Either she gives it up, or you resign. Conflict of interest.'

'But we're not married.'

Copper's voice had a decided edge. Rumour was right: it must have been Joss who refused legal matrimony. Strange for Copper, who had been the non-caring Don Juan for so long.

'Even so. You're living together openly.'

'Thanks for the advice,' Copper said coldly. In the language of the Metropolitan Police, advice meant a strong dressing down.

'You could be on dab,' Capricorn said, 'undesirable associates.'

'No, I couldn't,' Copper said through his teeth, glaring at his superior. 'There's nothing against Joss. She's clean as a whistle. Never broken any law, regulation, or even been accused of it. Not even a summons for driving. If anyone wants to have me up for 'undesirable associate' let him prove it.'

The lady in question was now back at the bar, talking again to Charlie Bo. Capricorn didn't want to aggravate a situation that was rapidly going from bad to worse, but he couldn't avoid glancing at the couple. Copper turned and followed his glance, and a vivid flush crept up his neck and suffused his face. "And if you've got anything to say, say it.'

Capricorn felt his own anger rising. He was merely trying to help. Then he caught himself, and put his brandy glass down. No one should understand better than a policeman that he who gives advice for another's good should expect a hostile reception. Nevertheless, they were treading on dangerous ground. The Metropolitan Police was an organization run under tight discipline. Through the years, there had been eyebrows raised about his relationship with Copper, a junior in rank whose familiar manner had seemed disrespectful to older and more conventional officers. Capricorn had never worried about it; their relationship was based on mutual respect and Copper's flippant manner was only a surface dress. In truth, he had amused Capricorn; a little levity was a welcome change from the ponderous manners of the Force.

But this attitude of Copper's was new. It not only bordered on disrespect, it had crossed the border. True, they were not officially on duty, but the detectives at Central were hardly ever really off duty. He could stop now, Capricorn weighed the matter, before Copper was provoked to a serious breach of discipline. Yet that would be shirking the job. The next step then would certainly be an official inquiry. It might even be scheduled already. Copper had been a good policeman. He deserved a chance to clear this mess up.

'You two have been spending a lot of money.' He started in low key.

'Together we earn it,' Copper said, wary but getting hold of himself.

'It causes comment, you must realize,' Capricorn tried to be diplomatic. 'People see you spending much more than your salary.'

'I don't see why,' Copper said. His tone was cold. 'I'm certainly not the only one. With due respect, guv,' he gave Capricorn a mocking flash of his green eyes, 'you do yourself. You got it from your old man,' he shrugged. 'Joss makes her own money and spends it.'

Capricorn, who had indeed received an inheritance from his father The Great Capricornus that had become more valuable as time went on, sighed. If Copper couldn't see the difference . . . Then he wondered uncomfortably if Copper had resented his comparative affluence in the past. Capricorn was a man of modest tastes, except sometimes in the salesrooms, but one of his pleasures was to entertain his friends and colleagues and to do it well. A detective's life was hard and often sordid. It was agreeable to provide a change. Copper had seemed to enjoy his hospitality over the years, but had he, after all, felt patronized?

Capricorn tried to continue. 'The car, your house,' he said.

'The new car is Joss's. The house is mine. You know I sold the one I lived in with Myrtle, and I made a bomb on it, I can tell you."

He didn't have to, Capricorn already knew. Copper would have been surprised, Capricorn thought, if he realized how much his affairs were already common knowledge. Yet, as a detective, he shouldn't be.

'The place you bought is charming,' he said. 'Sixteenth century, I remember, but with all mod. con. And quite a bit of land.'

'Joss picked it out,' Copper said. 'She has good taste. So it cost a bit more. Anything does, nowadays. You couldn't expect a girl like Joss to live in a modern box in the suburbs.'

Capricorn refrained from saying so, but he really didn't see why not. When he and Copper had first met Joss Parker, she had been sharing a slightly refurbished slum in Shoreditch. She was very happy to get

the room there, she had told them, when her friend, a
nurse, had moved out because her feet couldn't stand
the walk to Liverpool Street station.

That, however, was not the point. Copper was obviously in debt, and probably heavily in debt, but if he
could carry it, that was all right. Or Capricorn hoped
it was. He might as well get the worst over. 'You
don't have any ownership in the club, then?' he
asked.

'No,' Copper replied, but he did not meet Capricorn's gaze. Instead, he stirred his drink, a mild-look-
ing concoction with slices of fruit.

'Where did Joss get the money for the club? It's
known,' Capricorn tried to put it delicately, 'that she
wasn't a woman of means.'

'You have been buzzing about, haven't you?' Copper said sullenly. His chair was half-swivelled round;
he was still watching Joss and Charlie Bo, who certainly had a proprietorial air.

'I only put five thousand down on the house at
Wenmore. The rest was loans and a mortgage. I gave
the rest of the price of the old house to Joss.'

Capricorn closed his eyes for a moment, trying not
to add up Copper's indebtedness, and wondering
what a board of inquiry would think about that 'gift'.
'You gave her, that must have been about fifteen
thousand pounds. But you don't have a mortgage on
the club?'

'No. It wasn't a gift, exactly. Joss will pay it back
when she can but there weren't any—formalities.'

Naturally, Capricorn reflected, for with any hint of
legal involvement in this club, Copper would have to
resign. 'Joss has done well here. She certainly couldn't
have done all this on fifteen thousand.'

'Glad you're pleased,' Copper said shortly. 'She also
got a loan from the bank.'

Copper was perhaps being truthful about his own
transactions. He was just silly enough to make Joss

Parker a present of fifteen thousand pounds. For the rest, Capricorn could only believe him gullible. The place must have cost at least forty thousand. If he had given Joss fifteen, then she had had to raise another twenty-five. What kind of bank manager had given a young woman, with experience only as a secretary and a barmaid, a loan of twenty-five thousand, or more?

'Did you countersign her loan?' Capricorn asked. He didn't know what answer would be worse. If Copper had not, then the money probably came from some dubious source. Charlie Bo, at that moment, was putting his hand on the back of Joss's neck as she bent over the bar. The gesture seemed shockingly intimate. Fortunately, Copper was still gazing down at his drink, which he hadn't sampled. At least he hadn't taken to drinking, Capricorn thought mechanically. Copper had always been rather abstemious, except for beer. He wondered what Copper's answer would be to his question. If he *had* signed for Joss's loan, it would involve him in the club. And what kind of assurance could he have given the bank? Obviously, he couldn't repay the loan with all his other debts. The only inference to be drawn was unpleasant. Capricorn's fingers drummed against his glass. Many night places made money. They would be a good risk, except for the fact they so often ran afoul of the law. Licensing regulations were strict, and a steady stream of clubs opened only to be closed by the police. Copper, surely, would not have implied—'Protection' by the police was not a custom in England.

Copper set Capricorn's mind at rest, on that subject at least.

'What good would that have been?' he muttered.

Behind him Joss laughed. Charlie was amusing her.

'What are you after, anyway?' Copper asked, glaring at him.

The two men looked at each other over the table

glittering with false gold. Their uneasiness was resolving into grave doubt on Capricorn's part and open hostility on Copper's. To Capricorn, who had no family except his Merlino aunts, no brother or sister or even a cousin, Copper had become over the years very much like a younger brother, to be tolerated and encouraged. Copper's devotion to police work had never been questioned before; it had broken up his marriage when Myrtle decided that the lot of a detective's wife was not for her. But now it seemed as though Copper's love for Joss Parker was stronger than his love for his work.

If Joss had taken money from Charlie Bo, the case was clear. Copper could be brought up on charges and dismissed for consorting with undesirable characters. True, Charlie himself had never been convicted of wrongdoing in England. The Bonomis, a well-known Mafia family operating on the East Coast of the United States, had sent Charlie to England when a Senate Investigating Committee was becoming inquisitive, while at the same time England, under the Gaming Act, had become alluring. The Home Office, which had steadily refused residence to any known or even suspected Mafia character, could do nothing, as Charlie's mother had been tactless enough to give birth to him while on a visit to relatives in Soho: Charlie was British-born, and, as far as anyone could prove, clean with the law. His activities might not be desirable, involved as he was in clubs, pubs, gambling and doubtful health rooms, but he had never been caught doing anything illegal. There were no steps that could be taken to get rid of him. He had been watched but nothing had been discovered except that he liked pretty women and had a bad heart. 'The Yard's best hope,' the Assistant Commissioner had said.

Nevertheless, his family connections were enough to make trouble for Copper. 'Which bank gave Joss

the loan?' Capricorn pressed on. 'You use the Eastland, don't you?'

Copper looked up. At that moment Charlie Bo
reached out and gave Joss a big bear hug, perhaps
merely friendly, perhaps not. Copper smashed his
glass on the table. It shattered like a handful of ice.
'Mind your own bloody business,' he said. He got up
swiftly and walked away.

Capricorn, dismayed, looked down at the mess he
was left with. Liquid and sliced fruit from Copper's
drink oozed over the table top to drip on the golden
rug. Impractical that, for a drinking place, his mind
ticked over, avoiding for a moment acknowledgement
of a breach that was not only personal but of which
he should take official notice. Such behavior from a
junior was hardly to be borne, even in an off-duty interview. And even if Copper was being driven, apparently, out of his wits.

Copper grabbed Joss's arm and pulled her forward.
She was taken unaware and almost fell. Charlie Bo
expostulated. The leader of the trio, without seeming
to notice, nodded to the drummer who played a long
roll and made his cymbal crash. The group played
some kind of fanfare and then went into a very loud
chorus of 'Oh, when the saints come marching in!'

Copper pushed Joss as if she were a prisoner. Charlie Bo followed, his face dark and angry. The patrons
looked up startled as the three went the length of the
room towards the private office. Joss said something
loud and furious, but the trio were playing at the top
of their capacity and hid the noise.

Capricorn observed, almost without attention, that
the little mousy man was watching passively; Slope,
from his crowded corner, looked on, avid; while
Brenda, merry on drink, was oblivious of all but her
own party.

Motioning to the waiter, Capricorn asked for his
bill. There was no reason to stay longer. He had said

what he had to say; it was up to Copper now to clean his house. If he had been deluding himself before, he could obviously do it no longer. Capricorn hoped they wouldn't come to blows back there—Copper was angry and Charlie Bo had been drinking steadily. Should Copper manage to persuade Joss to give up the club, or if he decided to leave her and keep his job, then it would be time to consider accepting an apology.

To his surprise, before his bill was made out, the three of them returned. Whatever had been said and done, a certain sullen peace had been restored. More patrons had entered, and Charlie Bo's seat at the bar had been taken. A waiter hastily brought out an extra table and chair for him and squeezed it between the table of the lone mousy little man, who looked offended, and Len Slope's table, where the guests were already shoulder to shoulder.

Joss swept forward haughtily to greet the newcomers at the bar. Charlie Bo sat down, lit a cigar, and had a word and a smile for Brenda with whom, to Capricorn's further dismay, he seemed very familiar. Copper glowered at Charlie and then followed Joss and stood beside her, arms folded, his eyes hard and his expression implacable. Joss gave him a quick look of what seemed to be anger and dislike. She would get rid of him if she could, Capricorn thought suddenly. The food and brandy had been good but it was sour in his stomach. He felt almost queasy. All his policeman's special awarenesses were roused. It was a nasty scene, of a kind that could only end badly.

Fortunately, Charlie Bo was ignoring the quarrelling lovers. He had another drink and was laughing and teasing Brenda, who leaned across Len Slope to whisper in his ear. She seemed to be whispering for a long time, and his smile grew wider. Suddenly he started, with a jerk of his big body, looked round and then laughed. He held up Brenda's jet brooch, a lugubrious ornament, doubtless set with the hair of someone's dear departed, the light catching the long, wicked-looking pin in the back. He restored it to Brenda's dress, taking his time with obvious pleasure. One of the young men in the party raised an eyebrow, but Slope, Brenda's escort, only smiled and made himself ingratiating, huddling himself into the wall to make the intimacy more convenient.

Capricorn, at this point as depressed as he could be, motioned again to his waiter. He had failed in every way. There was nothing more he could do. The waiter, forgetting him, had gone off in a rush to a large party that was leaving. Their bill must have been complicated and it was paid, at last, with a credit card, involving a trip to the bar and a consultation with Joss. It was another four or five minutes before the waiter, abashed, returned. A group of people left the bar for the vacant table and Charlie Bo, with a last pat of Brenda's cheek, got up and, ignoring Copper, started towards his previous seat next to where Joss still stood. Copper looked murderous.

Nothing had been settled, Capricorn knew, or Copper wouldn't look like that. Joss had probably refused to discuss it, postponing the quarrel until after business hours. Capricorn didn't really believe that Copper would tear himself away from her. In the future, when things turned sour, but not yet. Not in time to save his career. The Yard would lose one of its best men, a man who might have risen very high. Yet, there was no help for it.

Charlie Bo had almost reached the bar. He stopped in midstride and clutched his chest. His mouth opened but no words came. He lost his balance, swayed and fell. His face, turning ashen, hit the bar stool. Capricorn jumped up and went over, pushing Joss aside. Charlie's eyes stared up in terror; his lips were blue as he lay caught in the spotlight from the golden calf.

Charlie Bo was dead. His heart had failed. The A.C.'s 'last best hope' had been fulfilled. Capricorn had been away from the Yard for a few days, cleaning up some old business and investigating the Barlow Road affair, and when he got back to the Yard, he found the atmosphere among the senior officers considerably less tense. As Sedgwick told Capricorn at a chance meeting in the lift, if Joss Parker now kept her nose clean and if Copper stayed away from the Golden Calf, the matter might be allowed to drop. Sleeping dogs.

Capricorn was not cheered. He did not subscribe to the theory about sleeping dogs. One old saw contradicts another, he thought. Murder will out. Then he told himself he could at least be thankful that there was no murder involved. Though not everyone believed that.

The night Charlie died, Capricorn had received another telephone call from Gyppo Moggs. Word had come to him from a certain quarter, he'd said mysteriously, that Capricorn had better not 'put the poison in' on Hake, the Barlow Road driver: in other words, try to make it easy for him. It was bloody lucky for Copper, Moggs had gone on, as if the two matters were connected, 'his old lady's boy friend turning his toes up like that.'

It was like the underworld to know about Charlie's death within an hour or so of its occurrence. The

Golden Calf was in Soho, of course, the centre of the grapevine. But what was Moggs trying to insinuate about Charlie's death, and why the implied slur on Copper? There was nothing mysterious about the death, Capricorn told himself; the insinuations were pointless.

Whoever was prompting Moggs was, in any event, wasting his time. The decision had already been made: Hake was charged with murder. And he had given nothing away, pretending he had been misunderstood when he had mentioned Brixton Jim, his friendly-puppy face expressing only puzzlement. Yet, Brixton Jim's war of nerves on Capricorn through the medium of Copper proved that Brixton Jim was worried—Hake must know enough to be embarrassing. Capricorn wondered what Brixton Jim could have promised Hake to keep his quiet, knowing that he faced a long sentence. Or was Hake frightened? Could Brixton Jim's influence reach right into the prison system?

It was no use trying to pump Moggs. His position in this matter was very delicate. For it had been Moggs who first connected the elusive Brixton Jim with the respectable Marcus James, though no one but Capricorn knew that, not even Copper.

Gyppo had been caught in the act of burglary. He had been very sorrowful about this because, as he had told Capricorn, it was to have been his last big haul before retiring from such arduous work. He was spotted by the occupants of a Panda car that had no reason to be around the street at that hour, according to Moggs, and had in fact been chasing another wrongdoer.

With Moggs's record, he had to go to prison, and it was during this stay that he had become fast friends with another inmate. 'A top crook,' Moggs had bragged later. 'A real brain. And a gent. Never been inside before and he took it hard.' A quiet, withdrawn man, he had apparently enjoyed the company of the flamboyant Moggs, although talking little about himself until he fell a victim to influenza. Before he was taken to the prison hospital, in his delirium, he had whispered some interesting things to the always-inquisitive snout. The man had recovered from the fever, but had later died in a fight with another convict. Gyppo held his tongue until his release but afterwards, in return for some little favours, and in gratitude for help that Capricorn had given Mrs Moggs during the absence of her provider, he had passed the information on.

Now Capricorn wondered about the convenient death of the talking prisoner, about Hake's apparent nonchalance, and how such an unimportant villain could have such vital knowledge, so vital that Brixton Jim would try intimidation of two CID men to insure Hake's silence. Certainly, none of the others on the Eastland job knew anything.

Henry Price, the 'peterman,' or safe-cracker, a well-known professional with two prison terms behind him, had recruited the other members of the team. He was a small, neat, bright-eyed Cockney of the sort that before the war would have worn a cloth cap and addressed a superintendent as 'Sir.' Now his dress, though sober, was a lot better than that of the CID officers in the division, and 'Mr Capperken' was the limit of his respect.

Not only Hake, but Jonesy the lookout, and Cock-Eye Bert, who carried both a cosh and a gun, had been well known to Price before the job. The bellman, or alarm-silencer, was a new entry in the criminal stakes as far as anyone knew. He was employed by the manufacturer of the alarm system used by the bank, and would never have been traced if he hadn't been in the car with Hake at the time of his capture.

'Bleedin' amachers, Mr Capperken,' Price had said in disgust. 'What did he want to go and get in that car for? Could've walked away, clean as a whistle. None of the others knew 'im. And you know me, Mr Capperken. I'm no snout.'

Unfortunately, it seemed for a time as if this were true. Capricorn probed delicately as to why a competent professional would have approached this gifted amateur.

'Got to 'ave 'em now, guv. They makes the bell system diabolical these days. A real grafter can't keep up. You've got to get someone from inside.'

Advancing technology causes problems to all classes, Capricorn reflected. In this case, apparently it wasn't a big problem, since the mousetrap worked for the mouse. He inquired further how the gang had known that this apparently respectable citizen could be approached.

'Well, that would be tellin'.' The bright eyes gazed up at Capricorn hopefully. It looked as though his ethics against informing might be open to compromise after all. Capricorn, who didn't blame the old man for the excesses of Hake, sounded, in turn, willing to be helpful, but the results were disappointing.

Henry Price had been approached about the job and given a description of the man and instructions to meet him only in public houses, and a different one each time. The description could have been that of thousands of middle-aged men, the name was almost certainly false. Capricorn remarked bitterly that Price had taken a lot of risks for this elusive character.

'Oh, I dunno,' he answered thoughtfully. 'Sweeter was all right. Lovely job. Piece of cake it was. Not Sweeter's fault that silly young bugger has to go and run over an infants' outing. Oo,' he said, disgusted. 'Fair turns my stomach to think about it. All these years and I've never been mixed up in rough stuff. Don't like it. That's for low-lifes. Rubbish. Pity he can't swing for it.'

The killings had certainly made this elderly villain sweat. If he had known about Brixton Jim, or the identity of Sweeter, he would have talked. Capricorn, always persistent, had gone on questioning, but came away convinced that Price knew nothing of value.

It had been a smoothly handled operation. And it would have gone off perfectly if it hadn't been for Hake's fondness for amphetamines and his fate in meeting the ice-cream van. Capricorn ran a check through the computer at C11 with the little information Price had given on Sweeter, but it was hopeless. He could be any one of a hundred known thieves or none of them.

Frustrated, Capricorn went to meet his friend Manning of Special Branch for lunch. He was glad his appointment was with Manning; of all Capricorn's acquaintance at the Yard, Manning was the only one who also believed that Marcus James, warehouseman, was the shadowy criminal Brixton Jim, and who also suspected the magnitude of Brixton Jim's operations and his pernicious effect on the life of the country. The A.C. was amused by Capricorn's long-harboured suspicions and referred to James as 'our conjurer's Loch Ness monster.' Certainly, James was well submerged in his life of rather drab respectability.

The two policemen had arranged to meet at a pub that had been a favourite of Capricorn's for years, a quiet, unpretentious place that served good plain food. He was disappointed when he arrived to find that, in the few weeks since he had last been there, it had changed hands and been drastically altered. The private alcoves, the round wooden tables, the comfortable chairs, had all disappeared. Now small plastic squares, each with two stools, were set in rows from wall to wall. The waitresses rushed and pushed their way through the crowded customers, carrying trays of pre-cut sandwiches wrapped in polythene. To add to the noise and confusion, a large colour televi-

sion set was blaring away on the bar: a news pro-
gramme was being presented, bombs were exploding,
but before Capricorn was able to identify the unfortunate locality, he saw Manning sitting at a table, quite
unperturbed by his surroundings—he cared little for
creature comfort. Manning, because of his nondescript appearance and chameleon-like quality, was
known as 'the grey ghost' of Special Branch. Now he
looked as though he ate in that same place every day
of his life, as if he were a clerk in a nearby office,
willing to endure what had to be endured to eat
cheaply and quickly, saving his money for his mortgage and his time for the extra work that he did in
his lunch hour.

Capricorn sat down, elbow-to-elbow with an elderly
man at the next table who was lunching with a young
companion, and tried to bestow his long legs without
tripping someone. He greeted his friend, and ordered,
but when his sandwich arrived, he found it inedible
and spent the time grumbling to Manning, a very de-
pendable listener, about the attitude of his colleagues
and superiors in the matter of Brixton Jim.

'It's not,' he said moodily, taking a pull at his beer,
'as if they don't know very well that such men exist,
even if we don't often get something to go after.'

'Merchant bankers of crime,' Manning said reflectively. Capricorn nodded. It was a good description.
Men like Brixton Jim bore the same relation to criminal activity that bankers bore to business. Financiers
and investors. Sometimes they took a hand in planning, as a merchant banker might help a management with special knowledge, but they were only
involved with top decisions and never with operations.

'It's easier abroad,' Capricorn said irritably, 'where
the big men run their own mobs. There's always a
chance of picking up someone high enough in the
chain of command to be able to testify against them.'

'The independent workman—part of the British way of life,' Manning grinned. He had placidly eaten his sandwich and now ordered pudding.

The pudding was something else in polythene, and the coffee seemed to have no smell. Capricorn had another beer. What Manning said was true in a way. English crooks were individuals, not soldiers in somebody's army. They had their 'minders,' or agents, who dealt with contractors of criminal labour for each separate job. The job planners would deal with the contractors, often through another intermediary. So even the underworld remained ignorant of its true masters, and the police were left with the more tangible villains to hunt.

'A lot of your people think it's better that way,' Manning went on. Special Branch thought of themselves as a group apart, though officially they were in the CID. 'A few steady older heads at the top who stay out of trouble themselves, keeping the reins on the young toughs. I've heard old Grinley say it a dozen times. "We're a small force. What would we do if all the bad youngsters went wild?"'

'Yes, but you don't think so, and neither do I,' Capricorn said soberly. 'If it was ever true, it isn't now. You know what's happening.'

The television set was blaring louder and claimed his attention. The announcer seemed excited. The scene was a loading yard—a big place, Capricorn wondered a minute, and recognized it as Burlinghame's, the big electrical appliance firm. Of course, it had been in the morning paper: there was a wildcat strike going on there. But his mind reverted to what Manning had said. They both knew that corruption by men like Brixton Jim was seeping into all levels of the national life. It wasn't a matter any more of cleaning women and nightwatchmen being bribed to look the other way; men of position and standing were accepting money to lend their names to boards of directors of companies that sheltered criminal money and sometimes criminal activities.

'You know John Osland was asked to give his name to some very strange outfit—John Osland! And Victor Manderby got a call, at home, offering him five thousand a year and a directorship of a company engaged in a business not fully explained.'

He was referring to a Member of Parliament and a high-ranking civil servant.

'Well, they didn't accept,' Manning said equably.

'Of course not,' Capricorn replied. 'But the way they were approached—so blithely. To me it points to a record of success elsewhere.'

He frowned. England was wont to boast of the incorruptibility of her civil service and parliamentarians, but in times like these, when moral standards were relaxed to say the least, he wondered if any group could be considered hermetically sealed off from the values of their fellow men.

'With the Inland Revenue chomping up everybody's pie and so often leaving just the crumbs, look at how many people now consider them plunderers to be quite properly, though illegally, evaded.' Capricorn spoke his thoughts aloud. 'And once that starts, with the weaker spirits, the cheating is likely to spread. Men like Brixton Jim know how to exploit that all too well.'

Manning nodded. 'True enough. Citizens without *civitas*. Sheep waiting for the wolf.'

'And the wolves get away with it,' Capricorn said bitterly. 'End up, very often, honoured by the same society that they prey on.'

'Look at that,' Manning said, with a change of voice. His attention had been caught by the monstrous set, and he wasn't liking what he saw. No wonder the cameras were present: Capricorn wondered if they had been tipped off. Management was trying to send out lorries already loaded with goods. Two lines

of uniform police stood by but did not attempt to
turn back the mass of strikers who poured through
the gates. The shouting men slashed tires, smashed
windows and hacked at the motors with crowbars.
The onlookers cheered; the police stood, impassive.

Manning put his cup of imitation coffee down and
watched, his round, bland face for once looking seriously upset. 'I suppose this is what we call selective
justice.' Capricorn noticed that no one else in the pub
seemed disturbed. They gaped at the screen but paid
little attention. 'Fair making a mess of Burlinghame's,' the elderly man at Capricorn's side observed,
but his companion merely called for another pint.

'If John Smith, private citizen, slashed a tire in
front of a policeman,' Manning said dourly, 'he
would be taken immediately to the station and
charged. But here you have Tom Brown, union member, doing the same thing in front of the whole country, thumbing his nose and walking away. What law
do we have left?'

Capricorn sympathized and agreed. 'But it's the
same thing you were talking about before,' he said soberly. 'We're a small force. And Uniform Branch
have a point. Their job is to keep public order and
they can only keep the public order that the public
wants. Since most people seem to feel that a crime
committed by a union member in a strike is not really
a crime, there is not much they can do. They are
there to keep the violence within bounds. Of course
the bounds get wider all the time.'

'And what about young Jimmy Green?' Manning
continued. 'If he sees his elders smash up a lorry and
get away with it, what's going to happen when he sees
a car on the street he fancies? Doesn't he have the
right to take it? At least he wants to use it, not
destroy it. What do we say to him?'

The two men stared blankly at the screen where a
smiling striker, in close-up, was making the V-sign.

Capricorn, who agreed with Manning, had no answer. He went back to his afternoon's work uncom-
forted. Well, at least, he thought, Manning hadn't
talked about Copper. He'd been spared that. But the
thought of Brixton Jim ran through everything he
did. At last he took his file out and went through it
again. There was nothing to hint, Capricorn thought
vexedly, let alone prove that Marcus James was not
an ordinary businessman. He was a gardener, and a
man of strong domestic habit. Only one thing was
slightly unusual: his bachelorhood. His sexual life
was normal, but his affairs were brief and usually conducted away from home. He kept no servants, only a
cleaning woman who came in by the day. Not so unusual, Capricorn thought with a grimace. All those
things could be said of himself. His own excuse for
not marrying was his involvement with his work. And
James? Did he think a double life too difficult to hide
from a woman? James senior had married a Cypriot
who spoke only Greek to the day of her death—a
good insurance against gossip with the neighbours.

Capricorn pushed the file away in disgust and then
told himself not to be foolish. He had waited a long
time to catch Brixton Jim; he could wait longer. The
feeling of driving urgency he had was not reasonable.
Time was on the side of the policeman. Or it was in
ordinary times. But these were hardly ordinary times.

Under the surface calm of the average Englishman,
there was an uneasiness that edged into fear. Beneath
the 'swinging' gaiety and the inflation-born illusion of
prosperity—a fading illusion—there was fear for an
England that could no longer defend herself from foreign enemies, and had trouble in governing reasonably at home. Fear, disguised by apathy, was as
prevalent in the air as the smell of rotting refuse.

The streets had been foul that morning when he
went to work, and that night, in Paddington, the
stench was overpowering. The aunts, elated at signing

a contract for yet another television show, were throwing a party and had insisted that he go. 'Come if it's just for half an hour, Merle,' Dolly had pressed him. 'You must see the place now it's been done up.'

Capricorn was still worried about sleeping dogs. Remembering his talk in the club with Copper, he was far from satisfied about Copper and Joss. With Charlie dead, he didn't know what was happening to that almost-married pair. Dolly was one of the few people that Copper might confide in. So Capricorn had agreed and gone to the party.

It was indeed done up, he found, after he had pushed by the dustbins that the Merlinos rarely bothered to take round to the back. Or perhaps, overflowing, they were just waiting for the dustmen that didn't arrive. The aunts' house—Dolly's Tod lived there, too, but no one ever considered him—had been furnished in what Capricorn thought of as Thirties' Hire Purchase. It had not aged well. Now, in the flush of their success, a young decorator had offered his services in refurbishing the place. They had not bothered with the plumbing or the wiring, which were in desperate need of attention, but had let the young man run wild in everything that showed. Only the front hall remained as it had been, with the exception of a deep carpet now laid on the floor. Photographs of the Merlinos in a hundred costumes and poses filled the walls from ceiling to skirting board, and not only Dolly, Nelly and Tilly but the pretty Milly, and Capricorn's mother, smiling out of the distant past. The Great Capricornus, in a dim corner, stared at Capricorn with a face that might have been a mirror image.

For the rest, the decorator had plunged into a heavy, Victorian style. No chink of light could enter, which suited the aunts very well. The dominant note was wine-red velvet, together with satin and plush. Almost every piece of furniture was draped, fringed or frilled, bric-a-brac was scattered over each horizontal surface, and there was no piece of wood that wasn't carved or dotted with knobs. There was nowhere for the eyes to rest, but they were drawn irresistibly to an alcove where immense bronze cupids held shaded lamps that showed Dolly and Nelly seated on a button-back sofa, while Tilly reared behind them, cooing softly.

Capricorn gazed and gazed. Each piece of furniture, as far as he could see, was authentic of its period, or at least a good copy like the voluminous curtains and flocked wallpaper, and yet the effect was not at all one of Victorian sobriety, but instead was raffish and deliciously comic. It was all he could do not to laugh out loud. The young decorator must have enjoyed 'sending up' his unwary clients. Yet the joke misfired. The aunts were pleased, the guests admired, photographers came and bulbs snapped through the evening. Such 'grand old ladies of the halls' could do what they would, their very confidence turned mockery to triumph.

'Such a gift for camp,' the editor of a smart magazine said reverently. 'Such a feeling for background.'

The aunts certainly knew how to pose for photographs; as usual Dolly was upstaging the other two. There the 'feeling for background' ended. Capricorn knew that by the next day they would cease to notice the new interior. They had never cared much about where they lived. The place would soon be littered with cigarette ash, the remains of odd meals on trays and a plentiful supply of glasses and bottles. The great beer jugs he remembered from his boyhood had only recently disappeared—and then he saw one, sadly disgraced, holding hot-house roses on a what-not.

Brenda Grey was there, dressed in the beggar-girl garments that were the fashion of the moment, crumpled, tattered and torn. She looked much too pale and tired for a girl just twenty-one and also rather forlorn as she was escorted by Len Slope, who was talking not to her but to a lean, dark, tight-lipped man whom Capricorn recognized as Pete Moletta, Charlie Bo's chief lieutenant; cold, furtive and the possessor of an unpleasant reputation, Moletta was a world away from the life-loving Charlie Bo.

Capricorn's aunts had no objections to having a few crooks among their guests—they preferred them to policemen, excepting Copper. Perhaps they thought the villains contributed to an interesting mixture, like the sprinkling of young people. Moletta, observing Capricorn's black look, was openly insolent. Turning to a giggly group, he observed, 'The Law might as well put on a clean shirt and go to parties. They don't like to dirty their hands these days. Pretty sight they were today at Burlinghame's. Made a lovely picture, didn't they?'

The people around him tittered. Lazily, he caught Capricorn's gaze, smiling faintly, with a gleam of something like triumph appearing for a second under his heavy eyelids. Capricorn could say nothing, just as he had had no answer for Manning. The business at Burlinghame's was a national disgrace. It might hurt Moletta as much as any honest citizen, and Moletta must know that, but there was something about the law held up to public ridicule that brought joy to that icy and vindictive heart.

Capricorn turned to go. Slope, the eternal syco-phant, sang, off-key, 'Oh, when the saints go marching OUT,' to the amusement of the crowd.

Capricorn's withdrawal did not give him satisfaction. Dolly followed him, complaining of his low spirits. 'Gawd, Merle,' she said, 'you was always a cold fish, but you're getting to be a right Misery Martin.'

'I'm not best pleased,' he was stung to retort, 'at meeting some of your guests. Moletta is a dangerous man, and that Slope is a nasty little villain. I don't know why you encourage such people.'

'Oh, a villain,' she scoffed. 'Everyone's a villain to you. Len's a poor little sod, he used to 'ave a stall at Leigh-on-Sea selling cockles, like 'is Mum. Now he's doing himself a bit of good with the nobs. That Brenda is stinking rich and she's been after 'im, I can tell you. Good luck to 'im, I say. Nice-looking boy.'

'He's not doing Brenda much good,' Capricorn said soberly. 'Look at the girl. She doesn't even look clean.'

'Pretty little thing,' Dolly said indulgently. 'Trouble with you, Merle, is you're too fussy. You and her ladyship and all that lot. I've told you, the kids is more like we were. When I was young there wasn't all this launderette and cleaners and baths every five minutes. Jug and basin and wash up as far as possible and down as far as possible, and poor old possible never saw soap and water all winter long.' She chuckled hugely. 'I thought you'd be in a better mood now Copper's old woman has lost her naughty boy friend. Gets the lot now, don't she, her and Copper, very cosy.' She shot him a mocking look.

Capricorn wondered what she was getting at. This was what he had come to learn. But she was too cross with him, and too excited, to talk straight out. Being Dolly, she hated to tell all she knew. She laughed at his discomfiture, and then the association of ideas took her mind off him and she obliged the company with a spirited rendition of 'She was only a bird in a gilded cage,' with some verses that Capricorn didn't remember hearing before and that had the party in stitches. Nevertheless, her words rang unpleasantly in his mind as he departed. 'Gets the lot . . . her and Copper, very cosy.' Like the message from Brixton Jim, they contained a puzzling, nasty innuendo.

Nor was that the end of the baying from the supposedly sleeping dogs. The next day he had to hear more about the Golden Calf. The morning started as badly as the one before. Mrs Dermott was much put

out with the accumulation of trash, and had been
foregathering with the porter of the British Legion
hall on the far side of the square about a private removal, which had made her late and his breakfast a
rushed affair.

The air was still sour in the streets and, in his haste
to dress, he had put on a coat too warm for the day.
He arrived at the Yard, and his box of an office, to
find a mountain of reports to be filled out. When he
was nearly finished, he was called up to see his Commander about the death of Charlie Bo.

'He died in the club. Heart attack,' Capricorn told
him. 'It came out at the inquest that he'd been ill a
long time.'

The Commander explained that he, too, had been
approached by General Grey who had just returned
to London. They were old school friends and the
General had complained to him about his errant
daughter, and his belief that she was taking drugs.
'She has her own money, but he has managed to tie it
up. Still, he says, she just laughs. Claims she doesn't
need much. He's sure she wouldn't go to the government clinics and he swears that someone in London is
giving them to her. She goes a lot to the Calf, and he
believes it's a den of iniquity. When he heard about
Charlie, he hoped that he might have been her
source of supply and that now it would be cut off.'

'I don't think Charlie was involved in drugs,'
Capricorn said. 'Drugs Squad doesn't have anything
against him.' Dangerous Drugs had watched Charlie
Bo since the day he landed. They were a very efficient
group, and it was hard to believe that they had been
bamboozled. But there had been talk—Manning had
mentioned it the other day. And certainly Brenda
looked like a girl with a drug habit. 'Surely,' Capricorn said, 'the general doesn't think that drugs are
sold at the Golden Calf?'

'Hard to say,' the Commander replied. 'Apparently

he went there one night, before he went on his last mission, all prepared to make a scene, but when he got there, he saw a lot of respectable bods, all dressed up, a toffee-nosed lot. Mayhew, from the Annerly Trust. Withers, the secretary of Gorton Finance—a lot of types you would never expect to see in a nightclub, let alone a dope den. He slunk away.'

'It is a pleasant enough place,' Capricorn said absently. 'Quiet. I dare say Joss is filling a public need. I'll check again with Drugs Squad,' he promised the Commander, 'I'm sure it wasn't Charlie Bo. I do have an idea—though the villain I'm thinking of does nothing for nothing. In any event,' he shrugged, 'if she's determined to get the stuff, you know she'll get it somewhere. Once they follow that Pied Piper . . .'

The Commander nodded gloomily, and Capricorn left, only to find that his friend in Drugs Squad was out to lunch. He looked at his watch in surprise. It was already half past one. Leaving a message, he returned to his office. Certainly, he wasn't hungry. And neither was he able to work.

Getting up, he paced about the room. Being a tall man, he couldn't go more than three paces in any direction, which didn't improve his temper. What was troubling him would no longer be pushed to the back of his mind; it was more immediate than even Brixton Jim, or foolish Brenda. He didn't have a temperament to let sleeping dogs lie. He had been asked to look into Copper's affairs; he had. The conclusion was clear. They were not proper for a detective at the Yard. Dolly, Gyppo Moggs—they were aware of it. If other senior police officers were satisfied, it seemed to Capricorn that they were too much indebted to events. There was no change of heart or mind on the part of the principals involved.

The scene at the club, over Charlie Bo's dying body, stuck in his memory. Joss had been tight-lipped, efficient and cold. Whatever she had felt for Charlie

Bo, her only apparent reaction was the wish that the patrons of the club not be disturbed, Copper had acted as any policeman would, taking care of all the details of sudden death. His manner towards Joss had been conciliatory, but there had been no response.

When Charlie had been stricken, Joss had wanted to move him, but Capricorn and Copper had intervened. They moved the guests back instead. Joss had a screen put in front of the bar and went on serving her guests from the kitchen. Charlie's doctor had arrived very quickly, but within minutes of his arrival, he pronounced Charlie dead. Then the three men removed the body to Joss's private quarters.

The office, Capricorn had noticed immediately on entering, showed signs of a violent quarrel. A vase was smashed on the desk, a chair had been overturned, a framed photograph of Joss and Copper lay on the floor, the glass shattered into fragments. The doctor, sweating with effort and perhaps nerves, took no notice of the scene, and it was not brought up at the inquest.

The inquest had been held as a matter of form. It was lucky for everyone that Charlie's doctor lived in the neighbourhood and had signed the death certificate. It was just as well and avoided scandal. The only ripple in the proceedings had come when Len Slope volunteered the information that there had been angry words between Inspector Copper and the deceased. Copper had been recalled to the stand and questioned. He testified that he had reproved Mr Bonomi for what he considered to be bad manners towards the proprietress.

The Coroner, a mild-mannered, rather frail-looking man, who nonetheless had all his wits about him, gazed sharply at Copper as though inclined to ask what business it had been of his. As Joss was present, the answer probably suggested itself. However, the postmortem had corroborated the doctor's findings;

there was no question of foul play, so he let it pass. Capricorn could imagine what the Coroner might say privately about the morals and manners of detectives at Central.

He tried to comfort himself with the reminder that the pathologist's report had not indicated any marks of violence on Charlie's body. The emotion of the quarrel may have contributed to Charlie's death, but at least Copper had not physically assaulted him. By the look of the office, though, it must have been a close thing.

The doctor, a good-looking man with a soothing voice, had told Capricorn he was not astonished at his patient's death. The degree of atherosclerosis had been marked for a man of Charlie's years. Death *could* have come at any time, he said, and then, overcome by medical caution, backtracked and said that of course there were cases of people walking around with such conditions for ten, fifteen years and more. You couldn't always tell, he said sagely, but he was not surprised. Charlie had never followed medical advice. Like so many Americans, he had only wanted pills and injections, anything to maintain youthful vigour. '*Una dolce corta vita,*' he'd said. Well, that was what he'd had, no doubt. Very sad for the wife in America: it would be a shock when she got the news. She was said to be older than her husband, and infirm.

Capricorn glared at the bare sheet of glass, permanently sealed closed, that was now his window. In the old building, a man could throw the sash up and get a breath of air off the river. Birds would light on the windowsill and quarrel over crumbs. Now there were no sills, no birds, nothing to distract a man from his problems for a moment so that he could come back refreshed.

No birds. Only sleeping dogs.

The habit of not putting off disagreeable tasks was strong in him. Even as he cursed his own persistence, he looked up a number and called the manager of a branch of the Eastland bank. Capricorn was cordial, and the manager was cordial in return. He gave the information requested without too much demur.

Yes, Miss Parker kept her account at that branch, but no loan had been granted to her. No application, the manager hastened to add, had been submitted. Inspector Copper already had a large mortgage and another loan—no doubt the Superintendent was aware—Capricorn assured him that he was indeed aware of the situation.

'Yes,' the manager said, 'yes,' no doubt relieved that his momentary indiscretion had not got Copper into trouble with his superior, and then no doubt wondering what the Yard was coming to.

'However,' the manager went on, 'no loan was necessary, if you're thinking of the Golden Calf.'

'No?' Capricorn said, very interested, but at the same time noticing the cooperativeness of the manager, quite a young man, by his voice. Not like the old days, he reflected.

'No. Miss Parker has made very large payments into her account that fully covered her initial expenditures, and left her a handsome working margin.'

'Perhaps you might give me the details,' Capricorn said smoothly.

'Yes,' the manager said. There was an odd inflexion in his voice. 'Well, there was a check for fifteen thousand pounds. That came from the Metropolitan Police.'

'The police?' Capricorn said, startled.

'Yes, signed over by Inspector—Sergeant he was then, Copper. I believe the Metropolitan Police had purchased his London house.'

'I see.'

'And the rest—the rest,' the manager hummed for a moment, 'there were three deposits of ten thousand pounds.'

'Totalling ten thousand?'

'No, ten thousand each.'

'And the source?'

'Ah, that, I'm afraid,' the manager's voice trailed off, 'I can't enlighten you. They were cash.'

'Cash? Actual notes?'

'Actual notes. Low denomination,' the manager explained. 'Miss Parker brought them in a suitcase.'

He made no further comment. Neither did Capricorn. He felt somewhat sick, thinking about the reputation of Central at the Eastland. To his mind, the death of Charlie Bo changed none of this.

Had Copper really been deceived? He concluded that he had. Not because Copper was stupid, far from it, but because his wish to be deceived rather than give up Joss was so strong. His love for Joss came before everything. Love—passion, rather. Capricorn remembered how much Copper loved his infant son, but he had divorced his wife anyway when she had insisted that he leave the Yard. He could still visit his son, of course. If he broke with Joss, that would be the end. Yet for him to stay with this woman, who was operating with Mafia money—

Capricorn sat back in his chair and stared at the ceiling. An extraordinary woman. Obviously, she didn't give a damn. There was no attempt at disguise. Just took the money, suitcase and all, to a branch bank in a respectable suburb. Was it a strange honesty of her own, or was she just too coarse-fibred to care? Her part of the business was legal, and it would be like Joss to shrug and say to hell with everyone.

He wondered to whom she owed the money now. Cash. There was probably no note, and no records. Unless Charlie had kept his associates informed about his dealings—and under the circumstances he most likely had kept quiet—Joss could be home free and clear. 'Gets the lot . . . very cosy,' Dolly had said, with some prescience. Now Joss owned her own gilded cage.

His telephone rang again: Drugs Squad returning his call. The Super was back from lunch. Capricorn went over and told him what he'd heard. He found the Squad aware of the increased traffic, but although they were puzzled by it, they had no knowledge of Charlie Bo being involved.

'Seems to me,' the Super told him, 'Charlie had tried to stay clear of that. I don't know what he did in the States, but here he wanted to stay out of trouble, as far as we know. Not,' he shrugged, 'that I'd recommend him to run the Scottish Widows, but he seems to have had enough with the gambling and clubs. He might have been in some other villainy, but if he had been in the drug game, someone in this Squad should be sent back to a beat. Me,' he grinned.

Capricorn laughed. The Drugs Super was on the young side of middle age, sharp, shrewd, hardworking and ambitious. If he said Charlie had not been in the drug business, Capricorn had to believe it. He then brought up his idea about Len Slope, which was a little more productive. Together, they went over all the information available.

Leonard Arthur Slope. Discharged from RAMC after reaching the rank of lance corporal. Stealing and selling drugs.

'Started young,' Capricorn observed. 'Any convictions?'

'None. He was much more careful after that. Arrested once on suspicion of theft on complaint of a customer in a gambling club. He swore that Slope had emptied his wallet after getting him drunk; he'd had a big win. The evidence failed to convict.'

'No regular occupation,' Capricorn remarked.

'No. As you see. A stint in a bookie's office, hangs around gambling clubs; he was known to have run a sauna bath of worse than doubtful reputation.'

'And now?'

'Apparently a gentleman of leisure,' the Super said drily. 'Though he's connected to a place called the Pompeian Rooms. We think he supplies cannabis, cocaine and maybe some other stuff, to that set he goes around with, but we don't want to collar him yet. We're watching to see where he gets it. Nasty bit of work,' the Super went on. 'Heard he tried to stir things up for Copper at the inquest. Full of grudges against the police, of course, like all that lot.'

It was a natural attitude for Copper's colleagues to take, but Capricorn was sorry to see Copper in the position of having his reputation at the mercy of any petty crook.

There remained the problem of Brenda Grey. He couldn't ask that Slope be arrested. The Commander wouldn't be pleased, but Drugs had to have a chance to catch the big fish, especially since Special Branch now had an interest. He thanked the Super and left, his mind occupied with what to do about the angry General Grey, with the oddity of drugs being sold for little profit and with the Golden Calf being run the same way.

When he returned to his office, a note lay on his desk, prominently placed. Sedgwick from Counterfeit had been in. But it wasn't a matter of counterfeit. Capricorn looked at the note written in Sedgwick's round, careful hand, irritably asking himself why this had been brought to him. Of course, he knew the reason perfectly well. Word had been received from New York that Mrs Carlo Bonomi was on her way to England to take her husband's body back to the United States and to wind up his business affairs.

Well, so much for sleeping dogs, Capricorn thought. Thirty thousand pounds. He had a strong suspicion now that with him or without him, those dogs were likely to turn into the very hounds of hell.

DUET FOR FLUTE
AND BARITONE:
PENNY WHISTLE AGITATO

Inside the fragrant, flower-bedecked room the day seemed brilliant: a golden autumn that felt like summer. Here the squalor in the streets could be forgotten. Capricorn sat at luncheon in a smart restaurant which was also one of his favourites. His table by the window overlooked a colourful garden, there was a pleasing hum of conversation and light laughter, together with occasional chinks of ice against glass. Capricorn, accompanied by a woman who drew admiring glances even in that place where lovely well-dressed women abounded, found himself cheerful, certainly more cheerful, he reflected, than he had any right to be. The natural man was enjoying himself, whatever the Chief Superintendent might think.

Long deliberation the night before had brought him to the conclusion that there was no point in talking to Copper again. Their last meeting at the Golden Calf left no room for friendly discussion. As long as Copper lived with Joss Parker the situation was hopeless: in Capricorn's view, Copper should resign.

Yet Capricorn remembered the look Joss had given Copper after their quarrel. As far as she was concerned, the end of the relationship might be in sight. In that case, the breakup might be hastened. If he were wrong, if it transpired that, contrary to appearances, Joss still loved Copper, then perhaps she might be persuaded, for his sake, to break away from her dubious occupation. Already, he believed, she could sell the Golden Calf for enough to pay off her debts, perhaps avoid difficulties with the heirs and associates of Bonomi, and still have enough left over to start another business on a more modest scale.

His resolution had carried over to the morning, buoyed up, no doubt, by an access of optimism. The piled-up rubbish had been removed by the combined zeal of Mrs Dermott and the porter from the British Legion so that he could enjoy his garden, faded though it was from the hot, dry summer. He telephoned his Commander before he left his country home and explained about Len Slope. The Commander, of course, agreed that Drugs Squad had to have their opportunity, though he was sorry he could do nothing for his old friend, the General.

'Wouldn't do any good for me to talk to the girl,' he said regretfully.

'No, I don't suppose she'd listen to old fogies like us,' Capricorn agreed. Certainly, he remembered, he had never listened to The Great Capricornus, except on matters he could hardly avoid, such as how to extricate himself from a coffin.

'She likes your aunts, perhaps they might have a word,' the Commander said. He was an admirer of the Merlino act, but so far, despite his hints, Capricorn had not made the introductions. Now he felt that the Commander was grasping at straws. The aunts had come from a time of drink, not drugs, but he couldn't see them assuming the mantle of responsibility.

'Let the kids enjoy themselves,' would be their watchword, and if a few fell by the wayside, well, that was the way things were.

'We could take them out to supper one night after the show,' the Commander said, cheerful at the thought. 'See what they think. Somewhere dashing—I'm vegetating these days. Wife never wants to come

to London any more. Hates the crowds worse than
the bombs.'

Capricorn made some polite answer, determined
never to do such a thing: if his aunts hadn't finished
off his career at the Yard before it hardly began, it
wasn't their fault. He would have to talk to Brenda
himself, for all the good it would do. But in the meantime, the Commander had given him an idea.

Guessing that Joss would be staying at the club, he
telephoned her there at an hour when an energetic
woman who stays up late might be expected to be
awake. Joss had answered him with coldness, and
turned down his suggestion for a meeting unequivo-
cally.

'If you want me to come to the Yard, Superintendent, you'll have to get a warrant. We have no possible
business, and you must know that I'm busy.'

As their relations had always been friendly, her
manner seemed graceless. She had as much charm,
Capricorn reflected, as a hostile porcupine. However,
it was not for nothing he had dealt with difficult
women from the time he could talk.

He laughed. 'Do I have to arrest you to take you to
lunch at the Florabel?' He named the restaurant, the
smartest and gayest in town at the moment, believing
that Joss wouldn't be able to resist the chance of
showing herself off in such company. 'I did want to
have a chat, but I promise not to bore you too much.
And on such a lovely day, even a Superintendent can
yearn for a more attractive sight across the table than
one of his own colleagues.'

She hesitated.

'I've booked a table for one o'clock. Suppose I
come for you at half past twelve?'

'Make it a quarter to one,' she said, already considering, he guessed, what she would wear. She had
hung up, not too agreeably, but he had gained his
point.

In the sunny restaurant, she had been quite different. She was beautifully turned out in trousers and a coat of white suède. The coat, of a severe cut, was open at the neck and as she wore nothing beneath, as far as was visible, her glowing throat pulsing against the leather gave her an exciting, feminine look. The general admiration made her sparkle. While they were eating, and as long as the conversation was general, she put herself out to appear pleasant, more from habit, Capricorn believed, than from any interest in her companion. Her charm was addressed to a wider audience; she was clever enough to know that Capricorn would never be a suitor of hers; he could be of no practical use, and she was not a woman to waste her powder and shot.

And, apart from her wonderful looks, she didn't please him. He wondered for a moment what Copper, who had a wide choice of women, had found so exceptional in her, after all. Apart from her own business, she was ill-informed, her opinions conventional and unexamined; her ambition, though driving, was crude; her goals, first for money, secondly for position, were understandable but in no way different from those of many thousands of others. Yet her sheer energy, her appetite for life, had its own attractions. When the pudding came, brandied and flaming and brought by a whole bevy of waiters, Capricorn noticed that the chef had outdone himself—the staff had succumbed to Joss's charms.

She seemed mellowed by the good food, the wine and the attention, and while he had a brandy and Joss was sipping a glass of port, he carefully brought up the subject of Copper and his embarrassment. Immediately, she stiffened. Any softness in her air was gone. Capricorn had arrested many criminals in his day but few had more hostility in their gaze than the steely-eyed Joss.

'Superintendent Capricorn,' she said coldly, 'let me

make this clear. I am not a dependent of Inspector Copper. My business is my own and has nothing to do with him.'

'Not a dependent, of course,' Capricorn murmured. 'But certainly, one could say, an associate. And Inspector Copper, as a detective at the Yard, is very much at risk in a situation where he is closely associated with a nightclub owner. Particularly where there are—certain loans involved.'

'It's nobody's business,' Joss said, 'but I can tell you, there are no loans. Copper gave me some money, and I raised some myself.'

'Thirty thousand pounds. From Mr Bonomi,' Capricorn said. 'It's a lot of money.'

Joss didn't blink an eye. 'It was a business arrangement. I turned the Hi-Ho into a success, and that place was started on nothing. Charlie made a lot of money when it was sold. I only got a salary and tips, so when I left, Charlie promised to set me up any time I liked. He was generous. He didn't want any formal partnership; there were no loan papers, but if he had lived, I would have paid him back eventually. I let Copper think it was a bank loan,' she said, frowning and grinding her cigarette into the ashtray, 'because I didn't want any more rows, but I was stupid. I should have told him then and if he didn't like it, it was up to him.'

'That would have been better,' Capricorn said, 'because such an arrangement certainly makes it appear that he has conflicting interests.'

'I can't make all of Al's troubles mine.'

It came as a small shock to hear Copper called by anything other than his patronymic, which he had always used alone. As Capricorn was among the few to know, his first names were Doodlebug Aloysius, a result of his birth at the end of the war in the midst of German rocket attacks, and a mother with a taste for the unusual. It was like Joss to ignore Copper's sensitivity. But that was unfair, Capricorn told himself. Domestic life, he had observed before, did strange things to standards of taste. The frostiest, most rigid superintendent he had ever known in all his years at the Yard had a wife who referred to him as 'the hubby,' and the man who was the terror of criminals and policemen alike had considered this habit endearing.

'Although I have taken on his troubles,' Joss went on angrily. 'A lot more than you probably know. His son. His mother.'

Capricorn wondered for a moment what the difficulty was with Copper's mother, but let it go. Possibly in-law problems, which seemed to be just as bad, if not worse, when the parties were not actually married.

'But I'm not giving up my business, my chances in life, for any man, and that includes Al. I've told him and I'll tell you, since you're interested, though I don't see that it's any of your business. If his 'association,' as you call it, with me means he has to leave the Force, then it's up to him to choose what he wants. It's his decision. I think a man with any brains is mad to stay in the police: I don't know why he joined in the first place. There's nothing to it; he gets less money than a docker, as much prestige as a dustman, the hours are worse than those of a peasant in the Middle Ages, and on top of that he's liable to be cut up or shot at. I think he's out of his head.'

Capricorn didn't think he could open Joss's mind to the concept of responsibility widely held by the Metropolitan Police, Instead, he tried a softer approach. 'You must think me very impertinent, speaking of these matters,' he said, 'but I do it as a friend. I have been asked, unofficially, to see what I could do to smooth matters out, before they become official, possibly involving Cooper's resignation. Although I understand what you say about a policeman's lot,' he smiled, with a smile that had been well known to melt the hearts of matinée ladies years before, and still, he knew, had great effect, 'Copper does love his work, and I think he would be very unhappy if he gave it up. And if he was unhappy, it would reflect on you.'

'Only if we were together,' Joss said sharply. 'Nothing lasts forever. I don't believe in "Till Death Do Us Part." And I can tell you, Al enjoys spending money as much as I do. But in any case,' she waved a hand imperiously, 'that's his business. He can stay with me as I am, or he can—he can go.'

It seemed to Capricorn that she stumbled for a fraction of a second over the word 'go'. She finished her port defiantly, and Capricorn nodded to the waiter, who refilled her glass. She made no demur and stared into the dark liquid.

'Of course, as you say,' he said gently, 'it's entirely your affair. Yours and Copper's. But, if you'll forgive an old acquaintance, it seems a pity that something begun with so much love on both sides should be broken up over something as small as a license to sell alcoholic drinks.'

As he spoke he was aware of his own insincerity, for he knew the difference between them was a lot greater than that, and he really didn't think the breakup would be a bad thing. He was afraid, in truth, that it wouldn't happen, and that Copper would give in to Joss's ultimatum. Then he reproached himself for a lack of charity; if Copper found something in her to love, who was he, Capricorn, to say it didn't exist, that Copper's feeling was by desire out of illusion? 'You're cold, Merle,' his aunts' ultimate complaint, echoed in his mind.

'Not so small,' Joss answered, voicing his own thought. 'That license is what stands between me and poverty—or suburban dreariness, at any rate, which for me is worse.'

'Copper bought you the house in the country,' Capricorn pointed out, with the awareness that he was fighting a losing battle.

She looked at him with scorn. 'Mortgaged until we're both ninety. He even had to borrow for the furniture. What d'you think we would eat, Meals on Wheels?'

'I can understand your wanting to be in business,' Capricorn said. 'But why must it be a club? If you sold the Golden Calf now, and took care of all the outstanding claims'—he thought that was as tactful a way as he could find of referring to Charlie's possibly suspicious heirs—'you would still have enough to go into another line, starting modestly.'

She laughed in open derision. 'Do you have any suggestions? You know, I'm sure, that Copper gave me fifteen thousand. What could I get, a stall in the Caledonian Market? Don't be a hypocrite, Superintendent. You know how much it costs to start up any kind of business now, and you know that most of them go under. If you leave out all the things the Yard considers 'undesirable'—pubs, clubs, gambling—there's nothing left. Unless you've got the capital of an oil sheik, you can't afford to operate anything with a small profit margin. Labour costs, supplies, the bloody accounting for VAT as well as the Inland Revenue—you name it. Can't be done.'

'There are some who do it,' Capricorn demurred, mentioning a well-known name.

'Yes, but you don't pretend he's typical?' Joss said, flushed with anger. It was very becoming, Capricorn had to admit. 'He's an electronics genius, who is also, and it's very rare, exceptionally canny in business. There hasn't been one like that since Edison. I've no claims to genius. I'm an ordinary woman with a lot of energy and ambition, and that's the end of it. And I'm alone. Copper is no real help to me, he's always too busy with the Yard.'

And Charlie Bo won't help any more, Capricorn reflected, but kept it to himself.

'My God,' she said, 'nobody has room to move these days. I hear that even the decent plumbers are emigrating now. The only people I know who can keep a small business going are Asians running neighbourhood shops and take-out restaurants, with the family, or more than one family, living in the back of the shop and all working fifteen hours a day and apparently no questions asked about child labour. They've been doing governments round the world for taxes for centuries,' she went on, 'so they're surviving better than most of us. And don't think I'm any sort of bigot,' she warned. 'I'm not. We all do the best we can for ourselves and I don't blame them for it.'

Joss had a good head for liquor, but she had had cocktails, two kinds of wine and the port. It was beginning to show, but not unpleasantly. She spoke frankly, quite unguarded, and Capricorn could see that in her directness lay a lot of her appeal.

'Don't pretend,' she said hotly, 'that England now is what it was years ago. The big unions can smash and grab what they want, the charity class is subsidized into comfort, and for the rest of us what's left? You can go and work for a big company, be a small, easily replaceable cog in a machine, and earn a salary chewed up by taxes and rotted away by inflation. "Be a good girl, work hard, save your money and when you're old you can paper your room, if you've got one, with pound notes." '

'There's more education now,' Capricorn said, his interest in Joss's argument almost making him forget his mission.

'Education,' she scoffed. 'For what? What do they do, these students, with their education? Most of them become servants. Corporate servants, or government servants, instead of domestics. A teacher in a council school is no more independent than a factory hand, rather less. A national health doctor is a post-man with pills instead of postcards. And a lot of women still find themselves slaving over a hot typewriter until they chuck it for a hot stove.'

'Even before the war, you won't remember,' Capricorn observed, 'not every little shop ended up as Marks and Sparks.'

'But you had a chance!' Joss cried passionately. 'If you had some brains and a lot of energy. I like to be independent. I didn't marry money, though I could have. And the only independence left is in what you call the undesirable businesses. Well, I'm keeping mine. And whatever I feel for Al, if he gets in my way, then I'll go it alone. No man is going to hold me back.'

She had never looked more beautiful, even in her softer moods when she played at coquetry, than she looked now when she was being completely honest. Or, he amended, as honest as she could be. Joss had her own blinkers. How independent did she think she would have remained with Charlie Bo in the picture?

Crooks always have an excuse for what they do, his policeman's mind suggested. Yet his sense of right pointed out that because circumstances were often used as an excuse, it didn't mean that at times the excuse was not valid. A busy detective didn't have much time to brood over public affairs. As far back as 1947, he had heard a lecture, quite unwillingly while he guarded a political prisoner, on how the Welfare State would destroy the independent middle class. The idea had seemed great nonsense then; it had a horridly prophetic ring now.

It was an uncomfortable thought that the only outlet remaining for a bright, energetic woman like Joss was the seamy, near-criminal or criminal world. Was crime to be the last bastion of the free enterprise system? He shuddered. In that case, what would that make of his own role as a policeman?

As he sat looking at the fiery Joss, a lot of scattered thoughts and feelings came together and collected into a grave misapprehension, far greater than his concern over the affairs of a valued friend and colleague. He thought of the prosecutions against British subjects who tried to smuggle gold to take the place of a currency no longer trusted. He thought of the laws prohibiting British subjects from sending any of their funds abroad where they believed they might be kept safe: he had himself received that day a thirty-page government booklet on the subject from his lawyer, and he had put it aside as being incomprehensible to the average man, determined to send it to his accountant. He remembered, at the same time, the figures he had seen in his morning's newspaper: the Treasury borrowing would be tripled this year, a governmental boost to inflation that amounted to confiscation of the funds of every citizen except the destitute. For some reason his mind served up a picture of Mayhew, the incorruptible manager of the Annerly Trust, a widows and orphans fund, spending an evening at the Golden Calf.

Copper had arrested the coiners. Other policemen were arresting smugglers bringing in gold coins, and citizens who bought the illegal imports. An old jingle ran in Capricorn's head:

The law locks up both man and woman
Who steals the goose from off the common
But lets the greater felon loose
Who steals the common from the goose.

Capricorn had become a policeman because he loved tradition, order, stability, and he had made it his life's work to protect them. Through that work he had come to realize no order was a mechanical structure that could be imposed and forced to remain. Order was a living thing, based on tradition but created each day by living men and women.

And what happens if order is changed, and a po-

liceman finds himself upholding law that no longer
reflects the good of society but its evils? It had happened before. Many police forces throughout history
had been formed, not to protect society but to tyran-
nize over it. The Metropolitan Police had begun in a
different spirit. Yet if society changed so much, as it
had in Germany when the Weimar Republic became
the Third Reich, when law and justice separate—
what then?

He had forgotten Copper, forgotten Joss who sat
across from him, forgotten even that he was sitting in
a public restaurant, but he was rudely awakened. An
all-too-familiar, very distinctive voice boomed in a
corner, dragging him back from his vision of a social
horror to the actuality of a personal one.

    Goodbye, my honey love, farewell my turtledove,
    You are the darling, the darling of my heart.

If he had thought himself safe from the Merlinos
anywhere, it was here. His aunts rarely went out for
lunch, and they had never been fond of smart restaurants; they preferred pubs where they could 'be themselves'. Alas, he realized, being themselves had
become 'the thing' in the smartest places. He looked
at them, in the table of honour in the corner that he
had seen occupied by members of the Royal house.
They were escorted by two men—producers, perhaps,
of their new show—but next to them the men were
nondescript.

The aunts looked, as usual, as if they were ready to
pose for their waxworks in Madame Tussaud's: Dolly,
in scarlet which matched her cheeks and clashed horribly with her Gorgon locks, resembled a saveloy with
curls; Nelly, in black, actually wore a bustle and bonnet; Tilly, in a scant white frock and a yellow cocks-
comb on her head, made him think of an emaciated
chicken. For once, he observed, Tilly wasn't trying to
pocket the silver. She was glaring at Joss as though

her leather suit of white—Tilly's usual colour—was a
challenge.

How he had missed their entrance Capricorn
couldn't imagine. Dolly's outburst was apparently oc-
casioned by the departure of one of the escorts who
had merely delivered them, as the table was set only
for four. If anybody else had made such a disgraceful
row, Capricorn thought gloomily, such a one would
have been asked to leave. But now that his aunts
were officially The Grand Old Girls of the Music
Halls they could probably strip down in the forecourt
of Buckingham Palace and get nothing but applause.
The new fame in television cast a curious glow on
their past; they were referred to as the last of the
great stars of the halls, yet, Capricorn remembered,
they had never been topliners in any but the third-
string houses. His father, who had indeed been a
great star in his day, and who was now forgotten, had
never failed to point that out.

As he saw Dolly, she saw him. Recognizing a friend
or relative was not, for Dolly, a quiet process. She
waved, halloo'd, rolled her eyes in a horridly ex-
pressive manner on observing Joss, roared in loud
laughter and poked Tilly in the ribs.

'You are the darling, the darling of my heart,' she
repeated, her short legs kicking against her chair in
delight at the mischief she was making. Her voice carried clearly, all too clearly, to where Capricorn and
Joss were seated, and their neighbours gave them
amused looks.

Joss looked amused also. She had been introduced
to the aunts by Copper, Dolly's favourite, and Capricorn had observed that, like a lot of young people
who seemed to respect nothing and no one revered by
an earlier generation, contrarily she had an overween-
ing admiration for anyone who made a success on television, no matter how tawdry they were or devoid of
talent. Perhaps it was because the young were born

into the television age, Capricorn surmised. It had been a magnet to them in their youth, and the occupants of the screen had more meaning for them than people they ordinarily knew in real life. Be that as it may, the tough-minded Joss was obviously flattered by Dolly's notice.

Capricorn, who could see as well as hear what Dolly was up to, was nervous on Joss's behalf. Dolly was playing a favourite game, praising Joss's looks in front of the very jealous Tilly.

'Just what we needed in the act,' Dolly was saying. 'If I'd seen her first, I'd 'ave left you in the 'ome, Till.'

Dolly loved to tease, and with Tilly it was easy. Normally, though eccentric, she was no trouble, but she was pathologically jealous, a fact which had led to her incarceration. She had been married, and her husband, apparently tiring of her oddities, had planned to run off with a dancer on the same bill. That night, when Tilly had been briskly sawing her husband in half, something had gone wrong. The police had been called, but the company, loyal to their own, swore that the couple had been happy as turtle-doves. The accident, they claimed, had been caused by new equipment, which was faulty, and the fact that Tilly's husband had been muzzy with drink, which last was fortunately borne out by the post-mortem. But although the verdict at the inquest had been 'accidental death,' the Merlinos, urged on by The Great Capricornus, had deemed it wise to put Tilly away 'for a while'. 'Just like the Merlinos,' The Great Capricornus had remarked, 'for a woman to saw a man in half. They should all be put away, if you ask me.'

A waiter had brought them drinks, which quieted Dolly for a moment, but Nelly, who was the sensible one, was watching Tilly with apprehension. Tilly drank her cocktail down in one gulp. Dolly, licking

her lips, returned to the charge. 'Quick she is, too,'
she was saying. 'I could teach her some tricks in no
time. Look at that shape. Can you imagine her in
tights with spangles? On the telly in colour?'

The tactful headwaiter buried them in large
menus. Capricorn breathed easier for a moment,
called for his bill and hoped to escape without further incident. But before his waiter had done his adding up, Dolly's head emerged, impatient as usual with
detail. 'You surprise us, luv,' she boomed to her escort. 'We're going to the loo.'

They always went together. Capricorn, knowing
that the ladies' room was at the other end of the
restaurant, and that the procession headed by Dolly
would have to pass his table, closed his eyes in apprehension.

The greetings between Dolly and Joss were enthusi-
astic, possibly even sincere. They did have a lot in
common.

'We're blocking the way,' Nelly pointed out, trying
to move her sisters on.

'Gawd, you look smashing in white, Joss,' Dolly
continued blithely. 'Girl your age can wear it and not
look alike a skelinton in a white sheet,' she looked at
Tilly and giggled.

Tilly's muscles jerked as if she were on wires. She
gave Joss a glance full of wild-eyed malevolence.

'Oh, do get on, Doll,' Nelly said uncomfortably.
She poked her sister in the rear, not gently, and Dolly
moved on.

But she was too late.

Tilly, breathing heavily through her nostrils, stayed
in front of Joss as if transfixed. The waiter presented
Capricorn with his bill, Capricorn swiftly put some
notes down and rose. Tilly blocked Joss's path. As
Joss made to rise, she smiled at Tilly quite agreeably,
and that was all Tilly needed. 'Finished, have you?'
she said in her high, small voice. It wasn't a question.

Without a visible twitch of her wrist, she did one of the oldest magicians' tricks—she jerked off the tablecloth, leaving the dessert things on the bare and surprisingly drab-looking table top. But whether by accident or more likely design, she upset the remains of the port so that it splashed over Joss's neck and throat and ran down, covering her white-clad breast like dark, swift-flowing blood.

TRUMPET SOLO:
CALL TO ARMS

'Blood,' Teresa Bonomi was saying. 'There was nothing wrong with his blood. No clot. No evidence of heart attack. So what I want to know, gentlemen,' (her voice, deep as a man's, held a trace of Italian accent, Capricorn noticed mechanically) 'is, what did my husband die of?'

The day that had seemed so pleasant at the Florabel was warm, airless and sour in the streets of Soho. Here even the brilliant sun was no longer visible. Capricorn sat with Sedgwick in a small, dark room. The windows were draped, the lamps had dark shades, the solid heavy furniture was of another era—not an English one. Teresa Bonomi, born Miraglia in Sicily, seemed to have brought her background with her. Actually she was staying in a house belonging to Charlie's cousins, the Cristoforos. The house was reminiscent of their home country during the period when they had left it; their nostalgia fossilized the manners already left behind by their countrymen at home. It was very hot and stuffy and Sedgwick was sweating, though not only from the heat.

Capricorn had escorted the startled and rather quiet Joss back to her club, after she had made a hasty but unsuccessful attempt to put herself to rights in the ladies' room. Tilly had been swept up and more or less sat on by her sisters. The attentions of the staff had flowed like unguent over the irritation, and the scene had been played down. Joss, who could take care of a deluge of drunks without turning a hair, seemed sickened by the unprovoked, nasty attack from someone she had admired and considered a friend, and Capricorn shared her feeling. He had hard thoughts about his aunts, feeling they had undone any goodwill he might have created during the lunch.

But all that was nothing compared to what awaited him at the Yard. Sedgwick was waiting for him, his fresh North Country visage grim. He didn't waste words.

'Mrs Bonomi arrived in London two days ago. Today she rang up and made a complaint against Inspector Copper and Miss Parker, accusing them of extortion. She had something to say about the inquest—says the whole thing was a cover-up for the police. I'm getting the complaint put into writing, and the matter will be referred for official investigation. Copper will be under suspension from now on until it's cleared up.'

'Must it be suspension?' Capricorn asked, one part of his mind automatically dealing with routine while another absorbed the significance of what he'd been told. He had a disagreeable awareness that he was shocked without really being surprised. A jumble of images crowded his mind: the Coroner's penetrating glance at Copper during the inquest, the scene in Joss Parker's office the night of Charlie's death. 'For the time, wouldn't it be just as well to have him use up some leave? That way, if he's cleared, there won't be a suspension on his record.'

Sedgwick, after some thought, had agreed.

'Though it might be done over my head,' he pointed out. 'Right now, I'm going to Mrs Bonomi. She's partly crippled, from infantile paralysis I understand, so we're not asking her to come in. The A.C. suggested you might want to come.'

Capricorn's eyesbrows shot up. 'Both of us? That's a lot of rank to take a complaint.'

Sedgwick grunted. 'The old man wanted you in on it. Said you'd been looking into this mess already for your Commander. Of course, it wasn't an order—'

So, of course, Capricorn had agreed to go.

On the way, the two men discussed the new development.

'Never heard of any of *them* calling on the police before. Would've thought it the *last* thing she'd have done.' The North Country 'a' seemed to add to his expression of incredulity. 'Even if she believes what she says.'

'Not the American or any of the European police,' Capricorn said meditatively. 'But they might look upon the Yard in a slightly different light. Caesar's wife and all that. And if she believes her story, it might be a sweeter revenge to disgrace Copper than to have him "taken care of," if indeed she has the facilities here to do that. As far as we know, she has no illegal business in England to keep from our prying eyes. If she believes she has the law on her side, she might decide to use it instead of bringing the Metropolitan Police down on her head for a gangland "rub-out." '

As he spoke, he reviewed what he knew about Teresa Bonomi. Capricorn's knowledge of the Cosa Nostra was augmented by his personal friendship with a former New York City policeman, who was now connected in some unspecified manner with what he called 'a federally funded agency.'

The Miraglias were a larger and more important 'family' than the Bonomis. Their business, though not confined to the U.S., had not penetrated to Great Britain and they had no connections there except through the Cristoforo relatives of Charlie, blamelessly prosperous importers of spaghetti, macaroni and other Italian foods. And whatever Capricorn may

have conjectured to Sedgwick, he certainly knew that
Teresa's behaviour was atypical. Cosa Nostra women
didn't usually take part in their husbands' affairs. He
had suspected that Mrs Bonomi was sickly, hysterical
and foolish and merely making a dreadful gaffe.

Looking at the woman before him, he had to revise
this view. Her black hair was intertwined with grey,
her lined face and thin neck, from which a heavy
gold cross dangled, suggested she was ten years older
than her husband. Infirm she doubtless was. Her face
testified to the experience of pain, and the jewelled
ebony stick that she still grasped while seated upright
in her chair, and the swell of muscle in her upper
arm, so out of proportion to the rest of her figure, visible even under the long sleeve, suggested her continued lameness. Yet in spite of that, and the weariness
she must feel from travel, she had made her investigation, marshalled her facts, come to her conclusions
and taken steps with astonishing speed. Her manner
was commanding and her eyes shrewd. This was no
meek Mafia wife, but very much a person in her own
right. The thought of Joss flickered through Capricorn's mind but was quickly forgotten as Mrs Bonomi
leaned forward.

Her black dress, unfashionably cut, was of heavy
silk with velvet bands and rustled an accompaniment
as she moved.

'So,' she said. 'What have you to say?'

Sedgwick spoke. 'I understand your distress, Mrs
Bonomi. But as you have already been informed,
there was a post-mortem and an inquest. Also your
husband was attended by his own doctor. Coronary
failure, I believe, was the term he used.'

Her mouth twisted and she gave Sedgwick a look so
directly scornful that Capricorn thought of Joss
again.

'We all die of coronary failure or heart failure,
whatever it may be. But what causes the failure?

Sometimes a blast from a gun, a cut from a knife, sometimes a method not so obvious.'

'But surely you are aware, Madam,' Sedgwick went on gently, obviously believing he had a demented woman on his hands, 'that his own doctor said he had been in danger of such a seizure for a long time.'

'Tch! That doctor is a fool. I have interviewed him.' Capricorn could well believe it was an interview, if not an audience. 'He knows nothing. He was the doctor of Carlo's cousin, who had never been ill. He is not even a specialist. Carlo's own doctor in New York is one of the leading cardiologists in the world, and I tell you that he did not believe him in any such danger. In many years, if he was not careful, yes. Possibly, if he were unlucky and clotting took place—but he was not liable to blood clot.' She picked up a pad that was lying next to the telephone on a small gilded table at her side, and read: ' "If clotting had been a danger, thinning agents, of course, would have been prescribed." So. I was also told it was unlikely that so much change would have taken place since his last examination. Copies of Carlo's records were sent to Sir Hawley Marcross,' she referred to an eminent heart specialist, 'who Carlo was supposed to visit here. Instead, he went to this local—quack.'

'The doctor is a qualified practitioner, though not a specialist, Mrs Bonomi,' Sedgwick said. 'I'm not a medical man, but the post-mortem confirmed his findings of atherosclerosis.'

He stumbled very slightly over the medical term. Mrs Bonomi's glance indicated she thought Sedgwick on the same level of competence as the doctor.

'Many of us have atherosclerosis,' she said. 'We may die of it, if we don't die of something else first. At seventy, seventy-five years of age. Certainly my husband had this condition, more than the average man of his age. But his own doctor says not to a dangerous degree as yet. If your post-mortem had found evidence of blood clot,' she said, 'we would not be together here. I am not an ignorant peasant. I know the unexpected can occur. But without any evidence of blood clot—and in the circumstances—' she added meaningfully, 'I tell you that his death is suspicious. Suspicious.'

She pounded her stick on the rug.

'And the New York doctor agrees. I spoke with him today by telephone. He suggested that as Carlo's doctor attended him, the post-mortem may have been a mere routine, and not likely to discover anything less noticeable than an axe wound in the brain.'

This was not quite true, but close enough to make the policemen uncomfortable. Capricorn wondered if the American doctor had really spoken so freely. If he had, he thought, it was refreshing.

'I came here, gentlemen,' her manner was dry, 'hardly forty-eight hours ago. And what do I find? I certainly knew that my husband had been under police surveillance since he arrived. Many of his businesses are under license, in the control of the police. Now I am told that one of my husband's employees, a barmaid, is living on the most intimate terms with a Detective-Inspector of Scotland Yard; and that these persons, previously poor and in debt, have acquired the funds to open a luxurious nightclub of their own. The woman suddenly obtained thirty thousand pounds, at the same time that sum is missing from my husband's accounts. I am not a child, gentlemen.'

She looked from one to the other.

At the mention of thirty thousand pounds, Sedgwick had started. Capricorn avoided his eyes. Sedgwick quickly recovered the poker face for which the CID is famous, but Capricorn could tell his extreme agitation by the tattoo his forefinger beat upon his knee.

'At the inquest,' Mrs Bonomi went on, 'it was testi-

fied that a quarrel took place in this club between
that same Inspector and Carlo over this woman.
Shortly after, my husband dies, in suspicious circumstances, with no questions asked. What, gentlemen,
does this look like to you?'

Capricorn had intended to be a silent observer at
this interview, but now he had to change his plans.
Sedgwick seemed incapable of speech; Mrs Bonomi
had to be answered. 'Questions have been asked,' he
said. 'I myself have interrogated the young woman.
The club is hers alone; she owns it outright. She
claims the money was advanced to her to set her up
in business.'

The hair on the back of Sedgwick's neck actually
bristled. Capricorn could feel the wave of protest: his
colleague must think that he, Capricorn, had been
withholding vital information from him. He was a decent, fair-minded man, and he was truly scandalized.

Mrs Bonomi gave Capricorn a glance that was
frankly contemptuous. Once more she reminded him
of Joss. 'And what does that mean, "advanced"?
There are no records of a loan. My husband had no
mortgage, no partnership. Don't think me naive. The
woman is young and beautiful. My husband was here
alone. I imagine she was his mistress. But he would
not have paid her over sixty thousand dollars for her
favours. My husband has many women,' she said with
a shrug. 'That is his business. Or was his business.
But sixty thousand dollars, that is family business.
This "advance" is incredible.'

Sedgwick had recovered somewhat. 'It doesn't mean
extortion,' he pointed out sturdily. 'For there to be
extortion, the girl would have to have knowledge of a
crime, and I don't suppose you're saying, Mrs Bonomi, that your husband was involved in crime in
Great Britain.'

She muttered something in Italian, not quite audible but obviously unflattering. 'My husband was en-

gaged in straightforward business, as you well know. But does that mean that evidence against him could not have been fabricated? The other lover, my husband's rival, was a Detective-Inspector of Scotland Yard. Knowing my husband's family background, who would be believed?'

Who, indeed, Capricorn thought. Mrs Bonomi didn't know it, but when there was an investigation of that sort, the policeman was treated with more hard-nosed suspicion than the worst villain known to Criminal Records.

'Your husband's death was abrupt, and as you say, unexpected,' Capricorn said gently. 'There may have been business arrangements in train that were not yet formalized.'

Which, translated, he thought to himself cynically, means that perhaps I can get her money back from Joss, if she would be satisfied with that. Her claim of extortion, though embarrassing, he considered merely a ploy. It might be unusual for Charlie to give a woman that much money, but it didn't mean it couldn't happen. Even a formidable woman like Mrs Bonomi might not be aware how much her husband customarily spent on his pleasures. Dolly had said of Charlie: '. . . and where he likes, he spends.'

If it hadn't been for Charlie's sudden death, Mrs Bonomi would probably never have known. Charlie had been careful. The money had been all cash. Capricorn wondered for a moment which of Charlie's underlings had known about it and been moved to inform the widow.

Mrs Bonomi didn't dignify his remarks with any reply. She merely gripped her stick and scowled. An imperious woman. Her profile was Roman, her bone structure fine. She had been good-looking once. 'Young and beautiful,' she had said of Joss. That was the rub. Probably she understood the situation better than she would admit, but she would try to get her pound of flesh.

'You have my complaint.'

Indeed they did. She had written it out herself and signed it with a firm hand.

'I demand an investigation and a second post-mortem. My husband was a British subject and he has a right to this.'

'He would have the same rights if he were a foreigner,' Sedgwick replied stiffly. 'An investigation is already being set in motion. I will forward your request for a second post-mortem to the proper authorities.'

Mrs Bonomi nodded. She rose with some effort and firm use of the bejewelled stick, but with dignity. The interview was at an end.

The two men found themselves rather quickly in the street, blinking their eyes against the bright daylight.

'My God,' Sedgwick said. He was a man who seldom blasphemed. 'Do you think he really did it?'

MARTIAL SOUNDS,
SFORZANDO

'Did what?' Capricorn replied calmly. 'We don't know that there's anything unnatural about Charlie's death.'

He spoke with an equanimity he didn't feel.

'Just because his wife is jealous—'

Sedgwick brightened, but then frowned again.

'Thirty thousand pounds,' he breathed. 'From that villain. I can't believe it. But you did,' he turned to Capricorn. Sedgwick's manner might be slow but his mind was not. 'You knew about it, didn't you?'

'Just today, for certain,' Capricorn replied. 'Copper didn't know it. The girl admits she lied to him.'

'Well, it looks bad,' Sedgwick said. 'It is bad. Natural death or not.'

The two men got into the official car and went back to the Yard in a state of gloom. There was a slight reserve in Sedgwick's manner. Obviously, he believed he should have been told at once and not left to discover unpleasant facts about his own Inspector from a villain's widow. Capricorn, uncomfortable about it, found he agreed with him. He sighed. Although so different, he and Sedgwick had through the years become friends, though they were not often companions.

The fresh-faced Northcountryman sat hunched in a corner of the car. Square of jaw, square of shoulder, chunky at the waist and broad of foot in clumsy shoes, with his pullover and tweeds that were too heavy for the season emphasizing his solid look, he contrasted sharply with Capricorn, tall, dark, supple and well dressed, whose air was naturally theatrical although subdued. Sedgwick looked upon his fellow officer as if he were seeing him for the first time—a member of an alien race.

Capricorn caught the suspicious glance and groaned inwardly. It had been many years at the Yard, more than he liked to remember, before he had been accepted by his colleagues and superiors, his work notwithstanding. The words, 'that damned conjurer,' echoed in his mind. The old wound was still sensitive.

It would be useless to try to convey to Sedgwick the scene at luncheon, to describe the impression made on him by Joss. Sedgwick was a family man, living on his pay, still supporting two boys at university, and with an ailing wife. He had come to Capricorn, in fact, for a loan when his wife had needed very delicate surgery and he had wanted a specialist of his own choosing.

Capricorn had given him the money gladly, but Sedgwick had insisted on repaying it, slowly and painfully, against Capricorn's wish. He knew too well how it was done. The giving up of every small pleasure: his pipe, the glass of beer, a few days by the sea in summer; a strict pruning of his meals when away from home—'No pudding, thank you'—even the clothes worn a few more times after they might have gone to the cleaner, a denial of all the little things that add grace to life. Sedgwick would have heard Joss's apologia unmoved, dismissing it with the phrase, 'A load of rubbish.'

At the Yard, Capricorn's Commander was concerned with the practical aspects. He inveighed at length about the Coroner and the Home Office. 'Anyway, it's been decided to do something about the post-mortem,' he said. 'A new one or a re-exam-

ination or something. You're to conduct an investigation on the death—the A.C.'s idea—since you've
started it.'

Capricorn protested, without effect.

'You're the only one available except Sedgwick,'
the Commander was too harried for sympathy, 'and
he has trouble enough of his own. Those damned
Krugerrands are still turning up. He's had to reopen
the case, after we hoped it was finished. A perfect
plague of the things.

'They've been picked up from the widow of a retired school teacher in Glasgow, who wants us to give
the money back—not the Scotch police, you notice—a
pensioner in Wales who lost everything he's got and
now has to go in a home and a housewife in Clapham
who's been putting all her food money into coins and
went on Social Security to feed the kids. Copper
should be handling it, but he's out until the investigation's over.

'And I can't give you anyone to work with either.
If it looks like anything, I'll have to get Lawdon back
from Wiltshire. And on top of it all, the Mafia wants
us to be nursemaid to them. I sometimes wish people
would stop thinking that British policemen are wonderful. I spoke to the lab about the body,' he said in
a fit of irritation, 'and they say there's not much more
can be done. Thank God they've kept his liver and
lights in their beastly jars. They can poke over them.
But the carcase has been embalmed by the under-
taker, so that's not much use. Mrs B had asked for
that herself because she wanted to ship the body
back.'

'She did?' Capricorn became thoughtful. 'That's
strange.'

'Not strange at all.' The Commander was peevish.
'Quite usual. I understand over there they embalm all
the corpses. Pickle themselves for posterity, if they

don't freeze 'emselves for the future. Rising at the Resurrection now considered too long odds.'

'I meant, sir,' Capricorn explained, 'peculiar in the light of Mrs Bonomi's signed complaint. She stated that she was suspicious about Charlie's death when she first heard about it, as his health was not considered precarious. Obviously, this isn't true if she sent instructions for embalming. If she wanted the body re-examined that's the last thing she would have done.'

'Whether she's lying or not,' the Commander said without enthusiasm, 'C5 will have to get on with it. And you will have to take care of your end. Talk to the lab when they've had a chance to poke their pickles.'

Capricorn accepted his assignment without more ado. This was no straightforward investigation he was dealing with. Going back to his office, he frowned down at his desk top and pushed all his papers to one side to clear his mind. Mrs Bonomi, knowing of her husband's condition, had accepted his death as natural and ordered his body embalmed, preparatory to having it shipped home. Then something she had heard had set her on a very different course.

It must have been a communication of some weight to have had so great an effect. A picture of Joss formed in his mind. Yes, a few words about Charlie's affair with the lovely Joss, his apparently giving her thirty thousand pounds, and the fact that her other lover was a policeman, that could have been enough. Mrs Bonomi's story might well be make-believe, or a gross exaggeration of the known facts, merely to cause trouble for Copper and the hated Joss.

He looked at the copy he had made of the Bonomi complaint before passing it on to the investigators of C5. Yes, she had definitely implied that she had spoken to the New York doctor before leaving for England. Remembering the scene in the Cristoforo

sitting room, with the message jotted down on the
pad by the telephone, he doubted that. She had given
the name of the doctor. On an impulse, he put a telephone call through to the New York City Police Department, directly to an old acquaintance. The New
York detective, now a captain, had been a lieutenant
of Capricorn's friend Happy Delaney, and had something of Delaney's breezy manner. 'The Bonomis and
Miraglias, huh?' he said, rather amused. 'You're getting some high-powered operators.'

Capricorn expressed a strong desire to be rid of
same, and the Captain promised to get an answer to
Capricorn's question at once, adding, though, that
eminent specialists were as hard to get hold of as the
tail of a monkey in the trees. In spite of that, he rang
back in a short time, having got the information from
the doctor's switchboard operator. There had been no
call from Mrs Bonomi that she knew of for a very
long time, not since Mr Bonomi had left the country—he was the patient. All telephone conversations
were noted, and the times filed. Mrs Bonomi had telephoned, however, from England, yesterday. She had
called early and insisted on talking to the doctor
when he came in. The operator remembered clearly
because it had been difficult to get the doctor to the
phone, and then there had been trouble on the line.
The conversation had lasted twenty minutes. Capricorn thanked the Captain, condoled with him over
the decimation of the New York Police Department
in the latest budget crisis and rang off, his suspicions
confirmed.

Now who among Charlie's entourage would have
told the widow about Joss and the money? And given
her the details of the inquest? The more he thought
about it, the more odd it seemed. Whoever had told
her had done it to incite her to action. But action of
any sort, even a private revenge which might have
been expected, let alone a public one, would end up

drawing the attention of the police more closely to the whole Bonomi operation. The attention of the police was the last thing desired by any of Charlie's cohorts: even though his businesses were legal, they always balanced precariously on the edge of the law, their greatest protection was to remain undisturbed. It could not have been done, Capricorn thought, even to curry favour with the powerful Miraglia family. The heads of that family would not be pleased by Teresa's action; the Bonomis would have a grudge against the troublemaking informant. It *could not* be one of Charlie's people. Leaving who?

His glance rested on the papers he had brushed aside. A heavy file on the work he had done when he was on loan to Special Branch. A lot of papers that needed attention still unsorted, swept together under Miscellaneous. Barlow Road. At first his observation was mechanical, then he suddenly took in the significance of what he saw.

What a damned fool he had been. Hake was going up for trial. Capricorn, in conjunction with the local men, was still trying to find the mysterious Sweeter. His attempt to connect Brixton Jim to Barlow Road and the Eastland job was apparent to any interested observer. He remembered the first call from Moggs. 'Take it easy with Brixton Jim. Otherwise they're going to make it awkward for Flash Copper, see.'

He had not taken it easy on Brixton Jim, and Copper was in very nasty trouble. Yet how on earth could Brixton Jim have involved himself in this affair? Capricorn's fingers drummed on his desk. He would have to question Moggs about the go-between. Perhaps he knew about Sweeter. He sighed, knowing it was likely to stir up a lot of trouble, but it had to be done. Like all detectives, Capricorn tried to take care of his snouts. Valuable adjuncts to his work, they had to be treated as well as possible, and protected from the notice of those whom they had laid information against.

Because of Capricorn's striking appearance, all his snouts were skittish about meeting him in the pubs frequented by detectives and informants, and through the years his measure of fame made them more careful than ever. The tendency to paranoia of the humblest criminals, who imagined that all their acts and movements were followed with intense interest by the forces of law and their fellows alike, in a constant searchlight which could only be evaded by immense cunning, was intensified in their dealings with Capricorn.

They would call him in the small hours, nearly always from a telephone booth—all villains believed their home lines were tapped. Their information given, they expected it to be acted upon, and if any tangible reward was due, they were likely to bump up against him unexpectedly in the street with elaborate casualness or to materialize ghostlike in his back garden at dead of night to collect. This had sometimes bothered his upstairs neighbours. Fortunately, Capricorn now had the second floor himself, and the tenants of the top floor, the elderly Miss Bints, slept sound.

Nor did any informant like being approached directly. Usually, if a job had been done in which Capricorn might be expected to have an interest, he would wait a bit, expecting a late-night call. This was one of the times when he would have to be the wooer, not the wooed. He dialled the number—ex-directory, of course—of Gyppo Moggs. The former burglar of note, now reduced by misfortune to petty theft, was a good family man living respectably in Dulwich.

Luckily, Gyppo—named for his Gypsy-like looks and possibly his ancestry—was at home and answered himself. He recognized Capricorn's voice and in shocked tones prevented him from identifying himself. Tersely, he said he would ring back. That meant, Capricorn knew, about three A.M., but he resigned himself to the inevitable.

There was nothing to do, really, until he had the report from the lab. It was at once too early and too late for that: the body would probably not have been delivered yet by the undertakers and the pathology people would all have gone home to their dinners. But he was too impatient to go home himself and rang up anyway. Whatever god or goddess presides over telephones was kind to him that day; there were late-stayers and among them was Hardy, who was to do the work. Capricorn was pleased it was Hardy. A pathologist was expected to be competent but Hardy was also good-humoured, a small, tubby man, able to talk standard English without hiding behind the arcane jargon of his trade.

'We won't get the carcase until tomorrow,' he told Capricorn, 'but I confess, just from curiosity I've had a look at the organs and Jencks's report. Jencks is on holiday, you know. But he'd done a complete autopsy. There's no sign of anything wrong. I've tested myself for everything except eye of newt and toe of frog. Perhaps it was the evil eye,' he chuckled. 'Overlooked, I think it's called. They still believe in it, in Sicily.'

'The Bonomis are citizens of the United States,' Capricorn answered, remembering that Mrs Bonomi had in fact been born in Sicily. 'Did you look at the heart?'

'Not a bad specimen for his age, and I had a few good sections of the aorta. Jencks found some lime deposits on the arterial wall and a certain amount of narrowing. I did more slides and came up about the same. Atherosclerosis, all right.'

'You wouldn't be able to tell if there was any clotting?' Capricorn asked.

'Not now. There's no clot present, anyway. Jencks

would have mentioned it if he'd found any, and there's nothing in the report about a clot.'

'He did die, then, of the atherosclerosis?'

It looked as though Capricorn's investigation was going to be finished before he had really begun. He was already feeling relieved when Hardy answered.

'According to Jencks, he didn't die of anything else. Sound in wind and limb. Jencks tested the viscera for poisons, but he only came up with a harmless quantity of digitalis in the blood—the doctor's two injections easily account for that. There was quite a bit of adipose tissue, but not more than a lot of us are carrying about. And he did die. So take away everything else, and you have to say he died of that. Of course, we just say what we find.'

Capricorn frowned.

'So to say that he died of atherosclerosis is merely a negative judgement? Because you haven't found anything else—as yet, anyway?'

Hardy laughed.

'Findings have to be interpreted—and sometimes misinterpreted. There are cases where the cause of death simply can't be established by post-mortem alone. I expect at the inquest his medical history was taken into consideration. We're none of us God,' Hardy said meditatively, 'and I'm not applying for the job. I'll give you a full report as soon as I've finished. But after Jencks I don't think there'll be any surprises.'

Capricorn thanked him and put the telephone down, disconcerted. It looked as though Teresa Bonomi's question: 'What did my husband die of?' was not going to be so easily answered after all. His frown deepened. And it was his investigation now. Charlie Bonomi had been no model citizen but he had a right to life like anyone else. If there had been foul play, he deserved the best that Capricorn could do, no matter how embarrassing and painful the affair became.

But Hardy hadn't said Charlie did *not* die of atherosclerosis, he argued with himself. There was no other apparent cause of death. It was just that his death came too handily. Convenient death is always inclined to cause suspicion in a policeman. His death was convenient for Joss to the tune of thirty thousand pounds, convenient for Copper who had lost a hated rival. Was it convenient for anyone else?

He thought again of Brixton Jim and his threats against Copper. Certainly, the death of Charlie Bo had served his purpose. Yet if Charlie's death had been contrived by some unknown means, in almost full view of Capricorn himself—no, it was too absurd. No one would go to such lengths to harass one policeman in order to influence another. There was no sense dragging Copper down unless it meant dragging Capricorn down with him, dragging him so far down that he was dismissed from the Force, something beyond the powers, Capricorn knew, of any villain.

Policemen were vulnerable in many ways. There was money, but Capricorn, who had always had means, found himself, by chance, a rich man. There was desire for women, but he had always been lucky in that regard, love had come to him as easily as money, lightly, pleasantly—if he had not experienced the great emotions, he hadn't missed them, he told himself. There was ambition to advance, but Capricorn had all the promotion he wanted—one more step and he would be confined to an office on administrative labours. He had already refused this. He was, in fact, a satisfied man, peculiarly free from any temptation. The villains certainly knew this. Brixton Jim understood that there was nothing he could do to Capricorn. Nothing at all.

That of course was why Brixton Jim had fastened on Copper. The great friendship that Capricorn felt for the young man with his obvious vulnerabilities, a friendship compounded by feelings both fatherly and brotherly, might perhaps turn out to be his Achilles' heel. But certainly no criminal of the calibre of Brixton Jim would go so far as to arrange a murder on so slender a chance.

Irritably, Capricorn wondered why he let Teresa Bonomi fasten his mind on the idea of murder, when murder was out of the question. If it could not be proved absolutely that Charlie had died of his coronary disease, there was no sign of any other cause either. Certainly, Charlie had been drinking. And there were poisons which could be administered that gave symptoms of heart attack—indeed, actually caused heart attack. But both Jencks and Hardy had given the organs a clean bill on poison. The whole business was just getting on his nerves, he decided. Copper had been a damned fool and would probably face suspension or worse, but there was nothing to be done about that now. He, Capricorn, should go about the routine of investigation, turn in his report and let the powers-that-be do what they chose, which almost certainly in this instance would be nothing.

He began making up his list of people to be interviewed, those who had been at the inquest, and some who hadn't. Brenda and Slope and the remainder of their party. Copper himself. There had been a man sitting almost on top of Charlie—the little foreign-looking man in the spotted bow tie. Joss would know who he was. If he was still in the country, he should be questioned also. The band, according to their statements, had noticed nothing until Charlie fell. The waiters had been rushing about, and the barman had actually gone off to the kitchen in search of extra supplies and missed the whole affair. Was there anyone else?

The telephone rang, shrill-sounding in the quiet. The Scots burr of his housekeeper, always intensified when she was cross, came heavily across the wires. 'Yu said dinner for eight o'clock. What am I to do with it?'

Capricorn's upbringing had been sketchy; he had never been reproved by his aunts for the usual childhood sins. He sometimes believed Mrs Dermott had been sent to him to make up for this lack—she could reduce him to an abysmal guilt in very few words. He had completely forgotten to tell her not to prepare dinner. Now he tried to placate her wrath.

Hastily, he went down and got his car and made his way home. Mrs Dermott's grievance was more than a spoiled meal. The neighbourhood where she lived was changing and she didn't like to go home late. At the same time, she had very old-fashioned views about the relations between employer and employed, or, as she preferred to say, master and servant, and she disliked having Capricorn drive her home. True, her feeling was reinforced by a suspicion of his driving and his sports car.

He considered the matter as he made his way through the streets, the litter slightly less obvious in the dusk. He already had two floors of his house. When the top floor and the attics came onto the market—the Miss Bints were talking about retirement to their country home—he would take his top flat and give it to Mrs Dermott. When annoyed, she threatened to return to Scotland on the basis of homesickness, Scottish Nationalism and, lately, great hopes of North Sea oil. As she hadn't been north of the border in over twenty years, he didn't put much stock in this threat, but her own flat might be an assurance of her staying, a convenience to them both. Besides, she deserved some soothing after Dolly's incursions.

As he had foreseen, her annoyance when he arrived home was audible: her radio was loud in the kitchen, proclaiming England's current misfortunes. She poured his sherry, not softening when he asked her to join him, and only looked less grim when he invited her to stay the night in the guest room in the flat above. He outlined his project for the future.

'It might du,' she said, unbending. 'But it'll cost an awful lot of money.'

'I'd like to do it,' Capricorn assured her. 'I need the attics for storage. And we'll have the house to ourselves then. You remember what it was like when the Harkness boys were upstairs.'

They shuddered together. The Harknesses had at one time owned the second-floor flat. They had been decent people, quiet neighbours, but they had two sons in college who came home during holidays accompanied by stereophonic equipment and a collection of rock records. There had been no peace by night or day, and a law suit was only averted by the departure of the Harknesses to larger quarters. Capricorn had thankfully bought their flat and at least assured his sleep. The Miss Bints themselves were quiet, but if they sold to someone else. . . As Mrs Dermott often darkly remarked, 'Yu never know.'

After dinner, which in spite of waiting was very good, Mrs Dermott, mollified but muttering about night things, went to prepare the guest room and Capricorn carried linen up for her. The sudden access of wealth that had made this purchase possible could not have given him as much pleasure in any other way. The upper flat did not have the fine twin-arched ceiling of the floor below, but the two principal bedrooms made one large room leading to the balcony that ran the width of the second floor and overlooked the garden. This he had made a library, his collection of books having long outgrown his small study. Another good-sized bedroom, also leading to the balcony, made a pleasant guest room, though Capricorn with his passion for privacy did not use it often.

He found Mrs Dermott a nightgown left behind by

a female guest, a very feminine bit of nonsense that she looked upon with disfavour. Her remarks echoed in his ears as he made his way down the elegant curved staircase laughing.

But laughter was soon gone, and sleep did not come easily. Reason fled as the night rolled on. The moon, appearing fitfully through the clouds, shone too bright into his room, and so he rose and drew the heavy curtains he had installed to make possible his sleeping by day instead of night which he still did at times, though not so often now as formerly. His lamp was out; yet he stared up at the ceiling as if he were tracing every intricacy in the plaster.

He saw Joss glaring at Copper with something like hatred; he saw Charlie, first proprietorial, laughing, and then enraged; he saw Copper standing over Charlie, looking murderous. And there was something else, something teasing his mind, something that would not let him sleep. He lay there, hopelessly awake, hearing his clock chime, the quarter, the half, the quarter, the hour, the quarter, the half, over and over again.

'So, gentlemen, what did my husband die of?'

'. . . the cause of death simply can't be established . . .'

He tossed and turned, and the voices clashed together. Mrs Bonomi's face swirled into that of Joss, then Hardy, patting his plump belly and smiling. 'Quite a bit of adipose tissue . . . harmless quantity of digitalis . . . the doctor's two injections . . .'

Capricorn sat bolt upright, wide awake.

'. . . two injections. . . !'

No wonder he had felt uneasy. How it had slipped his conscious mind he couldn't imagine. Could Hardy have made a slip of the tongue? No, he had been reading from Jencks's report. Two injections. Jencks must have seen two puncture holes. But Capricorn had been present all the time the doctor was there.

He couldn't have forgotten. He was sure he would have noticed. The doctor had given only one injection. He could see it now, the light from the golden calf glittering on the syringe. One injection.

He got out of bed. Hell and damnation. The phrase was in his mind and he uttered it aloud. The next moment it seemed as though someone had taken him at his word. There was a tremendous blast; the floor trembled; crashing sounds were all about him; smoke and an acrid smell rolled in with the cries of someone above. Glass shattered nearby. He made for the stairs, realizing that his heavy curtains had saved him from splinters, and ran up three steps at a time through the dust and smoke, rushing towards the high, thin scream that echoed from a world at war.

COUNTRY MUSIC, MESTO; QUARTET AFFETUOSO

Early next afternoon, through the heavy warmth, under an overcast sky, Capricorn was driving on the motorway to Wenmore. Of the people on the list he had made up the day before to be interviewed the little man, who turned out to be a respectable salesman of cheese, had returned to his native Zurich; Len Slope had disappeared and Brenda was not to be found in her lodgings at the moment. Copper was assumed to be at his cottage in Wenmore, although his telephone was either out of order or off the hook.

Capricorn hoped that his journey would not be for nothing—he had forgotten how far from London Wenmore was. He should have started earlier but there had been a lot to do. His house was being gone over by the structural engineers. He had been assured already that the damage from the bomb was minimal—it was an antipersonnel device, the bomb squad pointed out in the modern jargon, meaning it was intended to kill a man, not to damage property.

Mrs Dermott's staying the night had undoubtedly saved his life. His attacker, aware perhaps that he lived alone, seeing a light on upstairs, had assumed that the lighted room was his. Or so it was believed. The attacker, of course, had been away before the explosion occurred. Capricorn had not been able to get a good look outside very quickly. There had been Mrs Dermott to soothe—though that lady had soon recovered her calm, only fussing about her lost garments—and the Miss Bints to be rescued.

A footprint on the balcony showed how the intruder had gained access and placed the device through the open window. The respectable Mrs Dermott had been unable to sleep in the garment she believed to be that of a hussy, though actually the pretty thing belonged to the blameless Lady Theale who had shared that room with her husband the Dean. Fretfully, Mrs Dermott got up in the night, determined to exchange the offending garment for her own decent slip, and being Mrs Dermott, had gone into the bathroom and locked the door to make the exchange. Her extreme modesty had saved her life— her only injury had been small cuts from the broken looking glass.

So she had at last been driven home, more indignant than shaken, dressed in a medley of Capricorn's pullovers and scarves, with a pair of his socks pulled over her bare feet—she had a bunion, he noticed, he must get her to have that treated. The Miss Bints had been evacuated also, down to their country home. Though the damage had been confined principally to the second floor, and he knew he should be grateful, still he was ruefully aware that he was in for an extended period of work with all the noise that went with it. Dolly had called that morning to offer him a room in her house at Paddington.

'Bloody Irish,' she had said indignantly, having heard on the news about the incident, and that it had been ascribed to the Provisional Branch of the IRA because of Capricorn's recent work with Special Branch. 'What's the matter with you police anyway? Letting 'em come over here and blow people up and you don't do nothing. Well,' she said, 'I meant it's silly, it's just like during the war but no ack-ack nor sandbags nor nothing.'

Dolly, like many others, normally looked upon the

police as an enemy, but in times of trouble expected them to be there, functioning like a combination of the British Army and Jack the Giant Killer. He had answered her soothingly, if not honestly. To begin with, he was not at all sure he had been the victim of the IRA. Secondly, he didn't think he could explain to Dolly in the short time at his disposal the difference in legal status between the enemy in time of war and terrorists during a so-called peace. And thirdly, a part of him couldn't help agreeing with her.

He hadn't contradicted the report concerning the IRA but he and his friends at Special Branch had wondered about it. The Irish had not claimed responsibility, which they usually did, and though Capricorn had certainly been a possible target, he by no means had a high priority. The Special Branch regular men would have been more likely to be singled out, 'Although,' as Manning had said, 'you are certainly a sitting duck, usually alone except for the old biddies on the top, with gardens in the back leading onto the park, and that square quiet as death at night. A lot more trouble getting at me in my block of flats, for instance, or at Benson in his village, where any stranger sticks out like a sore thumb.'

The IRA, Capricorn thought, provided a marvellous scapegoat these days for anyone who wanted to get rid of a policeman or a politician. Of course, he couldn't be sure. He'd sent many men to prison but very few thought of revenge. Could it have been someone who wanted to prevent an investigation into an area where his interest was not shared by the Yard? And only yesterday, he thought wryly, he had been telling himself there was nothing the villains could do to him. He realized that he had missed his call from Gyppo. Gyppo had probably spoken to one of the local men and nearly died of fright. The Super had very nicely offered him a constable to watch the premises. That would certainly frighten his snouts away. He had declined, with thanks. Whoever was responsible would probably not try it again—the same way, at least.

He had turned off the motorway some distance back and was winding around interminable roads in flat, dull country. The sky was leaden. Capricorn hoped it would rain; he never remembered the grass so brown. Last time he had come down with Copper, before the purchase was completed, they had been discussing Copper's work, and he had not noticed the distance. His mind went back to the fake Krugerrands. A pity Copper couldn't have stayed on the case. He himself would very much like to know who the brain was behind that business.

Glancing at his watch, he realized that he had been travelling over two hours already. He wondered how on earth Copper, or Joss, had imagined they would be able to use the cottage, with their long hours of work in London. Though perhaps Joss had wanted the house for that very reason. With the other house, easily accessible in the suburbs, there would have been no excuse for spending nights away from home. Wenmore could never have been anything but a weekend reteat, a useful situation for a woman who liked her freedom.

When he finally approached the cottage, at the end of a long, dusty lane, it looked forlorn, without the charm he remembered. A thin, elderly woman in a cotton dress and long printed pinafore was in the desolate, neglected-looking garden, chasing two huge Great Danes who, in the intervals between jumping up and nearly knocking her down, were running round.

Capricorn got out of the car and brought the animals to heel. He recognized them from his previous visits to Copper; they had been well behaved but now they seemed to be running amok.

'Thank you, sir,' the woman said, frowning. 'Them

dogs is too much and I've told the Inspector so, time and again. They'll have to go, or I won't be able to do for him any more. When I made the arrangement there was nothing about exercising no dogs. I'm not up to it, as you can see, and my husband, he don't like the beasts.'

The front door was open and she preceded him into the narrow entrance. 'I don't mind letting you in,' she said, 'but he's not here, Mr—?'

Capricorn gave his name and learned that she was Mrs Twitchett who lived down the lane, and who only obliged because of her husband's illness.

'Emphysema,' she said dolefully, 'and he can't work. Never heard of it when I was young. Bronichal, yes. But if you was bronichal, you still went to work. A nice drop of cough medicine put heart in you, and none of these needles. Don't see any good in these needles if a man can't go to work. Can't go to work but can go down to the Rose and Crown and live idle.'

She opened the door to the living room and looked in doubtfully.

'It's not very tidy,' she said. 'Was you going to wait or something?'

It certainly wasn't.

'Last time the Inspector was down he left them dogs in the house instead of out in the garage like I asks him. He says its damp out there at night, but I ask you, in *this* weather? Don't know what *She* would have to say if she saw it, but we don't see *Her* much these days.'

Joss hadn't made herself loved by the cleaning woman, Capricorn observed, but perhaps Wenmore hadn't caught up with the new morality—if Joss called herself Miss Parker here, they wouldn't think too highly of her.

Mrs Twitchett sniffed, groped in her pinafore

pocket of her handkerchief and blew her red and running nose.

'Caught a cold,' she grumbled. 'Worst kind, hot weather colds. I'm supposed to spend a couple of hours a day tidying up for the Inspector,' she said defensively, 'but how can I if it takes all my time chasing those animals?'

When Capricorn had seen the place during the period of purchase, it had been very attractive. Two cottages made into one gave a living room that had warmth and spaciousness. The previous owner had furnished with some good old pieces, rose-coloured rugs and curtains and flowered stuffs on the sofa and armchair. An open fire had glowed pleasantly in the hearth.

Now those things were gone. The walls showed the places where the furniture had stood. Joss had put down a chocolate-coloured carpet, too modern for the room and much covered with dog hairs and dusty pawprints. A table and a few chairs from Copper's London house were scattered about with no attempt at arrangement. Joss had thrown this together and very soon decamped, that was obvious. Her interest had been elsewhere from the first.

'Do you expect Inspector Copper?' he asked without much hope. The place had an abandoned look.

'Oh, no, sir.'

The animals were quiet now but Mrs Twitchett seemed in no hurry to get on with her duties.

'I couldn't tell you when he'll come, I'm sure. He hasn't been here hardly at all the last week or so. Stopped in for a couple of hours one day, and then he was off again. You can see, can't you?' She regarded the scene before them morosely. 'And the garding, it's terrible. Mr. Locust who was here before, he left it beautiful. All them lovely flowers,' she leaned against the leaded panes and pointed a bony finger at the ground outside that was cut up into a

host of flower beds of ill-assorted shapes and sizes. 'I
expect he's out working. Always working, he is. Not
like my old man.' She looked dejected. 'But that
didn't please *Her*. Oh, no. Don't know what trouble
is, these young women. Carried on alarming. "They
don't pay you to work twenty-four hours a day," She
said. At 'im all the time about it, She was. In my
young days, a woman like that would have got a right
clout in the mouth, or worse,' she added darkly.

The dogs thumped against the door that Mrs
Twitchett had failed to secure and burst into the
room. Howling, they ran through, turning over a
small chair and scattering dirt as they went; they
jumped up against a door that proved to be closed
and hurled themselves against another that led to a
downstairs bathroom. Turning and leaping in the
small space, they knocked over everything movable—
talcum powder, lotion, a glass syringe—and a bottle of
nail polish fell and shattered on the tiles, covering
their paws with sticky red stuff.

'That Eva,' Mrs Twitchett panted, trying to hold
them, 'she's the worst. Adolph's not so bad by himself.
More mess to clean up; it never stops.'

Capricorn helped her pick up the pieces.

'Gone, that is,' she added. 'Mind your hand, sir. I'll
get the glass in my apron, not that that nasty red stuff
will come off.' She threw the bits of glass into the already overflowing waste basket. 'Plenty more where
that stuff came from. Dolls up like the Queen of
Sheba, she does. So it don't matter. Not like the time
when Eva broke some old pot *she* had brought in.
What a holler she made. Valuable it was, she said,
and I answered her. "I was taken on to clean, not to
be attendant to no wild animals," I said. "You'll have
to keep your stuff out of the way if you give them
beasts the run of the house." '

She gave the mess a desultory flick with a rag but
soon gave up and shepherded the animals into the

kitchen, where they settled down with some food. The hound nuzzled her hand.

'Adolph's all right, left to himself,' she repeated. Capricorn imagined she might say the same about Copper. 'A good watchdog as well. He don't like some of Her friends. He really takes against that nurse. Nurse Wallace, she calls herself. Animals know,' she added, meaningfully. 'Inspector Copper, he's a nice man.' She put the kettle on. 'I've got to have something wet or I'll have bronchitis myself—he always leaves a drop of something, and he says to me, "Help yourself, Mrs Twitchett. Good for the tubes," he says.'

She opened the cupboard and took down a bottle of whisky. 'Always a laugh and a joke with the Inspector, but she's something else, her and her fast friends. What they leave to clear up you wouldn't believe, drink and fancy foods, and men here and not a marriage license in the lot. And that nurse after the Inspector brazen as you please but *She* only laughs.' Mrs Twitchett sat down at the kitchen table and kicked off her shoes. 'I don't know how a nice young feller like him, in the police and all, ever got mixed up with a no-good like that one. We have a policeman in Wenmore,' she informed him over her glass of whisky, 'but he's a respectable married man with a family.'

'Now, the Inspector *might* have left a note upstairs saying when he'd be home, in their bedroom over the back,' she went on. 'He does that sometimes, in case She comes. I can't take you up because I'm not supposed to go up them stairs more'n I can help. It's the room where the bed is made. That nurse was in the other one and I'm not cleaning up after the likes of her and her fancy man, I'm not paid for that. Told young Doris down the lane she should have the Pill and gave her some, she did, and Doris not yet fifteen. Her mother was so upset she made a complaint at the police station in Dorkey, but they said it's not against the law. Don't know what good the law is any more, not much sense in having it.'

Judging that her monologue could go on for ever, or at least as long as there was something left in the bottle, Capricorn made for the stairs in hopes of finding a note.

'Nurse Wallace,' she continued in the same tone, merely raising the volume of her voice to follow him, 'she's the one started the Inspector on them needles. Not a real nurse now, you know, if she ever was. Works for that big lab'atory. Brings 'em in and he sticks himself with the stuff wholesale. It's not right.'

Capricorn looked back, startled at the implication. An ill-natured servant could cause a lot of gossip in a small place like this, certainly.

'There's nothing wrong about that, Mrs Twitchett,' he said. 'Inspector Copper tore his tendons and muscles in an injury he received in the line of duty. It's extremely painful, but he has kept on with his work. The doctor prescribed pain-killers and muscle relaxants for him, but unfortunately they made him sick. It was the doctor who suggested he take his medicine by injection.'

'Then he should get the injections from the doctor,' Mrs Twitchett said gloomily, refusing to yield. 'I don't hold with people sticking themselves.' The kettle boiled, with a piercing whistle, but she seemed to have forgotten its purpose and turned the gas off absently. 'And if the doctor ordered it, why should that nurse bring the stuff down in dozen lots? Overdoing it, he is, mark my words.'

'That kind of pain is most troublesome at night,' Capricorn said, knowing it only too well. 'I expect that's when he takes the injections.'

He made his way up the staircase, reflecting that the censorious Mrs Twitchett was quite right, Copper should get his supplies from his doctor. A friendly nurse with access to a lab made it too easy. He didn't know what the doctor was prescribing, but pain-killers could be habit-forming. He remembered his own surprise when, after a similar injury, he had found a prescription of his own that had been written out with the proprietary name was actually for a synthesized version of morphine.

There was, of course, no note. Only an undusted bedroom with some of Copper's clothes lying on the chair. The doors of the large wardrobe gaped open— there were very few of Joss's garments here. A weekend home, now abandoned. The death of Charlie had apparently not brought Copper and Joss closer. To her anger at Copper's possessiveness now was added his knowledge of her dealings with Charlie. Strange, Capricorn thought, gazing absently through the window at the dry, dun landscape, it looked as though that love affair was over, just as he had hoped it would be, but he felt no satisfaction, no relief.

He returned downstairs and noticed the telephone in the hall. The receiver dangled to the floor, probably knocked from its cradle by one of the dogs in a previous invasion. Replacing it, he bade good-bye to Mrs Twitchett, now nodding over the whisky bottle in the kitchen, and went back to his car. The dusty lane was narrow and full of ruts and it took some handling to turn his car and get onto a gravel-topped road. Copper would have to do something about that—if he stayed.

Capricorn's mind dwelt on the possible effect of the break-up of Copper and Joss. With or without her, Copper would have to go through the investigation now it was begun. A CID investigation was like the mills of God, it ground slowly and it ground exceeding small. And Capricorn still had to question him about Charlie's death. Mrs Bonomi's accusations were absurd, yet something bothersome was tugging at the fringe of Capricorn's awareness in that regard, with the usual accompaniment of a strong desire to think of anything else but that.

Apropos of nothing, he thought of the scene with the dogs, the syringe clattering to the floor. But that had no significance; Copper was no addict. A horn sounded behind him and he had to pull over almost off the road as a big lorry squeezed past him, churning up the gravel that struck his window sharply. He recalled his bedroom window, shattered from the explosion the night before. The explosion had broken into a night of worry—yes, that was it, that was the connection. He had been troubled by Hardy's report. Two injections, he had said. It had seemed ominous, considered in the wee hours.

Now, slightly relieved at remembering, he put his worry down to late-night nerves. Hardy had said there was no poison, and so had Jencks. Midnight nerves, the hour when old maids thought of burglars under the bed, and policemen thought every death suspicious. He could have been wrong about that second injection. Because he only remembered one, it didn't mean there couldn't have been two. He, Copper and the doctor had been crowded round Charlie's big body behind Joss's screen, the second might have gone unobserved. The syringe had glittered in the light from the golden calf; it could have sunk in twice. The doctor would remember.

In any case, what Jencks had seen was two puncture marks. Charlie might have had an injection that day for something quite different—though that wasn't likely. Then Capricorn remembered Charlie's sudden start from his seat in the club. He had groped and then held up Brenda's fallen brooch, the one with the wicked-looking pin. The bauble had pricked him as it fell. The punctured skin could have come from nothing more than that.

The motorway was already crowded with cars pouring out from town. Capricorn, driving back to London, had a fairly clear way ahead and drove fast. Having sorted so much out in his mind, he couldn't imagine why he still felt oppressed. Ideas scuttled in his head like mice: syringes, brooches, relaxants, atherosclerosis that might or might not mean death. Death that was too convenient. He wondered where Copper could be staying. Certainly not at the club. Probably not with a friend in the Force—Copper would not seek the company of a policeman while he was in what could only be thought of as disgrace. He might have gone to stay with one of his former girlfriends, to find solace for Joss's coldness. Yet, somehow he felt that Copper would not. Copper's feeling for Joss was too strong to allow such simple relief. He might have gone to a hotel, but Copper was not fond of staying at hotels alone.

Suddenly, he wondered if Copper might have gone to Dolly. They were friends; Dolly and the other aunts made a pet of him, and they had plenty of room. Dolly had run the house as lodgings, years ago. As he came near town he took the road to Paddington, stopping only for a moment to call Hardy at the lab.

Hardy was his usual cheerful self and told him that the carcass had been delivered, but nothing unusual had been found in the tissues, only, of course, the Formalin from the embalming process. 'Amazing stuff,' he said blithely. 'Pickles bodies. Saves the shirts from having to go to the laundry. Wonderful for everyone except hardworking pathologists.'

'But the amount of digitalis you found in the organs could not have been a lethal dose?' Capricorn asked slowly.

'We just establish quantities,' Hardy said, 'but I can't think of any circumstance where the amount we've been able to detect could kill. Perfectly within the limit of ordinary practice.'

Capricorn thanked him, and hung up. He thought

of calling his chief, there really seemed no point in going on investigating a completely normal death. But the chief would only tell him to finish a routine inquiry. So much for his midnight fretting, he thought. Hardy's mention of Formalin—horrible to think it was now in bed linen as well as winding sheets—struck a chord in his memory, some other case, he couldn't think what. Mentally he chided himself and went back to his car. Sometimes he wished The Great Capricornus had not trained him for his memory act. Bits of information cluttered his mind; sometimes he felt like a computer with a jumbled bank.

He sighed and went on with his disagreeable task. When Dolly had invited him that morning he had thought to himself that nothing would induce him to stay in that menagerie, even if his house were falling down and there were no hotel rooms in London. He would rather go to the YMCA. But he would visit her after all. She might have heard from Copper anyway. If not, he thought gloomily, he could probably get his address from C5; Copper would have to keep them informed. A strange way to have to find a friend and colleague of so many years. Almost as bad as having to look him up in the Criminal Records Office. He shuddered, and deliberately turned his mind to something else as he poked through the city traffic. Now what was that case where the outcome had depended so much on the presence of Formalin in the tissues?

'Treating me like a bloody criminal,' Copper was saying. He was stretched out on Dolly's wine-coloured satin sofa, too small for his length, his legs dangling over the edge uncomfortably. 'He might be your nephew, Scarlett, but he's a right bastard. After all these years. If he's coming, I'm off.'

'Always was a one for spit and polish and too fussy,' Dolly said. 'Even when he was a youngster he wouldn't eat black market. Don't know how he got

into our family. We've had all sorts, but never a law.
A Bill Sykes now—' She gave a china-toothed grin, lying in her big armchair with her feet on a velvet foot-
stool embroidered with the words: 'God Bless Our
Happy Home.' Her regular daytime costume, a tent-
like dressing gown, flowed about her, hiding everything except her head and its pile of false curls.

At number two lives Big William Sykes
she roared happily,
He goes to work whenever he likes
Last night a cop followed him down our court
And now the p'lice force is one copper short.

'Though not you, love,' she giggled. 'Copper by
name but not by nature. Why don't you forget the
p'lice and join us in the act? We could teach you in
no time,' she said, licking her lips and eying Copper,
whose tight-fitting trousers displayed his charms without reserve. 'Not like Tod,' she added, speaking of
her absent spouse with her usual lack of respect. 'In
all the years we've never been able to teach him to
pick a card.'

'You women,' Copper retorted. 'Always wanting to
change a man, take him from his work. First Myrtle,
then Joss and now you.' He grinned. 'All the loves of
my life.'

Nelly was sitting at a small table, riffling cards by
the light of a dim, globe-shaped lamp. Swathed in
black, hunchbacked, her hooked profile sharp against
the light, she looked like a gypsy fortuneteller, or so
it struck Copper at the moment.

'Come on Nell,' he said, 'tell my fortune. Are all
my women going to be like that?'

'She can tell your fortune all right,' Dolly giggled.
'D'you remember, Nell, that summer at Southend
when we was skint and you told fortunes on the front
and young Merle drew pictures sixpence a time?
Merle made as much as she did.' Dolly laughed at
Nelly's discomfiture.

Nelly glared beadily at her sister. She didn't care to remember what she considered her necessary, but unprofessional, activities. 'So happens I can tell fortunes,' she said, laying out the cards.

'Oh, tell mine, tell mine.' Tilly, wrapped in quantities of butter muslin, gibbered from the corner where she had been lurking, fiddling with a long silk scarf.

Nelly muttered something about straitjackets and otherwise ignored her. 'Pick a card,' she said to Copper.

He swung himself up from the sofa and made his way to the table with his usual swagger, but he took his beer and drank it down as if he were thirsty.

'Here's how,' Dolly said, joining him in a glass, but Nelly peered intently at the cards.

'Well, I see a lot of women and a lot of loves of your life,' she said drily, 'but no ancient Carroty Polls, or should I say Dolls.'

Dolly gave her a dirty look.

'Trouble,' Nelly went on, gloomy. 'I see trouble. But always a lot of women. A pretty, fair woman is the real love of your life, for a while anyway.'

'You've got that wrong, Nell,' Copper said thoughtfully. 'Joss isn't what you call fair.'

'Nor so pretty since you whopped her one,' Dolly said maliciously. 'And we asked her here to make up for Till's mucking up her clobber. You shouldn't have done it, lad. She'll have a lovely black eye in the morning.'

Copper moodily filled his glass from the open bottles of beer and ale that littered the sideboard. 'I know. It was lousy. I just did my nut. She's made me look a bloody fool, that's what I can't stand,' he blurted out. 'She lied to me about that money and the guv-ner, and everybody knew it. Everybody except me. So what do they think? They think she was carrying on with Charlie, which is bloody ridiculous.'

He paced about the room restlessly.

Dolly shot Nelly a knowing glance, but the two remained silent. Tilly, who had retreated to her corner, tittered *sub voce*. Copper noticed none of this.

'It was nothing like that at all. I know what he was up to, though none of the smart alecs at the Yard have any idea.'

He laughed harshly. 'With me out, it'll take 'em a year to clean up what I could've done in a week, the silly buggers.

'She should've told me, instead of getting herself in trouble,' he went on, with a quick change of mood. 'It was just his way of getting his foot in the door. Lend her money and then put the pressure on. That's the way they work it. And he was putting the pressure on her all right. Crafty sod. No wonder she was so jumpy, like a cat on hot bricks. Once she was in, she couldn't get out. Must have been awful for her, me poking around. Interfering. Just drove her up the wall.'

Nelly was staring at her cards, with the pack laid out before her. 'I see a death,' she said. 'Plain as day.'

Tilly whinnied in her corner.

'I found out exactly what villainy he was in, that he pulled Joss into with him. And I'm going out and prove it,' Copper said, his face set. He pushed his hands through his rumpled hair and picked up his coat. 'I'll bring in the rest of the bastards he had working for him and blow the whole operation to bits.'

'But they've chucked you out,' Dolly protested. 'What do you care? Why don't you just go after Joss and kiss and make up? You're better off out of that police lark,' she said disparagingly. 'No money in it and no thanks either.'

He paused at the velvet-draped doorway and smiled back at her.

'I know, Scarlett; I love you doll,' he said. 'But I suppose once a law, always a law. Anyway, I have to prove that arsel-creeper was blackmailing Joss and get her in the clear. The way it was,' he said defensively, 'there was nothing the poor girl could do. Nothing at all. She was in a corner.'

Tilly was making her high, squeaking noise.

'What are you gibbering about, Till?' Dolly said crossly. 'If you've got something to say, say it. And why don't you give Copper that scarf what you pinched off Joss? She never did nothing to you or anyone else.'

Tilly fluttered forward, gripping the scarf tightly, her shrill laughter stabbing into the silence.

'Yes, she did,' her pale blue eyes rolled. 'She did it.'

'Did what?' Dolly asked.

Nelly looked at her warningly.

Copper hesitated for a second at the door.

'She did him in.'

Tilly's words and laughter rolled maniacally after him as he flinched and then strode off, deathly white, his freckles contrasting oddly as if someone had flung a handful of mud that had spattered across his face.

Her voice echoed through the passage to the front door.

'She did him in. She did him in!'

'Bust her on the nose, he did,' Dolly giggled to Capricorn, half an hour later. 'So now he thinks she's an angel of Gawd. Men are like that. And she won't think none the worse of him for it either.'

'So you think he's gone back to her?' Capricorn frowned.

Dolly looked down her nose. 'Well, he might if you'd leave them alone. You make a lot of trouble for that young couple, Merle. You ought to be ashamed.'

Dolly in a righteous mood was particularly annoying.

'I only want to talk to him because I'm officially investigating the death of Charlie Bonomi,' he explained patiently. 'Copper was at the scene and it's just part of the usual procedure.'

Nelly flicked her cards and the sound crackled in the usually quiet room.

'Investigating?' Dolly pushed her lower lip forward. 'You mean there was funny business?'

She shot Nelly a glance that seemed mysteriously portentous.

'His wife thinks so,' Capricorn said.

'What do you think?' Nelly asked, glancing up.

'I don't know.'

The words were out before he knew what he was going to answer. He wondered at himself. There was no reason to believe there was anything wrong. Hardy had made that clear. No reason. Just his own nagging worry that he couldn't explain.

'Are you staying, Merle?' Dolly asked absently. 'There's plenty of room, even if Copper comes back. Gawd, we've got rooms here haven't been used since the war.' She took a long draft of beer and giggled. 'If you opened 'em up, you might still find some girl there with a Yank. D'you remember that Sylvie that was always getting into fights and trouble and bringing the police round? Went to the States, she did, and became a mayoress.'

She was almost dreamy with reminiscence and seemed not to notice the sound coming from above. Capricorn started. Surely it was no figment of his imagination; there was pounding upstairs, and a female voice shrieking for help.

'Is she back on a visit?' he inquired calmly, 'or is that one of her successors?'

Dolly howled with laughter. 'Oh, Merle, you're a card. You know we don't 'ave none of that 'ere any more, well, we couldn't, could we? That's just our Till. She got a bit excited when Copper was here, you know how she is about Joss. Above herself, Till was, so we shut her up in her room until she calmed down.'

'I see,' Capricorn said dubiously. When he had time, he worried about Tilly's release. She was a very strange woman. 'No thank you, Dolly, I don't need a bed after all. The glaziers have been in today and the downstairs will be habitable. It was kind of you to offer. I have to be off now to have a word with Copper.'

'You did ought to leave him alone, Merle,' Dolly said, her face darkening. 'He's a friend, isn't he? So the kids took some money from Charlie Bo. They had to get it from somewhere.'

'I'm not looking into Copper's ethics. That's out of my hands,' Capricorn answered. 'But it is unusual for a CID inspector to borrow money from the Cosa Nostra,' he added drily.

'Well, what do you care?'

He saw that Dolly was working herself up into one of her rages. Unfortunate that Tod, her almost-husband, was away on tour; she usually vented her rages out on him.

'Always got to pull a long face, you have, and talk like the Vicar of Wakefield. Jawed too much as a kid to that dog-collar up North, you did, him and his starchy wife.'

She was very red. Her agitation caused her head to tremble a little, jiggling the false red curls. Nelly yawned over her cards.

'Why shouldn't the boy have a few bob?' Dolly declaimed passionately. 'Just like your father you are, Merle. Always carrying on about some poor bastard who's trying to make a living. What your father called me one season in Oldham I'll never forget, just because I had a few gentlemen help me out when the management went bust. But he made sure his own nest was well feathered.' When Dolly was enraged her eyes protruded like marbles. 'He left you all right and you've done all right for yourself with poor Milly's oil wells that she didn't even know she had, and the big pots haven't come screaming down on you.'

Capricorn took his leave with as much dignity as he could muster. Dolly's bad temper had shaken him slightly. That was the second time in a week his fortune had been thrown in his face. It must cause more resentment than he had realized, though all the aunts, and Tod, had benefited from it in their needy times.

He drove towards Soho with the idea that Copper might be at the Golden Calf after all, but got caught in stopped traffic at the corner. The light blinked green, red, and green again, but still the constable on point duty waved him back. As he waited, in enforced idleness, he realized that Dolly's words had stung.

Capricorn had never considered himself particu-

larly fortunate in his inheritance from his father. He
had been an adult, in MI 6, when his father died. Although the income had been a pleasant addition to
his pay, the extreme of poverty in which his frugal father had left him as a child, the sordid and often terrifying life as a sorcerer's apprentice had seemed in
retrospect simply not worth it. The spending of some
of the money on the child would have made a difference that the legacy later on never could.

He had been too busy to do much with the money,
apart from buying his flat, and he had left his father's
investments as they were. The Great Capricornus,
perhaps from professional bias, had been fond of
treasure underground, and the shares of gold mines
that he had accumulated grew in value over a
hundred fold. Capricorn had found himself well off at
a time when most people were getting steadily poorer.

Dolly had said, suspiciously, that money came to
him as if it were going home. She proved to be right.
His Aunt Milly had died. Milly, as frivolous as all the
Merlinos, but unsuccessful. She had left all she
possessed to her nephew, a few shabby dresses, a pair
of sequined shoes and an old hat box. In the hat box
had been a stack of oil shares, quite worthless, shares
of leases on land that might contain some oil but that
never, as Milly's shabby little lawyer had said sorrow-
fully, would be worth drilling. It was the sort of
gamble a Merlino would enjoy. 'Never' had lasted until the Arab oil boycott. Suddenly the risk was worth
taking; drilling was begun; oil was found. Aunt
Milly's lawyer had proved shrewd and handled matters well for Capricorn who had given him, at his request, 'a piece of the action.' The shares were not
sold but were traded for an agreeable number of
shares in the consortium that took over. Capricorn
was rich beyond his needs and, he realized ruefully,
an object of envy to others, especially, it seemed, to
those he had helped.

Had his wealth, he thought uncomfortably, tempted Copper with desires he could not legally gratify? Had Dolly hit upon some part, at least, of the truth? He glanced back at the house, tarted up on the orders of Dolly's decorator with much bright and shiny paint, though the gutters and leaders were still in sad repair. One of the upper windows was open—unusual in that house. A long, pale leg appeared, then another, followed by the rest of the cadaverous form of his Aunt Tilly.

With a thrill of horror, he saw Tilly climbing down the pipe. While he considered abandoning his car in the middle of the press and trying to rescue her aging and doubtless brittle bones, she scampered down and landed on the window ledge below, agile as the girl she so curiously resembled, dressed as she was in a kind of sailor dress. She banged on the window, howled and catcalled at Dolly and Nelly inside the Victorian, boozy-smelling parlour, until the window was flung up and Dolly shrieked back. Capricorn averted his gaze and fortunately the policeman at last let him proceed. He found himself laughing helplessly and murmured, 'Oh, God,' to the suspicion of the harassed constable, who put on his official expression in accordance with the Metropolitan Police Instruction Book: 'Idle and silly remarks will be disregarded.'

By the time he reached Soho, laughter was over. On a narrow street, not far from where Teresa Bonomi was staying, a familiar redhead stood deep in conversation with Pete Moletta, Charlie Bo's former lieutenant, now perhaps his successor. Copper made Moletta laugh, a sniggering laugh that hardly moved his facial muscles. A moment later, Copper slapped him in a friendly way, threw an arm round his shoulder, and together they walked into a pub that was just opening its doors.

The corners of Capricorn's mouth turned downwards. Copper had already given up the Force, it seemed. He wasn't waiting for the outcome of the investigation. Was Copper making his peace with the Mafia—and Joss, too, perhaps? Angry, he pulled up and followed them inside.

It was not one of Copper's usual haunts. The place was drab: small without being cosy, shabby without being old. Nevertheless, Copper was chatting and laughing with the barmaid as though he was an old friend, while Moletta looked on with a supercilious grin. There was nothing about him to suggest a suspected criminal being interviewed by a detective, rather he had the confident attitude of a criminal who owns a 'bent law.'

At the sight of that nightclub-pale, smirking face Capricorn had a wave of disgust. He stepped forward, intending merely to ask Copper to come back with him to the Yard, but he was forestalled.

'' 'Ello, guv,' Copper greeted him jovially. 'Or shouldn't I say that now? Ex-guv. Worse than a bloody divorce,' he informed Moletta, who now smiled widely. 'You dunno what to call each other any more. Apart from a lot of hard words, that is. But I've got no hard words for the guv'ner—much,' he said. 'I'm just sick of the whole lousy Metropolitan Police and as far as I'm concerned they can all go and screw themselves, but aside from that,' he leaned back against the bar and tossed back half a mug of ale, 'what can I do for you?'

'I'm making inquiries regarding the death of Carlo Bonomi,' Capricorn said coldly. 'I would like you to come along with me to the Yard and make a statement.'

Copper gave him a sunny smile. 'What for? There was nothing funny about old Charlie's popping off. You can ask his best friend here, my mate Pete. Anyway, you were there yourself, you know all about it.'

Moletta looked at Capricorn, his expression blank.

'It was a natural death surely. Mr Bonomi's heart had been bad for years.'

Capricorn didn't want to explain anything to Moletta, who knew that Charlie's problem had been the vessels, not the heart itself, and who almost certainly knew about Teresa Bonomi's complaint. He might have been the one to inspire it, except that it would make no sense for him to get Copper thrown off the Force where he might have been a useful friend. Still, the machinations of the underworld could be Byzantine. Capricorn's mouth felt as though it were full of ashes, but he replied calmly, 'It's merely routine inquiry.'

'After the inquest?' Moletta inquired sarcastically.

Copper was looking at his watch. 'I'm afraid it wouldn't be convenient for me to come now, guv. Dinner time, I've got to see Joss. After all, the Yard isn't paying me any more, and it paid pissed poor anyway.'

He turned to Moletta. 'Cut me off without a shilling. Lose all my time in for pension. Worse than doing a stretch, they don't even give you a few bob when they let you out.'

'I've had considerable trouble finding you today,' Capricorn said. 'I would be obliged if you would come along.'

'Sorry,' Copper said amiably. 'Unless,' he gave a wink to the plump barmaid who wriggled in delight, 'you happen to have a warrant?' He smiled his surprisingly sweet smile, and Moletta giggled at Capricorn's discomfiture. 'I'll drop by in the morning, darling,' Copper went on. 'Not too early. Now I'm on civvy street I don't have to get up at the bloody crack of dawn. Me and my old lady like to get our beauty sleep.'

So he had gone back to Joss, or planned to. Capricorn was almost speechless at his manner. He had always known that Copper's feeling about police work was not the same as his own. It had little basis in love of order and justice; Copper had said himself that he liked the excitement of the game and if he wasn't a detective he might have been a villain: he wasn't born to be a nine-to-fiver. Copper had been such an excellent and reliable policeman, so devoted to duty, that Capricorn had dismissed much of his talk as youthful bravado. But all that had been before Joss. Could she have been the catalyst that brought about the transformation? Even seeing and hearing it, he could hardly believe what his senses proved. 'You can come in in the morning, if you wish,' he said. 'There is one thing I would like to know now. After Charlie's attack, do you remember how many injections the doctor gave him?'

He had merely asked the question because it had been on his mind. It was of no particular importance: he could get the information from the doctor at any time. Besides, Hardy had proved the injections were not significant. To Capricorn's amazement, Copper's face drained of colour and his eyes narrowed to slits. He looked as shocked as if he'd been kicked in the groin. The two men stared at each other. Copper was still a detective; he kept his face rigid and to the casual observer in the bar he would appear to have quickly recovered his self-possession. But to his long-time friend and companion the atmosphere about him was tense and almost pungent; it had the very scent of fear.

When Capricorn left the pub he was in a state something like shock himself. Copper had refused to go to the Yard, and he had been more than evasive about the question of the injection, claiming he didn't remember. It was impossible that he didn't remember. Copper's mind was of the neat and precise sort that wouldn't forget such recent events. Copper was procrastinating; he was lying and he was afraid.

In short, he was behaving like a man guilty of a serious crime. The crime of murder?

Capricorn sped homewards, his face grim. The doubts he had had about Charlie's death that had seemed so unreasonable now appeared well founded. The shock of Copper's behaviour, together with the chance meeting with Moletta, had jogged his memory. Moletta. Spingoletti. The case he had been trying to remember—or trying not to. He remembered now, all right. He wished he didn't.

It wasn't an English case, but he had the report in his library with all the details. When he arrived at his house, he left his car in the first open space—it happened to be a bus stop—and rushed in. He ran upstairs, without bothering to check if the glaziers had done their work and if any rooms were habitable. In the library some chairs were overturned, a vase was broken, a lot of books were on the floor and everything was covered with dust. The shelves on poisons still stood. He dusted the books' spines rapidly with his handkerchief, hunting for the case. Spingoletti, an American doctor. The case had been reported in England but not widely. Yes, there it was. A heavy volume. The doctor had been tried for two separate murders and found guilty of the second.

Capricorn remembered his friend Happy Delaney, then a New York City policeman, talking about it one night over dinner. 'A case like that is a nightmare for the police and the prosecution,' he had said. 'No wonder the first jury brought in a "Not guilty". The damned stuff isn't even on the Dangerous Drugs list. Anyone with access to lab supplies can get it. Looks like a heart attack—the hell of it is that is a heart attack. The drug breaks down in the bloodstream. The whiz kids from the lab couldn't really prove a thing.'

He took the book, sat at the library table and settled down to taking notes as carefully as if his mind were calm, although it was a whirling confusion of thought. He hardly noticed the destruction all round him, though his home and its carefully chosen contents were cherished possessions. 'Got that house instead of a wife,' Dolly often said derisively, but at that moment his home meant nothing.

There was a great deal of testimony, a lot of it not to the point. Almost an hour passed before he found what he needed. The testimony of the expert witnesses had been drawn out by the brilliant defense who had shown the pathologist to be only human and liable to draw inferences without enough fact to back them up. The indignant pathologist had pointed out that as the body had been embalmed, according to American custom, his task had been made almost impossible—which answer had suited the defense perfectly.

The evening was cool, but Capricorn found he was sweating. He put the book down and rested his head in his hands. Happy's words rang in his ears. 'It leaves no trace. Breaks down into succinic acid and choline, and you find that in any body. Not that anyone would have thought to look if Spingoletti hadn't caused a scandal, and then made the woman mad enough to give him away. The second jury brought in a verdict against him, but the state had never really proved the wife was poisoned. Proof, solid proof, is impossible.'

No, Capricorn thought, throwing the pencil down, his suspicion was running riot. Because he didn't want to think evil of a friend, his over-scrupulous conscience was badgering him into inventing it. The Catholic church, he remembered, considered scrupulosity to be a sin.

Yet it was true that Copper had reason to want Charlie Bo dead. Charlie was a rival for the love of his woman. If he had lived, Copper would certainly have lost his job, which meant something to him once. If he lost Joss, he would have lost the club as well and very likely his home. He would have drowned in a sea of debt. On the other hand, with Charlie dead he could have kept everything. And he must have thought himself safe. He could not have foreseen the arrival of Teresa Bonomi, infirm as she was, from three thousand miles away.

But—poison? Despite the weight of suspicion, Capricorn couldn't believe that Copper would poison anyone. It did not fit anything he knew about the man. He realized uncomfortably that he hadn't thought, 'Copper wouldn't murder anyone.' It was the method seemed unlikely, not the deed. Capricorn stirred uneasily. Certainly, the foolproof nature of the method would recommend itself to a detective. A detective, he remembered painfully, with easy access to lab supplies, a nurse conveniently enamoured, already supplying him with a drug of similar type without the lethal effect. Had his discussions with her suggested the crime?

So easy to picture the party at Wenmore, sitting round the fire after an evening of steady drinking. Copper flirting, according to habit, with the all-too-impressionable Nurse Wallace, who probably reacted, as so often happened, far more strongly than Copper ever intended. Nurse Wallace, with an eye on Joss, telling tales of men disposing of wives and mistresses by poison, the safest of all means. An idle question, and then the story of the Spingoletti case that had puzzled the best minds in forensic medicine for years. It was all too easy to conjure up the scene. Or Copper might have been familiar with the case from general knowledge. It didn't matter. Once the method was known, murder became horribly easy.

He could talk to Nurse Wallace, he thought, but at this stage, if she had been the supplier, she would only lie. Certainly, she wouldn't want to implicate herself in a death. And if Copper had wanted the stuff, he hadn't necessarily got it from her. A detective spends his life dealing with villains. If he wants to engage in villainy himself, he knows exactly where to go. Yes, murder was easy.

But there was a snag. Capricorn tapped his fingers on the table, deep in thought. Succinylcholine chloride was used in surgery to stop the action of the heart. As far as he knew, it could be given only by injection. True, it was prepared in solution, but there was nothing in the literature about its effects if taken orally. That, for any potential murderer, would be an unknown.

In the original autopsy, Jencks, the pathologist, had noted two injections. Grimly, Capricorn picked up his telephone, which had escaped the blast, and dialled the number of Charlie Bonomi's doctor. Surgery was over, he was told, the doctor had gone home to dinner. Capricorn called him at home and had to deal with a wife trained to fend off all demands at mealtime. While he was being gently agreeable to the loyal wife and persuading her to call her husband to the telephone for just a minute, he checked over what he knew of the man. Nothing to his credit. Ainsley Fairfield was a favourite practitioner among the wealthier people of the district. No longer young, but still good-looking, with a soothing manner and a pill or injection for all conditions. Sleeping pills, energy pills, tranquillizers for any untoward emotion. Stuff for your sex life and stuff to keep you young. A type familiar all through history, a purveyor of philtres and nostrums, with a medical degree now to ward off evil, not from the patients, but from the physician.

Fairfield came on the line. His wife had done the disagreeable work; he was all charm. Capricorn apologized for the intrusion, explained that he had to send in a report on Charlie Bo's death and asked directly about the injections. Naturally, he didn't get a direct answer.

'But, my dear Superintendent, I thought the inquiry was over. The verdict at the inquest, my certificate—'

'No one is quarrelling with your certificate, doctor,' Capricorn said patiently. 'It's merely a matter of routine. Something overlooked earlier. I hoped you might remember exactly what you gave him, or that you might have a note.'

'Oh, of course I remember,' Fairfield said more easily. He forbore to complain at being called away from his coffee for a mere matter of routine. 'The patient was *in extremis* when I arrived. The heart had stopped. I gave an injection of a strong stimulant, mostly digitalis, and tried resuscitation but, as you know—'

'Yes, of course. Certainly you did everything you could. My only question was about the injection. It was only one, you said.'

'Well, yes, one injection. The dose was larger than one usually gives, but in the circumstances—'

'Quite so. The pathologist confirmed it was within the range of safety. The only reason for my question was that he found two punctures. If you're sure you only gave one—'

'Well,' the doctor, aware now of the way the wind was blowing, took shelter. 'Well, I'm sure of the *amount* I gave. I have a note, and it could be checked against my books. As to whether I gave it in one dose, or if I gave first one and then, seeing no effect, gave another—I might have done that. It's hard to remember in detail. The difficult circumstances and the labour of the effort to resuscitate—I wouldn't want to swear to it.'

Underneath the veneer of charm, Fairfield had turned cautious. Capricorn would have taken a bet that he did remember. He had said quite distinctly, before he knew there was any question, '. . . an injection . . .' Fairfield knew about Charlie Bo. If there was going to be any trouble he wanted to stay out of it. Teresa Bonomi had summed him up quickly and accurately.

Capricorn thanked the doctor and returned to his notes. Copper *could* have given Charlie an injection after he was stricken. After the crowd had been moved back and the screen set up, Capricorn had left Copper with the body and telephoned for an ambulance when he found that Joss had only called the doctor. But it would presuppose Copper's walking about with a syringe full of the stuff—a large syringe at that, Capricorn reasoned, noting the quantity necessary for a man of Charlie's build. No, it was absurd. Copper had no way of knowing Charlie would collapse and there would be an opportunity—unless . . . Had the quarrel and the scuffle in Joss's private office been deliberately staged with that in mind? After a moment's consideration, Capricorn dismissed the idea. Nobody had believed Charlie to be dangerously afflicted. His whole manner of life was that of a man with no reason to worry about his health.

And yet, what had happened in that office? It would make more sense to assume that that was the place where the fatal dose was given. The attack was more easily explained as being the result of the fatal injection and not merely its precursor. But Charlie Bo would never have allowed Copper to give him an injection. Not under any circumstances. Not even if the row had made him feel ill and in need of medication. Charlie was no fool. He knew his rival to be his enemy. If he took an injection from anyone, it certainly wouldn't be from Copper.

But what about Joss? Had the quarrel between the young couple been staged to get out of their predicament? They might have been working in concert. No, Capricorn couldn't believe that. Joss's anger against Copper was genuine. Her sincerity had been as clear as her reasoning was muddled. She had thought she could be free and at the same time deeply indebted to Charlie.

Closing his eyes, Capricorn tried to picture the short scene in that office. Copper threatening, Charlie over-excited, Joss offering, perhaps in all innocence, a soothing injection, Copper seizing his opportunity to substitute the dose?

Yes, it could have been done. Capricorn remembered Copper angrily marching Charlie to the office. The dose had taken some time to have its effect. It must have gone into the muscle instead of the vein. The attack had come when—five, six minutes after Charlie had left the office? What a lot of conjecture, one part of his mind mocked, to try to prove a friend guilty of murder. Capricorn swore, something he rarely did, running through all the oaths he remembered without feeling any relief. He picked up the telephone again and dialled Hardy's number.

Fortunately, the pathologist was a good-natured man. To Capricorn's terse inquiry he answered that one injection had gone into the thick muscle of the upper arm and another into the brachial artery. Jencks had made a note of that. 'Doctor probably bungled the first one. Not unusual. A lot of G.P.'s get a mild case of nerves when they see a heart attack.'

Capricorn shivered, although the evening air that came through the broken panes was mild enough. Briefly, he told Hardy what he suspected, though not whom.

Hardy whistled. 'A nasty idea,' he said. 'If it's true, there's a problem. You can't find it in its original form.'

'I know,' Capricorn said, wondering if he was glad or sorry. He remembered one of the pathologists in the Spingoletti case had been forced to admit on the stand that the quantities of succinic acid and choline found in the body had been too small to quantify, let alone to judge more than normal. 'It would be the Spingoletti case all over again.'

'Not quite that bad,' Hardy said. Thank the Lord
for an intelligent man, Capricorn thought. It was like
Hardy to be familiar enough with the case not to need
any mental refreshing. 'The bodies in the Spingoletti
case had to be exhumed. They'd been buried for
months before a pathologist saw them. Before anything even slightly suspicious turned up, there were
four kinds of chromatographic tests and some others
made. We can do better than that now, but all it will
prove, if you're right, is more succinic acid and choline
present than usual and possibly more molecules of
choline—monocholine—in the area of the injection
than in a control area. What defense counsel will do
to us I have to think. I don't think a British jury
would buy it.'

Hardy agreed to run the tests the next day, reminding Capricorn about the presence of Formalin in the
tissues. Capricorn hung up and pressed his hands
against his aching temples. He was working awfully
hard to put his closest friend in the dock. What
Hardy said about British jurors wasn't entirely sound.
True, they weren't excited by months of sensational
reporting in the press so that their minds were made
up before the trial started. Nevertheless, they had
brought in verdicts before on tenuous evidence. He
thought of Edith Thompson, hanged for complicity
in her husband's death, though her husband had
been killed by her lover who never denied the act was
his alone. But Edith Thompson had written letters
about poisoning her husband. No poison was found
in his body; it may well have been purely imaginary,
but those letters put a noose around Edith's neck.
British juries were not fond of irregular relationships.
What would they think of a Scotland Yard detective
who shared a mistress with a Mafioso?

And yet, and yet. Capricorn sat there a long time
in the dust and ruin, grinding his pencil, without realizing it, into the fine veneer of the library table. He

gave a deep sigh that suddered through him. Whatever he might feel, he was a policeman and he knew where his duty lay.

Swiftly, he ran down the stairs and out into the street, ignoring the stained rugs and broken bannister, the shattered vase gleaming forlornly in the hall, the note from Mrs Dermott about the meal she had prepared for him in the kitchen—and the summons on the windshield of his car. He was back in Soho in thirty minutes. Another worry had formed in his mind, greater than the one he had before. If Copper had killed for Joss and found he had lost her anyway—Joss must know about the crime. She was quick, too quick, and she was no docile mate. Joss angry would not keep quiet. It was absurd, his thoughts were absurd, so Capricorn stopped thinking and concentrated on driving fast. He drove through several red lights until he reached the Golden Calf.

The electric sign was dark. Capricorn pushed the bell but, although he heard the sound echoing, no one came to answer. He pushed the door. It was unlocked and opened onto the dim vestibule. The overhead light was out but a glimmer came from the stairs and it was easy to make his way down. The main room of the club was bright with light from the golden calf itself. It shone down on the body of a woman slumped by the bar in the same spot where Charlie Bo had lain, a big woman wearing blue jeans and a white shirt, and Copper was leaning over her. Capricorn moved forward, automatically, for he didn't want to see. It couldn't be. His mind tried to reject the reality, to refocus his eyes, to blink the sight away, but it remained. The woman was Joss, or had been. Her throat was cut from ear to ear; the blood still dripped to the floor, glistened in a dark pool across her breast and on the hands of Copper as he started up, cursing.

LAMENT FOR A LADY

Capricorn was always to remember that evening and its quality of nightmare. The local men had arrived; the upper echelon at the Yard had been consulted, taken away from their dinners by the event, and the decision had been made to take Copper in charge. Sedgwick had been given the case, and he had come down to the club before Copper was taken away. He at once instituted a search for the murder weapon.

Copper denied the killing but without conviction. The usually vital, bubbling redhead looked like a different man. The male swagger was gone, and his body looked muscle-bound and brutish. His face was pasty white and dull, the jaw hanging slack, and those sharp green eyes were glazed over and vacant. He said little and what he had to say made no sense. He started one story and changed it to another. Nothing he said was borne out by any facts. He first denied, then admitted, that he and Joss had quarrelled earlier in the day and he had struck her. Her nose was bruised and her mouth puffy. At one time he said it was a bad quarrel. At another, he said it hadn't mattered. First he said he had gone to see her to take her out for a while before the club opened. Then he said he had gone to make up the quarrel. She was dead, he insisted, when he arrived. There was no one else present and no weapon.

Moletta, when found, did not substantiate this tale. He said that he and Copper had parted only a few minutes after Capricorn had gone, well before six o'clock, Moletta to keep an appointment and Copper 'to have it out with Joss'.

The woman in charge of the cloakroom, she who greeted the patrons with 'Hello, sucker,' had arrived about a quarter to seven and had heard a man and woman quarrelling loudly. Joss had been screaming: 'What's mine is mine and I'm going to keep it. You can go to hell!'

Not wanting to be involved in a row, the woman had gone to a café to get a cup of tea and wait till it blew over. The café was across the street, and she said she had kept watch to see if the club opened. She didn't see Copper leave or enter.

And that wasn't all. It was a minor matter compared with two murders but it was an added blow. When Copper was taken in charge he was found to have a quantity of the fake rands on him. Capricorn had to go and see the Commander, but before he left, Sedgwick had told him in disgust that there had been rumours of the traffic stemming from the Golden Calf.

'No wonder our bright lad managed to pick off the small fry so easy,' he said. 'Gave us two that didn't know him. He and the woman were in it together, that's obvious. The Golden Calf. Right under my nose. In the protection of the CID. This'll give us a black eye we won't live down in a hurry!'

The Northcountryman was grim with a cold anger. If he had found the knife, he would have had Copper before the magistrate in the morning. Teams of men were hunting through and round the premises. All the kitchen knives were sent to the lab in case one had been washed and replaced. Unfortunately, they were new and expensive, made in one piece of seamless Swedish steel that cleaned completely and easily.

The Commander was in a mood to match. By the

time they met, Capricorn had told his story so many times he was sick at heart. He realized, unhappily, how a witness must feel in a case where a friend or loved one is involved. A murder investigation was very different when it was a purely professional matter. Capricorn had been a detective all of his adult life, and yet now his mind was frozen.

It took this, he reflected, to make him know how much he had always thought of Copper. Copper, who took the place of all the brothers and sons Capricorn never had. A very different kind of man from himself, yet he could have sworn that Copper was a man of honour.

The Commander believed nothing of the sort. He was red with annoyance, and he had a look in his eye which promised that someone was going to pay for it. For all that he and Capricorn had been friends for many years, he gazed on him now without favour.

'You were asked to look into this business and clear it up,' he said. 'Seems to me you shilly-shallied. That young rogue has made a fool of you.'

He lit a cigar and smoked irritably. Smoking, Capricorn noticed with a remnant of his usual detachment, always made the Commander bad-tempered if he hadn't eaten. He must have been dragged from the table over this affair. He remembered that the Commander had been deciding between two honours, a promotion or retirement with the prospect of county work to his taste. A major scandal in the Department might change all that.

'You've let him get away with too much. It's been commented on before. His way of speech and addressing senior officers, his manner. Unfitting,' the Commander grumbled. He failed to take note that Capricorn had not always been Copper's senior officer in the chain of command, and that he wasn't now. Copper's swaggering masculinity, his success with women, had intrigued the Commander under his

guise of disapproval. Copper personified a secret wish
of many respectable men. 'It seems he's been running
the villainy the great British public was paying him
to stop, and now he's murdered his whore.'

Capricorn started for a moment at hearing such a
word from the Commander who didn't speak like
that, and at hearing the term applied to Joss. Joss, for
whom his feelings were mixed but grief was certainly
uppermost. Beautiful Joss, whom he had seen with
her lovely throat slit. That shocking, ghastly irrele-
vancy of severed tubes and tendons below her oval
face. It would have bothered her, he thought, his
mind veering off into absurdity, to have known she
would die with her face still swollen from Copper's
blow. Had she planned to work that night in spite of
her blemish? Capricorn had been painfully touched
at the sight of Joss in her working clothes. There had
been a bucket and a scrubbing brush close by. The
cleanliness and elegance of the club had been due not
only to Joss's finding workers willing to work, but because she, with her vitality and ambition, had not
been too fine to get down on her hands and knees to
make up for any deficiencies spotted by those sharp
grey eyes. Yet she would have carefully hidden the
fact that she did it. Joss. It was hard to think of her
as dead, her body a subject for the indignities of
post-mortem. Capricorn had a lump in his throat that
blocked his speech. He had an insane, totally unprofessional desire to hit the Commander in the teeth.

What he did was, perhaps, worse. During the inter-
rogation by his colleagues, he had committed the
cardinal sin of a witness, the sin that he himself had
inveighed against times beyond number. He had
withheld information. True, it was not directly involved in this case, but that was what obstructive
witnesses always said. He had told nothing of his suspicions about Charlie Bonomi's death. It was not only
silly; it was useless. He had discussed the matter with

Hardy. Hardy was no fool. When the story of Copper became known, Hardy would understand. It was past reason to expect he would remain quiet.

Capricorn had merely told Sedgwick he had gone to interview Copper about the Bonomi affair, and had let him assume it was routine inquiry. Now he was keeping both what he knew and what he suspected from the Commander. Capricorn didn't know why he was doing it. Why he wasn't doing the proper, the correct thing? He could have tied up Sedgwick's case for him nicely. Was it sentiment? He remembered Copper's face, ugly with freckles, lifeless, stupid, a fighter dazed in the ring. Perhaps the Merlino aunts were wrong, after all, with their lifelong cry, 'You're cold, Merle.' Perhaps he, too, could let his feelings warp his judgement. But he didn't believe it. Somewhere under the tide of grief he found a solid bedrock of certainty. He was following the dictates of reason. There was more work to do on the Bonomi case before he would be satisfied.

He had spoken briefly to the cloakroom woman the night Charlie died but she, with her mind divided between the pleasures of drink and company and the knowledge that she was scamping her duty in the cloakroom—'hardly any coats, though, in the warm weather'—had noticed nothing. But there was still Nurse Wallace, and there was Hardy's report. Slope, Brenda Grey and her friends—they had all been jammed next to Charlie for the last five minutes of his life and might have something to tell. They, and the departed commercial traveller. If he gave it up to Sedgwick now, that would be the end. Whether the murder of Charlie was included in the prosecution against Copper or not, it would be assumed at the Yard that he was guilty. And it was certain that if he told the Commander what he knew, he would be taken off the Bonomi case.

As it was, the Commander was by no means finished. 'It looks as though you've been shirking,' he said bluntly. 'Not long ago you recommended Copper for a promotion. Then we had to put A5 on him. You should have reported that he and the girl and Bonomi were thick as thieves. You haven't had much luck at all, lately, have you?' He eyed Capricorn with an unfriendly glance. 'Did you hear the news this morning?'

Capricorn, as it happened, had not. He had been putting matters in order after the bombing.

'That case you thought you finished up is wide open again. Barlow Road. Hake escaped from detention. Went over the wall during the exercise period—an elaborately staged affair. And we haven't found him yet.'

Only a very small part of Capricorn's mind noted that Barlow Road had not been the case, as the Commander well knew. He had only interviewed Hake because of his hints about Brixton Jim. The Commander was by nature a fair man. The events of the day must be prodding his ulcer. Capricorn had, in any event, little emotion left to respond with anger or anything else. What he felt, behind the annoyance of any policeman at a botched case, was a certain mental satisfaction. It had made no sense that Hake would have faced trial without giving up what he knew to try to make things easier for himself. Now the sense was clear. For his silence, Hake had been promised escape. He was stupid after all. Suddenly, Capricorn was certain about Brixton Jim. He had got Hake out, and Hake's life now wasn't worth three old farthings.

'We're watching the airports and the docks,' the Commander was saying. 'But—'

'I don't think you need bother, sir,' Capricorn pointed out. 'My guess is he's dead already, or trussed up for the kill.'

The Commander looked up sharply, no happier.

'Oh, yes, I'd forgotten your great theory. But you haven't pulled that rabbit out of the hat for us yet, have you?' he jibed. 'Time for one of your conjuring tricks. It might be true,' he added in dejection. 'So much the worse for us. No chance of finding him, then. "Scotland Yard baffled, and Scotland Yard bent," all in one week. We are going to look like fools of the nation. A smack in the eye for all senior officers. The A.C. is furious. P'raps you'd better stay out of sight for a while. Take some annual leave, you've got enough coming.'

'Is that an order, sir?' Capricorn said formally.

'It's a well-meant suggestion.'

The two men separated without the cloud lifting. It was the most dismal interview with his superior that Capricorn had had in all his years of service. The Commander believed that Capricorn had let the Department down by his camaraderie with the Inspector, failing to report his findings, trying to cover up Copper's indiscretions. Such conduct was entirely out of order in a highly disciplined force like the Metropolitan Police. And, Capricorn reflected soberly, the Commander didn't know the half.

When he left the Yard, the great glass edifice was glittering like a giant block of ice in the moonlight. The blade-sharp edges, the ruthlessly square line against the sky reflected neither sympathy with man nor hope of heaven. It looked what it was, a structure designed for the storage of machines and computers, with mortals left to scurry through the passages like mice behind a wainscot. Yet it was not the only building of that sort, by Bauhaus out of commerce, even in the neighbourhood of St. James's Park, let alone the rest of London.

He sighed, wondering how much of his distaste for the architecture of his day was due to middle age. Was it inevitable that at some point a man begins to feel out of place in the time stream? Could this be the beginning of the turning away from life that heralds the approaching of its end? Or was his a purely aesthetic withdrawal from the harsh uglification of a once-lovely city: was it mankind itself that in the twentieth century had taken a dangerous turn, inimical to its own life, presaging the destruction of the race?

Foolish, unpoliceman-like questions, he thought as he got his car. 'Havering,' Mrs Dermott would say. It was perhaps because for the first time in over twenty years he couldn't think where to go. After a busy day he enjoyed his solitude and had always turned gratefully towards home. Home, that reflected little of the twentieth century, except, he reminded himself, for its modern comforts: he was not a romantic. Yet now he hesitated. Home would be a shambles, between the bomb and the repairman: he had fibbed to Dolly and had no idea whether the windows were back in his bedroom or not. More than that, he felt so utterly dejected that for once he needed company. Someone to talk to before he took all his troubles to bed.

Though not a policeman. Capricorn's lips twisted wryly. He had a bad conscience; he'd better stay away from his colleagues tonight. Unfortunately, nearly all his friends were policemen. The life of a detective was too all-consuming to keep many close friends outside the Force. He wished for a moment that his friend Rose was in London; she would be the perfect companion for such a night, gentle, soothing and not a close inquirer. But Rose, naturally, was in Cicester being a perfect companion to her husband. At this hour most people would be comfortably ensconced in their domestic pleasures, relaxing, entertaining or being entertained.

On an impulse, he drove towards Paddington. His aunts, at least, liked Copper. They might be sympathetic for once. The journey was, of course, foredoomed to failure. The aunts weren't working, so

naturally they had guests, a small party in fact. Seeing
the cars outside, he was about to turn away, but
Nelly, admitting some newcomers, saw him and called
him in. Sharing an armchair in one corner were
Brenda Grey, her young beauty still tarnished and
bedraggled, and Len Slope, looking like a young, English version of Moletta. Brenda seemed somewhat
cooler to Slope; perhaps she was tiring of him after
all. Capricorn was about to leave quietly when an
oddly familiar voice came from the old wind-up
gramophone in the corner. Dolly's decorator had rescued that from the attic with cries of joy, and Dolly
was now playing a scratchy old record, a duet with a
male and a female voice in a tune he hadn't heard
since he was a boy:

Me and Jane in the 'plane, flying high in the cloud
Me and Jane in the 'plane, far away from the crowd.

The deep bass voice, how could he have forgotten?
It was The Great Capricornus himself. Who was the
woman with the sweet voice singing with him? It
must be Milly, poor dead Milly, the only one of his
aunts who could really sing:

Her kisses will show a million an hour
No traffic cop will ever stop me and Jane in the
'plane.

Capricorn smiled for a moment in reminiscence,
and Dolly, seeing him, hooted with laughter. Dolly
was in purple satin and velvet, with fake diamonds
sugaring her hair. Dolly was always at her worst in
purple—not only in appearance.

'You remember your father singing that, Merle,'
she screamed across the room. 'The pride of The
Ship and Blue Ball, his father was,' she informed the
company. 'Of course, he only sang so he could miss
standing his round. Oh, what a stingy sod.'

Her friends laughed. The son of The Great Capricornus tried not to look put out. It was quite true, he
reflected, but Dolly must still be annoyed with him

from the scene this afternoon to publish it. To him the afternoon seemed years away, but Dolly cherished her grudges. Len Slope was grinning at his discomfiture. Brenda Grey looked vacant.

'I just stopped in to see if Tilly was all right,' Capricorn said hastily and made for the door.

Dolly turned red. 'Why shouldn't she be?'

Oh Lord, Capricorn thought, she's in one of her belligerent moods. He wondered if she'd heard of Joss's death. It had been on the wireless news. Even if she had, it would be half-forgotten already. Except in matters involving her active ill will, Dolly lived in the moment. He made a sketchy gesture of farewell and strode down the passage, but Dolly tanked through the crowded room and ran after him.

'What are you hinting at?' she shouted. 'Always on about Tilly. Want to keep your own aunt shut up because you're ashamed of her, big pot policeman?'

Capricorn felt very tired and at the same time wished it were within the limits of civility to slap an aging aunt to shut her up. That's twice tonight you've wanted to hit someone, his inner voice reminded him. You must be losing your grip.

'She's upstairs,' Dolly went on. 'Been up there all afternoon and evening. I gave her her pills if you want to know, Clever Dick, and she's been asleep and not bothering anyone.'

Then her escapade on the drainpipe had done her no harm. Dolly obviously didn't realize he had seen it. She wouldn't want him to know either. She needed Tilly for the act and refused to admit that her mental balance was shaky.

'I suppose you've heard about Joss,' he said quietly.

Dolly calmed down. 'Yes. Gawd, it's terrible. Right in the club, the announcer said. A girl's not safe anywhere. To think she was here just this afternoon. "Come to lunch," I said to her, after that bit of fracas at the Florabel. And she turned up all right, but her old man was here and they had a set-to and went off. I liked her,' she said, melancholy. 'Not in the profession, of course, but she was like us girls. Independent. I'll go to the funeral. We'll all go. Well, maybe not Till,' she amended hastily.

She fiddled with her curls. 'But you see, Merle, we'd already asked people in for tonight and we didn't want to disappoint them. Joss herself would've said, "What's the use of making a fuss?" Why, she told me she wanted her body to go to science. What's Copper going to do?'

He looked at her, not knowing how much she'd heard.

'Copper's been taken in charge.'

'Taken in charge?' she said, incredulous. ''Oo took him?'

'The local men. I had to call them, of course.'

'You—' She stared with her eyes like light-green grapes nearly bursting from her head. 'What are you talking about?'

His weariness intensified and sat on him with the weight of the Tower, bridge and all. He must have been mad to come here, he thought in a moment of lucidity. He really could not bear to go through all this again. 'I found them, you see. Joss dead and Copper standing there over her.'

'You're bloody well mad,' Dolly said. She was truly and deeply shocked. Ethics did not figure largely in Dolly's life but he knew he had violated perhaps her only deeply held belief, loyalty to a friend against malevolent authority. 'Couldn't you 'ave given 'im time to get out?'

He looked at her. It was useless to try to explain and he longed for his bed, even if it was covered with glass and stone.

'No,' he said. It was the essence of a lifetime. Dolly rejected it with the same degree of meaning.

'You bloody piss-assed fool.'

'Yet Joss was your friend.' It wasn't his intelligence speaking, merely an emotion he didn't know he had.

'Well, it won't bring her back, will it? Even if he did it, won't he be sorry enough? He's been a friend for years and years, hasn't he?'

Dolly was mumbling now, her intensity somewhat diminished. In the dim hall, she looked about at the photographs of Merlinos past and present, as if for succor in this madness. She pointed to an old picture of Tilly as a soubrette. 'Didn't we have this trouble in the family and all of us shut our mouths, including you, although you was a rotten little monster even then?'

She seemed suddenly to become aware of what she was saying and glanced uneasily at the portières to the parlour, but the party had confined itself inside: delighted with the old gramophone, they were playing the record again.

Capricorn opened the front door and started to go. 'Me and Jane in the 'plane' followed him down the path. The light soprano against the bass voice caught his attention once more.

'I never knew that Milly made a record with my father,' he said, noticing at the same time the strange and complex web of family relations, screaming enemies one moment, reminiscing the next.

Dolly stood framed by the doorway, clutching her satin billows close and shivering in the cool of the night air.

'Milly?' she said, unbelieving. 'You thought that was Milly? She never sang like that. That was your mum, you bloody fool,' she told her nephew, who had never heard his mother's voice, 'That was your own mother.'

And she slammed the door in his face.

When he had driven far enough from Paddington, and the confusion stirred by Dolly had subsided, he paused. His weariness had changed into a tired wakefulness. His mind was overactive, while his feelings were stirred to a degree he rarely, if ever, experienced. His guilt at his somewhat unprofessional conduct mingled harshly with his grief for the dead Joss and his anguish at Copper's folly and crime. As well, however unreasonably, he responded to Dolly's condemnation of his action in turning Copper over to the authorities and, in a strange way, joined in that condemnation to some degree. And through it all, he was gripped by a poignant emotion that he could hardly identify, much less name, brought about by hearing his mother's voice.

He knew he wouldn't sleep that night if his bed were soft as angel feathers. There was a pub with a license to half past eleven where Manning was sometimes to be found, and he headed for it. Manning was always a good listener. And though as a Special Branch man he was officially part of CID, he was also part of a world other than that of the Metropolitan Police. Besides, Manning was a thoughtful man. He liked to ponder police work through the ages, and they had spent many evenings discussing King's men and village constables, the Sidney Street raid, the problems of detection from Daniel and the priests of Bel to the rogueries of Jonathan Wild.

However, though he found Manning in the pub, sitting in a corner looking like all the habitués that ever closed a place up, he was wrong. For once Manning the amiable, the kindly, who all through the years was a sounding board for all his friends and, it was said, the postman and the milkman, Manning was perturbed by a problem of his own and longed to talk about it. He began, as Special Branch men were wont to do, by saying that of course he couldn't discuss it, but by the time Capricorn had settled down with his drink and a limp sandwich, Manning was very ready to talk. Still he was a decent soul and allowed Capricorn to tell his story, beginning with the death of Charlie Bo. Manning had already heard about Joss's murder and Copper's arrest. He expressed his very strong regret. 'Thought he'd been sailing near the wind. We hear things, you know,' he went on reflectively. But you didn't say anything. Capricorn thought with appreciation. Manning continued. 'He's always been such a good man. It was the woman, I suppose. And then they fell out.'

'The woman tempted me and I did eat?' Capricorn said. He meant it sarcastically, but Manning nodded.

'I'm a true believer. Copper was always a bright lad,' he said reflectively, 'Good sort, the best to have a few drinks with. He could've gone a long way. But he's like a lot of bright and breezy types, not as simple as he looks. Two personalities there, I would say.' He was thoughtful. Capricorn felt rebellious. Manning was a sometime-student of psychology, a discipline that Capricorn believed to be ill-founded and inadequate for application. 'Policeman and crook,' Manning went on. 'The policeman was dominant, but the woman who didn't want a policeman, brought out the other.'

'Lured out the Hyde from the good Dr Jekyll?'

'Why not? It's happened before. And suffered the same fate as other consorts of Mr Hyde. It's not only Copper,' Manning looked at him tiredly. 'We all have a bit of it. Only we haven't met the circumstance that brings the lawlessness to the surface. Well,' Manning took in Capricorn's stern visage, 'perhaps not you.' He laughed, but the laughter soon faded. 'I feel that someone is bringing out my lawless side. And these days I'm not sure if it's my worst side or not.'

And so he led into his tale of woe. Although neither of the men was a heavy drinker, they sat in their quiet corner until the pub closed and drank a few whiskies while Manning for once was indiscreet.

'It's all of a piece, really, with what you were say-

ing before about the girl. She saw no wrong in
throwing in with the Mafia, as long as the government was trying to tax her out of existence and de-
basing the currency to boot. As you say, why
prosecute a few villains for drilling the gold from a
few Krugerrands, while the government is busy deval-
uing the pound? Joss wasn't the only one to end up
with an answer like that. I wonder how many of our
young people see our whole civilization as a sinking
ship? Every man for himself.'

He sighed. 'I'm not supposed to say anything, but it
doesn't matter really. If it's true, and I think it is, the
papers will have the story. And no one will take any
notice.'

Manning was worried about a persistent rumour
concerning a change 'Upstairs'. 'Not just us,' he confided, 'but a new head of all the intelligence services.'

The change was to come about because of ideologi-
cal differences with the Labour government, who, it
was said, deemed the former head not in sufficient
sympathy with the left. The change was considered by
Manning to be dangerous, if not outright disastrous.

'Of course, all of us old fogies feel like that about
change,' he said wearily. 'It's natural, I suppose.'

Capricorn nodded. 'It's always happened. Which
doesn't mean to say, of course, that at times the old
weren't right.'

The two men gazed at each other, uneasy, unhappy. At the same time, Capricorn noticed that
Manning, the 'grey ghost,' was greyer than usual. He
was not well. Worked too hard, of course, in the
emergency. But Manning's hair could no longer be
called prematurely grey. Yes, it was true, they were,
not old, but certainly middle-aged. This was the night,
he thought ruefully, for his being made very much
aware of it. And middle age was suspicious of change.
And yet—

'It's frightening,' Manning said soberly, voicing

Capricorn's own thought. 'We say we work for our country. Some of us have gone—far.' Capricorn met his gaze and thought of their wartime activities. 'We do it because we think we're working for a good cause. The British way of life. But in point of fact, we're working for the government of the day, pretty much. What do we do,' he said soberly, 'when and if the government of our day seems to be working not for the England we have known and agreed to serve but for an England that we never want to see? Resign, I suppose,' he said hopelessly.

The smoke curled about their heads, not dissipating but hanging in a thick pall.

A strange conversation for two English policemen, Capricorn thought. Yet Manning's worries seemed wellfounded. Capricorn's mind went back to his boyhood, when he had decided to join the police, because from his own life of vagabondage, order, stability, tradition had appeared infinitely desirable and far away from the sleazy, close-to-criminal world of the Merlinos, and he wished to spend his life protecting that order, that stability. But while he was occupied with defending it, the order and stability were changing fast. He felt like The Great Capricornus of the early days, who had distracted the audience with tricks in front of the curtain while behind it the stage was cleared and another, different scene was being mounted.

'After Philby,' Manning was saying with a shudder.

Capricorn looked at the proposition. 'He can be of the left without being a traitor,' he murmured unhappily.

Manning shrugged. 'I don't suppose Philby thought himself a traitor. Considered it was for the country's good, in the long run, no doubt. Treachery is decided after the event, and it depends who turns out the winner. Even in English history. Oliver Cromwell was aided by Scotch troops. Stuart kings were in the pay of France. Henry Tudor used French help to conquer England. And you know how he got rid of his enemies—made them legally traitors by dating his succession from the day before the battle of Bosworth field.'

'It's only a rumour,' Capricorn tried to cheer his friend. 'Service gossip. There might be no change at all or if there is it might be someone you can live with very well, even if he comes from the new boys.' And if not? He wondered. His mind leapt forward, considering the possibility of a government he would not wish to serve. He could always go back and work with his aunts, he thought grimly, as they wished. If he could not serve, he still had a talent to amuse.

Manning, not comforting and not to be comforted, muttered into his drink. 'Mene, Mene, Tekel, Upharsin.'

That night Manning was not in a state to soothe Capricorn's overtired nerves. When the pub closed, Capricorn found his depression had broadened and deepened. Copper's apostasy and the likelihood that he was guilty of murder—two murders!—seemed only part of the condition of a nation that had lost its values, a world that had lost its way.

The two bachelors were turned out onto the pavement unwillingly with no prospect of domestic comfort to alleviate their gloom. Capricorn went home with Manning to the grey man's rather drab and cheerless flat, and spent a night of restless wakefulness. He thought of the Commander's suggestion that he take some of his long-accumulated leave. It was the last thing he wanted to do. He wasn't going to give up the Bonomi investigation, nor, he decided in the first harsh light of morning, could he leave Copper to his fate. Sedgwick was a good man, but his mind in this matter was not open to thorough inquiry. His prejudice against the erstwhile 'Swingin' Skipper' was too deep. He was already certain that Copper had killed Joss.

The sun was shining strongly through Manning's skimpy blinds before Capricorn realized, very wearily, that he himself was not certain at all. Not only was he not sure of Copper's guilt, he didn't believe in it. Copper could have killed Joss by accident, in a rage; God knows, if maddened enough he might have killed her deliberately, broken her lovely neck. There were few men about whom it could be said they would never kill in passion, and Copper wasn't one of them. But he would never have picked up a knife and cut his woman's throat. With the confusion and emotion of the murder scene receding in his mind, that judgement stood clear. Never in the world. Nor, Capricorn's thoughts rushed on, had he poisoned Charlie Bo. Hake had escaped from prison: he had been promised freedom and he had risen like a fish to a lure, without seeing the hook behind. That event alone, Capricorn told himself, should have made things plain, if he had not let his feelings cloud his common sense. He remembered the night that already seemed a long time ago when he got the first mysterious call.

'Take it easy on Brixton Jim or they'll make it awkward for Flash Copper, see.'

And they had. Yes, he told himself drowsily, he had a lot to do. And the first thing was to talk to Gyppo Moggs. His spirits lifted, and at last he fell asleep, dreaming of rising above a blanket of sad grey cloud that lay over England, flying up in a 'plane towards the sun, with the voice of a woman he had never seen singing sweetly as he flew.

GYPSY GUITAR, MUTED

Day came, cool but bright. The sun shone harshly into Manning's dun and rather drab flat. He was already gone when Capricorn woke, and the place looked especially cheerless without its host. Manning was a monk, Capricorn thought, as he looked about him, smiling. A monk dedicated to Special Branch. He remembered Manning's doubts of the night before, doubts to him as serious as religious doubt would be to a monk of the spiritual orders. Still, Manning followed his discipline. He was already at work.

Capricorn put a call through to Gyppo Moggs, that slight tenuous connection between the gold robbery at the Eastland with the following massacre at Barlow Road and the strange, unpredictable events that had followed. Moggs answered, a very indignant, sleepy Moggs who did not keep early hours. He agreed, reluctantly, to meet Capricorn later but not at his house.

'It's unlucky,' he said gloomily. 'Never liked them houses stuck in the middle of all them trees and not a pub or a shop as far as you can see. Bad as the country. Only good for a blagging. I kept the meet with you that night, guv. Don't like this talking on the blower,' he sounded depressed. 'You shouldn't do it. I think I've been sussed out.'

'You were there?' Capricorn said, surprised.

'Saw the villain do the job,' Moggs said. ' 'Course, I

didn't twig at first. Thought he was just after blagging that Aladdin's Cave of yours. I was in the garden, just thinking to myself, I wonder does he know who he's doing. I thought something funny was going on when he went for the room with the light on, but before I could think 'Bloody Irish,' he'd jumped clear and scarpered. And then it went up, see, and me not even in a shelter. Gawd, we ought to get army pay just for living in this country now. What's the army for, anyway?'

Moggs shared Dolly's views, Capricorn observed without surprise. 'Did you see who it was?' he asked, taking advantage of Moggs's morning drowsiness to get a few words from him. If he had been wide awake he would have refused to talk at all.

'Oh, yes, in the middle of the night, dark as pitch. I could read the tea leaves and tell you,' Moggs said, heavily sarcastic. 'Why don't you go and find out from that computer?'

Moggs had a Luddite view of the computer in C11. He considered the electronic storage and sorting of information on known criminals to be detrimental to his trade as informer. At the same time, he had an almost superstitious awe of the device, as though it could give out information that hadn't been fed in.

'You said you saw him,' Capricorn remarked.

'Yes, when he was on the balcony in front of the light. Not clear. He wore something dark, nacherly. Didn't see his face. Moved like a young 'un.' He paused. 'Bit unperfessional, I'd say.'

'How is that?'

'I dunno—'course, I didn't know what he was up to—the way he jumped down,' Moggs said. 'Didn't think much of it, what with World War II starting up right after, but he jumped heavy for his size. Not noisy, must've worn rubber, but he doubled over for a minute like it hurt. Out of condition,' he added scornfully. 'Lazy like all the micks.'

Capricorn didn't believe the Irish were involved at all, but let it go. 'Have you ever heard of someone called Sweeter?' he asked.

But the sound of a name brought all Gyppo's natural caution back. He merely murmured that he would be, late that night, in a place that Capricorn knew. 'I'm going 'opping,' he said mysteriously and rang off.

' 'Opping,' Capricorn deduced, did not mean that Gyppo was contemplating anything as unlikely as going to Kent to gather hops very much after the season, but that he would be in a certain pub in the Old Kent Road. If Moggs knew anything about Sweeter, it would be worth paying a visit. The miraculous computer, unfortunately, was in total ignorance of that elusive go-between of Brixton Jim's and the bank robbers'.

The ultra-cautious Moggs would not arrive at the pub until near closing time, or possibly after. In the meantime, Capricorn determined, he was going to talk to Copper. Sedgwick might not be pleased; he might see it as interference in his case, but it had to be done. He rang the station where Copper was being held and learned that Sedgwick was there at that moment.

'They're charging him with murder,' the station sergeant, who knew Capricorn well, told him. He sounded aghast. Copper had been popular in the district. 'The Swingin' Skipper. Who'd believe it?'

Capricorn could believe the charge, though not its truth. He murmured something noncommittal and rang off. He would go around when Sedgwick had left. There was time, then, to go home and get fresh clothes.

Home was full of pleasant surprises. The house had been cleaned and tidied, glaziers were at work on the windows, Mrs Dermott apparently was cooking breakfast. The smell of coffee came deliciously to greet him.

As he ate breakfast, he congratulated himself, as he had done so many times, on his good fortune in having so admirable a housekeeper. But his pleasure did not last. Mrs Dermott was looking grim and, it turned out, not because of the damage to the house or the work it had caused her. She waited until he had finished his bacon and eggs and she had brought some more hot toast.

'There was something in the morning paper. About an Inspector Copper. It couldna be—'

'I'm afraid it is,' Capricorn replied. 'He was arrested on the charge of murdering Joss Parker. I don't think you knew her; they were very close.'

'Yu mean they were livin' together,' she said, her mouth primmed up. 'I know all about it. She was a loose woman. But the Inspector would never kill a woman. The very idea, it's daft.'

He noticed she had specified 'a woman.' Even Mrs Dermott then, always a victim of Copper's charm, believed him çapable of murder. But perhaps she believed everyone was capable of murder in some circumstances. He had known Mrs Dermott a long time, but she still, at times, surprised him.

'He had to be arrested,' Capricorn said carefully. 'It was known that Copper and Joss had been quarrelling and, unluckily for me,' he grimaced, 'I found him, in that wretched club, standing over her dead body.' He didn't mention poor Joss's cut throat; he had no desire to horrify Mrs Dermott. But she was not to be spared.

'And how was the Parker woman killed?' she asked.

Capricorn looked down at his plate where the toast was cooling. It didn't matter. His appetite was gone. 'A knife,' he said. 'Or a razor. It's not certain.'

'Hmph!' she said, her brow clearing. 'Then of course it couldna be the Inspector. For a minute there you had me thinking it might have been an accident. You said "quarrelling".'

Her gaze was thoughtful, as if reviewing mental pictures of domestic uproar, though to Capricorn's knowledge Mrs Dermott's brief marriage, which had ended with her husband's death at Dunkirk, had been a happy one.

'He's a big, strong man, the Inspector, and if that woman was playing him false and they had a row— well, she might have led him on until he gave her a smack. She might have fallen and hit her head,' she said judiciously. 'It's happened before.'

Capricorn remembered Joss's puffy face. Mrs Dermott wasn't off the mark there.

'But the Inspector would never take a knife to anyone, let alone a woman,' she said, satisfied, and went back to the kitchen. 'Anyone who would think that is a fool.' Her voice hung in the air after she had disappeared, like the grin of the Cheshire cat.

Capricorn felt cheered. Mrs Dermott was no detective but she was a reliable judge of humankind. It was pleasing that from her own observation she had come to the same conclusion that he had. But that was the end of pleasant moments for some time.

His phone rang, and it was his friend in Drugs Squad, calling from some place full of noise and hard to hear, belaboring him for unfair use of information, breaking his word, pernicious activity in the affairs of Drugs Squad and generally being a bane to the British public. When Capricorn could disentangle the story enough to defend himself, he was not much happier. Apparently men from Drugs Squad had been following Len Slope all night as he made a journey south of the river, to pick up supplies, they believed. They had not wanted to arrest him but merely to find his dealer. Much to their disgust, after many hours and much effort, the unmarked car in which they had been following him stalled and then devel-

oped further engine trouble, and Slope had been lost.
They had returned not too despondent; although they
had failed, Slope was unaware of the surveillance and
they could try again. But Slope, it seemed, in the
early hours of the morning had gone straight to
Brenda Grey, with all his purchases upon his person,
and had been seized by General Grey who had been
lying in wait, primed, Drugs believed, by Capricorn.

The General furious, had given the flaccid Slope a
thrashing, and then called the local police. Slope had
been taken in with all the incriminating evidence,
and Drugs were in high annoyance. They had to find
some excuse to turn him loose, or give up hope of
catching their bigger fish. 'And him holding cannabis,
amphetamines, and cocaine,' Drugs mourned. 'Of
course, he swears your friend the General planted
them on him, and we'll have to pretend to give some
credence to that tale. And Slope has the nerve to say
he'll sue him—our Len got knocked about a bit and
he's going to have a super black eye. He was afraid to
use some of his usual stunts with the General, no
doubt.'

Capricorn protested that he had spoken to no one
except his Commander, and knew nothing of the
General's visit. He felt a warmth that he had never
felt before toward the husband of Isobel Grey. There
must be good in him if he had blacked Slope's eye.
Drugs, bitter, eventually allowed himself to be convinced of Capricorn's innocence. Vexed himself,
Capricorn got his car and made for Soho. He might
as well see Brenda now and be done with it.

When he came to the dingy building where she
lived, in the vicinity of Ham Yard, he looked and
wondered. The house was dark, with a narrow entry.
It smelled of cats and cooking—foreign cooking, the
smell of garlic and coriander hung heavy in the stale
air. The stairs were uncarpeted. Brenda's room, he
believed, was on the second floor, but he found her

door with some difficulty as the landing light was out.
When he announced himself, she let him in, though
with no sign of pleasure or attempt to simulate welcome; nor did she show any confusion after the fracas
she had just been through.

She was a mess. The girl who had grown up in the
lovely old Grey house set in fifteen acres of orchard
land in Somerset, was living in a small dark room
with walls, divan cover and rug in various shades of
muddy brown. The carpet was unbrushed, the divan
cover was rumpled and dust lay thick in the corners.
The blinds were still drawn and the only light came
from a parchment-shaded lamp. In place of a kitchen,
Brenda had a gas ring, a kettle and a crudely
coloured mug with lettering 'A present from Leigh-
On-Sea.' Manning's rooms had been as bare and dun-
coloured, but they were clean and tidy. Brenda's
room was littered with her beggar-girl garb, and she
looked as though she might have slept in the dress
she was wearing. Her eyes were circled, her hair
limp. Capricorn felt a surge of impatience that anyone as loved and cherished as Isobel's daughter could
deliberately have brought herself to this.

'They took Len in,' she said. It wasn't a question.
She fumbled in what looked like a large saddlebag for
a cigarette, lit it and drew on it thoughtfully. Capricorn was relieved to see it was an ordinary cigarette.
Whatever the future effect on her lungs, at least her
mind was working at the moment.

He nodded.

'Silly, really,' she said without passion. 'He only
gives people what they want. I believe in letting
people do what they want.'

'Your father wanted to give him a good hiding and
he did,' Capricorn observed, 'but Mr Slope
threatened to sue.'

Brenda giggled. 'Yes, he did. But I didn't mean you
should *hurt* anybody. I think,' she said with some per-

ception, 'that Daddy would've liked to hit me, but he's too much of a gentleman. He writes me letters all the time. I don't open them.' She looked wary. 'I suppose he sent you to nag.'

'I came to ask you some questions about Carlo Bonomi's death,' Capricorn said firmly. 'You were sitting at a table with him moments before he died.'

'I didn't see much,' Brenda said. 'I had dropped my brooch, and I was pinning it back on and then there was a commotion. Before I saw what was going on Money Mum had a screen round and it seemed horrid, so I had another drink.'

Of course, she wouldn't know that Joss was dead. The nickname was the one that Len Slope had used, he remembered. 'I remember your brooch,' he said. 'Charlie pinned it back on, didn't he?'

'He tried,' she said, 'This one,' pulling out another crumpled dress like the one she had on and carelessly tearing off the jet-and-hair mourning brooch with the wicked-looking pin.

He took hold of it and felt the point of the pin. It was rusty and blunt, and it had made a hole in Brenda's dress as she tugged it. This pin would never have made a puncture that looked like the track of an injection; Charlie's coat and shirt had not been torn.

Carefully, Capricorn went through his list of questions, taking Brenda patiently up to Charlie's death and beyond. Her memory was deplorably vague; she confessed to having had too much to drink, and Charlie's last few moments of life were almost entirely forgotten in her excitement over having met a former admirer. She wanted to chatter about him and it was with difficulty that Capricorn kept bringing her back to the point.

'So you say that nothing struck you as in any way unusual that night? You saw the Inspector, Miss Parker and Mr Bonomi go back to the office for a few minutes—'

'I think I did,' Brenda said doubtfully. 'I wasn't paying much notice. I was having a few drinks with my friends. I was surprised at bumping into Johnny again—he's from Somerset, you know. And that woman from the cloakroom was telling jokes.' She giggled again. Capricorn despaired of getting any sensible answers. 'She's a lot of fun but old as the hills.'

She fished in the saddlebag for a looking glass and gazed at her face thoughtfully. 'Johnny says I look the same as I did when we were kids.'

'But Mr Bonomi sat next to you when he came back.'

'Yes. He fiddled about with my broach after it fell off but it's hard to work. I thought Len might say something but he didn't. Johnny pulled an awful face.'

'And then the bar cleared and Mr Bonomi got up to go back to his former seat, stopped and fell.'

'Yes, I think so. I wasn't watching. There was something—something funny.' She wrinkled her brow and stared into space, apparently back in her dream.

'Funny?' Capricorn asked.

'Weird. Well, I was drunk. Or I thought I must be drunk—although I have a good head, Len is always surprised—because the room started moving.'

'Oh,' Capricorn said, disappointed. Her testimony was quite useless. Apparently her self-centredness was of the sort that failed to take in impression of anything beyond her immediate circle of interest. He didn't know what he'd hoped for, but whatever it was he wasn't going to get it.

He rose to go.

'Funny,' she said, ignoring his action and continuing to address the place where he had been. 'It was different though.'

'Different?'

'Yes. You know when things start whirling about like that, usually they all go together.' Her hands sketched a circular motion. 'But this time, it wasn't like that. I was sitting back and the light hit—one of those coins, I think it was, as though it jumped up. Those things that looked like the old chocolate pennies with gold paper on, that Money Mum had stuck in the tables.'

Capricorn wondered if she would stop using that nickname if she knew Joss was dead. He didn't care to go into explanations now. And perhaps, in youthful callousness, she just wouldn't care.

'If they'd all gone like that,' she puzzled. 'Well, that's ordinary. But it was funny, just one coming up that way.'

Capricorn remarked that she must have been taking something more than drink to distort her perceptions.

She shook her head. 'Not that night,' she answered saucily. 'Hadn't got anything. That's why—' She stopped.

That's why she had met Slope. 'Did Slope give you anything in the club?'

'Oh, no, he's awfully careful.' Capricorn found her giggle irritating. 'I was *awfully* drunk, though. I got sick. That's why I didn't notice old fat Charlie.'

Old fat Charlie. Well, he must have seemed that way to her. Capricorn made to take his leave, but Brenda wasn't finished.

'You think I'm rotten, don't you?' she asked suddenly in a different voice, a little girl again. 'You're like Daddy and all the old respectables.'

She sat cross-legged on the divan, her feet, clad in thonged sandals, showing beneath the long Victorian dress. Pretty young feet. Isobel's violet-coloured eyes stared at him from the hostile face.

'They think I'm rotten because I like to have fun and don't want to get a job. But I'm not good at anything in particular and why should I be bored with doing something dreary that I hate? I have money; I get full control when I'm twenty-five, and I can manage somehow till then.'

'Wouldn't it be more pleasant for you at home?' Capricorn said, drawn into discussion against his will. It was time to go to Copper.

'But there's no one at home,' Brenda said blankly. 'The house is nearly always closed up, since Mummy died. I love it there.'

Capricorn was surprised; it was not the answer he'd expected.

'Daddy is hardly ever home. He's forever abroad, on some mission or other. I travelled with him, until last year. One horrible place after another. Hot and dusty or hot and muddy, with mosquitoes all over and hardly anyone to speak English. I loathed it, every minute. Mummy used to say that's army life, but it wasn't like that for her when she was young. She was in India and it was full of English people and she had a marvellous time. But even then, I don't think I'd have wanted to be abroad,' she said wistfully. 'I get homesick. I would go to sleep and dream of being home, somewhere cool and green.'

'Not so cool and green this year,' Capricorn said, smiling. 'Especially in Soho.'

'Better than abroad,' she said obstinately. 'And here you can go in any little shop and find what you want, or go in a pub and have a drink and meet people and—'

She stopped, at the end of her power to express her thoughts, despairing of any understanding from her parents' generation. Capricorn understood too well. He, too, when abroad had been wrenched with a longing for home. And he had had no home of his own then, he remembered, but England herself had haunted his dreams.

The telephone rang out in the hall; there were shuffling steps, a voice, a rap at the door: 'It's for Grey,' and the steps retreated.

Brenda jumped up with energy. Capricorn followed her out and began to walk downstairs; her voice, light and bubbling, came clear.

'Hallo, Johnny? Oh, no. I wasn't doing anything. Yes, I'd love to. Something fun. Daddy and Co. are being horribly drear.'

But by the time he had reached the street he had forgotten Brenda.

Capricorn sat in the interview room at the station, waiting for Copper to be brought up from the cells. He had been in this same rather small, drab room often enough. The scene was so familiar as to be hardly noticeable, but today there was a feeling of unreality about his presence and actions, as if the fox had suddenly become the hounds, leaving the huntsman stranded, irresolute.

For a moment he thought over the conversation he had had with Hardy directly after leaving Brenda Grey. It had been predictable. Hardy had tested for succinylcholine chloride, and then for succinic acid and choline. 'No di-choline. Looks like some monocholine in the area of the injection. Hard to qualify with the damned embalming. We *could* say that area of the right arm has more succinic acid and choline than a control area on the left.'

At this point even the plain-spoken Hardy went off into some technical talk about the merits of radioactivity for testing and chromatographic procedures. Capricorn, impatient, had interjected, 'But what do you make of it?'

'What did I see?' Hardy murmured. 'Enough to suggest to me that your guess was right. Whether that's enough to make it worthwhile to court—' He had sounded doubtful. 'Unless you have a very strong case otherwise—defense counsel could certainly make it plain what an overrated profession mine is. A great deal of guesswork, it will look like, from a small amount of fact. We do so hate the public to know. They might not want to pay our salaries. In your Spingoletti case, at least the jury knew that the doctor had been supplied with the stuff. Unless you have something as definite—'

But Capricorn had nothing at all, as yet.

He expected to feel strange seeing Copper, that once debonair but efficient policeman, a prisoner. When he was brought in, he looked odd enough, for his Carnaby Street clothes were replaced by a pair of ill-fitting overalls—of course, his own things would have been taken to be examined for traces of blood. Yet once their eyes met and the attending officer withdrew, all strangeness was gone.

They sat on opposite sides of the table provided for prisoners and free men, but before any words were spoken it was as if they were working together once more. Copper was still pale but the stupor had gone. Certainly there was none of his usual high spirits but he looked young and vital again, and his green eyes were sharp with intelligence.

'All right, guv,' he didn't bother with preliminaries. 'I'm stuck in here with all this grief so I'll give you everything I've got.' He made a faint grimace. 'Don't look like I can get a clear-up on my lonesome. I found Joss, like I said. I was only there about a minute before you.'

He was silent for a moment.

'You told Sedgwick you had just left Moletta,' Capricorn said. 'Moletta told a different tale.'

'I didn't want to publish what I'd been doing,' Copper said shortly. 'We'd been taken off the Kruger-rand job, but I'd been following up on my own, and you know what he is for going by the book and only by the book. I didn't think the bloody fools would have me off 'for Joss, not that I cared much about anything last night.'

His face contorted and twitched. Capricorn saw

that Copper, the Don Juan of the Metropolitan Police, the case-hardened detective from Central, was trying not to cry. He looked away, staring with great interest at a wall calendar, until Copper recovered and went on.

'It started when I was looking for the brains behind the coin lark. It was still going on, it was a dirty business and I didn't like it. And I had an idea. I thought it was that bastard from the beginning, but he was slippery as an eel, jelly and all.'

'Charlie?' Capricorn asked.

Copper nodded.

'Y'know, Charlie wasn't what people thought. Big Mafia operator. I soon got that sorted out. He was a Bonomi all right, but his family didn't think much of him—in a business way. He was too flashy, too much of a big spender, chased too many women. He made 'em nervous. When the investigation started over there, they sent him to England with enough money to start some straight business and told him to keep his nose clean.'

It seemed likely. Capricorn wondered how Copper had learned all this. He didn't have any special correspondents in the States.

Copper shrugged. 'Just put two and two together, guv. It wasn't hard. Joss told a lot—not that she knew what she was telling. She took his line, hook and sinker attached.' He paused for a moment. 'Joss is—was—clever as you like, but she'd worked in offices, a couple of clubs. She thought she knew all about it, but real villainy she didn't know. Any WPC knew more than Joss, but you couldn't tell her that. She thought she had it all worked out, and working for her. But she knew that Charlie wasn't afraid of us. He was only afraid the Bonomis and Miraglias would find out he was going against instructions. He didn't need to get involved, but once he got a whiff of the gold caper—I think it started in Italy—he couldn't resist. He took us for one of the developing nations that could use a foreign expert,' he said drily. 'Thought our villains were a bunch of bleedin' amateurs. Anyway, he liked having some lolly he didn't have to account for.'

Capricorn thought of Joss's thirty thousand.

'You couldn't catch him distributing the stuff. The boys I grabbed said it was a different place each time. The sellers got word where they were to make the pickup. But he had quite a system with the money. It would be brought into his clubs, then most of it was passed directly to runners who got it out of the country. He had a stable of 'em. It would have been about impossible to find anything on him he couldn't account for legally. So when Joss came up with her proposition to open a club, he liked it. A place he could control that wasn't connected with him or his people. He didn't do it only because he fancied her.'

Copper looked at him levelly. Now that Joss was dead, Copper could bear to admit at least some of the truth. There was a grimness about his face that Capricorn had never seen before.

'Did Joss know all this?'

Copper pushed his lower lip forward. 'Joss was never one to miss what was going on under her nose. Once it started she must've had a good idea. Not in the beginning, of course. Well, you can see, just the way she did the place up. Charlie must've thought it a big joke. Practically advertising. The other Bonomis would never have stood for that. Unprofessional. Joss was even going to call the place 'The Gold Coin,' he said, his mind wandering back, 'Till she found that damned calf one day on a stall in the Portobello Road. Got all excited and lugged it home, holding it like it was a baby.'

Capricorn found it necessary to study the calendar again.

After a minute, Copper continued. 'Joss really believed, I'm certain, that Charlie lent her that money on the up and up. 'Course, once she was well in he started putting the screws on. Using the place and getting her to turn a blind eye. Reminding her it was his money behind it. No wonder I made her nervous barging about.' He gave a harsh little laugh. 'She was really between the devil and the deep blue sea.'

'Yes,' Capricorn said. If it gave Copper comfort to believe that Joss's deception had caused her pain, he was welcome to it. Perhaps it was even true.

'It must've given her a shock,' Copper said, 'when Bo started bringin' in his villains. She couldn't stand Moletta.'

Capricorn didn't intend to ask, 'How could you have let it go on?' but Copper was aware of the unspoken question.

'I swear I had no idea for a long time. I had given Joss a lot of money to get started. It seemed like more than enough. As she got going she needed more—everything began going up and up before you could turn around. She said she got the rest from the bank and she was paying it off. She showed me the books. Monthly payments—to the Eastland, she said. I would never have thought to check. You know Joss. She wasn't a liar. Honest as they come. Too much for some people.' His brow clouded over. 'They thought her a bit, well, unkind, but it was just her way. Couldn't stand hypocrisy, Joss.'

'Until this,' Capricorn said.

'Yes.' Copper was silent for a moment and then spoke quickly.

'She did it for me, you see. She had to lie if she wanted to stay with me; she knew I wouldn't stand for that. And she did want to. Her nerves got ragged, that's all, with both of us hounding her. Charlie wanted to get her a flat. He told me that in the office that night and I—'

'You what?'

'Oh, I went for him,' Copper said. 'But I didn't hit him. Joss got in between and said she'd make up her own mind and we'd better go back in the club and act civilized. I felt like walking out, but I didn't want to leave him there. So I stayed.'

'Did Charlie take anything to calm down?'

'Nothing in the office,' Copper said. 'I don't know if he had anything in the club. He sat down next to Slope and talked to Brenda Grey and he had a drink. I wasn't watching him, I was watching Joss.'

'Was Slope working for him, do you know?'

Copper looked puzzled. 'I thought he was. A miserable little grafter and suddenly he's flush, hanging round the Calf, well into the drug game. Charlie didn't like him, though. And Moletta swears he's not in with them. And he says Charlie's people weren't running drugs. Not that you can always believe Moletta. There was one of Charlie's runners there that night,' he added. 'The little Nazi with the bow tie.'

Capricorn took this to mean the cheese salesman from Zurich, hitherto believed blameless.

'He took money out for Charlie through his business accounts. And he brings rands in, I found out, good ones; they're drilled out over here. Not sure where yet. Brings them in with the goods by train and ship—they can't use 'planes any more, of course. Moletta is keeping the business going. Sorry I had to give you so much lip, guv,' he said with a ghost of his former smile. 'But what with the investigation and everything, you lads have got the villains convinced that I'm bent. Moletta wanted to give me a job. Work with him in the Force if I could stay on, or be promoted to Villain First Class. Was a good offer,' he couldn't help gibing. 'Pay and prospects marvellous. He thought I had talent.'

Capricorn thought about Moletta. He and Joss could have fallen out over the coin business as well as the thirty thousand pounds. The words of Joss that the cloakroom woman had overheard, 'What's mine is mine and I'm going to keep it. You can go to hell!' could have been said to Moletta instead of to Copper as everyone had supposed. But that had been at a quarter to seven and Moletta, according to half a dozen witnesses, had been in a restaurant ordering dinner at that time. Certainly, he could have sent a minion. But if he had sent someone to negotiate, he would hardly have given the negotiator instructions to kill if disappointed. And the whole manner of the killing—Would an accomplished villain like Moletta send in a killer at a time when the kitchen staff was expected, the cloakroom woman was actually there and both front and back doors were open? The idea was absurd. And the cloakroom woman had said that in about half an hour of watching, she saw no one go in or out until Capricorn appeared.

'How did you get in the club?' he asked.

'From the yard in back,' Copper said. 'You know the yard in back of the club meets the yard behind the house in the next street. I had an idea, from plotting up those villains I hauled in, that they'd been working on those coins somewhere close by. I tried to get out of Pete Moletta where the work was done, but he didn't trust me that far. So when I left him, I got through an alleyway into those backs and sort of snooped, but it was starting to get dark. I didn't see anything worth breaking and entering, anyway.'

If the cloakroom woman was to be believed, the killer must have gone, if not come, through the back way. Sedgwick would have a large area to search for the knife.

'Did you see anyone as you came near the Calf?'

'In all the time I was looking around I didn't see anybody,' Copper said. 'They don't use those yards much. A few sheds. A couple of dogs chained up. Of course, it was dark by the time I got to the Calf, but if there had been anyone around I would've known.

You couldn't help kicking into a lot of rubbish that's lying around, and twice I trod on a cat. I thought I'd have some civvie yelling blue murder down at me'.

If Copper had been guilty, Capricorn thought, he certainly would not have told him that. Of course, he didn't know about the cloakroom woman's tale. Copper had, it seemed, effectively cut off the possibility that anyone else could have murdered Joss.

'Did you tell Sedgwick any of this?' he asked.

Copper shrugged impatiently. 'I did my nut. I wasn't going to tell him what I was working on. So like a fool I said I'd been with Moletta but not why, and I didn't tell him I'd been looking for the mint. I was feeling so bloody rotten about Joss.' His voice thickened. He fumbled in the pocket of his overalls for a handkerchief that wasn't there. 'I kept thinking, if only I'd got there a few minutes before. All the bloody years of protecting the Great British Public. And my own—' He stopped, as if words failed him. 'I never thought the silly bastards would try to lumber me.' He reiterated what he'd said before. 'And I couldn't have cared less, just then.'

'It's strange that you didn't see anyone,' Capricorn got back to the point. 'There's a problem how the murderer got away.'

Their eyes met. Capricorn could hardly, with propriety, tell Copper the results of Sedgwick's examination of witnesses. Even his remark about Moletta had been questionable, from the official point of view, but that had been something that Copper would have guessed in any event. Just as he guessed the trouble now. Copper was a detective and didn't need things spelled out.

He shook his head. 'I just don't know. I can't even think who'd want to do it. Everybody liked Joss, you know that. It makes no sense. And, God knows, she'd never do it herself, no matter what. And anyway, there was no weapon.'

Suicide was one thing nobody had considered.

'What about Moletta?' Capricorn asked. The business appointment Moletta had talked about could be a lie. The cloakroom woman could have been wrong about the time. But Capricorn remembered the pool of blood. He was no specialist but he could have sworn the death was very recent. And Moletta had been in that restaurant at six forty-five.

'He didn't have a grudge against her. Don't think he thought about her much. Cold fish. Didn't even fancy her.'

'There was the money,' Capricorn pointed out.

'I don't know if he thought that was coming to him,' Copper said slowly. 'But it would have made no sense for him to kill her. No way he can get the money now.'

If Copper was trying to make a case against himself, he couldn't do much better. Capricorn thought despairingly. Briefly, he wondered who would get the club. Not that it mattered.

'So you saw no one, heard no one, and you can't think of anyone who could possibly have had a motive.'

Copper's green eyes were thoughtful. 'Guv, it's ridiculous, but I can't. Joss was well liked, you know that. Unless—' His face darkened, and he looked down at his hands on the table.

'Unless what?'

'Oh, nothing,' Copper shook his head.

Capricorn looked at him with little patience. He didn't know how long his interview would last before someone officially on the case might come in.

'It's no time to hold back,' he said grimly. 'The whole world knows you punched her in the face yesterday afternoon.'

Copper rubbed his hand across his forehead and looked sick.

'Don't remind me. God, it seems a year ago already.

I was staying at Dolly's and she came—I wasn't expecting her. We hadn't been living together since the night that Charlie—'

He broke off.

'That Charlie what?'

'Died. The night Charlie died. We'd had a row. Then when she came in at Dolly's—she wasn't pleased to see me. She opened her trap and made me look like a fool and—oh, Christ.' He buried his head in his hands. 'What am I talking about? It was the last thing she ever said to me. "Why aren't you on your beat, Copper?" and I—'

He looked up helplessly, his red hair dark with sweat. 'You know I never hit a woman in my life.'

'Dolly thought that Joss understood,' Capricorn said gently, 'and Dolly knows about things like that. And you meant to go and see her?'

'Yes. I'd been worried about something and—'

Capricorn watched Copper's unhappy face. 'You were worried she did it,' he said slowly.

'Did what?' Copper looked guarded.

'Killed Charlie Bo.'

There was silence for a moment.

'What makes you think he was killed?'

'I have an idea about it.' Capricorn refrained from saying he had thought Copper was responsible. 'You remember the doctor gave him an injection.'

Copper nodded.

'The pathologist found the puncture marks of two injections.'

Copper didn't look surprised.

'What was in it?'

'The doctor claims to have given digitalis, which was found. The pathologist also came up with traces of succinic acid and choline. More than he would have expected normally to find, but hard to be specific about because the body had been embalmed.'

Copper whistled softly. 'The American case, what was it?'

'Spingoletti.'

'But you said he's not sure.'

'You can't be absolutely certain. From what Hardy said, I think he is sure, but it's a question of absolute proof. There's still argument about the American case, I know. But it would have been easy to do. Anybody with access to lab supplies can get the stuff. No books are kept. No one has to sign.'

'Used in chest surgery, I remember,' Copper said. 'Stops the heart.'

He was staring blankly, looking at images from the past.

'Yes. Why did you think Joss might have—'

'Oh, I don't know that I did, really,' Copper snapped back, wretched. 'It was just that, well, it was convenient, his dying, that's all. For Joss, I mean. Though I couldn't think how—and I didn't consider it seriously. But when I was at Dolly's—I was upstairs, and the girls were talking—and later Tilly started saying something.'

'Tilly's not all there,' Capricorn said. 'I think perhaps she should be back in the home.'

Copper gave him a look he didn't understand, but he let it go.

'I suppose Joss *could* have given Charlie something that night,' Copper said thoughtfully, 'but I'll never believe Joss was a poisoner. She couldn't have got hold of anything like that, and you said it was an injection. You know, I thought about that after we spoke in the pub. At first I wondered—but then I realized it was impossible. Joss didn't give him anything in the office, I would've seen it. And in that dress she had on, she couldn't have carried a pin without it being spotted, much less a syringe. If anyone did him in,' he said thoughtfully, 'I would have guessed Moletta.'

'Moletta?' Capricorn said, startled.

'He worked for Charlie, runs most of his places, and he's a lot shrewder than Charlie. It might have occurred to him he'd like to take over, and he's a cold fish—poison wouldn't bother him at all'.

'But Moletta wasn't there that night.'

'Nothing to stop him getting someone else to do the job.' Copper shrugged. 'Anyway, Charlie was a villain and he's dead and who cares?'

'I'm doing a special investigation,' Capricorn told him, 'on his wife's complaint.' He paused. 'I suppose the Wallace girl could have got Joss the stuff, if she wanted it,' he added casually.

"Mary Wallace? You *have* been looking around, guv. No. Not her. I mean, she'd do you a favour within reason. Sleeping pills for Joss—she had trouble sleeping days. My muscle stuff. But not poison, that's ridiculous. Mary's dead straight—in business. She wasn't all that close to Joss anyway. Might have done it for me,' he said, with a suggestion of his habitual swagger, and then he caught Capricorn's eye.

'Oh, I see. No, guv, if that's where you were, you were looking in the wrong hat for your rabbit. I didn't kill him. P'raps I should have,' he said grimly. 'But I didn't. A law to the last. And I didn't kill Joss, no matter what that Yorkshire puddenhead thinks. I wonder what he imagines I did with the weapon. Stuffed it, I s'ppose. But I don't even have a guess who it was. Could've been a stray nutter up to some nastiness,' he grimaced, 'who scarpered when he heard me come in.'

Capricorn tried not to sigh. As a theory it didn't fit in with what the cloakroom woman had heard. Of course, she might have been wrong. Witnesses so often were. It might have been that Joss was merely talking loudly on the telephone—to a hairdresser, perhaps, about a mixed-up appointment. Capricorn had known women who would get more angry about a missed session at the hairdresser than they would over a stolen handbag. Arguing with a man, she had said, but she had not heard any of the man's actual words. She could have imagined that. And she might have been wrong about no one having entered from the front. Capricorn knew the exact value of the observation of the average citizen while he or she was having a cup of tea. He wished he could interview the witness himself, but he would be treading on very thin ice. On the other hand, he had the usual policeman's disbelief in the peripatetic, vanishing lunatic. Still, he reminded himself, there was something very strange about Joss's killing. Capricorn couldn't remember a case like it in all his years at the Yard—except, he recalled over the decades, there had been the murdered land girl, just after the war. Found in a field with her throat cut. The killer was believed to be a prisoner of war with whom she had been having a love affair. Her stint on the land over, she had been looking forward to getting back to the gayer life of London. The story came back to Capricorn complete. She had no desire to return with the former prisoner to his village. The man was under suspicion, but there had been no proof, and with some reluctance on the part of the authorities, he had been sent home with the rest.

A crime of passion. As with Joss, nothing to suggest a professional killer. If Joss's face had been slashed, his mind ran on, speculating, it could have been an accident. A professional 'enforcer,' someone sent to frighten and threaten to disfigure her, who had gone too far. But that knife had surely been wielded with intent to kill, indeed, almost as if the murderer had wanted to sever Joss's lovely face from her body. Sedgwick had a good case, the detective thought dispassionately.

A policeman poked his head round the door to say that Sedgwick had arrived to see the Inspector. Capricorn rose to go, suggesting quietly to Copper that he repeat to Sedgwick the facts he had just given him. Then Capricorn left, hoping not to meet the other super who might suspect interference in his case. Things looked bad for Copper, yet Capricorn felt a great relief. He smiled benignly on a pretty, fair WPC at the switchboard, who stopped him to inquire anxiously about the Inspector. Copper's female admirers were legion, and his women caused trouble, but Copper was not a villain. He was the man Capricorn had always believed him to be. Somebody had murdered Charlie Bo, and Capricorn, with all his detective's intuition, believed that to be connected to the death of Joss. Perhaps she had known too much about it. Perhaps there was even a third lover. Having lived with the Merlinos as a boy, and followed them along the music hall circuits about the country, Capricorn did not neglect to consider any of the many-sided figures of love. Perhaps . . . Deep in thought, he almost walked into Sedgwick.

Sedgwick did not, after all, bother to give him any cold or suspicious looks. The Northcountryman looked tired and not too happy, but he wanted to talk. 'We've got a real problem with the weapon,' he said. 'I sent every knife in the kitchen to the lab, but they can't find anything. They told me, in the report, that any one of them could have been used and if it had been given a good wash under the hot tap there would be nothing to find. Miss Parker only bought the best,' he said grimly. 'Swedish steel, razor sharp, one piece and no serrated edges. I've had the men searching all day, just in case, but if he used anything else, he made it disappear better than you could—or your aunties.'

'You're still certain it was Copper,' Capricorn said slowly, 'You know, I can't believe it.'

Sedgwick shrugged impatiently, as though Capricorn's words were merely polite utterance and did not really express a policeman's view.

'Of course, you asked the chef and the other kitchen people if any of those knives were missing,' Capricorn went on diffidently. Sedgwick was his equal in rank and would resent even a hint of any questioning of his method. Fortunately, he took it merely as a comradely remark.

'Sometimes you wonder how the public live at all,' he grumbled, 'I mean how they grow up, marry themselves off, have families and get buried. You wouldn't think they could get out of bed without killing themselves. They don't see anything and they know less. Not one person in the kitchen—the cook, two helpers, the waiters—knew how many knives there were. The barman used his own little gadgets and had never even noticed the kitchen knives.'

Capricorn nodded. As a magician, he had been aware of the general public's dim observation. It was not owing to stupidity but merely that, in general, they had no need to be sharply observant. In the course of ordinary life, household objects stayed in their appointed place to be used when wanted, without the need of mental inventory. The chef would notice his knife only if it lost its good cutting edge.

'If the murderer had washed the knife,' he said slowly, 'he would have had to wash his hands so as not to bloody it up again. And yet when I saw Copper his hands were covered in blood.'

Sedgwick looked at him patiently. 'You're trying awfully hard, aren't you?' he said, not without sympathy. 'Don't think I wouldn't rather it was anybody else. I'd rather it was a Prime Minister than a CID man. If only we'd bounced him out before,' he said in disgust, 'it wouldn't be so bad. Of course he washed his hands. Then he bloodied them up again. I expect he was going to move the body. If he'd put it in the office, and emptied the safe, it might have looked like

murder in the course of robbery. Would have
muddled things, anyway. But we have the witness
that nobody else went in or out, and that ties it up,
even without the weapon.'

Capricorn looked at him with foreboding. 'What
did you find?' He didn't know if Sedgwick would tell
him, but Sedgwick was pleased to do so. From the
edge of his peripheral vision, Capricorn could see the
blond WPC, who was almost out of earshot, straining
to hear the conversation while her switchboard went
unattended.

'He had plenty of motive anyway,' Sedgwick said
heavily. 'She made him look a fool, got him in debt,
cost him his job and wanted to get rid of him for that
crook. Even after Bonomi died, she still didn't seem
to want Copper back. And we know he knocked her
about—we'll have to talk to your aunts. She'd told the
woman in the cloaks. We think he followed her after
he left your aunts, stopped off and had a few drinks
with Moletta, got his blood up and went down there,
tried to have it out with her; she wouldn't have it
and he killed her. Plain enough as it stands. The
Commander did mention, though, last night, that it
wouldn't have helped him even if he'd got away
with it. He'd still be up the creek as far as money was
concerned. He'd lost what he'd given her; the club
wasn't his, and he was almost certain to lose his
house—unless he planned to join Moletta, which
wouldn't surprise me. But it turned out he was more
artful than we knew.'

Capricorn waited in silence. Sedgwick showed a
gloomy satisfaction. 'When we went through her
things we found a marriage certificate. They were
married nearly two years ago at some little place in
the South of France. She was Mrs Copper and he in-
herits everything—or would have done if he hadn't
been caught. Out of his financial troubles, and rid of
the woman who'd ruined him. And you know,'

Sedgwick said reflectively, 'if you hadn't tracked him down that day, he'd probably have got away with it. We could have suspected, but there would have been no proof. That woman who heard them quarrelling never saw him, and she couldn't swear it was Copper. On her evidence alone we'd have no case.' Sedgwick gave Capricorn a friendly smile. 'It turns out that you're the star witness for the prosecution.'

By the time Capricorn left the station, his spirits had plummeted from cheerfulness to a deep gloom. Copper still hadn't told him the whole truth. Perhaps he was hiding even more. It seemed impossible to extricate him from this mess. Capricorn went about the necessary routine work without much hope, putting forward an inquiry about the cheese salesman from Zurich, interviewing the sneering, cocky Slope, who refused to give any answers and was released on the appearance of his solicitors.

Back at the Yard, Capricorn found a message from, of all people, Pete Moletta, but was unable to reach him at the number he had left. In fact, when Capricorn gave his name, the girl who answered the telephone got the giggles. Now what would Moletta want, he wondered irritably. Fishing for information, or trading something unimportant, no doubt, in return for a favour that Capricorn would be unwilling to give. Still, it was odd. Moletta had never been one of Capricorn's snouts, or anybody else's, he was sure. He tried a few places where Moletta might be found, and at last was told that Moletta had gone to Newmarket; was not expected back in London until the following day. Well, whatever it was could wait until tomorrow.

And tomorrow, he thought, he'd better get in touch with a firm of solicitors for Copper. It was a disagreeable idea, but it should be done. That was one thing, at least, he could do for his friend.

He looked impatiently out of the window, for it was nearly dark. Too late now to get a good look round the back of the Golden Calf. Now he wanted to follow up Copper's investigation, not primarily to find where the coins were being drilled, but to see who had access to the back door of the Calf. If the witness was right, the murderer must have left that way. If Copper was telling the truth, the murderer had gone just a moment or two before Copper himself arrived. Copper said he had neither seen nor heard anyone, but it had been dark, and perhaps the killer had known the area well enough not to stumble about. Copper had not been looking or listening for anyone. A slight sound could have been attributed to a wandering cat and forgotten. The killer, on the other hand, would have been highly aware and cautious. Hearing Copper, he might have hidden himself until the policeman was safely inside.

Leaving the place he always thought of as his glass cage, Capricorn took his own car and drove to Soho again. Even at this hour the streets were still warm, as well as littered and neglected-looking. When he came to the vicinity of the Calf he looked out but could not see any public access to the yards between the streets. He parked his car and paced up one street and down the next, checking all four sides of the enclosure. The only opening he found was a narrow side entrance to a pub on the street behind the Calf. There was a locked gate six feet high across the entrance. With the help of a convenient dustbin it was not too hard to scramble over. Copper had probably gone the same way. Capricorn realized, as he jumped over onto the other side, that he was not in the best state for gymnastics, and remembered Gyppo Moggs's sarcasm about the phantom bomber: 'Jumped 'eavy.'

He found himself behind the pub, in a yard smelling of beer and ill-kept w.c.'s standing in a row to the side. The pub yard was fenced off from its neighbour.

Capricorn, with the discreet use of a torch, found a place in the fence where the posts were rotten and breaking, and squeezed through. He made his way down and crossed to the adjacent yards with some inconvenience but no real difficulty. Like Copper, he expected that some tenant living above one of the ground-floor shops would look out of a back window at any time and be aware of an intruder; some light came from the buildings, and there was a fleeting moon. He passed a few sheds used possibly for warehousing, piles of rubbish that would not please the Fire Brigade and a few chained dogs who gave warning of his approach.

Capricorn was puzzled. It hardly seemed a route to be taken by an escaping criminal. He could be perceived, and easily trapped. Nevertheless, there was access to the back door of the Calf by the alleyway that Capricorn had just used or through any of the buildings in the quadrangle. He decided to come back by daylight and talk to the residents and shopkeepers—though he would almost certainly run into Sedgwick and his men, still searching for the murder weapon.

For tonight, Capricorn satisfied himself with calling in at the pub, only to learn that the night before had been busy, and that neither the barman nor his wife had so much as looked out at the back, a thing they rarely did in any case as all the bars faced the street and the back rooms were used for storage. In fact, they had nothing to do with the yard at all, except to leave notes for the cleaner who came in the daytime 'to scrub up those lavatories because they gets unsalubrious like you wouldn't believe, people all being pigs. And I will not,' the barman had added, 'have my wife going out there and cleaning up after 'em. But the cleaners you get nowadays they don't want to know nothing and half the time they don't put a hand to anything but the beer pulls, if you ask me.'

Capricorn went to have a quick meal, without much appetite, and thought of what he had learned that day, without much solace. Copper had suspected Joss of killing Charlie. That, Capricorn thought, was ruled out by the murder method. The poison had to be given by syringe, and Joss could neither have hidden one on her person nor had one handy in the translucent fixtures of the Calf. In any event, mechanical problems aside, Capricorn didn't believe that Joss had wanted Charlie dead. Copper might like to think so, but Capricorn remembered the way Joss had looked at Charlie in the club. Charlie could have made use of Joss, as she did of him, without any intimidation on either side.

Possibly Joss had been tempted by Charlie's offer of a flat. Certainly, Capricorn had got the impression she felt constrained by her relationship with Copper. And they were legally married, after all. Copper's wife. He remembered the glowing young woman who had looked at Copper with such frank, inviting delight when they first met. It had been obvious to Capricorn, the bystander, that that was the beginning of a romance. Now the end had come: Joss in the mortuary, Copper in a cell.

Irritably, he told himself not to be morbid. It was time to keep his rendezvous with Gyppo Moggs. Solid information was what he needed, and Gyppo must have something or he wouldn't have promised to meet him, however sleepy he had been in the morning. Remembering the cheerful sunlight that had shone into Manning's flat while he had talked with Gyppo on the telephone, Capricorn reflected that its promise had not been fulfilled. The day had been muggy and oppressive, and now with night there was no freshness, even in the light breeze off the river. Very un-English weather, he thought, after he parked his car and walked down the Old Kent Road to the pub favoured by his informer. He went inside the

public bar but there was no sign of the dark little
man, and Capricorn got a glass of brandy and settled
down to wait. Moggs, superstitious, ultra-cautious,
could come at any time.

He might have found a pleasanter spot, Capricorn
thought. It was a big old barn of a place that someone had tried to modernize with strobe lights and a
howling juke box. A group of young people were
gathered round what looked like a television set, jok-
ing and laughing. From the remarks that were called
to friends away from the screen, Capricorn gathered
that the film being shown was a private distribution,
even less inhibited than public television.

Capricorn waited. The crowd grew more hilarious.
A fight broke out when a gang of toughs appeared already drunkenly belligerent from another port of call.
The local police arrived and restored order. Capricorn drank more brandy. People surged in, milled
about and left. A few women and a rather sad-looking
young man accosted him. Capricorn checked the
other bars, although Gyppo always patronized the
Public, and observed everyone that entered. But although he stayed until the place closed, and then
waited outside for over an hour, Gyppo never arrived, nor did Capricorn see him alive ever again.

COCKNEY JAZZ

Gyppo Moggs's extreme caution and fear of daylight had proved to be his undoing. Venturing out after dark, walking through the back street south of the river, he had been the victim of a hit-and-run accident. Or so his death was listed by the local police. Capricorn didn't believe it for a minute, and neither did the unhappy Mrs Moggs, who, unfortunately, could not be persuaded to justify her belief. Capricorn left the neat suburban house the next day both depressed and alarmed. The murder of a snout, though not unheard of, was unusual. What information could he have had to make murder worthwhile? Capricorn would have wondered, why that night? but Mrs Moggs had made that clear. Moggs had been on the nervous side, she said, and staying in, unless he went to the local with a few pals. Nothing much doing anyway, she'd added cryptically, and gone on to say that Moggs had been looking forward to getting a little something from Capricorn to pay the bills. Capricorn took care of that, noticing with a rather melancholy pleasure that Mrs Moggs was pleased at his generosity in a simple and unenvious way. So pleased that when he had gone a little way down the street she called him back.

Capricorn looked at the fair, plump woman standing in front of the little pseudo-Tudor house, the front lawn dotted with stone figures of Disney-like animals. He wondered if the neighbours realized that

202 PAULINE GLEN WINSLOW

Moggs was—had been—a professional burglar. Very likely they all 'kept themselves to themselves' and had no idea.

'If it'll help,' Mrs Moggs said dolefully, standing in a little glass cage that protected the front door. She had been preparing an early dinner and still had a potato in one hand and a knife in the other. 'Moggs did say—I remember him laughing—that it was the first time he had ever been paid by a villain to tip a copper. Laughing on and on he was, until he went round that night and saw the fireworks. He didn't like that. Didn't like vi'lence. Not like these youngsters. Said he hoped it wasn't nothing to do with Sweeter. Just a minute.'

She darted back inside to the kitchen and came out again, without the potato and knife, but with a chequered cloth cap in her hands. 'I'd left the gas on. I don't know what I'm doing today,' she said. 'They run over Moggs so terrible I hardly knew him. His cap had fell off and the p'lice let me have it. I was so upset I couldn't leave him without bringing something home.'

She twisted the cap in her plump white hands.

Capricorn expressed his sincere sorrow and asked if she knew who Sweeter was.

'No, Gyppo wasn't one to talk business at home. The neighbours, nice quiet lot here, they all thought he was retired. Never heard of no Sweeter except years ago.'

Capricorn tried to find out how long, but her memory was vague.

'Oh, yers and yers. I don't know if it's the same one. Shouldn't think so. One of the top men, he was, in his day, but he went inside for a long time. Not from his work. It was because he had trouble with some little kids. Used to give 'em sweets. Nasty business, he did ought to have got the cat. Sweeter, they called him, or the Acid Drop. But that was yers ago.'

She had no more information to give, and Capricorn, after thanking her and making a handsome contribution toward Gyppo's funeral, expressed his condolences again and left.

His mind was racing. One of the top crooks who had also been a seducer of children. There could not be many such men. 'Yers and yers ago'—and he had got a long sentence for his practices. On the way back to the Yard, driving in fairly heavy traffic, he had plenty of time to search his memory, but he could remember only one such case. Could it possibly be the same man?

The war had spawned a lot of petty crooks, dealing in black market and stolen goods that could be sold at a very high profit to a public being paid good wages with nothing to spend them on. The 'spiv' doing a brisk trade in American watches had been a familiar sight in the West End. A lot of them had drifted back to normal life after the war, some had gone on to become serious criminals and earned themselves long sentences for their pains, and a few, very few, had become rich, successful 'minders,' the brains of the criminal world.

Bertrand Flowers had been the most noted example of that kind of success: he was almost the Brixton Jim of his day, but far more conspicuous than that careful man. Flowers had aped the gentleman. A well-made, handsome man, he was personally vain. Capricorn's memory, so well trained by his father in his youth to help him in his 'mystic' act, often gave him more help than Criminal Records. Now it served him up a picture of the debonair Flowers, dressed by Savile Row and the Burlington Arcade, in the lounge of a famous hotel, drinking with a young man of good family, who probably owed him money. Flowers had been a snob, and would have loved to gain entry to the private clubs of London as well as the hotels, but he had never risen that far. Not the police, Capricorn remembered wryly, but his own character flaw had been his undoing. His money and charm and his ownership of a drinking club, a successor to the near-beer bar of the war years, had given him easy access to women. The supply of beautiful young girls would have been ample for any ordinary man. But Flowers had not been ordinary. Even a pretty sixteen-year-old mistress had not satisfied his peculiar nature, for Flowers was one of the unfortunates whose passion was aroused by children. Nowadays, Capricorn reflected, as he made his way through the narrow, choked streets of the city, Flowers would be thought of as a man needing psychiatric care. In the years just after the war, his inclinations were thought of as disgraceful—even by Flowers himself. If the Yard had no solid information on his career in crime, many a local constable had him under surveillance for hanging round schools, ice-cream carts and sweet-shops, always in poor neighbourhoods, with a bright smile and a few sweets for the little ones. He had been cautioned by the police; he had once been taken before a magistrate, but was released; no complaints had ever come in from parents, and it seemed as though he would escape the consequences of his sex crimes as well as the others, until the affair of the Goresby Hotel. The Goresby was a smart, luxurious hotel in the West End, and there had been considerable stir one fine spring afternoon at three o'clock when a nine-year-old girl, partly undressed, had fallen from an upper window to her death in the street below. An alert young constable had caught Flowers rushing out of the hotel, where it was found he had booked the room from which the girl had fallen. Post-mortem had shown that the girl had sexual relations with a man just before her death. Perhaps the fall had been accidental, but public reaction had been strong against Flowers, and he had gone before old Satterthwaite who gave him a long sentence. Many people were indignant that he hadn't got the rope's end.

Could Flowers possibly be the Sweeter who had hired Hake and the rest? From the descriptions given, Capricorn had pictured an elderly cloth-cap type, a little brighter perhaps than Henry Price yet essentially the same sort of man. Flowers would be close to sixty now, of course, and he had done twenty years' hard labour. Capricorn thought he remembered hearing that Flowers had been unpopular in prison; he had not had any easy time. At the Yard, Capricorn went straight to Criminal Research and checked his memory against the files. The computer brought forth no other villain of Flowers's stature with the same aberration. Flowers had served his full sentence, and had been released in 1968.

Capricorn went to his office, trying to picture the change that could have come to a man like Flowers in those years. Yes, it was possible that he could be the Sweeter of the Eastland job. Ruined, coarsened, it was natural enough he should sell what talents he had left to someone like Brixton Jim. But where the devil was he to be found?

In the old days he had had a smart flat in Shepherd Market, with his young mistress, but there had been no sight of him in the West End since his disappearance into penal servitude. He was certainly living somewhere under an assumed name. Capricorn wondered that he had used his old nickname on the Eastland job. Very likely he hadn't; another ex-prisoner had probably pinned it on him. Still, it was a very long chance that it would connect in anyone's mind with the debonair Flowers of twenty years ago; lucky for Capricorn that Mrs Moggs's moral indignation had kept the matter alive in her mind.

It would mean setting up meetings with his various snouts, he thought, to try to track Sweeter down. It

could take time, and time was running out. If only he
had someone working with him—but the Commander
wouldn't spare him a man for an investigation Capricorn wasn't supposed to be running. If Sedgwick had
found the weapon, Copper would be before the
magistrate this morning. Even without it, Sedgwick
wouldn't wait long. Heavy-hearted, Capricorn picked
up the telephone and arranged for a firm of solicitors
to represent the Inspector.

Mechanically, he noticed two messages on his
desk—Moletta again and, surprisingly, Nelly Merlino.
His aunts didn't often intromit in the Yard itself; he
wondered with foreboding what was wrong now. Underneath his professional calm, he was assailed by a
feeling close to horror, at the thought of Copper
being bound over for trial on a murder charge. It
seemed unreal, yet he knew, whatever his private belief about Copper's innocence, Sedgwick was right; he
had a strong case.

His prediction proved accurate. As he put the telephone down after speaking to the solicitor on the
subject of bail, Sedgwick himself poked his head
round the door to tell Capricorn that he was taking
the case before the magistrate the next morning, and
that Capricorn would be required to give evidence.
His men were still conducting a search for the knife
all round the back of the Calf, Sedgwick told Capricorn, but he was going ahead anyway. He had made
extensive inquiries that morning, but none of the
householders or shopkeepers with yards leading to the
back door of the Calf had noticed anyone outside
that night—not even Copper, he added fairly. 'Trust a
civvy not to notice a strapping six-footer with red
hair and leather boots banging about his back yard,
treading on his cat.'

While he grumbled, someone who had been standing behind him fidgeted, and Capricorn caught a
glimpse of a buxom woman with dyed-blond hair

showing from under a scarf wrapped about her head. She peered round Sedgwick's shoulder and gave him a flirtatious glance, rolling a pair of rather prominent brown eyes. Her face was familiar, though for a moment Capricorn couldn't think who she was. Sedgwick took her arm firmly and moved off down the corridor in the direction of the lift. A witness that he was seeing out, probably, and then the figure re-arranged itself in Capricorn's mind. He saw those rolling eyes in a well-made-up face surrounded by a halo of fluffy blond hair, the buxom shape in a low-cut evening dress. Of course. It was the cloakroom woman from the Golden Calf. He recalled that 'Hello, sucker!'

Swiftly, he jumped to his feet. Sedgwick would probably not accompany her down. He forced himself to wait until Sedgwick with his measured, ponderous tread had returned to his office, and then took the lift to the ground floor, catching up with the woman while she was still in the vestibule. Turning, she saw him and gave him a friendly, indeed more than friendly, greeting. Gallantly, he escorted her to the entrance, while she chattered away. Her resonant voice contained traces of East London, larded over with a vaguely American accent, and she used both Cockney and American phrases.

'What a terrible thing,' she said, getting to the subject of her visit, 'I really can't get over it. Gee, it's awful. I've hardly slept or been able to keep a thing down.'

She looked quite healthy in spite of this. Not as striking as she had looked in her make-up and the soft light of the Golden Calf, she was heavy-featured with quite a good figure but without the height of Joss or her imperial bearing. In daylight, Capricorn judged her to be in her middle forties. At the door she looked about her pensively. 'It took me hours to get here,' she said. 'All the way from Finsbury and I didn't dare call a mini-cab now, with the club closed.

I took two buses and I hurt my ankle gettin' on. Look.'

She displayed her ankle, calf and some of her thigh for Capricorn's inspection, much to the controlled but visible amusement of some of his juniors who were entering the building. Capricorn commiserated. Perhaps, he said soothingly, transportation could be provided to take the lady home, and, he added, as it was almost lunch time, perhaps she would join him for a meal.

Pleased, she laughed in a roguish way, and rolled her eyes again. Taking his arm possessively, she insisted they go to a certain pub where she had hopes of getting a job as barmaid.

'I live from week to week,' she said frankly. 'No do-re-mi. I got this flat and the furniture and everything when I got the job at the Calf, and Gawd knows how I'll pay for it now. "Won't some kind gentleman see me home,",' she sang.

Capricorn hastily called a cab. Although his witness had pretensions to sexual charm, she reminded him of his aunts. He was aware, as if he had eyes in the back of his head, of the interest of the policemen guarding the entrance to the Yard.

On the way, against his will, he had to listen to her complaints about Sedgwick. 'That one from Ilkley Moor,' she said with resentment, 'Do you know he wrote me down as Mrs Beeton? I haven't lived with Beeton for over ten years, and nobody ever called me Mrs Beeton in my life. If it gets in the paper, who's going to know who Mrs Beeton is? They'll think it's a cook. I've always been Miss America—that's my real name, you know, not a stage name. You could've told him,' she informed the startled Capricorn. 'Known each other for years, I said, but he wouldn't listen. I remember you from when you used to come to the Hi-Ho Club,' she leaned close to Capricorn, 'You remember, I used to take the private parties upstairs when Joss was running the downstairs. I shared it with that Gertie, who wasn't any good. A stick, Gertie was,' she went on, patting her own more-abundant charms.

When they arrived at the pub, a fairly busy place off Piccadilly, she introduced Capricorn as her new boyfriend from the Yard. 'Always wanted to own a law—again,' she said with a rich laugh. Her voice was clearly heard by all the patrons. The barman who was friendly, indeed familiar, was also amused. 'You need it, America,' he said.

After she had attended to her business, which consisted of drinking two large gin-and-limes very quickly and getting assurance from the barman that Harry, the now-absent owner, was considering her application, she allowed Capricorn to order sandwiches while she removed herself to the Ladies'.

As he took the food to a corner table, where he hoped for a little quiet, he tried to remember having seen her before, but except for a brief glimpse at the Calf, the memory eluded him. He had been very busy with two warring youth gangs when he visited the Hi-Ho, and, anyway, when Joss had been present other women were inclined to be overlooked. Joss. He sighed. So she had taken the aging Miss America with her. Joss had a soft spot in her heart after all.

Miss America—could that really be her name? He suspected that she was not unknown to the Yard, and later when he looked her up he found that to be the case. She had started life as Maisie Merker, though there was some doubt as to whether she had been entitled to Mr Merker's name—

Miss America returned. She had taken off her scarf and fluffed her hair, and she had been busy with her make-up kit, including, he noticed, a set of long eyelashes. He was getting the complete treatment. She had removed her light coat, and her walk was as much a movement from side to side as it was forward.

There were a few appreciative whistles from the other patrons, who seemed to know her well.

Capricorn couldn't help thinking of his lunch at the Florabel with the more discreetly but sincerely admired Joss, with a pang of regret for all that eagerness and glowing vitality now quenched forever. For a moment his witness seemed a very poor substitute for Joss with her statuesque and classic beauty; the sexual signal she emitted was just as strong, but without the same ability to evoke a response. He had to reproach himself, however, because as he well knew, no one human being is a substitute for another, and this woman had her own special quality, a simple and undemanding gaiety. She was humming and snapping her fingers as she walked across the room, calling to one friend and another—her rhythm was perfect and he guessed that Miss America had been a singer. Joss had enjoyed life, too; she had devoured it; she had been direct and intense but never really gay.

Somewhat to his relief, Miss America switched to lager and lime with her food, and although animated, she was sober enough to answer any questions. First she had to tell him about herself, with a few omissions. She had, indeed, been a singer and had worked with small bands, but, she shrugged philosophically, she had never really 'made it.' Once she had gone on a tour of the United States, but it had not gone well and she had had to pay her own way home. That was when, very hard up, she had married Beeton.

As she talked, telling him funny stories about her life as a rather unlucky performer, a life he himself knew very well, he couldn't stop comparing her with Joss. Joss had had beauty, ambition, if little humour, and she believed she had the world before her. Miss America was wary behind her gaiety, if not cynical—she knew her chances had passed her by. But, for all that she enjoyed what the good Lord sent and ate her food with appetite. He didn't think of her as callous, either. It was natural to her, after an unpleasant shock, to go on with a shrug. No strong emotional bond had tied her to her late employer. Perhaps envy had played a part, but he doubted that—except an occasional pang, perhaps. She was an open soul.

When Miss America arrived at the subject of Dolly Merlino, whom she had seen and admired—they would get on, he thought parenthetically—he steered the conversation to Copper's quarrel with Joss at Dolly's house, and then to the time of the murder. Was she quite sure it was the Inspector that Joss had been quarrelling with, he asked. He mentioned his idea that Joss could have been talking to someone on the telephone.

'Oh, no,' she was regretful, but quite positive. 'I wouldn't have said a word if I wasn't certain. I liked the Inspector, I thought he was a great guy.' She chuckled. 'He could've left his shoes under my bed any time he liked. But he never gave me a tumble. No, I heard him—well, a deep voice, a man's, and who else could it have been? I don't know if I told old Ilkley Moor,' she went on, frowning, 'but I think Joss said about the thirty thousand pounds—that's what upset him so, you know, her taking that from Charlie and lying about it. I knew all along. Charlie'd had his eye on her since the Hi-Ho, and that money business was his chance. I couldn't hear what Copper was saying because Joss was shouting. Carrying on alarming. She could be a right bitch, you know, though I shouldn't talk ill of the dead. Anyway, when I heard 'em rowing I thought, well, I'd better stay out of the way until it's over. You know what I mean, between man and woman like that, they both want to tell you their sides, and then afterwards if they make up they're sorry that you listened.'

Miss America was sensitive, much more than Joss had been, Capricorn perceived. But Joss had died young. It was clear to him, though, that however cer-

tain Miss America might be that it was Copper arguing with Joss, her certainty was not founded on
fact, merely on assumption. That was important.

She was still talking about Joss, who, after all, had
been on her mind. 'She would have everything her
way, that was her trouble. Of course, she was gor-
geous, that I won't deny. But she played up the Inspector and made him look a real fool. I don't say it
was right what he did,' she took out a cigarette and
Capricorn lit it for her. She smiled, a broad smile
showing a good set of teeth, except where they were
yellow at the gum line—bad dentistry, her practitioner had used cheap material for patchwork. 'But
she asked for it. Carrying on with Charlie in front of
everyone, and at the same time getting Copper in
trouble with the Yard.'

Capricorn wondered who else she knew at the CID.
The investigation hadn't been public knowledge.
Well, the villains had known quick enough. He
remembered the sneering Moletta. What the devil did
he want?

'She took all the kid's money and then wanted to
chuck him out for that foreign ponce. Thought she
was clever,' the more experienced woman shook her
head. 'I could've told her, but of course she wouldn't
listen to me. You know how it is with girls,' she said
resignedly. 'By the time you get a few wrinkles and a
double chin, if you don't have jewellery, a sable coat
and a flat in the West End, they're not going to listen
to you. I expect you thought we were friends,' she
told Capricorn, 'but we weren't. She just thought of
me as the help. Paid well, she was very generous, but
never asked my opinion on anything. "America do
this," and "America do that." I'd been round clubs
a few years longer than she had and I could've told
her a lot. But she never listened to me or the Inspector, come to that. And now look where she is.'

She took a good bite of ham roll. Capricorn

couldn't help thinking of where Joss was and pushed his own plate away. Dolly had spoken, just as casually, about the disposition of the body. Of course, neither Dolly nor Miss America had seen Joss as she lay in the light from the Golden Calf. The lovely neck of a lovely woman, suddenly turned to butcher's meat. The dreadful halitus of blood. Capricorn had been a policeman for a long time but he had never become inured to such scenes. He understood Copper's stupor that night and his total lack of self-protection. He had loved the woman.

'And that was about a quarter to seven, I think you said.'

'That's right. The club doesn't open till eight, but she always liked me to come in early and take bookings on the phone, and get everything ready; the char doesn't always leave it looking so hot. This time of year I look after the Ladies' as well as the cloaks, see that the dressing table is neat and tidy and put out towels—there aren't many coats in the evening yet. Usually, I go in the back and get myself a cup of tea and a sandwich—Joss never minded, I'll say that for her. She even used to tell me, "have some of the smoked salmon if you like," but I wouldn't take advantage. So I remember looking at my watch, it keeps good time,' she brandished her watch proudly, an expensive-looking affair set in diamonds, and then, catching his rather scrutinizing look, took her wrist away hastily and rested it on her knee under the table. 'And I went to get a cup of tea across the street—not a drink, because I can't keep my mind on my work if I start drinking early, though Joss never minded if I had a couple later on. The customers are always asking me to come to their tables for a drink; they get to know me. So I went to Luigi's because he wouldn't charge me for a whole dinner. I thought Joss could answer the phone herself if it rang. And I waited for the Inspector to go.'

'But nobody went in or out until I came at just about seven?'

'Not a soul,' she said positively. 'I was sitting at the window table and I had nothing to do—a few fellows tried to chat me up, but I'm not interested in the sort that goes into Luigi's—so I was watching all the time.'

'But he might have gone out the back way,' Capricorn said.

She stared, her bold eyes under the long false lashes for once quite serious. 'There is no back way out. A back door, yes, but it only leads to a yard with a fence. There's an outside toilet that they used when it was a Chinese restaurant, but Joss had all new ones put inside, that lovely ladies' room, all gold, and wee-wee places for gentlemen. Cost a fortune.'

'Yes,' Capricorn said thoughtfully, 'but perhaps, with you on the other side of the street, and so many people going back and forth at that hour—some going home for work and others going out to dinner and the theatre—and the light fading, you might have had trouble spotting them all.'

He sounded like a defense counsel with a poor case, he thought despairingly, trying to impress the jury by making a witness doubt her story for a moment, a story that she really believed. He had raced after Miss America when he saw his chance to approach her unofficially, not because he thought Sedgwick to be less than thorough but because he considered him to be too biased at this point to see the alternatives clearly. Sedgwick hadn't liked the 'Swingin' Skipper;' to the good family man that meant promiscuity. He had liked 'Flash Copper' even less, indicating as it did a detective who was spending more than his pay. Last and worst, he hated a Yard man who had dealings with the Mafia. Sedgwick would never manufacture a case against Copper, but if he had a strong one he wouldn't be trying to poke it full of holes.

Miss America saw where he was leading and shook her head. 'No, there weren't that many. I could see all right. There's a lamppost next door but one. The Super said I gave a marvellous description of you.'

She blinked at him under the false lashes, and moved her left hand confidingly close to his where it lay on the table top. With all his dejection at her answer, he felt a pang of pity as well. Her fingernails were gaily painted, but America's joints were swollen with arthritis.

'Tall as Gary Cooper,' she went on, 'only younger, of course. And dark and good-looking. I'd know you anywhere.'

'Too noticeable for a detective,' Capricorn said soberly. The fact had annoyed him all his working life. 'People always notice a man of my size. But perhaps someone less conspicuous—'

She was adamant. 'Oh, no really, I couldn't be mistaken. Old Ilkley Moor did ask me over and over, though between us I don't think he likes the Inspector much. Old-fashioned,' she said scornfully. 'I'll bet he goes to bed with his old woman in his nightshirt.'

Capricorn wasn't interested in Sedgwick's nocturnal habits and drank his ale gloomily. He hadn't managed to shake her story at all. He had wasted time. He wondered if Sedgwick's men had found the weapon. It wouldn't make much difference. If they found it, Sedgwick would say Copper had hidden it, and if they didn't he would call his experts to say it must have been one of the knives in the kitchen, well washed.

Rather wearily, Capricorn reminded himself that he was supposed to be investigating Bonomi's death. Miss America was informative on the subject of Charlie. She was quite shrewd, and she had been suspicious of criminal activity in the club.

'A funny lot would come in, as well as the smart

types,' she said. She wasn't happy about naming names, but she did mention Slope. She was also suspicious, he found, of some of the more respectable clients.

'There was one old fellow, Withers, you know, waistcoat and laced-up shoes, grey and stiff and never look at you when he's with somebody, but at three in the morning if he's alone, he tries to get you in the corner and have a feel—after a few drinks, of course. Old bastard. Well, anyway, one night I was dying to go and I couldn't get in the Ladies', it was jammed, so I took a quick peek to see if there was anyone in the Gents', and who should be there, jawing away and not doing anything else, but old Withers with Charlie Bo and that funny little foreign fellow like Mickey Mouse. Funny, if you ask me,' she said.

Capricorn took Mickey Mouse to be the little man from Zurich in the spotted bow tie, now believed to be a currency smuggler. Withers, of Gorton Finance. Work there for Fraud Squad, most likely. 'Did Joss use a syringe to take any medication?' he asked abruptly.

'Joss?' She looked at him, rather nonplussed at the sudden change in subject. 'No, I don't think so. Copper did, he had a few in the drawer of the desk, because his pills made him sick. He was always forgetting to use 'em, though. I remember Joss saying she wished he'd clear the stuff out. But I don't remember her sticking anything in herself.'

'I didn't mean a dangerous drug necessarily,' he said.

'She did tell me she'd taken shots, Vitamin B12, for energy,' Miss America said thoughtfully. 'But she got them from her doctor. Joss loved going to the doctor, she was funny like that; she enjoyed being pulled about in the surgery. She wouldn't have given them to herself. She did take pills, ups, if you get me.'

Capricorn understood her to mean amphetamines.

'She took them after midnight. Not that she really needed more energy, Joss could go forever—she could wear me out,' Miss America said thoughtfully, 'and I always figured I was a real night owl. But, of course, I had a few years on her. She would take them to give her extra sparkle, she said. Joss always saw herself as being on stage, in the club,' Miss America explained. 'It was a performance with her.'

Well, none of that would be any help to Copper, Capricorn realized, in great dejection. Unless he could dig up Flowers and find some connection between the killings and Brixton Jim, all his work seemed to prove Copper guilty of both murders. Then his own phrase reverberated in his mind. 'Dig up Flowers.' He thought of Moggs and the missing Hake. For all he knew, Brixton Jim had rid himself of Flowers already.

He eyed the witness in front of him, so chatty, so cheerful, so sure: aside from Capricorn himself, Sedgwick's chief witness. Buxom, solid, immovable. If it wasn't for Miss America, counsel could certainly get Copper off, even if the real murderer were never found. But she was a fixed obstacle in the way.

All round him the noises of a pub went on, talk, laughter, the clinking of glasses, and his nostrils were full of the familiar smells, beer, whisky, tobacco smoke. He had a sudden longing for a cigarette. It was in such an atmosphere that The Great Capricornus had liked to talk to his son, many years ago, when young Merlin had been tall enough, if not old enough, to go inside. He explains how other magicians' tricks were done and taught his professional heir to see for himself. 'It's always in front of you, if only you look,' he would say with a cunning wink. 'Anything that seems solid, heavy, like it don't move—the floorboards even might be part of the trick. Take the last thing you'd ever think of, and watch it like a woman trying to get in your trouser pockets. That'll be it.'

But there was no trick in Miss America, Capricorn thought soberly. In this instance, she wasn't trying to cheat. If she could, she would have let Copper off. Nevertheless, if there was one particular quality that Capricorn was known for at the Yard, it was his refusal to give up.

He smiled at his witness ingratiatingly. 'You see a lot. Your eyes are sharp as well as beautiful. You really don't miss anything, do you? I'm supposed to be observant,' he said, 'and yet I passed you, sitting there in the window, without seeing you at all. I don't know how I did that.'

'Oh, well, you weren't looking my way,' she said tolerantly, 'I'm sure you're usually sharp. But I was watching close because I wanted to get started. I knew there'd be a lot to do when I saw the char go in and come out right after.'

'The char?' Capricorn said softly.

'Yes, that old girl the agency sent. Looked like a real crazy Jane. Tall, skinny old bag in a dress with a sailor's' collar, high heels and no coat or anything. Hair dyed blond. I hate to see an old woman with dyed-blond hair,' she said patting her own locks nervously. 'Silly buggers—I told them at the agency when I phoned that afternoon to send someone with brawn because Joss liked the place done up shining. She rang me in the morning—woke me up, actually, to be sure and get someone because she was going out to lunch. Our usual had called in, she got a bellyache or something. But Joss threw this old girl out in a couple of minutes. It was too late then, anyway. Cookie was due in. Joss must've cleaned up herself.'

'When did she arrive?'

'The char? Oh, just after I sat down in Luigi's.'

'While the quarrel was going on. Did you mention that to Superintendent Sedgwick?'

Miss America looked at him, affronted. 'He didn't ask me anything about the char. He wanted to know if anybody had gone in or out who could've done the murder. She was hardly there three minutes, and she must have had the strength of a starving hen.'

'Of course,' Capricorn said hastily. He ordered two brandies. He didn't know about his guest but he needed a drink badly. She was telling the truth. He understood very well how witnesses rearrange questions in their minds, according to their own preconceptions, before they answer. 'Had you ever seen that char before?'

'No,' Miss America said scornfully. 'They really got that one out of the Ark. Fit for nothing. Joss must've given her money to go away. 'Course, she was in the middle of having a row and wouldn't want her there anyway. Gave her a jacket as well,' she added.

'A jacket?'

'When she came out she had a sort of knitted jacket on, a long one. It had been hanging in the cloakroom for ages, someone left it and never claimed it,' she said. 'It was like Joss. She was good-hearted.' America was very mellow now. 'Gave the old girl something to eat, I think. She came out with a brown paper bag.'

Capricorn wasn't feeling mellow at all. A loathsome idea had dawned on him, but he had to persist. 'So the charwoman must have gone in after six forty-five, then?'

'Not much after. I didn't look at my watch, but by the time I got my sandwich—Luigi was doing dinners, you see—she'd gone. What a funny old tart.'

'Why do you say that?' Capricorn asked, not really wanting to hear the answer.

'Wa-al,' she said, thoughtfully—the American accent came and went—'she was sort of skipping along when she left, practically dancing. I suppose she was pleased, poor old cow, not having to work. And singing.'

'Singing?'

'Yes. Some hymn it was. I told you, the street was quiet then. She crossed the street and passed right by me. A thin, funny squeak she had. "Washed in the Blood of the Lamb." '

Miss America sang in a trembling falsetto, wringing her hands and rolling her round eyes to the amusement of bystanders, who laughed aloud. She joined in their laughter, but she was not a stupid woman, and perhaps observing something in Capricorn's expression, the significance of her words dawned on her. Laughter fled and she glanced at him uneasily. She wasn't nearly as uneasy as he was. He suggested he take her back to the Yard so that she could amend her statement to Sedgwick. It was possible, he pointed out, that the char had seen the quarreling parties.

She agreed to go, but said it would have to be after closing time, as she had to wait for the owner. She needed the work, and told him virtuously, but from glances that passed between her and some of her bolder admirers, he took it that she had some more immediate relief in mind. He wrote down the name and number of the domestic employment agency she gave him, and left her making her way back to the bar, while he went to the telephone. Miss America was already restored to good spirits. Relieved, no doubt, by the absence of the law, she snapped her fingers again and obliged the company with a song and dance, arthritis notwithstanding. The strains followed him, faintly, into the booth:

Happy feet, I've got those happy feet
Two little happy feet, that never stop dancing
Happy toes, ten little snappy toes . . .

As he expected, the employment agency denied, indignantly, that they had sent anyone.

'Calling in at three o'clock,' the manageress exploded, 'what do you expect? We tried our best, let me tell you, and it cost money and time phoning, but you won't get one of them out at that time of day and I don't blame them. We're not back in the Middle Ages, you know. We don't keep them sitting around in rows in case someone has a fancy to call in at five o'clock. I told that Miss America, but all I got out of her was a laugh, and an "Oh, do your best, duckie." '

Capricorn thanked her and hung up, feeling actually queasy. The bit of ham roll he had eaten lay in his stomach like a lead pellet in an acid bath. He told himself that this would probably save Copper—Sedgwick's important witness had changed her testimony: someone other than Copper had been present in the club during the time the murder was presumed to have taken place. He remembered that Joss's blood had already begun clotting when he himself had arrived just after seven, yet according to Miss America, Joss had been paying off her charwoman, finding her clothes and packing up food shortly after a quarter to the hour. He wondered if Miss America's assumptions about that had been wrong. 'The strength of a starving hen,' she'd said.

He thought of Tilly, climbing down the drainpipe with more strength in those skinny arms than he could have believed. Tilly in her sailor dress and high-heeled shoes. Tilly who hated Joss and had assaulted her in the Florabel. Dolly said she had taken her sister back to her room and given her tranquillizing pills, but Dolly had lied before. He remembered, with awful clarity, the scene from his boyhood—the policemen, blue-uniformed and in plain clothes, backstage in the shabby old music hall; the cast, nervous, upset, yet bound together by their loyalties. Dolly had lied, claiming that Tilly and her husband, who died from the accident, had been like two turtledoves, though even Capricorn had known that the husband had planned to run off with one of the dancers on the bill.

A shriek of laughter from the bar, brought about by Miss America's performance no doubt, penetrated the glass booth and brought his mind back to the present. He was being overly imaginative, he told himself. After all, Miss America had made it clear that she had seen the Merlino act on television—she would have recognized Tilly, surely. But would she? The policeman wondered. Not surely. Dolly, yes. Dolly would always be recognized because she always looked like herself. Stolid, ham-faced, she was as impervious to the make-up man as she was to the costume maker. Nelly, though, could be transformed from a little, dark old woman to someone Gypsy-like and mysterious, while Tilly, with her thinness and childish face properly covered with mesh and make-up, looked slim and still attractive. Besides, on camera as on stage, the aunts had sparkle and poise. It was possible that off stage Tilly might be unrecognizable.

A red-faced fat man in a loud suit with a racing sheet in his hand was banging on the door of the booth and opened it slightly, irritated, no doubt, at the sight of Capricorn sitting staring at the receiver, doing nothing and depriving him of contact with his bookmaker. The voice of Miss America wafted in:

. . . I can't control

Those dancing heels to save my soul.

Capricorn started to leave and then remembered, with foreboding, that Nelly had tried to get in touch with him. He would go to Paddington instead of ringing up, but in the meantime, he thought wearily, he had to find out what Moletta wanted. This was the time to catch him at lunch in his favourite pub.

Moletta's voice came over the line, flat and bored, but instead of his usual undertone of sarcasm, Capricorn thought he detected some amusement.

'Seems I gave that young law some grief,' he said. 'Between you and me, if I'd known what it was all about when that Yorkshirepud Super came round I would have lost my memory.'

Of course, Capricorn remembered, Moletta still thought of Copper as a 'bent law,' and a possible future partner. But his statement had been taken. What did he think he could do now?

'Thick clod,' Moletta was still concerned with Sedgwick. 'If he hadn't played that stupid CID game, keeping mum and poker-faced, I could have told him something. So when I found out what was going on, I thought I'd tell you.'

'You have some information about Miss Parker's murder?' Capricorn's heart leapt, whether in anticipation, fear or both, he didn't know.

'I'd hate to have to go to court,' Moletta grumbled peevishly. 'If you can save me that I'll be glad. And don't forget that you'll owe me a favour, Superintendent.'

Capricorn knew he wouldn't forget. Moletta would remind him.

'Well, what is it?'

'I might be able to get the Inspector off,' Moletta said triumphantly. 'Exactly when was Joss killed?'

'She was dead at about five past seven when I arrived,' Capricorn answered, wondering what was coming. Had Moletta cooked up some sort of alibi for Copper? 'And it's believed she saw a woman, thought to be a char, about twenty minutes before that.'

'Oh.' Moletta sounded deflated. There was a pause. Perhaps he considered rearranging the tale he was about to tell, but if he did, he gave it up. 'Then I suppose I can't do him any good. I thought I was the last person to talk to her before she was killed, and I know Al wasn't there then.'

Al. Joss's name for Copper. It still struck Capricorn's ear as odd.

'When was that?'

'Well, I'd got to Dominetto's before half past six. I was having a drink with some people before dinner. One of them was a whisky dealer; he offered me a special price. I thought Joss might be interested, so I gave her a ring. They take a long time to get to the food in Dominetto's and I don't take more than a couple of drinks,' he explained. 'The telephone at the bar is next to that damned great clock that chimes so that you can't hear yourself speak. While I was talking to Joss, it chimed the half. It was right, too. I was getting hungry and looked at my watch.'

'You were talking to Joss at half past six,' Capricorn said slowly. 'Do you remember for how long?'

'Quite a while,' Moletta said. 'My table wasn't ready, and Joss was full of chat. Women,' he added. Capricorn could imagine the supercilious lift of the shoulder. 'She'd answered herself, none of the staff were in. She said it was one of those days. They'd called in with excuses right and left and she was stuck being head cook and bottle washer. But she laughed; she was in a good mood,' he said reflectively. 'Roared with laughter telling me that she'd walked into a door and she'd have a black eye in the morning. Big joke. Then she told me she heard someone in the kitchen and I remember her saying, "Oh, Christ, it's some old cow. What the hell have they sent me? As if I haven't got enough old cows with Miss America." She meant that cloakroom woman, that's what they call her. Fat tart, long in the tooth. Anyway, that's when I heard the clock strike. Joss said she'd have to go and see to the old girl and she said she hoped I'd still fancy her with a black eye, and she rang off.'

Notwithstanding his sick despair, Capricorn noticed the discrepancy in time between Moletta's story and Miss America's; he said it was half past six when the woman entered, but Miss America had said it was gone a quarter to seven. But Moletta, who had a lot of business, was more likely to keep accurate time than Miss America, with her fancy stolen watch, and her attention, despite her protestations to the contrary, on the men in Luigi's who were trying to 'chat her up.'

'What made you certain that the Inspector wasn't there?'

'The way she talked. "Darling, angel, lover"—always pushing sex, Joss. Good for business. Didn't care who heard her at it—some of the women guests didn't think it so hot, I suppose, but she went on anyway. The only time she didn't do it was when Al was around. He hated that stuff. Just what you'd expect with Al after all the women. But she wouldn't open her trap if he was anywhere in the building—afraid he'd catch her at it. A few looks is as far as she'd go. So when she started kidding around about a bonus if I gave her the rock-bottom price on Scotch, I knew Al couldn't be there.'

Capricorn thanked him and asked him to make another statement for Sedgwick, despite his feelings, as Sedgwick was in charge of the case. Moletta reluctantly agreed. 'But don't forget you owe me.'

Capricorn promised he would not. 'Go as soon as you can,' he said. 'Your evidence might help to get the Inspector released.' He didn't tell the Soho villain that he might be getting the Superintendent's aunt arrested instead.

He left the telephone booth, and the pub, not without noticing Miss America, now surrounded by a large circle of admirers, giving a reprise of her comic version of a song from—when was it, the 20s?

I keep cheerful on an earful of music sweet
'Cause I've got those hap-hap-happy feet.

Capricorn caught a taxi back to the Yard, wishing grimly that such a light-hearted song was all he had to think about.

'Washed in the Blood of the Lamb.'

Miss America might be vague about time, but she wouldn't mistake that. She had the tune quite correct, he remembered. He had heard it before, often enough. The home where Tilly had lived for so long was a good one, with a religious-minded board of governors. They had believed in prayer and hymn-singing every morning, and he had been greeted many times by a brisk rendition of 'Washed in the Blood of the Lamb,' as well as 'Onward Christian Soldiers' or 'We Plough the Fields and Scatter the Good Seed on the Land.'

He remembered Dolly's anger when Copper was arrested, her excited protests when Capricorn had inquired, innocently as it happened, as to Tilly's whereabouts on the day of the murder. He wondered about Nelly calling him at the Yard. Had she wanted to tell him something, perhaps away from Dolly's influence? If his suspicions were justified, would Nelly be truthful? She was not as violently emotional as Dolly and was more reasonable, but still, he thought, she possessed the same strong loyalties. He fancied she might try to warn him, but he didn't believe she would testify against her own sister—who was also a valued member of the act. Underneath the confidence stemming from their success, both Dolly and Nelly were well aware of their age, and the slippery affections of the public. Neither would want to risk a drastic change.

The key to his aunts' door hung in its usual place on his keyring. They had given it to him years before, for his convenience when he was a struggling young sergeant, and he had kept it in case they ever needed help. He used it now, letting himself in quietly and feeling with his present purpose, like a traitor. The house was quiet.

As he switched on the hall light he at once observed a photograph, which had been hanging there doubtless for over twenty years without his noticing it before, of the young Tilly and her dead husband, smiling rapturously at each other.

He went up the stairs, trying to make no sound. The aunts were probably having their post-luncheon nap.

Tilly's room was empty. This room had not been redecorated. It was as it always had been. The lino-leum-covered floor, whitewashed walls, plain chest of drawers and narrow metal bed gave it an institutional look. All it needed was bars on the window. Tilly's clothes were still on hooks in the corner, with a scanty green curtain half-drawn across. The only concession to her new life was a wooden wardrobe to hold her stage costumes.

Capricorn searched methodically through the daytime clothes and then the costumes, looking for the sailor dress. He found a lot of strange-looking garments but not the frock with the square collar, reminiscent of the 20s, that he remembered seeing her wear. The drawers of the pine chest were crammed to the overflowing and jamming stage, and he dragged out an incredible assortment of underclothes, fake jewelry, salt cellars and spoons bearing names of hotels and restaurants, men's cuff links, a few brittle wishbones, a Salvation Army bonnet, and a fine old porcelain box, reputed to have belonged to the Marquise de Pompadour, from his own collection. He stared for a moment, fascinated. Tilly had filched that from a glass cabinet fitted with a special lock, and had got it out of his house under the eagle eye of Mrs Dermott. Next to it was a heap of old pennies, sixpences and shillings, an apple, and a large grubby collection of cigarette cards held together with rubber bands. A navy-blue garment was caught behind a drawer; it revealed itself to be not a dress, but, incredibly, a pair of gym bloomers with elastic top and bottom.

Glancing around the room he saw, carelessly flung

across a kitchen chair, a long, knitted grey cardigan, or jacket. He looked at it doubtfully. There was a label from a big London shop—the garment was probably sold by the hundreds.

He turned his attention to the bed, and lifted the wide, heavy quilt. It overhung a great, undusted heap of Tilly's treasures. There were about a dozen pairs of shoes, a heap of scarves that all looked new, an article of bedroom furniture no longer in common use, three bags of sweets, four cameras and a tennis racket with a broken string. He stacked the stuff on the bed for a closer look and examined all the pairs of high-heeled shoes. The left shoe of one of the pairs, though clean to the ordinary glance, had a suspicious stain on the front of the sole and an almost imperceptible smear where the sole met the suède of the upper.

Steps shuffled along the corridor. The door opened. Tilly, dressed in a gown made of white Turkish towel, her hair foamy-white with bleach, stared first at him, as he stood with the shoe in his hand, and then at her treasures on the bed. She giggled at the unusual sight.

'Where's your sailor dress, Tilly?' he asked gently.

'Till—' a voice roared. A door banged, and then another. Tilly had woken her sisters.

'They took it.' Tilly smiled widely.

Dolly, grey under her fiery topknot of corkscrew curls, glared at Capricorn, a true Gorgon.

'Shut up, Till, and go and rinse your hair before it falls off.'

Over Capricorn's energetic protest, she bundled her off into the bathroom. Nelly, quiet and more sallow than usual, came in and grabbed Capricorn by his lapels, but Dolly was back quickly, regarding them both, her arms akimbo.

'What are you doing here this time of day?' she asked. 'Did *she*,' looking at Nelly suspiciously—per-

haps there had been some argument between them—
'get hold of you?'

Before he could answer, Nelly interjected. 'I rang
him up to talk about young Copper,' she said coldly.
'I heard he'd been taken in charge, and I think it's ridiculous. If you weren't so excitable, Doll, you'd say
the same yourself.'

'Yes,' Dolly sniffed, a little quieter. 'So you had to
come here for that?' She still looked at Capricorn
searchingly, her gaze hostile and wary. 'Why are you
pulling our Till's stuff about? What are you up to?'
She turned to her sister. Suddenly they were allies
again, regarding Capricorn as they had when he was
a boy, and a hindrance to some cherished purpose.
'Imagine us going to his posh place and going
through his things. Call a constable, he would. As it is
that Mac practically searches you before she lets you
out.'

'Where's Tilly's sailor dress?' Capricorn asked
bluntly.

' 'Er dress?' Dolly was full of malevolent sarcasm,
her pebble-like eyes shining with anger. 'Where do
you think? In the wash, with her brassiere and knick-
ers, do you want them as well? Turning funny are
you?' she went on, her face getting red. 'No wonder,
living by yourself with just a char and a picture of
her bloomin' Ladyship. It's unnatural, that's what it
is and—'

'Leave him alone.' Nelly was the only person who
could control Dolly's rages. 'No need to upset him.
We want him to get this rubbish about young Copper
stopped, that's all, isn't it?' She addressed Capricorn
very coolly. 'I don't know why you're so interested in
Till's things,' she said. 'We always have to put her
dresses in the wash after she's worn them once, except
her costumes that I put away. She gets her things in a
state, as you've seen yourself. I put that dress in the
washing machine.'

Capricorn looked at her doubtfully. None of the aunts had ever been interested in laundry. In the old days, it had gone out in a haphazard fashion, and was often lost when they travelled. He believed that nowadays, although they had a washer and dryer in the basement, it was only used by the cleaning woman. But if that was Nelly's story she would stick with it—she couldn't be trapped like the excitable Dolly.

'So it's in the house, then?' he asked.

'Oh, I don't know,' Nelly sounded casual, too casual. Dolly was breathing hard down her nose. 'The woman that does for us hasn't been in all week and I had to iron a few bits myself, and you know me, Merle, I was never much good at ironing. Give me a pack of cards and I'll do anything you like, but an iron is a nasty thing. Burnt my fingers,' she grumbled, 'and half the stuff got scorched. So we had a bit of a clear out. Slung some stuff away. Might have been that old dress of Till's, I don't know. You could look at the stuff in the basket in the basement, I didn't sort it out. But the dustman's been—and about time, the rubbish has been lying about, I'd swear, for a fortnight—so if it's gone, it's gone.'

'What, my dress?' Tilly, who had come back still frothing, was indignant. 'What did you do that for?'

Dolly grabbed her and pushed her out again. 'Go and stick your head in the basin, you silly mare,' she roared. 'And don't take it out until I tell you.'

Capricorn had been looking at the pile of scarves. One of them was of real silk, long and purple-striped. He had seen that scarf before. It had been lying on the back seat of a car, Joss's car, in front of the Golden Calf.

'And where did she get this?' he asked.

Before Dolly could speak, Nelly said quickly, 'That's Joss's. She left it here when she came for lunch. Tilly must have nicked it. She's a bad girl. You know she didn't like Joss.'

Dolly, who had been calming down, got red again. 'Till didn't mean nothing,' she said. 'She pinches from everybody, you know that. Look, the cow,' she screamed suddenly, looking in the drawers that Capricorn had left opened, 'My best tiara with the marcasites.' She crammed the bauble on her head for safety, careless of her appearance in flannel nightgown and plaid wool slippers.

'And whose cardigan is that?' Capricorn asked.

Nelly looked at the garment on the chair. By her expression Capricorn could swear that she had never seen it before, but she didn't flick an eye. Before he could stop her movement, she had it in her hand and he knew, although she had hardly looked down, she had seen the label. Nelly was the best magician of them all. 'Mine,' she said. 'You know she's a tea-leaf. I got it on Oxford Street one day, it turned cold, but I never liked it. Not my style.'

'It's no use,' Capricorn said wearily. 'You told me that Tilly never left the house the day that Joss was killed, but I saw her myself, climbing down the drainpipe. I was in a taxi on the corner.'

Dolly turned purple and lifted her hands, and he thought she would actually strike him. He stepped back, instinctively, but Nelly caught her firmly. 'I can understand your being upset, Doll,' she said coldly, 'at the implication. Coming from our own nephew, it's a bit thick. But you don't have to say anything. What you're referring to,' she addressed Capricorn, 'was a silly lark that we both knew about. She hammered on the window and called us names. We let her in, and then took her upstairs and gave her pills, and after that she slept all day. We didn't even get her up for the party. If you think she could have got up again after two of those pills, then you'll have to talk to her doctor. One of them's enough to knock a horse out.'

Capricorn looked from the enraged Dolly to the calm, but more deadly, Nelly. Bits of her story he knew to be true, but most of it he was sure was a lie. He was certain if he looked for the missing dress it would not be with the rest of the wash. But the aunts would stick to their story. He had no chance to shake it unless Miss America could make an identification that would stand, which was doubtful. Out of the corner of his eye he saw Tilly again, lurking furtively in the doorway, a towel round her head, listening avidly, her mouth open. He spoke suddenly, swiftly. 'Why did they take the dress?'

'It was the blood, it was the blood,' Tilly answered, laughing madly.

Dolly turned like a fury and slapped her across the face while Nelly, small as she was, pulled the tall Tilly out of the room and hauled her down the corridor. Tilly jerked her mouth away from Nelly's restraining hand. 'Slit a chicken's neck!' she yelled. 'Slit a chicken's neck!'

The front doorbell pealed loudly across Tilly's yells and her sisters' exclamations. It was a steady, persistent sound.

'Slit a chick—'

Capricorn looked out of the window. A large, official car was parked at the curb. On the porch, pushing the bell and looking about him with interest, was a CID sergeant first class whom Capricorn knew well, and next to him, pink-faced, square and solid looking, with his usual air of being prepared to wait all day if necessary, was Sedgwick.

Behind him, in the corridor, Tilly was still screaming.

'Slit a chicken's neck!'

MOONLIGHT SERENADE

Sedgwick had come to take a statement from the Merlinos about Copper's quarrel with Jóss. He stood stolidly in the aunts' stage-Victorian parlour, his stern glance quelling the sergeant who was inclined to stare about. Capricorn received them alone for a long, uncomfortable ten minutes. Dolly and Nelly had refused to come down until they were properly dressed, and Capricorn, reluctantly, had had to leave them to admit his colleagues.

To have said that Sedgwick was cool would now be an understatement. He had already heard, by telephone, from both Moletta and Miss America, and was showing all the signs of a Superintendent who believed that another officer was interfering with his case. Capricorn wondered whether a complaint had already gone to his commander. Finding Capricorn at his aunts' house during the working day made Sedgwick even more suspicious.

The stories of Miss America and Moletta about a charwoman had impressed him very little. Sedgwick sent his sergeant back to the car, ostensibly for some forgotten cigarettes, and then attacked Capricorn roundly. 'Getting these people to ring me up with these tales, trying to get Copper off, is that it?' he demanded furiously. 'I took a statement from Beeton myself, and she swore up hill and down dale that nobody went in the place after she came out until the "handsome Super." You,' he added, with a snort,

meaning there was no accounting for tastes, and at
the same time there was something wrong with a CID
Superintendent who could be thus described. 'Now
she comes up with this tale about a char that the
agency never heard of. I don't put much stock in Mrs
Beeton anyway—she's been done for soliciting, did
you know that? She's as much good as my old boots—
and her story doesn't hold up. That villain Moletta
puts the char inside at half past six when Beeton was
trying to cadge a free meal from Luigi. Luigi remembered, all right; she tries it on often enough. I don't
see how a char going in and out around half past six
stopped Copper cutting his wife's throat before seven
o'clock.'

'Not just before seven, I should think,' Capricorn
replied. 'The blood had started to clot when I got
there.'

He still was carrying the shoe he had found under
Tilly's bed, the shoe with the stain that might, or
might not, be blood. Sedgwick should be told what he
suspected, but his natural reluctance to involve his
family was buttressed by the certain knowledge that
the Northcountryman would laugh in his face. Yet
Sedgwick was planning to bring the case before the
magistrate. He had to be informed.

Slowly, patiently, with a heavy heart, Capricorn
tried to confess his suspicions. He told Sedgwick of
Tilly's jealousy, her lack of balance, her quarrel with
Joss. He described her escape from the upstairs window in her sailor's dress, and the matching description of the charwoman by Miss America. There was
the paper bag that Miss America had seen her carry
out, which might have contained food, or hidden a
weapon. He told him of Joss's striped scarf found
among Tilly's treasures, possibly stolen from the club,
together with the cardigan—that must go to the lab,
too, he thought. He displayed the shoe. The mark on

the shoe, in the light of the parlour, could not be seen. Sedgwick stared, his face a blank.

Capricorn, feeling more and more like a male Medea, went on to explain what had happened to Tilly's husband, how Tilly had not been charged with any crime but that her worried relatives had arranged for her to go to the home and how she had been released under medical supervision.

He paused. There was a moment's silence, broken only by the loud ticking of the clock on the chimneypiece. Then Sedgwick spoke, his words preceded by an ominous, slight whistling sound as he breathed down his nostrils. 'Are you telling me,' his voice was loud and clear, 'that Copper, who you caught with his hands still bloody, didn't kill his wife, but that she was murdered by your own aunt, who's a homicidal lunatic?'

Out in the hall, the front door slammed. The sergeant was returning.

'Ah, ha, ha, ha, ha!' A dreadful laughter grated on Capricorn's ears. Not only was the sergeant in the doorway, but two of the aunts preceded him, in full array. Nelly had come down in a stiff black taffeta jacket and skirt, heavily sprinkled with jet, a Spanish shawl and round, glittering earrings. Dolly was even more impressive in billows of scarlet satin, an Elizabethan ruff, her hair done up with the tiara on top and blazing from head to foot with fake gems.

The sergeant and Sedgwick regarded them with respect. Capricorn had noticed this curious anomaly before. Music hall performers had been objects of suspicion to the police, landladies and shopkeepers, but the advent of television made a great difference; they were now respected citizens, objects, indeed, of a kind of veneration: 'the tube-change,' he called it, a compound of familiarity and ignorance.

'Oh, Merle, you're as bad as your father, you'll say anything! Well, what I always say is anything to help a friend, but you're going a bit far.' Dolly smiled richly at Sedgwick. 'Which one of us did he say did it?'

Sedgwick made a sound between a gargle and a cough.

'Well, young Merlin,' she said, deliberately using the name that he had legally changed as soon as he was old enough, 'You mustn't tell fairy stories. He was always an imaginative boy,' she spoke with fondness.

'A liar,' Nelly said flatly.

The sergeant looked as though he was sorry he'd come back, and in his embarrassment crushed the cigarettes in his hand.

'Could I speak to your sister Tilly?' Sedgwick asked, with an appearance of calm.

'I'm sorry, Commander,' Nelly took over, as the better strategist of the two. 'Can't we help you? Merlin got Tilly so excited, she took a sedative so that she could have a nap. We're doing a performance tonight, a show for charity, at the Palladrome. The Actors' Fund,' she explained.

'Chief Superintendent Sedgwick, Miss Merlino,' he murmured. 'Where was your sister on Friday afternoon and evening, if you know?'

'Of course we know,' Nelly said, mildly surprised. 'Won't you sit down, gentlemen? We can give you half an hour. A glass of sherry?'

The aunts were doing their best grandes dames act, Capricorn thought bitterly. He could bet there was nothing in the house but Guinness and gin.

'Not on duty, thank you,' Sedgwick answered. 'I won't trouble you much longer. Where was Miss Tilly Merlino on Friday?'

'We had been rehearsing a new act here in the afternoon,' Nelly said, 'and Tilly's part requires some climbing. She was practicing up and down the pipe outside this room. We performers don't get older, you know,' she smiled a vicious little smile, 'but we do get

tired a little sooner than we did. Tilly was very tired,
so she took a relaxing pill and went to sleep. I think
our Merlin—he'd come to visit us that afternoon, he
does that very often, I don't know quite how the Yard
can spare him so much,'—she gazed at him with
deadly fondness, 'he saw her from his car and wondered about it. You must forgive him, Commander,
he's been so confused, with poor Inspector Copper—
that bright young man—in trouble.'

'And did Miss Tilly have an argument with Joss
Parker in a restaurant, on Thursday was it?'

Both the aunts laughed. 'One hardly has arguments
in the Florabel.' Nelly swished her taffeta skirt. 'It's a
very fine, quiet restaurant. Tilly was showing poor
Joss a trick, and some wine spilled, that was all.'

Sedgwick nodded solemnly. 'But there was an argument between Inspector Copper and Miss Parker in
this house, early Friday afternoon?'

The aunts had the grace to look ashamed, and as
the sergeant took their statements, they gave the information reluctantly.

'I don't think that meant anything,' Dolly said
uneasily. She forgot the grandeur. 'He bashed her,
but she took it like a good 'un.'

'Liked him the better for it,' Nelly said, nodding.

Sedgwick didn't reply to that but had them read
the statements and sign. 'By the way,' he said. 'Just to
get things clear, was Miss Tilly in a mental hospital?'

'She was not,' Dolly said indignantly, her flushed
pink face over her white ruff like a ham on a doily.

Nelly remained calm. 'Many years ago, my sister
was involved in a terrible accident, on stage. I daresay
Merlin was telling you about it. She was a very young
girl and it was a bad shock. There was no blame attached to Tilly, the equipment was a new model with
a bad fault, and something broke. The model was removed from the market. Also I must say, though I
hate to speak ill of the dead but it came out at the in-

quest, Barney, her husband, was extremely careless because he was, to put it bluntly, drunk.'

'Bad that,' Dolly sighed. 'Never drink before going on.'

'Poor Tilly was so upset, as any woman would be, she had a nervous breakdown. Living as we did then, Commander, travelling from town to town, we couldn't look after her, and we put her—we and his father—' she nodded to Capricorn, 'in a nice rest home. It was for convalescence, but she liked it and stayed. Travelling round was so hard, we didn't want to put her through that. And there was enough money for her upkeep—rich as Croesus, that side of the family.'

She glared at Capricorn, her gentility slipping a bit, but her words, as Capricorn well knew, striking a sympathetic chord with Sedgwick.

'Of course, once we got this house, and got ourselves settled, we brought Tilly home. You must have seen her on London Saturday Night,' she said to Sedgwick, who was a fan of that variety show, 'as good as she ever was, better really.'

'I wish I had a chance to see you tonight,' Sedgwick smiled, fatuously, Capricorn thought. With many kind words on both sides, Sedgwick and his sergeant were seen off. Capricorn, thinking he would be lucky to escape being sliced in half himself, left at the same time, grimly keeping hold of the shoe, which Nelly had been trying to pry surreptitiously from his hand, and the grey cardigan. Neither Sedgwick nor the sergeant looked at him as they went to their car, but Capricorn heard clearly a sort of stage mutter from Sedgwick about 'Madness in the family.'

He walked to the place where his own car was parked with as much dignity as he could muster, feeling emotionally sore and almost sick. With a little of his usual detachent, he observed that his pain in betraying poor mad Tilly—a betrayal forced upon him by his sense of justice as much as his friendship for Copper—was not lessened now that Sedgwick refused to believe him. Of course, Sedgwick thought his story just a play to gain time, to prevent Copper from being charged. Yet Capricorn and Sedgwick had been colleagues for many years with respect for each other's abilities. Before this, it would have been hard to believe that so much accumulated trust could disappear so quickly. And Capricorn noticed that of all his emotions, by no means the smallest was his humiliation of being diddled by his aunts, a state he remembered so well from his childhood.

Sedgwick, parked the closest, got away first. As soon as his tail lamps disappeared at the corner, Dolly and Nelly appeared as if by magic outside the front door, hooting and doing a kind of victory dance round the dustbins.

It was fortunate then that thoughts couldn't kill. Nelly gave a war whoop and plucking a flower from a neighbour's bush, stuck it in her lapel. In all his misery, her action reminded him of something he had wanted to ask the aunts. He was, he found, a detective first and a human being second. After carefully locking up his evidence in the boot, he walked back to the gate.

The aunts, perhaps fearing violence, withdrew inside and he went after them.

'What d'you want?' Dolly brought to bay in the parlour, turned and faced him.

'I only wanted to ask you something,' he said calmly. 'I'm interested in finding a man called Flowers, Bertrand Flowers, and I thought perhaps you might have heard of him. He was quite a dandy in the West End during the war and shortly after. Had a fancy for little girls. He's dropped out of sight but I want to ask him some questions.'

But he had swallowed his pride and shamed him-

self for nothing. Nelly was silent and sullen but
Dolly, scarlet-faced, her eyes popping, let herself go.

'Turn in your own auntie, would you,' she
screamed. 'After we brought you up and looked after
you, you lousy, rotten little sod. Six foot four of our
grub and drink and you want to put our heads in the
rope,' she was getting confused but that didn't stop
her. 'And then while we're dangling with our necks
broke you want to come and ask us to work for you?
Call yourself a detective?' she was purple now. 'You,
you couldn't find a killer if he kicked you up the arse.
You told these tales, you think Tilly's the only jealous
woman in the world, you're up the pole, that's what
you are, up the pole.'

She looked round frantically, for some object
suitable for throwing. A china shepherdess shattered
at his feet but she wasn't satisfied.

' 'Ere,' she yelled. 'I'll find your Flowers!' She was
screaming at the top of her voice. A vase of artificial
roses came sailing across the room and missed his ear
by an inch. Her eager gaze lit on the pile of telephone books. As she reached down, he beat a hasty
retreat.

'Dolly,' he said, 'don't be silly.'

Dolly, with Nelly in tow, had reached the curtained
arch. He saw Nelly grin as the books started coming.

'You look in there, you wet-arsed detective!' Dolly
roared. 'Be a real Sherlock 'olmes! Look in the phone
book!'

He ducked, but the last volume struck him on the
neck as he fled.

The late sunlight was pleasantly gilding the trees
in Hyde Park as Capricorn sped eastward, facing a
steady stream of oncoming traffic, city workers going
home after the working day, back to the bosom of
their families. Family life, after all, was not such a
bad thing. His anger against Dolly and Nelly had

disappeared as if by magic. Magic, he reflected, was of course the family business.

What a fool he'd been! It was a good rule not to work on a case in which you were personally involved—friendship, family feeling had tossed his emotions and clouded his vision. He had been acting like an audience, mystified by appearances, staring in the wrong direction, until Dolly, bad-tempered, outrageous Dolly had hit upon the truth. He had been actually running away from that yodelling pair, pursued by bits of furniture and books, when the sense of what she had said struck him.

There were still questions to be answered, but Capricorn knew with sudden certainty what had happened to Joss. The gathering of evidence would take time; the proof—he shrugged. Perhaps guilt could be proved, perhaps not. The great puzzle was how the killer had found the strength. An agent might have been employed, but he was sure that hadn't happened. The grudge was too personal. Murder may not have been the plan: the opportunity was probably the temptation, Joss alone, with no one to witness— Capricorn thought of his evidence, locked in the boot, the shoe, the cardigan, and he shivered, though the evening was warm and close. He must talk to Tilly, away from the other aunts, when her head was clear of sedatives—as clear as it ever was—and to her doctor.

A van with a young driver at the wheel cut across Capricorn's path so suddenly that he had to jerk on the hand brake, thankful no one was too close behind. The van sped on, and Capricorn hoped it finished its run without mishap. As he bent down to release the brake, his hand brushed something on the seat beside him—a book. While the driver behind him hooted impatiently, he realized that in his confusion he'd carried off one of his aunts' telephone directories, clutching it with some vague notion of not causing scandal if the neighbours were watching. 'Always worried about the neighbours,' he could hear Dolly's mocking voice in his mind. It was volume E-K. When he sat waiting at the next red light, and had to wait to inch along through two changes, idly he looked up Flowers. There, sitting in the place where it might be expected, was Bertrand J. Flowers, at an address in Dulwich.

With all his worry about Copper, all his grave misgiving about poor mad Tilly, he was seized by a sudden, enormous fit of laughter. The driver who had been honking his horn was still behind him, and took the first opportunity to pass, shouting an uncomplimentary remark. Oh, God, Capricorn thought, whatever Dolly had said about him was true. He considered for a moment. He had to see Flowers, but he couldn't go to Dulwich now; his other business was more urgent. If only he had Copper, or *someone* working with him. He pulled up and made for a row of telephone booths, found an instrument that worked, and while he read the praises of Che Guevara scribbled on the wall, together with detrimental references to Her Majesty's government, and some blunt sexual suggestions from a more traditional artist, he got through to the local men. He explained the situation, and received a promise that they would investigate and hold Flowers if he proved to be the man. They were very willing to cooperate as, they told Capricorn, they had reason to believe that he was. 'The old dog's still up to his old tricks. Too many mothers going to work these days, don't keep such a sharp lookout. No complaints but he's been seen loitering in a suspicious way.'

That settled, Capricorn resumed his journey to Soho. He went first to the street where the Golden Calf stood, and leaving his car, had a good look at the two solid rows of buildings on either side. To the right of the Calf was the Berwick Quick Wash, a

coin-operated laundry filled with busy housewives, to
the left a small dusty grocery with faded lettering, J.
Cristoforo, Importatore. The shop was closed, the
window unlit, but Capricorn could see boxes of spaghetti, green peppers, strings of garlic bulbs and
cheeses hanging from the ceiling. Capricorn looked
upwards. Most of the upper floors along the street
were lived in by the shopkeepers or let. There were
no lights above the grocery, only outlines at the window of boxes and crates. Warehousing, Capricorn
thought. The pattern fit.

Daylight was fading. He took a torch from his car
and went and made himself agreeable to the ladies in
the laundry. They giggled at his request, but they
pointed to a door through the back.

'I hope it's all right,' the manageress said. 'We
don't use it much. I live upstairs and use a private
one.'

Capricorn reassured her and went out to the back.
A strong, high fence ran on the left side down to the
end of the yard. There were no rotten posts, no gaps,
and the top of each post was peaked and sharp. Not
the way an intruder would have chosen. The back
fence was almost unscalable, but Capricorn got a foot
in a loose brick on the outside w.c. and scrambled
over. He hoped the ladies weren't peeking; they
would certainly think him odd.

The yard behind the house on the next street
wasn't as well guarded. He easily got over the fence
into the yard on the left, and was about to go over a
trellis fence into the back of the Calf when he banged
into an old dustbin, filled with refuse that had turned
rank, and brought a curious and disapproving tenant
to a back window.

She would probably call the police, Capricorn
thought, resigned, but he held on to his torch and
went over anyway, and soon was out of sight as he examined the inside of the old w.c. It was whitewashed

and clean, though the bowl was full of rust and the flush no longer worked. It had not been a luxurious facility. The floor was of rough concrete that wouldn't take a footprint easily, unless the shoe were muddy. There were no finger marks on the walls. He flashed his powerful light into every corner. The seat was wooden and had rotted. Little splinters lay along the edge, holding a shred of something dark. Capricorn looked closer and pocketed the bit of dark stuff with sober satisfaction. He believed he knew the dress from which the scrap was torn.

No one was guarding the back of the Calf— Sedgwick's team was finished. Capricorn examined the fence between the Calf and the grocer's shop carefully, in particular the spot where there was a handy gap. Sedgwick's men must have looked it over, but they didn't know what they were looking for. But although he searched every rough edge and splinter by the light of his torch, he had no more luck.

The back door of the grocer's shop was locked. The windows were both locked and barred. He could let himself in easily, of course, but with that indignant woman at the upstairs window probably summoning the local men, it could be embarrassing. He patted his pocket, making sure his handkerchief with the scrap of cloth was still there, and returned to the laundry by the same roundabout route. The ladies giggled again, and Capricorn was glad to bump his way between the carts filled with wash out into the street, where he was at once accosted by an unpleasant, familiar voice.

'Got the old dears all in a flutter, haven't you?'

Len Slope, with his sharp suit, his carefully arranged hair, his pale face and cynical smile, was leaning by the door.

'Out already, are you?' Capricorn said shortly. He knew very well when Slope had been released, but saw no harm in reminding him that his liberty shouldn't be taken for granted.

Slope was not a whit disturbed. 'You're not going to put me away so easy, guv'nor, you know that. My minder's too much for you. You'll never get him, either—unless I give you a little tip, see.'

Capricorn paused.

'Let's go somewhere and have a little talk,' Slope said. 'I've been trying to get you by yourself since they let me out.' He smiled, showing a lot of excellent teeth—the villains could afford the best dentists, Capricorn reflected, wondering what on earth Slope was up to. 'I've got an idea about going legit, guv,' Slope confided. 'Inside isn't for me. I couldn't stand it. Do myself in, I would.'

'Thought you said you were too clever for us,' Capricorn said tersely. He didn't want to talk to Slope now, he had another call to make and he was in a quiet fever of impatience.

'Well, you know what it's like once those bastards in Drug Squad are after you,' Slope said gloomily. 'It's true they could never really do me on the straight, but they'll fit me up, that's what they'll do. So I thought p'raps you and me could make a little arrangement.'

He was very meek and mild.

Capricorn, in a hurry, ignored the slur upon Drug Squad. 'Come to my office tomorrow,' he said, and moved to go.

'Don't be in such a rush, Super.' To Capricorn's annoyance, Slope put an arm out to detail him. 'I didn't meet you here accidental. I've been traipsing around after you since you left the Yard—I know that little bus of yours inside out by now. Good little job—I could hardly keep up with you part of the way back from Paddington. Caught up with you when you went in the phone booth, but I couldn't find a place to park quick enough.'

So Slope had seen him assaulted by his aunts.

Capricorn looked upon Slope's zeal to reform with suspicion and on his person with no favour. 'I'm in a hurry. Tomorrow will do.'

Slope hung on his arm. 'Just a few minutes. My place is right near here. Look, I'll give you a phone number and you call up and see what I'm offering. You've been after it for years. You didn't know I was in with the particular party.'

Capricorn hesitated. Drug Squad had been working for weeks to try to find Slope's 'minder'. And Manning and Special Branch were possibly interested. 'Where is your place? I'll give you half an hour,' he said.

'Just down here.'

They walked to the end of the street and round the corner. A garish sign by an open door proclaimed:

THE BATHS OF POMPEII
Sauna and Massage Emporium

London's Luxury Rooms!
Health Food Bar—Solarium
Fully trained maidens
Visiting service available

Inside, large coloured pictures of nubile maidens in languorous poses adorned the walls.

'It's all right,' Slope said with aplomb. 'It's a straight place.'

Capricorn gave him a look, and they went down the crimson-carpeted stairs to a lounge and reception room. The lights were low, the benches around the wall were deeply upholstered. Pornographic magazines were conveniently placed for anyone awaiting services. On a counter was a case of unpleasantly pallid-looking health foods of a sort usually favoured only by the young. Capricorn pondered for a moment the mores of the younger generation, so oddly reversed from the Victorian: they were libertine about the loins and ascetic in the stomach. Would they produce a subculture of the chaste who lurked in teashops and gourmandized on chocolate eclairs? His attention was soon snapped up by a coffee-maker. The liquid percolating through the machine was dark, strong, fresh and aromatic. He was sharply reminded that he had had no breakfast, and only a bite or two of lunch. He craved coffee above all things, but he kept his mind on his business.

'The booths are up there, three to a side.' Slope might have been an agent, showing off a good let. 'Anyone working?' he inquired of a dusky maiden behind the bar. 'Luna, this is Superintendent Capricorn. This is Luna, Superintendent. She's a highly trained masseuse.' He waved a hand at the wall where framed certificates of some sort were hung.

Luna gave him an appraising look, a wide smile, and shrugged. Amused by charades, no doubt. Capricorn wondered, from her look, if she thought he had come in for services. She showed Slope a list. 'And there's a gentleman in the solarium, waiting,' she explained. 'I didn't want to leave the desk.'

'Run along dear, I'll take care of things.' Slope watched her disappear into a room at the end of the corridor. Capricorn, his mind buzzing with other matters in which the Cristoforo family figure prominently, nevertheless wondered about a solarium in the basement.

'Sunlamps,' Slope explained obligingly. 'Would you like a drink, Super? We don't serve spirits here, but I've got my private stock.'

Capricorn was getting irritated. 'No, thank you. What is all this about a phone call?'

'Are you sure?' Slope poured himself a stiff one, taking the bottle from a locked corner cupboard. 'Here.' He wrote something down on a card from a stack on the bar depicting the club's activities, and handed it to Capricorn, smiling. Capricorn recognized a South London exchange. After Slope had swallowed

a long drink, he nodded to a telephone sitting on a
table by a bench. To reach it, Capricorn had to sit
down and lean back—it was meant for customers in a
reclining mood. If anyone walked in, he would certainly look like a waiting customer, he thought with
irritation, sure that that was why Slope had asked
him to use this instrument, instead of the one conveniently placed on the wall behind the bar. But
when a voice answered, a Cockney female voice,
rather loud and harsh, as though its possessor might
be slightly deaf—'Hullo? Hullo? Mr James isn't home
yet. This is his housekeeper. Can I take a
message?'—his irritation fled.

Capricorn hung up and stared at Slope. It looked
as though Copper were right after all. Slope hadn't
been working for Charlie Bo. But was it really Marcus James, Brixton Jim himself? It didn't seem possible. Could this plum be dropping in his lap at last?
It was unbelievable. Marcus James, who had foxed
the police all his life as his father had most likely before him, could he really have made himself vulnerable to a cheap little grafter like Slope?

Slope watched his reaction with a satisfied smile.
'Surprised? I told you I had something you wanted.
Now, how about it, Super? I can give you enough on
him to put him away until they carry him out in a
box. Gyppo Moggs. Hake.'

'Is Hake dead?' Capricorn asked mechanically, his
mind racing.

'Hake's last job was Gyppo Moggs, and that was
the last of him. From what a little bird told me, you
won't see him again unless he gets washed up at
Southend. To tell you the truth, guv,' he leaned forward towards Capricorn who was still seated, 'that's
one of the reasons I want to get out, see? Makes me
nervous. Just give me a clean bill, that's all I ask. I'd
rather not go to court, it would be very unhealthy,
but I can give you plenty, barring that. Do we talk?'

Capricorn thought of his other business. He had no warrant; he didn't even have Sedgwick with him—he supposed it could wait. 'All right,' he said.

'I'm going to fill up. Are you sure you won't take anything?' Slope was playing the gracious host. Capricorn hesitated. The smell of the coffee was torture.

'A cup of coffee, if I may.'

'Good. Cream?'

'Please.' Capricorn liked it black at this hour, but cream would be nourishing.

'I'll get you some fresh.' The obliging Slope took the cup behind the bar, and leaned down. 'Nice little fridge we have. Always plenty of cream and ice.' Eager to please, he offered sugar, but Capricorn declined. Slope, his drink refilled, sat down next to him.

'Is there anywhere else we can talk?' Capricorn asked, restive.

Slope smiled. 'Only the solarium or the booths. This is better. Don't worry. I'll close the door upstairs. The girls take the customers out the back way—they usually prefer it.'

Capricorn drank some of the coffee while Slope ran upstairs. It was almost as good as it smelled. Capricorn was a great lover of good coffee. A slightly bitter aftertaste, perhaps. That was the trouble with percolators, they were inclined to overbrew. It still seemed incredible that Brixton Jim was delivered into his hands, with so little trouble on his part. Not that such things didn't happen—for all the hard work and efficiency of the CID, most villains were brought to book with the help of informers. But there was a quid pro quo. If the cash paid out for information was small, and it was, favours were supposed to even the balance. Slope was offering the crown jewel of information, in return for Drug Squad's easing up on a charge that hadn't even been brought.

It must be the business of Moggs and Hake. Slope was afraid. That was the only answer that made sense. But how had that cagy old fox been taken in by Slope to let him know so much? From never trusting anyone to trusting him—Capricorn gave a mental shrug. Perhaps it was the same trouble that plagued lawful business. Lack of aspiring young men in the trade. Brixton Jim had had to use the aging Sweeter to set up the Eastland job, after all.

Slope, when he came back and sat down, talking sixteen to the dozen, strengthened this view. 'You see, Super,' he said, 'it's just not worth it nowadays, taking chances. Oh, a bit on the side now and again is one thing, but I don't want to be mixed up in rough stuff. Hake today—it could be me tomorrow. Of course, I'm not a bloody fool like he was, but the old man's had to rely on me, and he might decide I know too bloody much. And what do I need it for?'

He shrugged.

'This place is all mine now. And I've bought a half interest in a pub. I run with a pretty fancy crowd and I know a couple of nice girls. I can marry money if I want.' He smiled, a self-satisfied smile that made Capricorn want to kick him, while he wondered grimly if Slope meant Brenda Grey. She had money of her own, and in time would have full control of it. 'I only have to pop the question.'

Slope's voice droned on and on with his excuses, his requirements and his offer. He not only named names, he gave dates, places and times. Capricorn took notes. His pen raced. It was difficult, in the dim light. Writing was awkward, but the bench was comfortable to sit on, more comfortable than he would have believed. It had been a long day. Pleasant to relax for a moment. With an effort, he pulled himself up. He needed to be alert. The solid information Slope was giving, if it checked out to be true, would put Brixton Jim behind bars for a long time. Capricorn's quest had come to an end, after so many years.

The pen slipped from his hand, and he fumbled

for it among the cushions. He was abominably
drowsy. It would be delightful to put his feet up for a
few minutes, once Slope was finished. Then Capricorn pictured marching Slope off to the Yard. How
amazed the Commander would be. He saw the Commander's face, when at last he admitted that Capricorn had been right. It was a satisfying image.
Capricorn smiled to himself. Slope went on, telling
him more and more, much more than Capricorn
needed, faster than he could write. Incredible really,
Slope should offer so much. Sleepily, Capricorn saw
the Commander's face, Sedgwick's face, blurred together with Dolly's that afternoon. Sedgwick's face
and Dolly's, rather similar.

Capricorn's heavy head leaned backwards and he
saw Slope smiling and setting his drink on the bar.
Dolly had been rude. She had said things about
Capricorn and his father. His father. The thought
was like a tiny drop of cold water in his mind. Slope,
smiling, amazingly voluble. His father. 'There's nothing that's amazing if you look sharp.' With a great effort, he opened a heavy eyelid to watch Slope. Slope
was doing something with the drinks cupboard. The
brass knob gleamed in the light: it was as though the
light danced off and moved forward. Scattered points
came together in Capricorn's mind. Brenda Grey saying, '. . . one of those coins . . . jumped up
. . . the light.'

In his drugged mind, Capricorn knew that he was
drugged, and why. He saw Slope, frowning now, advancing on him syringe in hand, and knew he was to
die as Charlie Bo had died. And now he could not lift
his eyelids, let alone his body. He was going down,
down into sleep, but with an effort that he couldn't
possibly make, from some last, grimly held reserve, he
thrust out one of his long legs and kicked at the advancing Slope, catching him in mid-stride. Startled,
Slope missed his step and fell, the syringe dropping

from his hand. Capricorn could not do more for a moment than throw himself forward over the body of the smaller, lighter man, but the effort cleared his head slightly so that he was able to reach up, find the whisky bottle on the bar and bring it down full force on the head of the struggling Slope.

Slope was, for a moment at least, still. Capricorn blinked his abominably heavy eyelids. A little fat naked man ran rosy and alarmed, from a booth, followed by a handmaiden, somewhat disheveled. She took one look at her employer and ran to the door screaming, 'Police, police!' as Capricorn fell back into his sleep.

ARIA FOR CONTRALTO VOICE

The Metropolitan Police, Capricorn decided later, were still attracting a good calibre of men. The two that answered the maiden's call, when she flagged down their passing Panda car, behaved with admirable calm and dispatch. Entering the house of ill-repute, ready to deal with a drunken client who was assaulting the owner with a broken bottle, they were able, after hearing Capricorn's explanation mumbled with some difficulty, to adjust their ideas and cope with a drugged Chief Superintendent and a dangerous villain.

Slope was given first aid and put under restraint. A bottle of chloral hydrate was found in the refrigerator under the bar. The quantity missing did not seem enough for a poisonous dose. Before the doctor arrived, Capricorn was drinking a fresh brew of black coffee and briskly walking up and down to stay awake. The syringe, and what was left of its contents, were carefully packed up for the lab.

A call was put in for Brixton Jim to be taken into custody. Once he learned that Slope had failed and was facing both a charge of murder and attempted murder, he might well take to his heels. Drug Squad was notified as interested parties and Capricorn himself, still drowsy and having to mouth his words carefully, got hold of Manning. Manning listened quietly and, with his usual economy, merely replied: 'We'll put a watch on the airfields and the ports.'

Slope had a case of violent hysterics and the doctor,
who had been called for Capricorn, had to attend to
him. The doctor gave Slope an injection to quiet him
down, whereupon he went into a crying jag.

'I didn't want to do it, Super,' he sobbed. 'Gawd's
truth. I wouldn't tell you, I was frightened out of my
life. 'E made me do it. Always frightened of him, I
was. I 'ated the bastard and that's the truth, an' all.
But he had me under his thumb, see.'

Sitting on the crimson bench, with his bandaged
head in his hands he looked as harmless as a
hairdresser's assistant and as pathetic as an orphan,
which, he went on to explain, he was. 'Never gave us
nothing when we needed it,' he whined. 'Could've
starved to death for all he cared. Grandpa always
kept us down at Leigh, and Jim let Mum marry a
cloth cap. She died when I was only five,' he said pite-
ously—Capricorn wondered if he was rehearsing a
speech for the jury—'and do you think he bothered to
come to the funeral, her only brother?'

Muddled as his head was, Capricorn started. In all
his investigation of Brixton Jim, he had come across
no mention of any family. It was believed that he was
quite alone. Certainly, his father had married only
once, and his Cypriot wife had borne him one child,
according to the records at Somerset House. Slope's
mother must have been born the wrong side of the
blanket. No wonder Marcus James the elder had kept
this family down on the coast. So Slope was the
nephew of Brixton Jim. That was the reason a master
criminal had given responsibility to an inept weak-
ling: the family tie, plus, perhaps, Slope's Army medical experience. The Army trained apprentices for
many trades. Nepotism had been the Achilles' heel of
a vicious, but perhaps lonely, aging and childless
man.

Slope didn't see it that way; he continued with his
catalogue of grievances. 'Never gave me a helping

hand. Took no notice till I got started on my own account. Then he got his hooks into me. But I didn't mean no 'arm.' He looked round wildly. 'I swear.'

The doctor wanted Capricorn to go immediately to the hospital for tests. Capricorn insisted on giving his statement—no one was going to release Slope while the doctors played detective with Capricorn's body. The terrified clients in the booths, after having their names and addresses taken, were allowed to go. The maidens were kept to make statements, but only Luna, who was Slope's mistress, had been involved and she claimed she knew only part of the scheme. The Chief Superintendent was to have been found in a booth with one of the girls in a compromising position. She swore she knew nothing of the planned murder.

That was probably true, Capricorn told the man from Drugs Squad who had arrived post haste. If the plan *had* worked and Capricorn was supposed to have died from heart failure, Luna would have been more convincing if she had believed it. She was taken in charge and the other maidens were sent home.

Drugs was puzzled by the knockout drops. 'If they went to so much trouble to give something that couldn't be found on post-mortem, why spoil it with chloral? Chloral doesn't dissipate in the blood. Any pathologist would have found it first crack.'

Capricorn rubbed his forehead, trying to clear his drug-dazed brain. 'You're making very free with my post-mortem,' he grumbled. 'Slope's not a doctor; he was only a medical orderly. He might not have known that. Probably made a habit of using the stuff to smooth his rotten little path. Brixton Jim would know, but I'd bet his orders were only for the injection of the succinylcholine chloride.' They both looked at Slope, who was still snivelling. 'I don't suppose,' Capricorn added, 'he was supposed to drug Charlie Bo in the main room of the club, either. He was probably told to get him alone in the men's room, or somewhere. But when Charlie was dumped next to him in the corner, he took his chance. And nearly got away with it. If the Calf had been just a little darker, he would have. As it was, only one witness noticed the glitter of the syringe and she was too drunk to know what she saw.'

Drugs fancied Slope might be a sampler of some of his own provisions. 'Cocaine. It induces that kind of euphoria.' When Slope was taken away, Drugs commended the young constable on his quick recognition of a drugging. 'Time was they would've thought you were drunk,' he said to Capricorn afterwards. 'They recognize it much sooner now. Good work on their part. Bad on ours, I suppose.'

Drugs departed to see about getting a search warrant. The huge James warehouse in Commercial Road was to be searched, as well as his house. The room emptied out; the noise lessened; the concentrated activity subsided. Capricorn felt cross, cranky and had a desire to lie down. He agreed to be driven to the hospital, but not in an ambulance. While a constable went to his car, he looked at the notes he'd made earlier. Most of the writing, except at the end, was legible. He had wondered why Slope was talking so much. It was disquieting to realize it was because he thought he was talking to a corpse.

Once again Capricorn, now on his way to the hospital, traversed the narrow winding streets of Soho, aware of all the familiar night sounds around him. Laughter and talk from customers leaving the pubs; shouts for taxis from audiences pouring out of cinemas. Young people drifted about, in and out of coffee houses, talking in loud, earnest voices. On the street just past the one where the Golden Calf was housed, Capricorn roused himself to look out of the window. A local villain on the prowl caught his gaze and took himself off quickly. A burst of rock music floated by as the door of a discothèque opened and banged shut. But the house he studied, belonging to sober, law-abiding people of the neighbourhood, was as quiet as that of any sleeping suburban family, as quiet as the house of Gyppo Moggs, as quiet as the house of Marcus James.

The doctor at the hospital was of the extreme-caution school. Capricorn might well be all right, in danger of nothing more than a good night's sleep, but 'it was better to be safe than sorry.' Capricorn groaned at this chestnut, and found he was to be both safe and sorry, since the treatments given to him were undignified, unpleasant and extremely uncomfortable. Once he was thoroughly and completely awake, with no desire to sleep left at all, he was put to bed with orders to stay there until morning. Annoyed at having been talked into all these, he was sure, unnecessary precautions, Capricorn got into the hard narrow bed, not really long enough for a man of his size, prepared for a wakeful and wasted few hours. His last thought before he fell asleep was that although it was a good thing that he had at last implicated Brixton Jim, so far nothing had helped to clear Copper. There was a lot of work ahead before Copper could be released: Copper, who was still thought to have killed Joss.

He woke very early, surprised and pleased to see that well-known red head looming over him. 'Going to sleep all day, are you?' Copper said agreeably. It was five A.M. 'They haven't found him yet,' he continued, answering the first question that came to Capricorn's mind. 'Don't worry. There's a call out to watch every airfield—even the two-Cessnas-and-a-cow. He couldn't move in a helicopter. They're turning his place over already.'

'What are you doing out?' Capricorn asked, rubbing his eyes. His mind was quite clear. Copper was looking very smart, he observed. 'Escape, did you?'

'Sedgwick—Ilkley Moor, as our Miss America calls him—let me go. Decided he'd come a cropper with me. Mrs Beeton cooked him up a lovely tale and he turned me loose.'

'Miss America,' Capricorn said suspiciously, sitting up. 'What's he been talking to her about?'

Copper sighed. 'Guv, I'd rather not tell you just now. There's been a bit of a mix-up, but it'll all come out in the wash. Look, that terrifying head nurse says you've got to eat their breakfast. I've seen it and I pity you, is all I can say. What with one thing and another, you'd better have a tranquilizer. Take two.'

A nurse appeared with his breakfast. It looked as advertised. Capricorn had some tea and toast while Copper chaffed the nurse in a fair imitation of his usual manner. Copper's grief for Joss was suggested by the shadows under his eyes and the new lines round his mouth, but he wasn't going to parade it. He remained evasive about Sedgwick's change of heart.

'I'll tell you later,' he said. 'I thought I'd come with you to see Slope.'

'You're still under suspension, aren't you?' Capricorn asked. 'Pending the outcome of investigation?'

Copper explained while Capricorn found his clothes, bathed, shaved and dressed. 'Miss America showed 'em Joss's private set of books. There was the lot Joss kept to show me, with the payments listed to the Eastland on the loan, and another that she'd kept locked in her desk with no payments to the bank. That was the set she'd showed the tax people—she was straight with them,' his voice had a bitter note. 'But whether she intended to pay Charlie back or not, we'll never know. Naturally,' he went on, his tone lightening, 'as Miss America is known not to be much good, she was listened to with a lot more attention than a detective inspector from C1. Quite right, too. Anyway, they found out I was skint which cheered 'em up no end—all honest Englishmen must be broke to the wide. So now the old man thinks I didn't do in my own wife, the mills of God will probably stop grinding, though the paperwork might take another three weeks.'

Capricorn was happy, though still puzzled about whatever it was that Copper was holding back. While he was waiting for the hospital to go through its usual routine before letting a patient escape, he called the Dulwich police to find out how they had progressed with Flowers. The information they gave would have been a bitter blow the night before— Flowers was dead. Now it merely caused him to shrug. He had Slope; that would be enough to get Brixton Jim convicted—once he got his hands on him. Although the case had now broken wide open, that name still filled him with a sense of fury, a cold rage at the man who for so long had sown the corruption whose growth could choke the life of the nation while he remained a sheltered, respected and honoured citizen. The extent of his villainy, Capricorn reflected, was hardly explicable, it seemed to go further than could serve James's purpose. The robbery at the Eastland, even with the ghastly concomitant of Barlow Road, was a piece of ordinary criminal work, but drug-running, hardly profitable in England, was difficult to understand. Well, it would all come out now. James wouldn't get away. He was as finished as Flowers. 'Are you sure his death was natural?' he asked. If it hadn't been for Slope, things would have worked out conveniently for Brixton Jim.

'Oh, yes, no doubt about it,' he was told. 'He died in the hospital here. He'd been ailing for years. The emphysema started in prison and gradually worsened ever since, his doctor said. Anything else we can do for you?'

'No, nothing.' Capricorn thanked them, and put down the receiver, with the picture of Bertrand Flow-

ers of the 40s still in his mind's eye—a debonair handsome man, smiling with a bright flower in his lapel
for show and his dark secret hugged close. A rotten
way to live. A lonely way to die.

Next he tried to get hold of Sedgwick. He had
plenty of time while the hospital searched for some
misplaced record, but Sedgwick had left home and
was not in his office. While they tried to find him,
Capricorn hung on the telephone, crossly conscious
that his clothes were crumpled and his linen was yesterday's. But much as he wanted to go home and
change, there was too much that needed to be done
urgently. He eyed Copper's dapper presence, and inquired if he had been to Wenmore.

'No,' he replied, 'I came straight here. Meg
Hardcastle went down and brought me some stuff.
Said she cleared up a bit, thank God. That char's
only good for finishing up a bottle.'

'Hardcastle?' Capricorn said, wondering.

'Nice little WPC, you must have seen her at the station. She got friendly while I was in there. Nothing
like that, guv,' he noticed Capricorn's expression, 'I
can't look at a woman without seeing Joss. Just a
friend.'

'Any relation to the deputy A.C.?' Capricorn asked.

'Daughter,' Copper answered succinctly and Capricorn shuddered. Well, that wasn't the problem now.
He was released with a clean bill of health at the
same time that the Yard informed him Chief Superintendent Sedgwick was already out working on a case
and could not be reached.

'Now where the devil is he?' Capricorn muttered.
He walked with Copper to his car while Copper tried
to dissuade him from continuing the search. 'Leave
him alone for a bit, can't you? For one thing, you
know what he is for Regs, he'll chuck me out until
the investigation is officially closed. I don't feel like
sitting on my duff in Wenmore until this caper's fin-

ished. Second—well, you'll only get in a lot of fuss. Stay out of it, and it'll clear up by itself.'

The day was already warm, with the unusual, oppressive heat. Even at the hospital the rubbish had not been picked up and stood in odiferous piles. In the car park, a sweeper was leaning on his broom discussing the weather with a colleague. 'They say the poles are melting,' he said gloomily. 'In years to come, all of England will be flooded out.' His companion was thoughtful. 'Might as well go for our tea break now.' They ambled off. A car backed up in front of Capricorn and knocked over a mess of tin cans.

'What is all this?' he said, irritably. 'How the hell did you get out and what's going on?'

He would go ahead without Sedgwick and without the warrant, he decided recklessly. He was in good standing at the moment, having been proved right about Brixton Jim. It was worth the chance.

'You were better off not knowing,' Copper said, staring through the windshield at the streets already burdened with early morning traffic. 'You won't find Sedgwick anyway—unless they've got him locked up. I wouldn't put it past them.' He was grinning faintly. Copper was resilient, Capricorn observed. Whatever his inner turmoil might be, no one would guess looking at him now that only yesterday he had been imprisoned on a charge of murdering his wife.

'Past who?'

'If you must know,' Copper told him, 'Sedgwick let me go, because after he left you yesterday, he hauled in Miss America to check on your story, although he thought you were nuts. He didn't put it that way to me, you understand, but I got the idea.'

Capricorn could well believe it, but what was coming?

'He's quite a fan of the old girls, and he had a picture of them from La Belle magazine. He blotted out the other two and just left Tilly, and Miss America identified her as the woman she'd seen go into the Calf. So while you were getting yourself all sorts of attentions in The Pompeian Rooms—lovely girl that Luna, I know her well—Sedgwick had auntie picked up and brought in, after the girls finished their turn at the Palladrome. I understand,' he said, with a straight face, 'that Nelly and Dolly were a bit vexed.'

Capricorn shuddered.

'You might well feel the draught,' Copper went on. 'They assaulted the officers, incited the audience, which was just coming out, to riot, there was a scrimmage and I hear they've got practically half the Bar battering the walls down at the Yard. It was all on the late news, and I expect there's quite a bit about it in the morning papers—haven't seen 'em yet. Sedgwick is now convinced that Tilly did it, silly old—You're going the wrong way,' he said.

Capricorn thought of the sniggers and titters he was going to have to put up with from his colleagues and juniors. It was bad enough they would learn he was found drugged in a brothel—such things got about with the swiftness of drum signals. Even if he achieved his long-held ambition to catch Brixton Jim and put him away, he still might have to leave the Force. It was too much. 'No,' he said, 'Slope can wait a bit. I've another call to make. You can come if you wish. By the way, you're not grateful to Sedgwick. You don't agree with his deduction.'

'Tilly kill Joss? Ah, don't be daft. She wouldn't do that. I don't know what she was doing there, but she wouldn't kill anyone. You don't know women, guv,' Copper was grimly amused. 'Tilly's a hairpuller, a hatpin-sticker, not a killer.'

'There was that business with her husband,' Capricorn said slowly.

'So I've heard, often enough,' Copper said. 'But I'd lay you ten to one that between 'em they buggered it up, that's all. She might have been excited and not careful, and the trick didn't work right, and that was that. You didn't investigate it, you were just a kid then and frightened, and the others probably got you all worked up. I know a bad one when I see one, and old Till isn't it. Can't we get to Slope first, guv,' he said in a fit of impatience, as Capricorn tried first one congested street and then another in an effort to get to his destination. Lorries delivering loads blocked most of the narrow ways, and stanchions placed by a road-mending gang barred yet another to through traffic. 'I've got to go to Tring this afternoon. It's my day for Greywillow. And I want to get it out of that bastard about Joss.' His face was set and hard.

Capricorn looked at him, his mind balancing a confusion of thoughts. 'You believe it was Slope,' he said.

Copper stared.

'It wasn't,' Capricorn said soberly. 'Only indirectly, perhaps. We're going there.' He nodded to the house he had looked at the night before on the way to the hospital, not far from the place where the patrolling constable had referred to 'Flash Copper'.

Copper gave him a look of puzzlement, worry and something close to dread. He jumped out of the car and, seeing nothing much wrong with the road surface, swept up the yellow stanchions barring the way, let Capricorn through and replaced them. The shades in the house were up, the curtains parted. A respectable household, that kept respectable hours. Capricorn knocked at the door and asked for Mrs Bonomi. Giving the maid his card, he explained he had news. He had come none too soon. Already a trunk with a ship's label stood in the hall. Mrs Bonomi planned to sail home on the *Queen Victoria,* it seemed.

Sounds came from the dining room on the first floor. The family were still at breakfast, but the policemen were shown up to the same room that he and Sedgwick had been in on Capricorn's last visit. Mrs

Bonomi sat in the same chair, in the same spot, in a dress looking very much like the one she had worn then, of heavy black silk, but trimmed with lace instead of velvet bands.

'Good morning, gentlemen,' she said, in her very distinctive voice, unusually deep for a woman's, and rose to greet them, if not with ease, without too much difficulty. The lameness in her right hip, although it made her step halting, did not incapacitate her. She used her stick, the ebony stick with the gem-encrusted gold head. Again Capricorn noticed the swell of her upper-arm muscle under the sleeve as she rose. She laid the stick aside to shake hands with him. Capricorn met her firm bony grasp with reluctance, observing at the same time the practiced ease with which she leaned against a small table and distributed her weight until she was as well balanced as a woman with two good legs.

'I've come to tell you that you were right: Your husband was murdered, and the killer has been discovered and arrested. If you stay with us a while longer, you could attend the trial.'

Her eyes gleamed. 'You have arrested the woman's lover?' she said eagerly.

Of course, she had never seen Copper.

'Perhaps I should introduce Inspector Copper,' he said. 'The husband of the late Joss Copper, the owner of the Golden Calf.'

Teresa Bonomi didn't move a muscle, but her face went grey. Her dark eyes glinted with hatred at Copper, who looked from her to Capricorn, mystified.

'Your husband was killed by a man named Leonard Slope. Slope was the agent of a man who was your husband's—business rival, shall we say.'

For a moment he thought he saw something flicker behind her steady gaze, but it vanished before he was sure.

'You mean,' she said scornfully, 'you have decided

to cover up for the *gornod*'—Capricorn hoped that Copper didn't understand the word. 'You pretend it was done by some criminal you wish to get rid of and you save your own man.'

Copper's jaw was rigid, but he was well controlled.

'I notice you don't mention Mrs Copper,' Capricorn said. 'You accused her, the last time I was here.'

'Certainly, I accuse,' Teresa Bonomi said coldly. 'But I know the woman is dead. Killed, they say, by this man. I am surprised he is not arrested. The police in England are supposed to be honest. But it seems that police are the same the world over. Perhaps he gave you some of the money his woman got from my husband.' She muttered something that Capricorn didn't catch. It was probably just as well.

'We know that Inspector Copper didn't kill his wife,' he said calmly. 'We have a witness to the murder.'

'You lie,' she responded. Her scorn and anger were real. She was very sure that what she said was so, and that Capricorn must be lying. Her certainty shook him for a moment. He thought of his only piece of evidence. If he searched her trunk, would he find the dress from which the black silk had been torn, or had she sensibly got rid of it? As for his witness, even if she made the identification, she could be discredited on the stand. He needed more. Carefully, he watched Teresa Bonomi, observing how she had stood without difficulty and without her stick, wondering how much of her invalidism was a pose. Her face certainly had the marks of pain, the lines and sallowness of constant ill health.

'I believe you've made a dreadful mistake,' Capricorn said. The severity of his tone was mitigated by something close to compassion. 'Mrs Bonomi, where were you between six and seven on Friday night?'

'Where would I be? I was here. I didn't come to England as a tourist,' she said sarcastically. 'I came to

take my husband's body home. The arrangements are
made. I sail at ten o'clock tonight on the *Victoria*.'

'Was anyone here with you?'

'Naturally. My husband's cousin and his wife. Mr
Moletta came some time in the evening—I am not
certain of the hour. I think before dinner.'

Moletta had said nothing about that, but then,
even if it were true, he would have kept a discreet
silence. He could have come to the house after he left
Copper and before arriving at Dominetto's.

'And what time was dinner?'

'My husband's cousin is a man of routine. We have
dinner at seven each night.'

Two relatives and Moletta. Three biased witnesses.
He might be able to shake their stories, but they
might not even be aware of the truth. If Moletta had
left her as late as six-fifteen, and the others hadn't
seen her until seven, she would have had time
enough. Even a lame woman could walk from here to
the Calf in ten minutes. Moletta's call placed the
murderer there at half past six. Pete Moletta was
likely to be one very embarrassed villain.

'And an excellent dinner, I'm sure it is,' Capricorn
said pleasantly. 'Mr Cristoforo imports special food-
stuffs, doesn't he?'

'He does,' Mrs Bonomi said impatiently. 'Gentlemen, if you have come to discuss pasta you must excuse me. It is time for me to attend to my packing.'

'And Mr Cristoforo has shops of his own,' Capricorn went on. 'For instance, in the building next to
the Golden Calf.'

She was almost as poker-faced as the CID, Capricorn thought, but now there was a wary look about
the eyes. He felt, rather than saw, Copper stiffening
like a dog that catches the scent.

'My husband's cousin has many shops and—what do
you call them, warehouses. He is still here if you wish
to make inquiry, in the dining room.'

'I am sure that while you were here, even if you did not see the sights, your husband's cousin showed you his shop and warehouse in the next street,' Capricorn said. 'A very natural thing to do. A neighbourhood shop that stays open quite late for the local housewives who need something just before dinner. No one would notice one particular woman going in, or notice that she didn't leave with the other shoppers when the lights went out. Even the man behind the counter, at his busiest time, might not notice that someone had not gone but had slipped into the back room, out of the door, through the rotten fence into the back yard of the Calf, and through the rear door into the kitchen.'

'You accuse me?' She laughed in his face. 'You think I, a cripple, killed that big whore like a horse?'

Casually, Capricorn put a hand on Copper's shoulder, but Copper was oddly still. Capricorn realized with a strange pity that Copper, for all his own jeopardy, was sickened by the truth. He was a man tender to women, and this crime he now understood too well.

'She was surprised,' Capricorn said quietly. 'She had been working and thought you were a helper, come to work in the kitchen. She saw a lame older woman and was hardly on her guard. She probably looked for her bag to give you money to go away,' he said, remembering Miss America's account of Joss's proclivities. 'She stood next to you by the bar at first with nothing but charity in her mind. She was not prepared for the cripple to turn into a criminal, the older woman into a madly jealous wife, the cane into a weapon.'

The only thing that stung, he saw, was the phrase 'a madly jealous wife.' Two small spots of red blotched her sallow cheeks.

'You are mad,' she said, with seemingly little interest. 'In your desire to save your—confederate, you make yourself ridiculous. To pretend I could have the strength, I, who can hardly stand—'

'You have learned to stand quite well,' Capricorn said. 'And with surprise you need very little strength.'

'This is just talk.' She turned away, picking up her stick and making for the door. 'Idle nonsense. If you had any witness you would not keep me here a quarter hour with fairy tales. I am going about my business. It is time for you to leave—or do I have to call the American consul to protect me?'

'Telephone your consul by all means,' Capricorn said, 'although you say this is nonsense. Perhaps you are confident because you have destroyed the dress, the one that might have bloodstains, the one you tore when you hid in the yard, after you heard Inspector Copper approaching.'

He took the piece of black silk from his pocket, but she refused even to glance at it.

'You waited there, didn't you,' he went on, 'until he had gone inside, before you made your way back through the shop.'

'Get out,' she said contemptuously, 'I have no more time for you.'

She leaned on her stick, her hand covering its jewelled top. Between her fingers, the emerald caught the light. The stick was a fine object, old and perhaps irreplaceable. He nodded to Copper who was quick, if puzzled, and caught Mrs Bonomi by the upper arms. Capricorn took the stick. He turned the handle but nothing happened. He tried turning the handle clockwise, but there was still no loosening, no movement of any kind. Could he have been wrong? The idea made him feel almost sick. If he was wrong, he'd made a terrible botch of things, and what was worse, he realized belatedly, implicated Copper who was just getting out of trouble. Perhaps the mechanism, not used too often, had jammed. He pulled as hard as he could, and he was a strong man, but stick and handle remained obdurately in one solid piece, an innocent crutch for an old lady.

Pausing, he looked up. Teresa Bonomi was watching him and he saw the muscles round her mouth relax slightly. He took a breath, loosened his grasp and reminded himself that he had been a magician. His fingers remembered without direction. With the tenderness of a mother caressing a newborn baby, they slid up and down the fluting, probing for a hidden spring, a concealed catch—nothing. He pressed and twisted, he felt the tip, but nothing moved even with his expert probings.

He was sweating. If it hadn't been for that slight relaxation of Teresa Bonomi's mouth, he would have felt certain now that he was wrong. A childish, entertainer's notion. If it had been a weapon, certainly she would have destroyed it. Yet it was a beautiful stick, and valuable with its many jewels. His fingers caught the idea before his mind. They pressed and turned each of the larger stones as he slowly twisted the base of the stick. All were firmly set by a master craftsman, and immovable, until his finger lightly tapped the glittering emerald. It did not turn, but as he twisted the base, it sank almost imperceptibly. His searching fingers then turned it in a clockwise movement. The tip of the stick moved counterclockwise in his other hand, smoothly and easily as if it had been turned that way not too long before. The eyes of the woman in front of him widened. It had been such a little vanity. A lovely thing in its way, a consolation for her lameness, perhaps a gift from someone dear. The bottom of the stick slid away, revealing seven inches of sharp steel blade.

'You might have more time for us, Mrs Bonomi, than you think.'

MARCH FOR A
TUMBLING CLOWN

The person most deeply affected by the arrest of Teresa Bonomi for the murder of Joss Parker was Copper himself. The prisoner remained calm, even scornful; it was the detective who was close to breakdown.

'You see, guv,' he said, 'even when I found Joss's body, even in the jug, I always thought in the end I'd get the bastard who did it, maybe Moletta, maybe Slope. It was something to look forward to, to put right. And now—nothing.'

'We've got the killer.' Capricorn tried to comfort the bereaved husband. He himself still would like to know who told Teresa Bonomi about her husband's dealings with Joss. Slope, he felt almost certain, on Brixton Jim's instigation, but Mrs Bonomi would never tell him, and Slope wasn't likely to implicate himself in one more murder. 'Tilly gave a surprisingly good identification. The lab will almost certainly find some blood on that dagger: she won't get away with it.'

This was no consolation to Copper.

'The old girl,' he shrugged. 'I dunno. She thought Joss and me did in her old man and we were getting away with it. She was putting things right.' He sighed deeply. 'You know, Joss was a mug. She could've taken care of that crippled old girl, with one hand— she's given me a few shoves that nearly knocked me over. She knew she'd taken the old woman's husband, her money, and that Charlie had died at a time very handy for herself. So when she realized who it was had come into the place, what did she do? Run? Try and say she was sorry? Not her. She argued about the money. Miss America heard them at it. Joss would've given a char she didn't need money to go away, but she argues with Teresa Bonomi.'

Capricorn pited him. There was no catharsis in the discovery of the truth, only more bitterness. Joss, he reflected, for all her flirting with criminality, had been at bottom a very ordinary English girl, and that had been her tragedy. Whatever she had said and done, she had always lived in an orderly tradition. She had believed that crime would help her get to the top of her tree; she had not imagined that the solid ground of lawful behaviour could suddenly slide out from under her feet. She had fancied she was something she was not, and she had met death at the hands of the real thing.

Copper didn't even had the pleasure of taking Moletta in as an accomplice. Investigation quickly showed what Capricorn had surmised was true: when Mrs Bonomi had hinted about revenge, Moletta had done his best to dissuade her, and thought he had succeeded. Revenge would cause a fuss, and fuss was bad for business. But Teresa had been born in Sicily, in an older school, and revenge for her meant more than business, more than freedom, more perhaps than life itself.

Unlucky Copper could not even have the drug of work. The Metropolitan Police has its own bureaucracy, and until the investigation officially wound down, he could not be reinstated. But before Copper left for Greywillow, Capricorn asked whom he was visiting, and the whole story came out at last, the elder Mrs Copper's illness and the money troubles it had brought. Capricorn, unhappy for the sake of Mrs Copper whom he had known and liked, nevertheless now understood things that had puzzled him before.

'You bloody fool,' he said, 'why didn't you tell me instead of—' He didn't complete the sentence, but Copper understood and shrugged. Capricorn knew why, without an answer. Cockney pride, a strange, tough plant. Rather than ask a friend for money, Copper had tried to carry that appalling burden alone. Well, he would have to accept help now. There would be very little until the estate was settled, and heaven only knew what would happen then. Inspector Copper couldn't run the Golden Calf, or own it either. In the meantime, Capricorn was sorry to see him go. He could have used Copper's help because he was taking charge of the search for Brixton Jim.

Capricorn's hopes of finding him were high. He believed Brixton Jim to be too cautious to try to leave the country in the first enthusiasm of the hue and cry. From all he knew of the man, it was much more likely he would go to ground for a while. A cordon had been thrown around the British Isles, and reports came in constantly. As Brixton Jim was of average height and build, of healthy middle age, had unexceptional features, and was driving one of the most common makes of car, he was of course seen everywhere from the Hebrides to Penzance. All reports were checked and sifted, but Capricorn's best hope of information was from someone with personal knowledge of the man and his habits.

His life divided neatly into two layers, contiguous and distinct as two geological strata. Marcus James, warehouseman, city businessmen, had a wide acquaintance but no close friends. To his neighbours in South London he was known as the son of Marcus James who had married a foreign woman and been left a widower with a son. He was a good householder, a reasonably assiduous gardener, but he neither visited nor entertained, was not a church-goer, and did not take part in any local activities. It seemed unlikely that anyone who knew Marcus James would offer him shelter from the police and prosecution.

There remained Brixton Jim. All his known criminal acquaintances, named by Slope, were questioned patiently with surprisingly little result. The men taken in charge would have been glad enough to give evidence to save their own skins, but they knew less about him than the police. Slope and the dead Sweeter had been the go-betweens. Slope was questioned, to the point of weariness on the part of the questioners and near-hysterics on the part of Slope, and it was obvious he had no idea where Brixton Jim might have fled.

'I don't know nothing,' he had said, turning surly. 'Only told me what he wanted. Never asked me to a meal in his house, not even a drink or a cup of tea.'

The social slight had weighed heavily on Slope. Capricorn believed he would have betrayed his uncle's whereabouts if he could. Detectives burrowed in the underworld, each talking to his own snout. Villains all round the country found their premises 'turned over,' to their great indignation, but without result.

In the meantime, other matters went forward at the Yard in the usual way. Sedgwick stopped in Capricorn's office to talk about the Bonomi case. Fortunately, he was no longer angry at Capricorn's interference, he was too relieved at getting rid of the Merlino aunts. Tilly's being taken into custody had become a *cause célèbre*. Now that her status had changed from suspect to chief witness, Dolly and Nelly were happy and had withdrawn all charges against the police. Tilly seemed to be enjoying the proceedings vastly. Enough blood had been found on her shoe and on Teresa Bonomi's dagger to be typed as human, and under the Nobel process as female and of Joss's type. While Sedgwick talked about the use of the fluorescent microscope, ultraviolet light and special dyes, about XX chromosomes, the different evaluations of the Nobel process made by experts and the possible effects on the jury, Capricorn's mind went for a moment to the problem of Tilly. When he had time, he thought, he must talk to her doctor. But he forgot her medical problems when he got a final report that no contraband or sign of wrongdoing of any kind had been found in James's home or warehouse. The Mersey properties and those at Harwich turned out to be equally innocent. The container traffic at Tilbury had also been searched, causing much disruption and delay to the annoyance of shippers and port officials, but all to no purpose. Even the police of Bremerhaven were alerted, and were extremely cooperative, but they had no more luck than their English counterparts.

The Commander, however, was cheerful. 'We'll get him,' he said, 'and with Slope testifying we can put him away.' His ill-temper with Capricorn had quite gone with the prospect of this prestigious arrest. Slope's volubility had caused a sizable proportion of London's top criminals to be brought in. 'It's like going through Method Index and ticking them off,' he said with great satisfaction. He actually whistled— Capricorn hadn't heard him do that for a long time. The old man was relieved, he thought. Copper was going to be given a clean sheet by the investigating officer. 'Though there are things that will have to be talked about,' the Commander added thoughtfully.

Like thirty thousand pounds of ill-gotten gains, Capricorn considered briefly, before he was called away to check on a report of a middle-aged man at Southampton who was attempting to get his hair dyed. He proved to be an actor, but obtaining the proof wasted a lot of time. Sedgwick drifted in and out, rather worried by what he considered to be unnatural calm on the part of Teresa Bonomi.

Capricorn couldn't tear himself away from his command post, and just caught a few hours' sleep as he could at the Yard. But he might as well have gone home for all the progress he made. Not one useful lead came through. Day followed day, and Capricorn's hopes flagged. It seemed to him that something was wrong. Perhaps he had been mistaken and Brixton Jim, already possessed of a false passport, had gone to the nearest airport and got away before the net was tightened. His arrangements were certainly efficient. He had learned of Slope's arrest and vanished before the CID could get to his house—in not much more than thirty minutes. He could have taken a helicopter and gone to a waiting 'plane at a small, private airfield before the local men had responded to the general alarm. Capricorn couldn't think of any other reason why not one snout in the country had got wind of his whereabouts. There was always information, even if too little and too late, but about Brixton Jim there was only silence, a silence so complete it must be based on real ignorance. Interpol had been alerted but so far, at least, had no information to give.

Capricorn stood in his office, weary and puzzled, staring out of the sealed glass at a London still in the torpor of the unseasonable heat. It couldn't last much longer, part of his mind noted. A good storm to clear the air, and the country would slip gratefully into the accustomed cool of autumn. But most of his attention was on the search. He had conducted many searches, and he had a feeling for them. And though anyone could say with reason that a few days meant nothing; villains were caught after weeks, months and sometimes years, his feeling grew that James would give him the slip. Everything possible was being done, yet Capricorn felt somehow he wasn't searching in the right places.

Apart from the scale of James's activities, Capricorn tried to think what was different about James that made him fail to follow any of the usual patterns. He had not tried to find refuge in the underworld. As far as the police knew, he had not tried any of the smaller hotels or lodging houses where he might have expected to go unnoticed. Capricorn paced the room, trying to think himself into Brixton Jim's skin. Although he seemed a city man like any other, he was really of a particular breed. His family had come from the river and the docks. Despite the careful watch Capricorn had arranged at the airports, the railway stations and on the roads, his mind kept returning to the ships.

It was the Port of London that the James family had dealt with longest, and the Port of London had been Capricorn's first object of scrutiny. Thames Division and the Port police had been provided with a photograph of Brixton Jim—not too clear, Capricorn thought but the only one available. A picture taken with a group at a Lord Mayor's banquet was singularly unhelpful on a criminal hunt. Every shipping line that the James warehouse had ever dealt with had been visited and investigated, their employees questioned, their ships gone over by the Port police before departure. It had not been difficult. The great days, when over a hundred different lines had used the Port on a regular basis, and a warehouse like James's could have stored cargo from almost any one of them at some time or another, were gone. The dockers had resisted containerization; the Port was in decline. Not many man hours had been needed for the search. Tilbury, down river, with its passenger traffic and brisk container trade, was more time-consuming but the efforts there were fruitless, too.

There was no reason to think that James would take the slow way out of the country—it was just an idea, a persistent idea. As far as he was able, Capricorn had, with the help of local men, put a watch on canals and waterways, only to be landed with inno-

cent souls like the American tourist who was hauled
off a sightseeing barge at Camden carrying a bag of
bric-a-brac he had just bought from a stall in the
market. Then there had been a tip about a mysterious man, identical to the one in the photograph, trying to board a private pleasure boat at St. Catherine's
Dock. But he turned out to be merely a visiting German who had wandered off from a new hotel while
his room was being made ready: tired of the company
of his fellows in the lounge huddled deep amid the
flight bags, he had tried to arrange an airing for himself on the river. Brixton Jim, middle-aged, spare of
figure and slightly balding, might have been a standard model, Capricorn thought bitterly. There seemed
to be thousands like him wandering around the
streets, a dozen a day leaving the country, all taking
up the time and energy of the searchers, and all for
nothing.

Well, not quite nothing. A few odd villains that the
Yard wanted had been picked up, among them the
suspected cheese salesman from Zurich, who had been
taken off a boat at Tilbury. The little Switzer, it
seemed, had sharp eyes, and in return for accommoda-
tion on his currency dealings was quite willing to give
information against Slope in the murder of Charlie
Bo. Capricorn felt the Yard didn't need to make a
deal, but that wasn't his worry at the moment.
Higher-ups would decide in any case. One more bit of
unpleasantness came from that arrest. Although the
Switzer was as discreet as he could be, Treasury officials, poring through his minuscule notations and
matching them up with figures they had collected in
their own investigations, believed they had found a
connection not merely with underworld figures but
with Gorton Finance and the Annerly Trust, both of
whom they had been watching for some time.

Capricorn found that news uncommonly de-
pressing. Withers of Gorton Finance might have been

278 PAULINE GLEN WINSLOW

involved in currency smuggling on his own behalf; Mayhew of the Annerly Trust most definitely would not. He was a man of the very highest integrity, undoubtedly trying to protect his widows and orphans. He wasn't the only person in the country who had come to believe that financial instruments based on the pound sterling had too much measure of risk. Capricorn remembered Joss and her complaints and wondered what was happening to the country when the best men were driven to look on the wrong side of the law.

Fortunately, at this juncture he had a piece of unexpectedly good news in a telephone call from Manning, who would have been jubilant if he ever allowed himself to be. Capricorn had almost forgotten that Manning was interested in the case, but he was quickly filled with joy by Manning's story.

Days before, Manning had accompanied the team who had searched the warehouse in Commercial Road. Manning—'never a one to dirty my hands if I don't have to'—had left the team to their labours, and turned his attention to the local pubs and eating houses, where, posing as a lorry driver, he quickly became hail fellow well met with the drivers from the James warehouse. So much for procedure, Capricorn thought with resignation, because all the drivers had been questioned meticulously, and sworn statements had been taken which seemed to prove the James business, management and employees, had a standard of probity that could serve as an example to the Boy Scouts.

To Manning, under the warming influence of a few beers with whisky on the side, the usual stories of pilferage were soon told. 'Amazing really,' he commented to Capricorn, 'when you think of the efforts of the Port police, let alone our own men. Practically impossible, but they manage, the bastards. Gives you hope for human nature.'

He sounded as though he was grinning as he spoke. Capricorn waited patiently, in the knowledge that Manning wouldn't take his time for the sake of a few goods stolen between port and warehouse. 'I'll tell you one thing though, they never suspected their old man, and they're a suspicious lot. A bit tightfisted, they said, and as hard a governor as anyone can be now with the unions, but they thought he was straight. I was ready to give up last night. Then I had to buy a few drinks for one of my new pals. Just came back from a funeral, he was a pallbearer and got in a heavy sweat. Bad thing that, it goes to the chest. One funeral leads to another, like weddings. Took three doubles to restore him to health. You know, I don't get paid nearly enough for this work,' Manning interjected sadly. 'My friend had buried his brother, a former seaman, who had been living for the last few years in a sailors' home on the Isle of Dogs. Not a bad place, my friend told me, all things considered. He'd been going to see his brother there regularly when he was off work and he was going to miss those visits now. Not a bad place at all, his brother had liked being close by the river and the docks. "It was near that other place at the old man's," he said. "What other place?" I asked, never having heard of James's owning another warehouse, not since the war. "Oh, the one by the West India Docks," he said. "I don't know if James's own it, but they have some carry-on because once or twice, when I went there on the late side I seen one of our lorries parked by the loading platform."

'You wouldn't think,' Manning said meditatively, 'that they would know one of those lorries from another. No name on 'em, and he hadn't even noticed the license plate. Could've been changed, come to that. But it's all one, for those boys know their lorries the way a mother knows her own pram. So I went down with a few mother's helpers and a search warrant and we found all sorts of jolly stuff tucked away in pallets that had just come in. Drug Squad can hardly believe it,' he said. 'You don't see heroin of that grade often. But that wasn't all. Your friend had been doing a bit of gold-running, too. A bit short after you nabbed his haul from the Eastland, no doubt. Shame the trouble the boys have to take since the airports got nosy, isn't it?'

'Bullion?' Capricorn asked, puzzled.

'Believe it or not, those little ten-tola bars. The ones they're so fond of in the East. Funny how often it goes together.'

Capricorn thought about it as he congratulated Manning on his success. Gold and drugs—they had gone together in the East, in all countries where the local currency wasn't trusted, where distributors and pushers liked to be paid in gold. Was the pound sterling now becoming like the currency of a banana republic? Capricorn's mouth turned down gloomily.

The master and crew of the ship that had been unloaded were taken in for questioning, as were the river pilot, the dockers, the warehousemen. Officials of the steamship line were brought in, but after days of exhaustive investigation nothing useful was learned. The line had a good reputation, and not a breath of suspicion had been heard about her officers. The Captain was well known to the Port of London Authority and they believed him, and probably most of his crew, to be innocent.

'It's not unknown,' the Port police told Capricorn. 'As far as the Captain is concerned, he loaded a straight cargo. The stuff is slipped in with the connivance of the dock gangs—and *they* often don't know what it is.'

The mixed cargo, mostly fruit, potatoes and sherry, taken on at different ports, was bound for different merchants, who had to be investigated also. The warehouse used by Brixton Jim belonged to a company of good reputation, and the only arrest made was of a night manager who had been one of Brixton Jim's men. Slope had known nothing of him, and Capricorn became depressed again. Not surprising they had failed in the nationwide search: there was too much about the fugitive still unknown. Not merely seller of drugs but an importer; an international dealer in drugs and gold. No wonder he had killed Charlie Bo. James might have had his own connection with the Organization, that cartel of crime, but whether he did or not, he would have viewed a semi-freelance Cosa Nostra operator on his territory without joy.

After this excitement, the routine of the search went on. James's car was found, abandoned in a parking garage in North London. The license plate had been changed to cause confusion, but it was identified by James's fingerprints inside. He didn't know about that set on file. It was the only satisfaction Capricorn had in days. The arrested warehouseman turned out to be a man only recently corrupted. It had happened around Christmas, as those things often do. He had been bribed to turn a blind eye to some small pilferage, almost, it was put to him, in the spirit of the season. Once he had fallen into that trap, of course, he was finished. He had to go on doing as he was told, or face the threat of exposure. To Capricorn's disgust, the go-between had been the departed Sweeter.

Despite the arrests, the life of the underworld went on. More crimes were committed daily, and the police were needed to deal with them. The search continued but of necessity the amount of action had to be curtailed. Even Capricorn was beginning to long for a good meal and a decent night's sleep. The young people who had sat near Charlie Bo in the Golden Calf on the night of his death, including Brenda Grey, came in but Capricorn, swamped with work, had somebody else take their statements. The windows of his glass cage suggested confinement, not illumination. He had never liked administrative labour and, he thought broodingly, the only break in the case had come from Manning working alone.

Piles of reports sat on his desk still to be checked, the telephone messages, all the evidence of activity which he suspected was useless. He had thought that Brixton Jim's life was like two geological strata: the green and fertile topsoil representing the businessman, the sand below the criminal. Now he suspected there was a third stratum, previously unknown, that the private, solitary James had sunk back to with the greatest ease.

The son of The Great Capricornus looked about him at the heaps of papers, and felt like part of the audience at a magic show, puzzled by one flourish after another, while, before eyes too distracted to see, the real business was going forward in routine fashion. He thought about it while he smoked a cigar, in defiance of his resolution, the first since his night with Manning. It was time, he told himself, to stop being an audience and to do something.

He went to wash his face with cold water. Looking in the glass above the basin, he noticed himself for the first time in many days. He was pale, his eyes were red-rimmed, his hair awry. Dispassionately, he thought that the man he saw was a mess.

After arranging for a fresh, clear-eyed Inspector to take his place at the telephone, he got his car and, like a dog looking for a scent as he put it to himself, drove to Brixton. No more precise reason could be given for his journey; the house had been well and truly searched and it had contained nothing that did not properly belong to Marcus James, honest warehouseman.

It was a very ordinary house, such as might be seen on almost any London street, a rather gloomy Victorian building, detached from the neighbours but not imposing. The garden behind was well tended. Capricorn made himself known to the men watching the house and went inside.

The interior, like the exterior, was surprising only in that it was so ordinary. Nothing to indicate the wealth or status of its owner. His legal, acknowledged wealth would have justified a much larger expenditure than these surroundings implied. The wallpaper was clean but dull, either flowered or striped. There was polished linoleum, a rug in the living room, mass-produced and well-worn, furniture that would have been usual enough in the home of a minor clerk about fifty years ago: one or two old pieces, and some machine-made reproductions. The interior had neither beauty nor comfort, but there was an air of respectability.

Capricorn roamed about, alert as a cat in unaccustomed surroundings. The file he had so carefully built up on Brixton Jim over the years seemed to be of no use now. What did he know of the man, besides his City dealings, his acting as a financier and planner of major crimes?

The near-austerity of this place was reminiscent of the monk-like Manning's quarters, but what god did Brixton Jim serve?

Photographs on the chimneypiece dominated the living room: obviously, the family group. To the left, Marcus James the elder, resembling his son but with the stern look of a Victorian pater-familias. In the centre, the boy, at about six or seven, very solemn, his hair parted down the middle of his crown with ruler-like precision. He was carefully posed with the right ankle on the left knee and formally dressed in a dark coat and trousers, knee-length socks and a stiff collar that seemed to cut his neck. To the right, in a more elaborate frame, a stout woman of about thirty, comely but not overly attractive: the Cypriot mother.

There was no photograph of any sister. If Slope's mother had really been a bastard daughter of the house, there was nothing to show it here. 'Kept us down at Leigh,' Slope had said. That must have been the last of the James's coast properties, sold when Slope had gone into the Army.

If it weren't for Slope, Capricorn thought, this house might have convinced him that he had made an absurd mistake. The house could have belonged to a family whose highest ambition was to join the local tennis club. The books behind the glass doors in the parlour, Scott, Thackeray, Dickens, had their pages stuck together—James was no lover of literature. The water-heating system was an old-fashioned geyser in the kitchen; there was a bread bin with half a loaf, and the cheese sat in a dish with a slanting lid. The clothes in the bedroom were respectable, durable garments, not of the finest quality.

The study, already taken apart by a search squad and put together again, was small and contained only an ugly oak desk and chairs, a few bookshelves, a wall calendar, a telephone. Capricorn recognized the number that Slope had written down in The Pompeian Rooms. The desk drawers contained nothing of interest. Printed business stationery, plain paper and envelopes, stamps. VAT forms, some filled in. A book of telephone numbers. Railway timetables. Shipping schedules. All these had been carefully vetted. Accountants had been brought in to study the VAT forms, but everything was in order. Everything in the desk belonged to the surface stratum, Marcus James, businessman.

The cellar, once Capricorn, stumbling about, had found the light switch, showed itself to be typical of a Spartan, old-fashioned household. A lawn mower stood next to shelves of various garden implements. Earthenware pots for planting sat in a row. Rakes leaned on the wall, next to a defunct copper in the corner. A ladder.

Capricorn carried the ladder up to the top floor, and, with its help, scrambled up into the attic. The attic was merely a depository for old furniture, of the same sort as downstairs, perhaps in a little worse condition. No trunks—the James's were not travellers, or else they travelled light. A mangle was carefully draped in a sheet. There seemed to be nothing personal, not even a rack of old clothes, except perhaps, next to the mangle where there were piles of old comic papers, carefully corded and tied. Capricorn leaned down to pick one up, but the paper was dry and crumbling. The print was fading but the characters were still legible—someone in that household had followed the saga of Weary Willy and Tired Tim. Capricorn smiled, for a moment back in time with The Great Capricornus chiding him that if he did not apply himself to a thorough study of his craft he would end like those two amiable but unenterprising men. 'Too light for heavy work and too heavy for light work,' The Great Capricornus had said morosely. Then Capricorn sneezed and was back in the present, wondering if the papers had been saved for sentiment, or had been bundled up for charity and then forgotten. At any rate, they were no help to a puzzled policeman. He took the ladder back down to the basement and by the time he returned to the ground floor, a shower was pattering against the windows.

Capricorn hoped that a real storm would come at last and clear the air. He wandered aimlessly from room to room. From the parlour he could see, even on this respectable street, the overflowing dustbins waiting in the front gardens. London was smelling like a large dump. Pacing back, he looked out of the study window. There was the typical London small garden, lawn in the middle, crazy paving path, flowers planted all round behind a border, rose bushes trained along the fence. Marcus James spent his Sundays like any other small householder, only more silently, pottering about when the weather was fine. Nothing here to give a hint of where he'd gone to earth. This house was only an inherited family house, with no reflection of the individual man.

Or was there? The books on the study shelves, though old, had a worn look—unlike the matched sets in the parlour, they had been read. An atlas. A few offerings of the Left Book Club. Marx, Engels. Capricorn glanced through. No nameplates in the books, no inscriptions. Had James bought these himself, Capricorn wondered, or had they been left by his father? Some were just a few years old, for instance, an account of the events in China during the revolution written by an American general. In this volume someone, perhaps Brixton Jim himself, had made marginal notes of a pedantic kind, mostly in agreement with the author, who was not unsympathetic to the new regime. The handwriting was small and tight. Only one comment, near the end, was written in a less-controlled hand. Perhaps it was an afterthought of a man ready to doze in his chair. 'The East Wind is prevailing . . .'

Capricorn remembered the boast of Mao Tse-tung, '. . . the East Wind is prevailing over the West Wind.' He also remembered Manning's concern that had brought him into the case, the possible political aspect of the drug-running. He thought of the heroin in the warehouse brought in by James's men, heroin so pure it was worth a fortune abroad but comparatively little in Great Britain, unless it was to be reshipped, and that was unlikely. He remembered the small bars of gold, useful for corruption on a small scale. He sat and thought while the shower poured down, slackened off and left bright pools in the garden.

Then he telephoned his office, and checked his memory against the list he had prepared of all the ports of call of the ship that had carried the contraband. She had made a leisurely voyage, stopping at many ports including Corfu, Brindisi, Naples, Genoa, Lisbon. Then he called Manning, tracking him down in Drug Squad. He was still working with them on the smuggling—just in case, he told Capricorn.

'It might be a good case,' Capricorn said, and shared his suspicions.

'Hope you're wrong,' Manning said. 'If it's business, we can make it not worth their while, but if it is politics—cut off one head and another will spring up. Not much chance of finding our friend now, I take it.'

'Do you believe he might be in an embassy?' Capricorn was thinking aloud.

'If your guess is right? It would be unusual, in such a case,' Manning answered. 'Of course, our friend might be considered very special—but I would tend to think not.'

'Then all that's left is luck,' Capricorn said moodily as he hung up. He only believed in the help of luck when the last bit of effort had been made to deserve it. But now he could think of no more effort to make. If James's illicit dealings in cargoes from the East Mediterranean did involve political consideration, that meant very little in this search, except to make it harder. It certainly indicated a whole new area where he might be hidden, but not where he could be found. The police could get away with 'turning over' the dwellings of known criminals in a general search; they could not go into the homes of thousands of people because of their political beliefs.

He looked through the drawers again, any action seeming better than none. The telephone book—every number and address had been run down. The VAT forms were merely copies of those at the warehouse— James was a careful man and checked his own accountants' work. The railroad timetables were up to date, for all points in the country, as might be expected of a warehouseman. Nothing unusual there. Shipping schedules—all the lines involved had been questioned and re-questioned, and to be on the safe side, a special watch was being kept on all ships of those lines during loading and departure, as well as ships from other lines that James did not deal with directly but had connection with through his interests in other ports.

The Silver Stream line to the West Indies, the Conway line to Australia and New Zealand, the Black Star to Africa; the ships that mostly served the Mediterranean, the *Andromache* and her sisters, the Crowell line, the smaller lines like the Mariposa and the Hepworth that still came into the West India Dock. The Hepworth—just two coalers now—and the Mariposa ships, growing shabbier every year, the once-smart white upperworks and red-and-green funnels dingy as they came up the tidal Thames.

The Mariposa. He paused. He knew about that line from seeing its ships and hearing gossip about her losing business to the new Minassis combine, but—he thought of the painstaking check of the lines just completed and didn't remember the Mariposa line being among them. That didn't necessarily mean anything, he told himself. A warehouseman was a middleman. Cargoes were booked onto lines by the firms of ultimate destination. On any day, a warehouse could get cargo from a line it had never dealt with before. There was no reason why Brixton Jim should not have had schedules from any line that came into the Port of London, as well as Tilbury, Liverpool and Harwich—he probably had, somewhere at the warehouse. But it was odd that he had that particular one at home.

Capricorn rubbed his head. Or was it? He was so tired that his mind was blurred. By this time, he knew, he would think a bus ticket for Wapping found in the gutter had a strange, esoteric significance. Nevertheless, he telephoned the Mariposa line, or tried to. The London office was merely a desk in a shared space, and the agent had gone out for a coffee. But when he returned, he tried to be of help. The name Marcus James was unfamiliar to him. He took care of land arrangements for importers only on request, and used the warehouses on the wharf. Naturally, most of the importers made their own arrangements once their goods were through the Port. Any schedules made up for the Mariposa ships were only approximate. If one of the ships got a chance for extra cargo and she had the space, she would make an unscheduled stop. Waxing very frank, the agent told him that the line was four old buckets and only one of them had been through the Port of London, or any other British port, in the last six weeks. The *Santa Lucia* had been expected a week ago. Held up by engine trouble out of Piraeus, she had come in yesterday. She had already unloaded and was now taking on cargo for Naples and Brindisi.

Capricorn thanked him and could hardly hang up fast enough so that he could get hold of CID at the Port. Then he called Manning again, but Manning, who was polite, obviously thought he was chasing straws in the wind—or bus tickets. However, he agreed to meet him at the dock. 'Drugs are getting very boring about all this,' he remarked. 'They trace back where the stuff comes from by the grade, what can be cooked up where. They've explained to me so thoroughly that I could open up a quick-lunch for addicts.'

Capricorn's spirits were high as he sped across London. He refused to consider the odds. There was a chance. If his hunch was right, and James had had illicit dealings with one or more of the Mariposa ships, it was possible he would wait for one of them to take him out. Certainly, they could take him where he wanted to go.

Manning was sceptical. 'Seems too kind of our friend,' he remarked when he met Capricorn in the CID office on the dock. 'Leaving you a handy schedule and then popping off to catch the ship. With so few ships coming in now—it amounts to co-operation with the police.'

'He left schedules for just about every line that comes in,' Capricorn retorted, stung because of the truth in Manning's jest. 'And they are things he saw every day of his life. To be seen without being noticed, except when wanted. Like a calendar or a clock.'

He spoke, however, without conviction. They stood on the quay watching the crew board the ship in the warm afternoon. The gulls were screaming, swooping down to feed on debris spilled during loading. Capricorn had assumed that the Port had its own rubbish removal system, but there was a lot of piled-up trash on the quays and wharves—perhaps the men had joined their city brothers in the unofficial slowdown. The smelly heat exacerbated Capricorn's already tense nerves. Perhaps, he thought, that was why he took such an unreasonable dislike to the Captain of the *Santa Lucia*.

The man was surly, it was true, but then, he was behind schedule on his run. He told them he was returning with the same crew; no new men were being taken on in the Port, but to his obvious irritation, Capricorn stopped each man and personally examined his papers. Although only the first mate had remained on board while the *Santa Lucia* had been docked, Capricorn and Manning went over the ship with the Port men. The ship was loaded with cases of light machinery, and Capricorn, backed up by the assistant harbour master, ordered some of it moved round as, despite the Captain's fury, he searched the ship on each deck from the square of the hatch to the skin. Most of the crew were Italian and Manning, fluent in that language, chatted with them during the search. He could report only that they were all regular seamen and appeared to know each other well.

There was nothing more to do. Capricorn crossed the wet and slippery upper deck with some difficulty, grasping the ropes to keep his long legs from sliding out from under him. He heard the deckmen laughing and making jokes in Italian and Greek that he partly understood. He felt like a fool, and a double fool. The Captain and the assistant harbour master wore almost identical expressions—landlubbers who held up their schedules and the work of the Port with harebrained notions were hardly popular. Even Manning grinned as Capricorn slipped on the gangway. The magician had tried to pull a rabbit out of the hat but instead, in the terms of the old vaudevillians, he had laid a monster of an egg.

SEA CHANTY,
WITH PERCUSSION

Capricorn, always stubborn, after a discussion with the Port police, requested a still-closer watch on outgoing ships. Merely because he wasn't on the *Santa Lucia* didn't mean that Brixton Jim, if he was still in England, wouldn't choose to escape by way of the Port. Dutifully, Capricorn returned to the Yard, only to find nothing significant had come in during his absence. His Commander took one look at him, told him he resembled a landed fish and suggested he get some proper sleep.

Tired and defeated, Capricorn got his car and turned homewards. He would sleep a few hours and get fresh clothes. Overtiredness was exciting his imagination and making him see everything out of proportion. He still smarted from the tolerant politeness of the assistant harbour master, the frank amusement of the deckmen, even Manning's grin. Manning had been brought up on the coast, messing about in boats. In his own childhood, the only time he had been on the water was in a rowboat at the pier where he had worked with his aunts. He had to laugh at himself; he was becoming positively maudlin with self-pity. It was interesting, the detached part of his mind noted, how lack of sleep broke down character. Now he could understand exactly how it worked in brainwashing.

He had also been lying to himself. His late Majesty had sent him on a few voyages, and now he came to

think of it, there had been some glorious sails in a
fishing smack at Leigh-On-Sea when his aunts were
playing Southend. Leigh-On-Sea. Brenda had had a
souvenir cup from there in her room, its bright crude
colours striking in that drab place. He had seen it the
day Slope had been found there: Slope, who before
the war had sold cockles from a stall. Slope, who had
lived in the house at Leigh owned by Marcus James
until a few years ago. The James family, who knew
the river and the coast. Capricorn remembered sharply his dislike of the Captain of the *Santa Lucia*—was
that in part distrust?

He pulled over to the side of the road, and for a
moment sat with his head in his hands. Was it another attack of nerve-strained fancy? He didn't have
time to sleep on it, that was certain. The *Santa Lucia*
would already be steaming down the tidal Thames.
He might ask Customs and Excise for assistance, but
for what precisely? They could hardly be asked to go
out and dog every small craft in the estuary as far as
the twelve-mile limit to see if one of them was about
to rendezvous with the *Santa Lucia*. He'd already
made himself ridiculous once that day. A blast of
hornblowing behind him suggested he was doing it
again—Horse Guards Avenue was no place to park.
As he moved on, he observed that his hands weren't
too steady on the wheel, and his eyes were twitching
and felt sandy. Accepting the inevitable, he made for
a garage, and called the Yard for assistance—a sergeant from C1 and an official vehicle. 'And have the
sergeant come armed,' he said as an afterthought.

While he waited, he drank three cups of strong
black coffee and soon felt somewhat better. It was a
pity he couldn't have Copper with him, he thought
when the sergeant arrived—a good man, but middle-
aged with a wide girth and ponderous tread.

As they were driving down the road to the coast
the sky darkened. The storm was coming at last. Still,

from the rise by Hadleigh castle, Capricorn could see the estuary before him, and he took in the magnitude of the task. The James's had owned property at Leigh, but certainly they must have been familiar with the entire area. Southend, Westcliff, Leigh-On-Sea, Thorpe Bay and Shoeburyness. The area was nearly as large as Brighton.

The sergeant, who had been driving in silence, looked at him questioningly. Capricorn faltered, unsure now which way to go. Lightning flashed; thunder rolled and the rain began to come down. No pleasure boats would be out now. There were hardly any people to be seen, even in the heavily built-up Southend. Visibility was so bad that Capricorn thought, miserably, he might as well stay in the hotel by the pier and watch the *Santa Lucia* come down and follow her by boat. But then if she met no small craft for twelve miles out, what then?

First they drove to old Leigh, once a fishing village, where the men still went out after brown shrimp. It must be the only place where Brixton Jim could expect to find a boat and a boatsman now. Leaving the car, Capricorn and the sergeant looked over the embankment down at the beach and were quickly drenched in the pouring rain, driving by a wind off the water. A few boats were beached along the shore, but no small craft were visible on the water. No humans, no animals even, were to be seen or heard. After the policemen had patrolled the entire length of the embankment, Capricorn gave the order to drive along the cliffs to Westcliff and Southend, and for the next two hours they searched every beach around the estuary.

It was a solitary, fruitless search. Neither man nor beast had chosen to go out in such a storm. Even the gulls were hidden and silent. Capricorn routed out a renter of boats at Southend, whose sign was still displayed by the pier. When Capricorn asked if anyone had hired a boat that day, the man, although protesting at being torn away from his tea, looked at Capricorn almost kindly, as if he were an idiot. His boats were rowboats, paddle boats and a few small outboard motors. The season was over and they were all hauled in until the spring. No one had inquired about a boat, and certainly none were out. The only craft to go out at this time of year were the fishing boats at Leigh, and they would all be in by this time.

Capricorn thanked him, and grimly made his way back to the old town to search again. He had wasted too much time. If Brixton Jim had ever come here, which was beginning to seem more and more unlikely, he was almost certainly gone by now. Capricorn regarded the one long crooked street with its houses, quays and wharves that had changed very little since its village days. Someone had parked a large van so that it was blocking the road and the policemen had to leave their car and walk.

No one was on the street. 'Rooms to Let' signs were all over the boarding houses. The stalls selling shellfish were closed up or had vanished altogether. Only the tower of St Clement's stood indifferent to weather or season, overlooking the estuaries of the Thames and the Medway as it had done for centuries past.

Again the two men lingered on the top of the embankment, trying to peer through the driving rain. The beach was still deserted, but they walked its length, turned back and walked its length again. Nothing could be seen on the water. Soon the *Santa Lucia* would be at the river's mouth. Capricorn knew he was already, without a doubt, too late—if his idea had ever been more than a wish, a fancy. He had come on a fool's errand.

Aware of the sergeant's patient but inquiring looks, Capricorn had nothing to say. No more ideas, except to return to London and pick up the threads of the routine he had so precipitously abandoned. He stared

out to sea, with nothing but the Lobster Quadrille
echoing through his otherwise empty head. 'The further off from England the nearer is to France . . .'

'So turn not pale, beloved snail,' he murmured, and
the sergeant started. 'We'll go down on the beach.
Might as well make a thorough job of it.' They went
down the steps to what looked like sand, to enter a
world strangely different from the one above. On the
embankment, with all its view of the estuary, one was
still part of the world of village and town, close to
the roads and railway stations and all the works of
man. Here one's angle of vision was abruptly
changed. The spray stung his eyes. The beach,
though much less of it was visible, with sea and cloud
became the universe, a universe not friendly to mankind.

Small craft, upended, lay all along the shore. At
one point, visibility was totally blocked by a pub
built out over a jetty. Capricorn, squelching in his
shoes, deployed the sergeant to reconnoitre on the
other side, more to get rid of his polite but wondering gaze than because of any real belief that he would
find anything. As he plodded away, his usual
measured tread slower and heavier on the beach,
Capricorn remembered the gun, but let him go. It
wouldn't be needed today. The sergeant's clothes,
meant for a dry day in town like his own, were hanging from him like washing hung up without being
wrung. Capricorn guessed that once out of sight, the
sergeant if he found a bit of shelter might take it, and
not further court rheumatism for the sake of his eccentric superior.

Capricorn leaned against the embankment, a little
out of the force of the wind. He watched for ten, fifteen, twenty minutes. He thought he heard the sound
of a car above. Then the sound stopped; but no one
came down the steps—imagination, perhaps. That too
active imagination. Yes, surely the *Santa Lucia* was al-

ready making her way out to the open sea, heading for the straits. The storm continued. As the thunder seemed to die away, lightning would flash again and another roll crash overhead.

Of course, the whole town was huddled inside its houses. He wondered which house had belonged to the James's. He could have found out from Slope, but he had been in too much of a hurry. There weren't that many boats, either. He could have made inquiries about the owners instead of rushing about to no purpose. His plan had been ill conceived and foolishly carried out. Now it was time to find the unfortunate sergeant and let him go back to town where he could be useful—once he was dried out. Capricorn moved away from the embankment and immediately barked his shin on a broken piling. It was sharply painful and he cursed roundly, pausing before he turned towards the steps. In that instant, a brilliant flash of lightning lit up the whole shore, and Capricorn saw at the opposite end of the beach from the jetty a low groyne that cut off his vision from the furthest point. He had seen it from above, of course, but time had passed. While he was down here, he might as well take another look. He could get no wetter. His bruised leg protested, but he ignored it and went on. Funny about pain, he reasoned, it must like companionship because now every tooth in his head was aching in sympathy.

As he came closer to the groyne, it seemed as though something was moving on the other side. Wishful thinking again, he told himself sourly, but no, it was the figure of a man tugging a boat. Capricorn picked his way between puddles of oil-slicked water. He was too close to the embankment to be seen, but the beach seemed to consist entirely of bits of cockle shells and even in the wind and rain he was afraid that the crackle underfoot might be heard. He stopped, took his shoes off and continued. The shells cut into his feet through his thin, townsman's socks, but he reached the angle of the groyne and the embankment without being observed.

Two youths were pushing a small craft into the water, a battered tub, but it carried an engine as well as sail. A man was already aboard, handling the ropes. Even with his vision obscured by the pouring rain, Capricorn saw it was not, of course, Brixton Jim. The man was bigger, more powerful and looked much younger. Capricorn's disappointment was so sharp it felt like a pain in his belly. Anger followed disappointment. He was about to ask officiously what the boys were doing risking their lives in the water, when the group was joined by another figure, looming up from the mist of spray and rain, a man of medium height and spare figure, looking with his jersey, sea boots and fisherman's cap like an ordinary seaman except, as he drew closer, for his eyes, too sharp, too full of authority and command.

Quickly, he was in the boat and it was moving. Capricorn looked round for the sergeant but he was still out of sight. I should call for help, Capricorn thought. He can't get away. But his heart was thudding. It was Brixton Jim there, a few yards away, almost within reach, if—

Capricorn lept over the groyne, waded through the water, grabbed the side of the boat and, hauling himself up, heard his own voice saying, 'You're under arrest.' Brixton Jim grabbed for his belt. He's got a gun, you bloody fool, Capricorn told himself savagely and hollered to the sergeant, but his voice was carried off, thin in the wind and the waves. The boatman's hand dropped uncertainly from the tiller, but the craft continued to chug slowly forward. Brixton Jim pulled, his pistol caught in the voluminous folds of the heavy jersey. Capricorn snatched at him, catching him off guard as the boat rolled and Brixton Jim pitched forward and down on the deck. The boatman

reached for an anchor. Capricorn ducked and
swerved, catching his breath in relief as one of the
lads from the beach climbed over the side and caught
the boatman's arm.

Capricorn was rolling in the bottom with Brixton
Jim, grappling for his gun, finding the other man
unexpectedly tough and agile. Lightning ripped
again over the water and Capricorn, through the
sting of sea spray in his eyes, saw the boatman knock
the lad over the side and take up the anchor again,
lifting it over Capricorn's head. Capricorn grasped his
ankle, but Brixton Jim took the chance to untangle
his gun. The boatman staggered, Brixton Jim
steadied the gun; Capricorn, despairing of the sergeant, thought he was done when a shout came from
on top of the embankment.

A flash divided the sky and showed not the sergeant
but a red-headed figure pointing a gun from above—
too far, much too far, Capricorn thought, but Brixton
Jim looked up for a fraction of a second and that was
enough. Capricorn twisted Brixton Jim's wrist and
grabbed the pistol and then both of the lads were in
the boat, holding the boatman and switching off the
engine. For a weary moment Capricorn feared that
Brixton Jim might break away and jump overboard,
but he was a man who knew when he had lost a
battle, if not the war.

A battle? Perhaps he considered it just a skirmish,
Capricorn thought ruefully at the local station. For
the first time, he actually saw how effortlessly Brixton
Jim could slip from one identity to another. The man
taken into the station spoke no English, only Greek,
and produced papers made out to Kimon
Kazantzakis, assistant cook. He was convincing
enough to have foxed the local men, with his helpless
gestures and bewildered gaze. When an interpreter
was found, Kazantzakis explained, with great volu-

bility, that he had missed his ship at the Port and he had paid a man to take him out to join her at sea. The man he had found was a stranger, he looked brutal—Kazantzakis shook his head—he had demanded a great deal of money, all that Kazantzakis had in fact, and so, fearful, he had armed himself with a pistol borrowed from another seaman. They had heard rumours, he said darkly, of foreigners being robbed and drowned off the shores of England.

He had planned well. The police spoke by wireless to the *Santa Lucia*, still in British territorial waters. The Captain replied that it was true Kazantzakis had failed to rejoin the ship. No, he hadn't mentioned it to the Port police. They had not asked about missing seamen. A drunken lot, the Captain said, apparently referring to his men and not the police. It happened all the time. His vessel sailed on its course but without Brixton Jim.

He might have got away, Capricorn reflected, that flood of Greek was very convincing—if you didn't know about his Cypriot mother. But it was the set of fingerprints that nailed him, the fingerprints he hadn't known the Yard possessed. The fingerprints that Capricorn had surreptitiously obtained—that had to be his consolation for being saved by the appearance not of the armed sergeant he had taken down with him but of Copper, almost restored to his usual state of genial impudence.

'I was up at CO to be jawed,' he said, 'and I heard your call come in. Sounded interesting, and I knew you couldn't manage without me, so I followed you down. When I saw you were expecting a Dunkirk, I took a look round myself. Gawd, it's quiet down here. Could've knocked off a couple of kids for pot, high as a pair of kites they were, and giggling, with water up to their knees under the pier. But lucky for you I took a gander at what you were up to. I do like to be beside the seaside,' he added. The rain had slowed to a steady drip.

Capricorn looked at his gun. 'But you're still under suspension.'

'Not any more,' Copper replied cheerfully. He told a joke to cheer the sergeant, who was aching with mortification at having followed orders and missed all the glory.

Before they left the station to take James back to London, Capricorn was happy to clear the two boys who had tried to help when they knew they were dealing with the police. They had been brought in quite innocently. The boatman, a heavy, stupid brute, was something else and was charged with attempted assault of a police officer. He had taken all that risk for two hundred pounds, and now claimed he had been attempting to subdue Brixton Jim with the anchor after it turned out he was not the simple seaman in a little trouble with the authorities that he had claimed to be.

Back in London with the matter of identification cleared away, Brixton Jim still refused to make any statement. His shrewd cold eyes rested on Capricorn without expression. He showed no sign of defeat or even apprehension, and asked for his counsel with the air of a man facing an inevitable, but annoying, delay of a business appointment. Despite this calm, Capricorn was surprised to notice that when Brixton Jim spoke English he had a decided stammer. Of course, they had never talked together, but Capricorn had not even heard it mentioned. He had known that Brixton Jim was rather silent by habit, perhaps the disability explained the silence. It was not from nervousness certainly, the flood of Greek after his capture made that plain. He was well aware of all his legal rights. The law: That would be his next line of defense. He would fail there, Capricorn thought, would there be another? Manning was to think of the answer to that, later.

'You were bound for Corfu, according to your papers,' Capricorn remarked. 'A short trip from Corfu to Gjinokaster.'

At the mention of the Albanian port, Brixton Jim looked at him appraisingly. He knows I didn't get that from Slope, Capricorn realized. Brixton Jim had never let Slope know about his third persona. Had that been the real man, the bedrock of this strange personality, or were politics, for him, merely another profitable enterprise?

'Today West Wind is prevailing over East Wind,' Capricorn reversed Mao's phrase.

'N-not for long,' Brixton Jim retorted deliberately.

Capricorn raised an eyebrow. 'You're not doing too well. Your own nephew has let you down.'

Brixton Jim didn't move a muscle. 'Th-there are no y-young people worthy of trust in this c-country.' He was full of contempt. 'Th-they don't know the meaning of d-discipline. Nobody has t-taught them. It's time for a ch-change. It's being done elsewhere. S-soon it will come here. Th-they will learn to obey.'

Capricorn wondered if he had considered the Red Guards. Well, so he was a political after all. A large-scale crook and swindler turned political through an illegal association; or perhaps he had been politically minded from the beginning. A boy brought up in that austere, so-early-motherless household, taught nothing but hard work and to live between two worlds, contemptuous of the society he preyed on— Who could say? Some of both, perhaps. As Manning pointed out, after his own session with Brixton Jim, at the very top crime and politics often meet.

'De Gaulle and Union Corse in Action Service against the Algerians. The Americans with the Mafia against the Axis in Sicily in World War II. You should read Fleming instead of Flaubert,' Manning mocked.

'He knew all about it. My guess,' he shrugged, 'James might have been a Communist of the puritanical, old-fashioned sort. His business with the Chinese might have led in that direction.'

Capricorn sighed. His dealings were usually with a lower echelon of criminal, who at least were for the most part refreshingly apolitical. Or perhaps they had a reasonable wish not to kill the goose that laid their golden eggs. He thought of James's stammer: the doctors said, nowadays, that a stammer came from fear. It was English that held James's tongue; it was his father he had feared, then, not the Cypriot mother. Well, James's mental progressions, thank the Lord, were not his problem. James could wait for his Brave New World behind bars.

'If he loses in the courts,' Manning warned, 'he might still try to get exchanged, after a terrorist kidnapping.'

But Capricorn refused to worry. 'Now he's blown he's of no further use to them. Not political enough. He's no young leader with a following. A discard. Rubbish.'

For once Manning agreed. Not that he was happy. 'The man's a traitor, but he won't be shot. He's a murderer, but he'll never hang.'

It was true, but Capricorn couldn't worry about that either—not for the moment. Chief Superintendent Capricorn, he promised himself luxuriously, was going home. It was time. Copper, who had driven behind him on the way back to London, had called out many a jeer about his ragamuffin looks, unimproved by oil, sea water, cockle shells and tar from fighting in the boat. Capricorn found his own car, noticing, despite all that had passed, he felt rather less exhausted than when he had left it in the garage. He was ravenously hungry and wondered if Mrs Dermott was at his house and if she would have anything for him to eat. Then he thought of Brixton Jim in prison.

Despite what Manning had said, he felt a great, glowing satisfaction.

A long piece of work had been brought to a successful end. Brixton Jim, a master criminal, perhaps a member of the Organization, possibly a foreign agent, had been captured and, with the evidence against him, Capricorn was sure he would be out of commission for a long, long time. Brixton Jim, who had tried to stop his investigation with threats against Copper and attempts to bring him to ruin, had been thwarted.

Copper's troubles were almost over. He would always grieve for Joss, but he would find consolation. His only remaining problem was financial, and Capricorn could help him there. For tonight, Capricorn refused to worry about anything, not even what was going to happen to Brenda Grey. That could wait for tomorrow.

The quality that Capricorn loved best in his home was its silence, and the quiet of the square in which he lived. He thought of Gyppo Moggs's distrust of the lack of bustle, the sheltering trees, the proximity of the park. Poor Gyppo. His busy little suburb hadn't saved him.

Tonight the country-like quiet was broken, just a little. The British Legion hall, usually decorous and mute, was brightly lit and sounds of Roll Out the Barrel came from within—an ex-servicemen's get-together. An annual outing, perhaps. A coach was parked just behind his own space. Tonight he could put up with Roll Out the Barrel; he felt an affection for the world. A dim light came through his own front windows: Mrs Dermott must still be there.

With his mind full of enchanting thoughts of hot baths, clean clothes and probably cutlets for dinner, he smiled benignly at the ex-servicemen who were leaving the hall, still singing, walking four abreast and straggling into the road. He closed his policeman's mind to their illegally parked coach. It was too big to be where it was, and it blocked the vision of any car coming from the other side of the square. But there was almost no traffic at that hour, and it looked like the ex-servicemen were going home.

He was almost at the curb, his keys in his hand, when he saw a car approaching from behind the coach. Automatically, Capricorn jumped on the curb and turned to wave the ex-servicemen up onto the pavement. They let out an indignant roar: a sports car was coming down the street the wrong way. The driver had been going at a good speed but slowed up, swerved, saw the other car with its driver slamming on the brakes, and swerved again, his own brakes squealing. He bumped up on the curb, and his mudguard sideswiped Capricorn on his already bruised shin before the bonnets of the two cars became hopelessly entangled. Capricorn felt a sickening pain in his leg, but pain, confusion and astonishment did not prevent him from recognizing his attacker as the stoppe driver Hake, the report of whose death had been, obviously, premature.

ENGLISH LYRIC —
CLOSING CHORD

Capricorn woke next morning a happy man, or almost. The storm had cleared the sticky heat away at last. Earlier, half asleep, he thought he had heard the rumble of the dustmen's carts. Brixton Jim was in custody. Today he could rest. And perhaps he would call some charming friend to be his guest for dinner.

The pain in his leg, still deep and fierce, had localized itself and the rest of him was fresh and cheerful, but it brought back the events of the night before. The ex-servicemen, not too merry for good sense, had helped to grab the raving, baby-faced Hake, who was dutifully trying to carry out orders just a little too late, had he but known it, for Brixton Jim. Capricorn, for all his weariness, hunger and pain, had been obliged to go through more official procedures, make a statement and be trundled off again, protesting, to the hospital for X-rays. While he was waiting without much patience for the verdict of the orthopedist, drinking a cup of stewed tea brought to him by a kindly nurse, he saw the doctor who had treated him for chloral poisoning not so long before.

He had been horribly facetious. 'Well, well,' he said, quite interested, 'chloral hydrate, assault by a BMW—you're not a very popular policeman, are you?'

'He's a lucky policeman.' The bone man, thank heaven, was matter of fact. 'The driver must've been almost stopped when he touched you. You've got a nasty bruise, and it'll hurt like the devil for a long time, but the bone isn't broken. Get some rest, keep your weight off, and come in twice a week for hydrotherapy. I'll give you some pills to make you sleep and some pills for the pain in the daytime.'

Having no broken bones, Capricorn proposed to take little of this advice. He had swallowed a pain pill but, refusing to stay, had arranged to be driven home to a street restored to its usual quiet and peace, where he at last made his way into his house with nothing to worry about until the morning but his aches and the wrath of Mrs Dermott.

The night, as it happened, had not been without further interruption, but now all was peace. Mrs Dermott's wireless announced that cool, clear weather was general over the British Isles. All his sins of omission to that lady had been pardoned, as he was classified as walking wounded.

He enjoyed his breakfast, while Mrs Dermott informed him that the Miss Bints were staying in the country and had let her know they were interested in selling their flat. Belatedly, he thanked her for her work after the bomb damage, and in cheerful spirits they discussed improvements and alterations. Capricorn tried to walk on his injured leg, and found it did not hurt appreciably more in motion, except that the soles of his feet were still sore from treading on the cockle shells. He was interrupted several times by congratulatory calls of various sorts.

The Commander was much impressed with the skills of Hake. 'He would have got you, all right,' he said cheerfully, 'if it hadn't been for the Legion bunfight getting in his way. Wonder why he waited so long.'

Capricorn pointed out the difficulties of an escaped prisoner trailing a Chief Superintendent. 'Last night was the first time he could have caught me alone since we picked up Slope. Not that I'm giving him a reference,' he said somewhat acidly.

The Commander giggled. 'Pity. All that talent will go to waste. And that good-looking handmaiden loses two lovers at once. But when we let her go I imagine the vacancies will soon be taken up.'

So that was how Hake had found out about Brixton Jim, Capricorn reflected. The easiest, oldest way there was. He had shared a mistress with Slope. 'Lovely girl, that Luna,' Copper had said, 'I know her well.'

But Capricorn forgot Luna as the Commander went on to talk about the Merlinos. Long had the Commander wanted to meet them; long had Capricorn thwarted this wish. They had met, at last, over the Tilly affair, and Dolly had invited the Commander to join the studio audience at the Peter Playfair show that evening where she was making a surprise appearance. 'It's quite early,' he went on, 'and I thought of taking her to dinner afterwards at the Florabel. But she has to go down to some inn near Tunbridge Wells tonight: they're shooting some location shots for her new film early in the morning.' How quickly the Commander was picking up the jargon, Capricorn thought crossly, guessing what was to come. 'Unluckily, I came in this morning by train. Dolly mentioned she had thought of asking you—'

Capricorn said dutifully that he would be happy to join them at dinner and later drive Dolly to somewhere near Tunbridge Wells. The Commander rang off, a happy man.

A more sombre note came from Manning. He still believed the changes in officialdom that he feared were coming to pass. Incredibly, Manning, who lived for his work, spoke of resigning—even going abroad. Manning, who was so English he was like part of the landscape. Capricorn tried to cheer him up and urged a good long sleep. Weariness could make one see things out of proportion. Changes might not be to his liking but were probably not as dire as he thought. And he might be quite mistaken. But Manning, in the thick of a hunt for a letter-bomber, was not cheered.

As Mrs Dermott was ready to clear away, Copper arrived, sending her back to the kitchen for more coffee, bacon and eggs.

'Managed to get on the sick list, have you? Soldiering off again,' Copper said. He flung himself into a chair at the table and crossed his legs comfortably, grinning up at Mrs Dermott as she ministered to him. She bridled happily as if expecting to be pinched. 'I stopped in to see the aunts. Woke 'em up. What a lot,' he said in admiration. 'Offered me port and brandy for breakfast.'

Only Copper would be allowed to wake the aunts with impunity. Another caller would have got the bottles without the drink.

'I told them what a clever little super you'd been, but they weren't impressed. That Dolly,' he chuckled.

Capricorn knew that Dolly was not impressed. She had got him on the telephone at three in the morning exuberant about Tilly's having a starring role in the forthcoming trial of Teresa Bonomi. In response to her inquiry as to where he had been hiding, he had told her a little about the hunt for Brixton Jim. Nothing had caught her attention but Copper's appearance on the embankment at the vital moment.

'Now *he's* what I call a detective,' she'd said with appreciation. 'I'd marry him myself now Joss is gone if it wasn't for Tod.' Tod had been on tour for six weeks and Capricorn would swear it was the first time she'd thought of him.

'I told her how you got the woman that slaughtered Joss,' Copper went on thoughtfully, 'but she made nothing of it. More excited about what they'd wear for the trail.'

Capricorn had heard about that, too.

'Well,' she'd said, and he had imagined her standing in a characteristic pose, with one hand on her hip, curling her mouth downwards, 'they might think you clever at the Yard, but I don't know how it took you so long to work that out. The way you were brought up, you must've been a grown man before you saw a stick that didn't have something in it, even if it was only a few flags.'

And now he had to take her to dinner and drive her somewhere near Tunbridge Wells.

Capricorn asked Copper if he would like to join the dinner party, but he excused himself. 'Just not feeling up to larking about,' he said. 'Don't want to spoil your fun. Thank God I'm going back on the job. Someone's coming for me soon—my car's back in the garage. I'm going to see Sedgwick; I'm still working with him. We stopped the rand business for a while, but you'll see, something like that'll soon start up stain, unless the inflation stops. People are frightened. You heard about the Swiss cheese and the Annerly Trust, I suppose.'

Capricorn nodded.

'Anyway, I've had my reprimand,' Copper said. 'Got it hot and strong for keeping quiet about being married to Joss when she took on the club. As soon as the estate is settled, it has to go, of course. Until then, I'm letting Miss America have a shot at running it— under supervision,' he added, seeing Capricorn's look. 'She's changing the name to The Giddy Goat. And she can sing with the band—she's good, all right.'

So Miss America was to have her chance after all. Capricorn fervently hoped she wouldn't ruin it.

'I've seen those solicitors you sicked on me,' Copper continued. 'I've got an idea about that thirty thousand.'

He unfolded his plan, which was to set up a trust to repay at least in part some of the people who had suffered most from the swindle in counterfeit rands. 'Some of the poor old bastards were pathetic,' Copper told him. 'And the idea sat all right with the high muck-a-mucks.'

'But what about Mrs Bonomi?' Capricorn said, puzzled.

'No legal claim,' Copper replied shortly. 'Let the money go to the people her old man thieved it from. The Guv'ner's worried about the case, by the way. She won't confess—says nothing. But it makes no never mind.' He gazed at Capricorn thoughtfully. 'We didn't do much there, you know. Lot more wrong with her than a gammy leg. She's dying and she knows it.'

'I see,' Capricorn said. Both men were silent for a moment.

'Poor old Joss.' Copper had a new expression, a sober sadness. 'Couldn't do anything for her at the end. She never got anything out of all her shenanigans, even the say about her own body. She hated funerals, and she wanted to be a donor for transplant surgery. Signed cards and everything. But, of course, what with the postmortem, it wasn't any good. So I let her mother do what she liked, and they had a big funeral, and Joss is in a great fancy metal casket with all the brass trimmings.'

'I'm sorry I wasn't there,' Capricorn said sincerely. He had been so involved in the search he had forgotten everything.

'I had to talk with the doctors at Greywillow,' Copper went on. 'Mum's much better. They told me there wasn't a lot wrong with the old girl except she'd been lonely—you know, all the neighbours had moved away from where we lived, and the new lot weren't the sort she could get to know—and she hadn't been eating properly. She's coming home to Wenmore for a few days—Meg found me a good housekeeper who'll keep an eye on her. We're going to see how she does. Might be all right. Couldn't have done it with Joss home,' he sighed. 'Funny world, ain't it?'

It was. Capricorn wondered if the bright, ambitious Joss would have grown in compassion if she had been allowed to live. Teresa Bonomi, who wore a cross over her heart, had taken more than Joss's life, she had stolen her opportunity for grace. Then Capricorn told himself that was bad theology, and turned his thoughts to the present. He knew that Copper had no serious thoughts of Meg Hardcastle, but dropped him a hint that the lady might be misled.

'Don't think I'll ever get married again, guv,' Copper said. 'Couldn't fancy it. Unless it was your aunt Scarlett,' he gibed. 'She'd keep you on the hop.'

Copper's ride announced itself at the door, and of course it was Meg Hardcastle, in an open two-seater. Capricorn watched them ride off, the sunshine sparkling on Copper's red head and on her golden one. Even in his grief, Capricorn reflected, Copper was a lucky man. He was a natural man, and whatever came, he would adapt to it. Not like the intellectual Manning, or himself for that matter. For a moment he was back in the night filled with Manning's gloomy foreboding. Had all that been strained nerves, and overtiredness, he speculated, or was Manning really thinking of resignation? He thought of his own job, and what he would do if Manning's worst fears became fact. Go back to being a magician, once more trailing in the wake of his aunts? The idea seemed absurd as the sunlight streamed in cheerfully from his garden to brighten his breakfast table. Or was a rested body and a fine day as much a deceiver on the side of optimism as weariness and the dark was on the side of despair? Nature herself was the great conjurer, to the mystification of men, her actors and audience. He shrugged and got ready to leave. Sufficient unto the day . . .

The soles of his feet were very painful as he drove, and his leg ached, but he was anxious to talk to Tilly's doctor. Copper was not the only one to be concerned about madness in the family. It turned out to be an uncomfortable talk. The doctor, rather rushed, granted him an interview punctuated by telephone calls and urgent messages from his nurse. He stared at Capricorn solemnly from behind the barriers of a large desk and heavy spectacles. In much prosier terms he agreed with Copper, which made Capricorn feel he had been very dense. 'Emotional state at pre-puberty . . . no evidence of psychosis . . .' It all amounted to Tilly being a hair-puller, and not a murderess. 'Nowadays,' the doctor was a young man and very sure of himself, 'we would never have encouraged the family to keep her in a home.'

'But she stood there and saw a woman murdered, and all she did was take a couple of things she fancied—some apples, I think, and a cardigan—then walked away, singing. She never turned a hair.'

The doctor went off again in heavily Latinized language to say that Tilly was a jackdaw, which Capricorn already knew. 'A little childish, certainly,' he concluded. 'We know that. We wouldn't advise her living alone.' Capricorn wondered about the medical 'we,' but was not inclined to question it. 'Irresponsible, a little callous, like a child. But after all,' he looked less medical and more human, 'what about the rest of us? We would have cringed at the killing, but how long would it be before our next good meal?'

Capricorn left, not too pleased with himself. He couldn't remember, but he supposed he had eaten breakfast the morning after Joss's death. Yes, he thought, the difference between Tilly's childish callousness and his own adult sensibility was about twelve years.

The pretty little bar of the Florabel cheered him as he waited with some apprehension for Dolly and the

Commander. The late-afternoon sun glowed on the flowers inside and out in the garden. If the rubbish in the streets had not yet been cleared away, here at least was the illusion of freshness, an oasis of fragrance and charm.

Dolly roared in, still in costume and full make-up. She was explaining to the staff, who were hanging on her words, how she had totally demolished a young singing star who had tried to 'upstage' her, and showed them what she had done while the girl was singing. The Commander was hooting with laughter. Dolly shuffled a pack of cards around one knee and then the other, showing off her ruffled red drawers. She caused her hair to glow with a greenish halo, produced two snakes that wriggled down her arm, and, to Capricorn's horror, had certain rubber appendages that looked like bodily parts jump out from her bodice to the tune of Pop Goes the Weasel.

She had not yet greeted her nephew. Capricorn breathed a sigh of relief when she pressed some female into service as a dresser and marched off for the Ladies' to readjust her gown.

The Commander, very gay, told how the young star had been reduced to tears, how Playfair had vowed never to invite Dolly for a live show again, and how the studio audience had given her a standing ovation. Then he had to talk a little shop. Sedgwick's men, on a great search round Soho that afternoon, had found the workshop where the Krugerrands had been drilled and, in early fulfilment of Copper's prophecy, work was now being done on Hungarian crowns. Moletta was still being questioned. The Commander also hoped to show that Moletta was the one who had instigated Teresa Bonomi to murder. The killing would then take on the aspect of gang warfare and less scandal would reflect on the Yard. It was a comforting thought, but obviously wrong. If Moletta had known that Mrs Bonomi, with her powerful underworld connections, had been the killer, he would never have made his call to Capricorn at the Yard. No possible future favours from that source would compensate for the wrath of the Bonomis and Miraglias.

They had a drink while they waited for Dolly— shrieks of laughter were coming from the ladies' room—and the Commander told him the story of Tilly's arrest. Callously, he enjoyed Sedgwick's blunder. He described the impact of the aunts on the Yard very graphically, from Dolly storming the entrance in full theatrical wig, looking, in a feathered dress, like some great bird of prey, up to the next morning when Tilly was released from detention and Dolly, restored to good humour, entertained the police, the lawyers, the crowds in the street, together with a fine sprinkling of pressmen, with an impromptu but spirited version of 'She was only a bird in a gilded cage, a pitiful sight to see.'

Dolly, appeared refreshed, gave them a reprise, to the joy of the Florabel's early dinner patrons. The Commander was in stitches over the whole affair, but Capricorn knew how he would tell the story afterwards, to a different audience. The pain in Capricorn's leg was nothing compared to the emotions he felt. Never, even if he became Commissioner, would he be anything other than Dolly Merlino's nephew. Gloomily, he saw the aunts giving 'a turn' on his grave.

When Dolly was quieted by the appearance of her food, the Commander went back to the Bonomi case, which was very much on his mind. He didn't share Copper's feeling about the *lex talionis* nor was he worried about Mrs. Bonomi's health; he wanted a tidy prosecution. 'It's not a bad case, as it is,' he told Capricorn, 'but the experts can fuddle the jury about the Nobel method, and Tilly *could* get mixed up on the stand. You know they're getting Sir Peter Margrave for the defense.' Margrave was the most redoubtable barrister of the day in criminal cases. 'It would be a help if we could show that Moletta had talked to her, worked her up about Joss and her husband,' he sighed.

'With the greatest respect, sir,' Capricorn said politely, 'I can't see it makes much difference. She certainly knew about the affair, that's the point. We know that because she told Sedgwick and me all about it when we were at the Cristoforo house. And she mentioned it in her signed complaint.'

'Police evidence,' the Commander said, not looking very happy.

Perhaps it wasn't the verdict in the court that was worrying him so much; possibly there was some fuss from Mrs Bonomi's countrymen. There was always a certain awkwardness about trying a foreign national. In this instance it couldn't be helped. Teresa Bonomi was guilty of premeditated murder and that was that.

At the appearance of the brandy, Dolly became lively again, taking over the conversation, gossiping and humming old tunes. Capricorn was glad they were enjoying themselves; he didn't want to inflict his own sudden sadness on them. Dolly's singing, earlier, had taken him back to the day just before the telephone call from Gyppo Moggs and the start of all the violence; the two policemen standing near the Calf, talking of Flash Copper and Mrs Copper; the sarcastic reference to their newly acquired wealth in that same song, '. . . only a bird in a gilded cage . . .' And now Joss, that handsome woman who had sat with him at this same table so bursting with life and hope, was buried in a brass coffin shovelled deep under the earth.

It would be Miss America who took her place. An ill wind, he sighed later as he drove Dolly out of London. Dolly's exuberant chatter distracted him from what he recognized as an after-the-case melancholy, a feeling that not so much had been accomplished after all, a melancholy that would soon be forgotten in the constant pressure of work. Brixton Jim was out of harm's way, that curious man, so eager to discard the civilization that had nourished him for the sake of his strange ideology, by a German materialist out of Asia's convulsions, but, as Manning said, there would be others. Marcus James's conviction would be not an end, but perhaps only a beginning.

As they roared along the motorway, Dolly, tired out by the last few days, fell asleep and snored peacefully at his side. But when he turned off near the town and pulled up for a traffic light, she woke with a start, in a different mood.

'Was you worried about what His Nibs was saying tonight, Merle? About that woman what carved up Joss? I wasn't going to say nothing to him—never trust a rozzer—but it was young Len that stirred it up.'

'What makes you think so?' Capricorn said, startled.

Dolly was yawning. 'Brenda told me, you silly arse. Always nagging about that kid, I told you she was all right. She came to the show at the Palladrome with her new boyfriend. One of her own sort, he is, and she's starting to look like one of the nobs again. She's going to share a flat with a girlfriend in Belgravia, she told me. Very la-di-dah. Brought the young feller round between the acts. A smasher.'

'But what about Len Slope?'

'She told me on the quiet why they bust up. 'Course, she didn't know what it was all about. You was there, not that you'd notice anything. Any man what would think our Till went round to Joss to carve her up, when all she wanted was to scratch her eyes out—made a right fool of you there, didn't we?' She giggled happily.

'Where was I with Brenda and Slope when they broke up, Dolly?'

'At our housewarming, where d'you think?'

They were outside the small town and into the country. Dolly's voice spilled harshly into the quiet air.

'Brenda and Len had a row. He'd just brought her and he said he had to go. Brenda had an idea for a long time he had another girl,'—Capricorn remembered Luna—'and she was wild. But Lenny boy said no, he had an appointment with some ancient Itie bird. Rotten way to talk, but of course he's common as dirt,' she remarked with one of her frequent swings of loyalty. 'Going to ginger her up, he said he was. He would really make her jump when she knew about the carry-on with Joss and her old man.'

Brenda's evidence. The last link in the chain. It showed up both killings as part of the war between two criminal organizations. And Brenda was a private citizen—no connection with the police—the Commander would be pleased. One more act of villainy to charge to Slope. Capricorn didn't think Teresa Bonomi would care very much. The verdict of a British court would not affect a woman who was prepared to face with composure a higher judgement.

He consigned Dolly to her friends at the inn, and drove back, avoiding the main roads and taking each byway as he fancied. The autumn night was cool and fragrant. The wheat had been harvested but the trees still held their leaves; the apple orchards were heavy with fruit. All was fresh from the recent rain. In the hedges sweet-brier still bloomed. Perhaps there would be a St Luke's Summer, he thought, a last burst of clear, sunny spring-like weather before winter came.

The moon shone from a clear sky, turning the river he followed to silver and the landscape to magic. He, a magician, knew himself to be enchanted as he looked at the England he loved, as it might have been for centuries. Cottages sat by the road; a farmhouse stretched back into the fields; a church with a Gothic spire reached for heaven. He slowed down as he approached the churchyard and lingered there, contemplating the dark old graves, the long-dead resting peaceably. Then he moved on to the top of a rise, and stopped and gazed around him, down at barns with their sleeping animals, the houses dark with curtains drawn. The land seemed a haven of peace, yet those who were buried in the churchyard, in the older burial mounds to the west, and in the new cemeteries nearer town with headstones still white as bleached bone, all those who had gone before could tell a different tale.

As he sat there in the quiet night, it was as if he could see them live: the men who had watched in fear and wonder the Romans marching forward with their red cloaks fluttering in the breeze; men who waited for the conquering William, with Harold and their known world dead at Hastings; the good Christians, huddled in the shadow of the church spire murmuring when Henry broke the tie with Rome; Elizabethans preparing to meet the ships of Spain; the simple countrymen caught between Cromwell and the King; the men who left to fight Napoleon and keep the island safe as in his own time men had fought Hitler and kept England free. So many men and women, their hopes and dreams and passions gone and put to rest, and only the earth itself remaining, sleeping in fragile peace under the deceptive moon.

He thought of Copper and poor dead Joss and their cynicism; he remembered Manning and his despair. For himself, he was like Brenda, naughty Brenda who had no great dreams or passions, but who had simply longed for home. Whatever was to come, he would stay. He would do what he must, but he would remain. With the motor silent, he listened to the small night sounds all about him: the flutter of a dying leaf, slowly falling, the croaking of a frog in a nearby pond, the purring chirrup of a nightjar from the distant wood. This was England and his dwelling place.